THE LOST ASCENDANT

Christopher Mitchell is the author of the epic fantasy series [illegible]s. He studied in Edinburgh before living for several years in [illegible] where he taught English. He returned to study classics [illegible] and lives in Fife, Scotland with his wife and their four children.

By Christopher Mitchell

The Magelands Origins

Retreat of the Kell
The Trials of Daphne Holdfast
From the Ashes

The Magelands Epic

The Queen's Executioner
The Severed City
Needs of the Empire
Sacrifice
Fragile Empire
Storm Mage
Soulwitch Rises
Renegade Gods

The Magelands Eternal Siege

The Mortal Blade
The Dragon's Blade
The Prince's Blade
Falls of Iron
Paths of Fire
Gates of Ruin
City of Salve
Red City

City Ascendant
Dragon Eyre Badblood
Dragon Eyre Ashfall
Dragon Eyre Blackrose
Dreams of Kell
God Restrainer
Holdfast Imperium
World's End

The Magelands Dominion

Serpent Dominion
Demon Witch
Death Seer
Blood Burden
Kin Strife
Tempest's Edge
Creator of Worlds
Palace of the Almighty
Sapphire Throne
The Lost Ascendant
Yearning for Evermore

Masters and Makers

Fall Seldom Kings
The Making of Abigone
Whalebone King
Lies the Prince
Suffer the Heir

Cover Design by Sasha Almazan and Gene Mollica, G&S Cover Design Studio. LLC.
Maps by Irina French

Brigdomin Books Ltd
First Edition, July 2025
Ebook Edition © July 2025
ISBN 978-1-915978-63-9

ACKNOWLEDGEMENTS

I would like to thank the following for all their support during the writing of the Magelands Empire - my wife, Lisa Mitchell, who read every chapter as soon as it was drafted and kept me going in the right direction; my parents for their unstinting support; Marilyn Hopwood for reading the books in their early stages; James Aitken for his encouragement; and Grant and Gordon of the Film Club for their support.

Thanks also to my Advance Reader team, for all your help during the last few weeks before publication.

DRAMATIS PERSONAE

Plateau City – Imperial Court

Thorn Holdfast, Empress

Kelsey Holdfast, Herald of the Empire

Lucius Cardova, Imperial Constable

Brogan ae Bridget, Chamberlain

Martius Claudian, Imperial Adjutant

Fenu, Imperial Chief of Staff

Nardini, Chief Jurist

Slaeon, Imperial Treasurer

Bedig ae Brannig, Lord Marshal

Rosie Jackdaw, Imperial Quartermaster

Cael Holdfast, Imperial Secretary

Arrosa Holdfast, Aide to the Empress

Plateau City - Others

Carden Holdfast, Karalyn and Cardova's Son (10)

Caitlyn Holdfast, Karalyn and Cardova's Daughter (9)

Caelius Logos, Retired Quartermaster

Calpurnia Holdfast, Kelsey and Van's daughter (15)

Caelius Holdfast, Kelsey and Van's Son (13)

Cowie Holdfast, Cael and Arrosa's Son (2)

Van Logos, Ambassador from the City of Salve

Nestorian, Rosie Jackdaw's Husband

Colsbury

Shella, Imperial Chancellor

Olo'osso, Retired Pirate

Frostback, Silver Dragon

Halfclaw, Blue/Green Dragon

Clackenbaird – Marchbrae Holdfasts

Aila Holdfast, Purveyor of Whisky

Naxor, Aila's Cousin

Killop Holdfast, Corthie and Aila's Eldest Son (20)

Konna Holdfast, Corthie and Aila's Eldest Daughter (17)

Cairney Holdfast, Corthie and Aila's Son (16)

Carter Holdfast, Corthie and Aila's Son (14)

Clova Holdfast, Corthie and Aila's Daughter (12)

Carron Holdfast, Corthie and Aila's Youngest Son (10)

Ceres Holdfast, Corthie and Aila's Daughter (8)

Carla Holdfast, Corthie and Aila's Youngest Daughter (6)

Rainsby

Cole Holdfast, Imperial Agent; Son of Keir Holdfast

Alva Longhold, Imperial Agent

Audrey Longhold, Imperial Marine

Hold Fast Estate, Holdings

Celine Holdfast, Estate Manager

Ulna, Dragon Eyre

Blackrose, Queen of the Eastern Rim

Maddie Jackdaw, Blackrose's Rider

Beth Jackdaw, Maddie's Daughter (15)

Oto'pazzi (Topaz), Maddie's Husband

Sable Holdfast, Retired Agent

Alara'osso (Lara), Sable's Partner

Anaj'osso (Joss), Sable and Lara's Son (13)

Alindi'osso (Lindi), Sable and Lara's Daughter (9)

Athumia – Nom Karta

Kyra Holdfast, Karalyn and Lennox's Daughter

Edgar, Brother of Edmond

Edward, Kyra and Edgar's Son

Alfred, Kyra and Edgar's Son

Elmhirst, Ancient, Edgar's Aide

Famula Min Gahad, Queen of the Dominion

Abda Min Gahad, Famula's Sister

Saphben Mon Gahad, Famula's Brother

Konran Mon Gahad, Famula's Brother

Tirna Min Gahad, Famula's Sister

Sigra Min Sigmund, Lord Sigum's Niece

Athumia – Zamata

Bailey, Theodora's Brother

Bauchlie, President of Zamata

City of Salve

Emily Aurelian, Queen of the City

Daniel Aurelian, King of the City

Elspeth, Emily and Daniel's Daughter

Maxwell, Son of the God-Queen

Others

Karalyn Holdfast, Immortal Dream Mage

Lahnos Laimos, Former Commander, Imperial Army

Sigum Mon Sigel, Dragon, and Friend of Lahnos

Ora'lya, Dragon Rider

Dermot Laimos, Lahnos's Son (6)

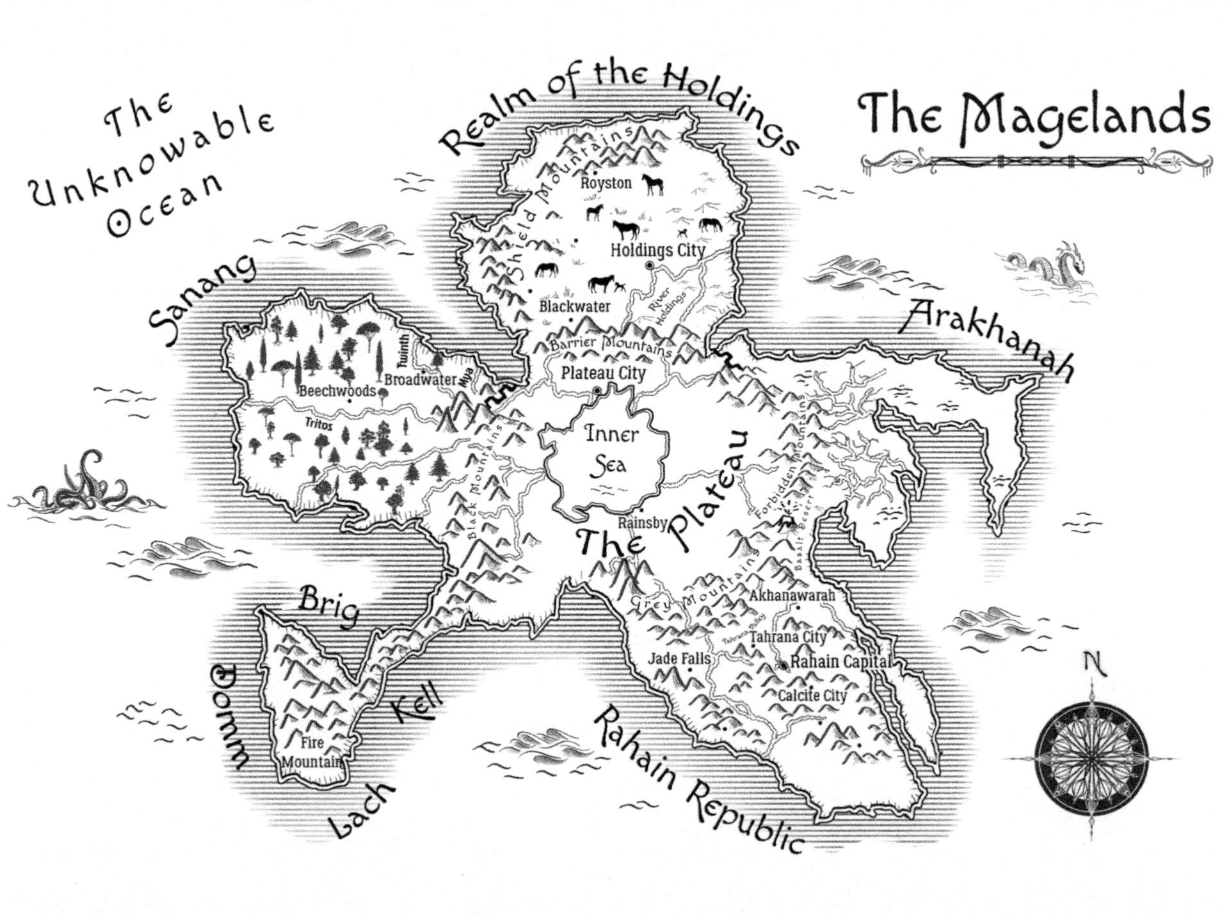

The Magelands
The Unknowable Ocean
Realm of the Holdings
Shield Mountains
Royston
Holdings City
Blackwater
River Holdings
Barrier Mountains
Plateau City
Sanang
Twinth
Broadwater
Mya
Beechwoods
Tritos
Inner Sea
Black Mountains
Rainsby
The Plateau
Arakhanah
Forbidden Mountains
Basalt Desert
Grey Mountains
Akhanawarah
Tahrana City
Rahain Capital
Jade Falls
Calcite City
Rahain Republic
Brig
Kell
Domm
Lach
Fire Mountain
N

The Plateau

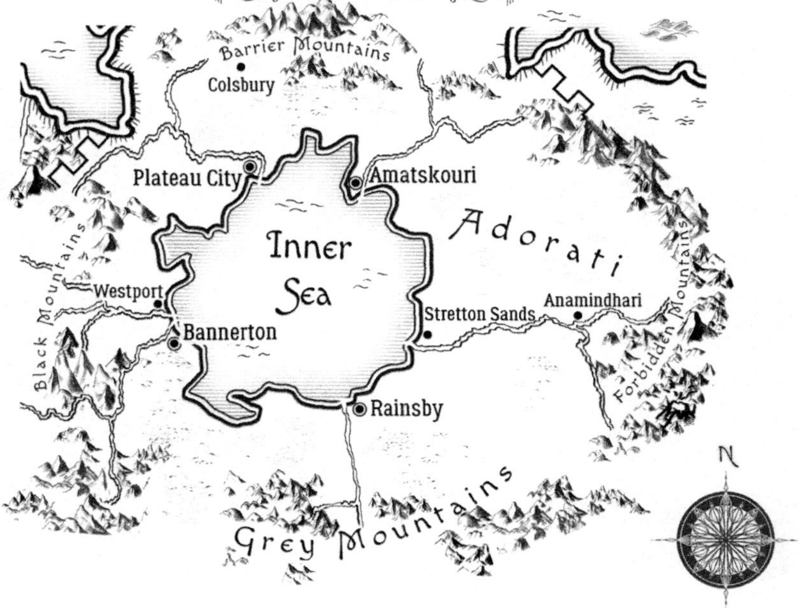

Barrier Mountains
Colsbury
Plateau City
Amatskouri
Adorati
Inner Sea
Black Mountains
Westport
Bannerton
Stretton Sands
Anamindhari
Forbidden Mountains
Rainsby
Grey Mountains
N

CHAPTER 1
REPLACEMENT

Rainsby, Southern Plateau – 15th Day, Second Third Summer 552

Cole Holdfast's vision soared above Madden's Tower. The port town of Rainsby lay still and quiet beneath him, and the oil lamps in the streets were illuminating a few soldiers on guard by the harbour. Cole turned towards the north, and his vision shot over the calm waters of the Inner Sea. The sky in the east was beginning to lighten, and Cole could see several ships, their positions marked by the glistening foam of their wakes. Cole increased his speed. He had crossed the Inner Sea with his powers every day since being posted to Rainsby, and he reached Plateau City in under a minute. He slowed as his vision flashed over the southern districts of the great city. The Blue Palace dominated the centre of the imperial capital, its twin, curved towers rising hundreds of feet into the air. It looked finished from the outside, and the tens of thousands of blue ceramic tiles encasing its outer surface were already picking up the first hues of dawn.

Cole veered away from the enormous, unfinished palace, and aimed for the Ministry of the Plateau, where the Imperial Court was based. His vision went through an open window, and he saw Marshal Bedig sitting at his desk. The red-haired Kellach man looked tired, and he was sipping from a cup of coffee, a lit cigarette in his left hand.

Cole entered his mind.

Good morning, sir.

Good morning, Cole, said Bedig.

Cole placed a vision of himself into the man's head, so that it would seem as though he was physically standing in front of him.

'That's better,' said Bedig. 'How are you this morning?'

'Everything is fine in Rainsby, sir,' said Cole. 'Do you have any messages for me to pass on?'

'I have a brief message for the Matriarch of Sanang,' said Bedig, 'but my main messages are for you.' A tired smile touched his face. 'First of all, happy birthday – did you think I would forget?'

'Thank you, sir,' said Cole.

'Twenty-seven, is it?' said Bedig.

'Yes, sir. I'm getting old.'

Bedig laughed. 'Just wait until you're as old as I am. I'll be thirty-five next third. When I was your age, I was already a member of the Imperial Court. You have been reporting to me for several years, Cole, and so I can probably guess the answer to my next question – have you ever entertained the possibility of joining the Imperial Court? You have the longest range of any vision mage in the Empire; are you honestly happy with being stuck in Rainsby?'

'I prefer the quiet life, sir.'

Bedig frowned. 'I thought you would say something like that. I'm moving on, you see. I have served ten years as Imperial Marshal, and I'm ready for a new role.'

Cole's eyes tightened. 'Have you resigned, sir?'

'I requested a transfer,' Bedig said. 'I'm being posted to Ulna in the Eastern Rim, as Imperial Legate. It's time to enjoy some Dragon Eyre weather. Anyway, I was asked by Her Majesty if I could suggest a replacement, and...'

'Please don't tell me that you suggested my name, sir,' said Cole.

Bedig laughed. 'Calm yourself, Cole; I did no such thing. I recommended that Cael take my job, but that would leave your cousin's position as Imperial Secretary vacant. It's the lowliest role on the Imperial Court, but it would get your foot in the door.'

'What if I don't want my foot in the door?'

'That would be a great shame, as the Empress seemed quite taken with my suggestion. Should I inform Her Majesty that you are refusing to do your duty?'

Cole gazed down at the carpeted floor, and shook his head. 'I will do whatever the Empress commands.'

'Come on, Cole; did you really believe that a mage with your power would be allowed to languish in Rainsby forever?'

'I don't see it as languishing, sir. From Rainsby, I can contact every major settlement on the Star Continent, from Holdings City to Threeways. I wouldn't be able to reach Domm if I was based in Plateau City.'

'How do I put this politely?' said Bedig. 'The Empire now has over fifty working Quadrants in its possession. As Imperial Secretary, one of those Quadrants would be yours, and you wouldn't need to use your vision powers to send messages. A few finger movements, and you would be in Threeways. That brings me on to my second message for you – your replacement as Rainsby's vision mage is being sent out to you today. I want you to train this mage to take over your responsibilities, so that you are free to be recalled to the imperial capital.'

'But... You mean the decision has already been taken? Don't I get a say in this?'

'Did you not just tell me that you would do whatever the Empress commands? Her Majesty feels it is time you were brought into the inner workings of the Empire. You have two thirds, Cole. Train your replacement, then get your arse back to Plateau City.'

Cole suppressed his emotions. 'Yes, sir.'

'Thank you, Cole,' said Bedig. 'Right – your message for the Matriarch. Let her know that Cael will be joining her in Broadwater tomorrow to take over the investigation into the assassination attempt. Reassure her that the Empire will do whatever it takes to keep her and her family safe.'

'Yes, sir.'

'Try not to look so unhappy, Cole; this is a major opportunity for you. The Blue Palace will be ready by the time you get to Plateau City, and you will have your own quarters in the Western Tower.'

'Yes, sir. When will my replacement be arriving?'

'At some point this morning; Claudian is organising it. Have a good birthday, Cole, and I will speak to you tomorrow.'

Cole inclined his head, then he severed the vision connection. He rubbed his temples, and gazed out of the window of his small, cramped office. For four years, he had enjoyed the peace and quiet of Rainsby. He had carried out his job, behaved himself, and kept his head down. The port town had been a backwater for decades, its economic importance eclipsed by Westport and Stretton Sands; and its strategic significance had faded into irrelevance with the annexation of Rahain into the Empire. Destroyed and rebuilt many times over, Rainsby was the least attractive of all the cities bordering the Inner Sea. As many of the marines based in Madden's Tower never failed to remind him, Cole's father had been responsible for obliterating the entire town over two decades before, when Cole had been a baby. At twenty-seven, Cole was older than his father had been when he had been killed by an Ascendant in Kell. Keir Holdfast had been involved in several wars throughout his short life, and yet his son had done nothing of any note since helping the Empress destroy the Wystians on Gyle seven years before. His cousin Cael had been the opposite – always keen to prove his worth to the Empire, while Cole had preferred to remain out of sight.

He remembered what he was supposed to do, and sent his vision out through the open window again. When he had delivered his message to one of the Matriarch's chief advisors, he got to his feet, and left his little office. He walked through the quiet hallways of the tower, then he descended a level to the marines' large mess hall, where breakfast was being served. Everyone in the building knew who he was, but he had kept himself aloof from the others, and had made no new friends. The marines respected him, but they also thought he was standoffish and a little cold, and he could get through entire days without speaking to anyone face to face.

He queued at the food counter, and nodded his thanks when the marine cook handed him a loaded tray. He walked to a quiet booth and sat down, placing his tray onto a wooden table. A marine officer eyed him from a neighbouring table, then she got to her feet and walked over to where he was sitting.

Cole tried not to show his annoyance as the marine stopped by the booth.

'Captain Holdfast?' she said.

'I am having breakfast, Lieutenant,' he said. 'Can this wait?'

The marine smiled. 'No, sir; it can't. I got a letter from my little sister this morning.'

Cole frowned. 'Do I know you?'

'Not particularly, sir; though we have met. I was in your cousin's class in Pebble Strand; Cael and I were good friends back then.'

Cole eyed her. 'Audrey Longhold?'

'Yes, sir,' she said, the smile remaining on her face. 'Anyway, my sister told me that she is coming to Rainsby.'

'Is she also a marine?'

'No, sir. She has no battle-vision.'

Cole grew impatient. 'Why are you telling me this?'

'She has inner vision, sir,' Audrey said. 'She's coming here to replace you.'

'Oh. I see.'

'It came as a bit of a shock to her, sir. She had no idea she was a mage until she was twenty-two. My uncle swooped in, and my sister was commissioned as a junior officer in the army.'

'Your uncle?'

'Yes, sir. My uncle is Holder Long. He is very pleased to have two nieces who are mages, and he wanted us both in uniform; my poor old dad didn't have a say in the matter.'

'I know how he feels.'

'So where are you off to, then, sir? You know, after you have trained my sister.'

Cole shrugged. 'I don't want to talk about it.'

'Fair enough. When my sister gets here, I'll bring her up to your office. She's shy, and she's bound to be homesick, so I intend to take care of her until she settles in.'

'Then I guess I will be seeing you later, Lieutenant.'

Audrey eyed him, then she returned to her table. Cole turned back to his tray, and picked up his mug of coffee. It was turning out to be the worst birthday he had experienced in several years. He was being forced out of his job, and the marines would be keeping a close eye on how he treated his replacement. Why couldn't the Empress understand that he wanted to be left alone? She was almost as bad as Cael, who was forever encouraging him to *fulfil his potential*, whatever that meant. Cole had done his duty during the short war with the Dominion, but the Empire had enjoyed seven years of peace since then. Cael had spent that time working as an agent of the Empire, using his Quadrant and his powers to flit from place to place, sorting out problems and acting as the Empress's eyes and ears across the vast territories under imperial control; while Cole had sat in an office, passing on messages, and growing ever more insular.

He left the tower for his usual long walk after breakfast. He went by the harbour, where merchant vessels were unloading produce from the other ports lining the Inner Sea, then he walked down to where the massive city walls built by Bridget had stood. A few sections were still standing, and Cole gazed at the magnificent ruins. His father had held back the tide of Agatha's Rahain forces from those walls when he had been seventeen. He had also fathered Cole by that point, and was betrothed to the woman who would rise to become the Empress. Dead at twenty-six, Keir had moved into the realms of myth – a peerless fire and vision mage; a hero of Rainsby, Colsbury and the Kell Pass. Everyone had forgotten what a terrible father he had been, and Cole never sought to remind people that his father had walked out on his mother while she had been pregnant. No one wanted to hear about that; instead, they continually asked Cole to tell them about the great things his father had achieved.

Cole turned away from the ruins and walked through the narrow streets in the centre of Rainsby. Some parts had survived, but most of the town had been rebuilt in the previous decade, replacing the old segregated quarters that had previously existed. In the new Rainsby, Holdings dwelt alongside Kellach and Rahain, their old animosities not exactly forgotten, and their differences tolerated rather than celebrated.

When he returned to Madden's Tower, he decided he would read for the remainder of the morning while he waited for Audrey's sister to arrive, but Adjutant Claudian was already there, standing outside Cole's small office, with a young Holdings woman by his side.

'Good morning, Captain,' said Claudian.

Cole frowned. 'Sorry if I kept you waiting, sir.'

'That's fine,' Claudian said; 'it gave me a chance to give Lieutenant Longhold a quick tour of the facilities in Madden's Tower.' He gestured to the woman next to him. 'Might I introduce Alva Longhold to you, Captain? I trust that Marshal Bedig has informed you as to why she is in Rainsby?'

'He told me, sir,' said Cole.

'And this, Lieutenant Longhold,' Claudian went on, 'is the finest vision mage in the Empire – Captain Cole Holdfast.'

'It's nice to meet you,' said Cole.

Alva Longhold said nothing.

Claudian dug into a pocket and withdrew two items. 'These are for you, Captain,' he said. 'The first, as you can see, is a Quadrant. It is now yours. The Empress wishes you to have it, in anticipation of your new role. The second item is a letter that Her Majesty wishes you to deliver, in person, to Konna Holdfast in Kell. Konna's eighteenth birthday is five days from now, and you are to present her with this letter on that date.'

Cole took both items. 'Understood, sir.'

'Excellent. If there are no questions, then I will leave Lieutenant Longhold in your capable hands.'

Cole inclined his head. Claudian took out another Quadrant, glided his fingers over its surface, and disappeared.

Alva exhaled. 'That man intimidates me a little bit,' she said. 'I don't know what it is about him, but my mouth clamps shut in his presence. He's like a strict headmaster or something. Are you going to invite me into your office?'

Cole gazed at her.

'My sister said you were quiet,' Alva went on. 'Have you seen her? She said she would be here to greet me when I arrived, but I haven't seen any sign of her. Where is she?'

'I don't know,' said Cole, as he unlocked the door to his office.

He walked inside, and Alva followed him in and closed the door.

'This is a very small office,' she said. 'Are we both going to fit in here? It's very dreary. As soon as I take over your job, I'm going to clear it out and redecorate; I hope you don't mind.'

Cole sat down by his desk. He opened a drawer, and dropped the Quadrant and the letter into it. Alva walked over to the window and gazed out at the view.

'What is your range?' said Cole.

'A hundred miles,' she said.

'That's not good enough,' said Cole. 'Any vision mage based in Rainsby needs to be able to reach the major regions of the Star Continent, and you can't even reach Plateau City.'

Alva laughed. 'I thought you might say something like that. This time last year, I could barely range five miles. This time last third, I could only reach fifty miles. Herald Kelsey said I must be a late developer.'

'You've met Kelsey?'

'She interviewed me for this job,' said Alva. 'Under your guidance, I have to be able to reach Plateau City in the next two thirds; that's what she said.'

'What about Threeways in the Domm Pass?' said Cole. 'And Holdings City? What about the Rahain Capital?'

'I don't need to be able to reach them,' she said. 'Herald Kelsey told me that we have so many Quadrants these days, there is no need for the Rainsby mage to be able to reach everywhere. In fact, you are the only one who has ever been able to do it. She said you were wasted down here. When she said that, I thought she meant that you were getting wasted down here; you know, getting drunk and smoking dreamweed all the time; so I said that sounded like fun. She gave me a really funny look.' She cleared a pile of books from the room's only other chair, and sat down. 'What are you going to teach me first?'

'How old are you?'

'Twenty-three.'

'And you didn't know that you were a vision mage until recently?'

'That's right. How could anyone know if they don't try? My mother said that priests used to routinely check all teenagers in the Holdings, back in the olden times; but no one does it any more. I did try to see if I had battle-vision, like Audrey does, but I don't. I'm quite pleased about that. If I had battle-vision, I would have been sent to the marines. Do you have battle-vision?'

'Are you ever going to call me *sir*?'

'I don't think so. I'm here to take over your job, so I see us as equals, even if you are a Holdfast. Is that why they made you a captain – because you're a Holdfast?'

'I've been in the army for seven years.'

'My sister has been in the marines for seven years, and she's still a lieutenant.'

'I don't have battle-vision,' he said. 'I have upper vision and fire powers.'

Alva laughed. 'Fire powers? I didn't know that.'

'Why would you?'

'Well, your father had fire powers; everyone knows that. He burned down the whole of Rainsby.'

'I am not my father.'

Alva eyed him. 'No, I can see that now.'

'Where are all your things? I assume you didn't arrive without luggage.'

'Claudian has already taken my luggage to my new quarters. I have my own room, and it has a private bathroom attached to it. He also took me to the mess hall and introduced me to a few marines. They seem nice; but, you know, I wouldn't want to get on their wrong side.'

Cole frowned as he looked at her. She seemed completely unsuitable as his replacement.

'Try to get into my mind,' he said.

'All right,' she said. She stared into his eyes, and he felt a slight tingling at the back of his head.

'I can't,' she said. 'Something is blocking me. How are you doing that?'

'Try to work it out.'

Alva smiled. 'Did Karalyn seal up your mind? Is she really as crazy as everyone says?'

'I haven't seen her for years, but don't call her crazy. She has saved the Star Continent more times than you can imagine.'

'Three times,' Alva said. 'Karalyn Holdfast has saved the Star Continent three times. I learned about her in school. What's she really like?'

'I don't know, and that's the honest answer. You should have asked the Herald when you had the chance.'

'I did ask her,' said Alva. 'Kelsey laughed and told me not to concern myself with such things.'

'How many languages can you speak?' he said.

'All of them.'

Cole raised an eyebrow.

'It's what I was best at in school,' said Alva. 'I was studying languages at Holdings City University when I discovered I had vision powers.'

'Do you know Gunstian?'

'I meant all languages used in the Empire,' she said. 'Gunst isn't in the Empire, yet.'

'Do you think it should be?'

'I think all lands should be in the Empire, but only if they want to be. I wouldn't force any nation to join us.'

'I have one last question,' he said. 'What do you think about the Empress's plans to bring democracy to the Empire?'

'I think...' She trailed off, and her eyes tightened. 'What will happen if I say the *wrong* answer?'

'Tell me, or I will read it from your mind.'

'That would be quite rude,' she said. 'I was told that you were quiet and polite. One of the harmless Holdfasts.'

'Who calls me that?'

'Most folk in the Holdings, as far as I can gather. I mean, unlike Cael, you look like you could be from the Holdings, apart from you being so tall, of course. They say that you are the opposite of your father. He was ruthless; you are harmless.'

'Your opinion on the promised democratic changes, if you please.'

'All right,' she said. 'Are you ready? I think they are stupid. What's wrong with letting each province govern itself in its own way? Look how rich and peaceful we are right now, before these so-called *improvements* are forced upon us. Do you know how many people live in Rakana and Rahain? There are so many of them that they will be able to dictate what happens in, say, Kellach Brigdomin. That can't be right. I have nothing against the Rakanese, but the population of Adorati is set to explode in the next couple of decades, and the rest of us would be easily outvoted. My uncle said that I wasn't to worry, though, as the reforms will never happen. The constitutional convention has been bickering and procrastinating on the island of Colsbury for seven years, and they still haven't found a solution to the contradictions inherent in bringing full democracy to the Empire. As a Holdfast, you should be pleased about that. Democracy will hurt your family more than it would hurt mine. How will you keep control of the Empire if the masses are allowed to vote you out?'

'What makes you think I want anything to do with power?'

'Well, as I said, you are the harmless Holdfast. Is that why you have been hiding down here in Rainsby? I look upon this job as a stepping stone to something better; is that not how you see it?'

Cole said nothing.

There was a knock on the door, and it opened. Audrey Longhold walked into the small room, a huge smile on her face. Alva got to her feet, and the Longhold sisters embraced, laughing.

'Look at you in your army uniform,' cried Audrey, 'but don't be scared; the marines will protect you.'

'From whom?' said Alva. 'Cole?'

Audrey laughed louder.

'He's been asking me all kinds of questions,' Alva went on.

'Has your big mouth been getting you into trouble again?' said Audrey.

'No more than usual. Are you free this evening? I want to see what the taverns of Rainsby have to offer.'

'I'm free, but what about you?' said Audrey. She glanced at Cole. 'Is my sister working tonight, sir?'

Cole shook his head.

'Thank you, sir,' said Audrey. She turned back to her sister. 'Let's drink until we fall over. We can start after dinner in the mess hall, then we can rustle up a few marines and go out. Rainsby only has about a dozen decent places to drink – we'll see if we can hit them all.'

Alva laughed. 'Sounds like a good plan. Have you got any spare cigarettes?'

Audrey pulled out a half-used packet from her uniform and gave it to her sister.

'Thanks,' said Alva. 'I'll buy some for you in the mess hall later.'

'All right. I'll see you at dinner.' Audrey saluted Cole, then she left the room. She turned before closing the door. 'I just remembered something,' she said. 'Happy birthday, sir.'

Cole nodded, but kept his mouth closed.

Audrey shut the door, and her sister glanced down at Cole.

'Is today your birthday?'

Cole nodded again.

'What are you doing to celebrate?' said Alva.

'I have nothing planned,' he said.

'Do you, uh... do you want to come along with me and Audrey tonight?'

'No, thank you.'

Alva sat back down, looking a little relieved.

'I don't drink,' Cole went on; 'or smoke, so I would be obliged if you didn't light a cigarette in here.'

'What do you do, you know, to pass the time?' she said.

'I read. I go for long walks. I have a horse stabled in the cavalry compound, and I sometimes take him out of Rainsby for a ride into the hills south of here.'

'That sounds a bit dull,' she said, 'apart from the horse-riding. I wonder if the cavalry would lend me a horse; I had to leave all four of mine behind on the Hold Long estate. What about friends? Do you have any friends in Rainsby?'

'No. Cael visits every third or so, to catch up, and he sometimes brings Arrosa. She's his wife.'

'I know who Arrosa Holdfast is,' she said. 'Why are you not married?'

'I have no interest in seeing anyone, and I don't care if you think my life is dull. I'm not here to make friends, or to find a wife.'

'Then why are you here? I heard that you could easily get a job working for the Empress in Plateau City.'

'That's none of your business.'

She narrowed her eyes. 'Are you hiding from something?'

'You know nothing about me.'

'That's not exactly true, is it? The Holdfasts are the most famous family in the Empire. We learn about you at school; did you know that? I did a class project on the Holdfasts when I was fourteen. Does Sable ever visit? I'd quite like to meet Sable.'

'I haven't seen Sable for about five years. She's busy raising her two children on Dragon Eyre.'

'That's a pity. Maybe you should do more to keep in contact with your relatives. Right – what are we going to do this afternoon? Should we have lunch first? What's the food like here?'

Cole glanced away, half-tempted to give Alva the entire day off so that he wouldn't have to talk to her.

'We're going to be working on improving your range,' he said. 'You have two thirds to reach as far as Plateau City, which is about six hundred miles from here. If you can't do that, you won't be able to take over my position.'

Alva nodded. 'All right. Should we get started?'

CHAPTER 2
GIFTS

Marchside, Kell – 20th Day, Second Third Summer 552

Konna sat on the soft grass by the tomb of her father, her gaze on the view of Southern Kell. The hill upon which Corthie's cairn had been built was as high as the one that bore Clackenbaird Farm, and she had a perfect view of the surrounding countryside. To the south, a higher range of hills spread out into the distance, and the town of Marchside lay nestled by their feet, while, to the north, east and west, the farms and fields stretched out into the horizon. The sky was blue, and the sun was shining down. Even the wind was still, for once, and Konna savoured the warmth on her skin. There weren't many days in Kell as sunny and pleasant as that day had become, and she felt reluctant to walk back down the path that led to the farmhouse, despite the fact that her family would be waiting for her.

Her eyes went over the green lands of her home. Apart from a small time on Colsbury, she had lived her entire life in Kell. She shuddered as memories of Colsbury ran through her. She hated the place. It had been upon the isle of Colsbury that she had seen her father's body after it had been brought back from Dragon Eyre. Until that moment, she had never grieved for anyone, nor had she harboured any hate within her heart. She had been ten when her father had been killed fighting for the Empress, and she had spent her eleventh birthday in a fog of grief, when each day had run into the next, and each night had lasted forever. Her mother's tears had been unending, and were it not for Uncle Naxor, Konna believed that her family might have fallen apart at that time. While the family had held together, nothing had been the same since, as though a light had gone from their lives, snatched from them by the greed and selfishness of Thorn, Kelsey, and the rest of the Colsbury Holdfasts. They had stolen Corthie from his family, and had sent him to die on a strange world that Konna had grown to hate.

She felt Naxor trying to get into her head. She narrowed her eyes, and allowed him in.

I am sorry to disturb you while you rest by your father's tomb, he said, *but your mother is starting to get a little worried about you. Do you think you might know how long you will be?*

Tell her I'm coming, Uncle, she said in her mind.

Thank you, Konna.

Naxor's presence vanished from her thoughts, and she got to her feet. She glanced at the large cairn, and placed a hand onto one of its rough stones, where moss was starting to grow.

'Sleep well, Father,' she said. 'I love you.'

She set off down the hillside, following the well-trodden path to the road that led up to the farmhouse. She passed a junction, where another road ran round the base of the hill towards the vast collection of buildings that made up the Marchbrae businesses – businesses that had made them the richest family in Kell. Smoke was rising from the chimneys of the distillery and the copper-works, and a wagon loaded with barrels was being pulled along by a team of four ponies.

A tall Kellach man waved down to her from the driver's bench.

'Good morning, lass,' he called out, 'and happy birthday.'

'Thanks,' she called back.

Konna left the junction behind, and climbed the hill to the farmhouse. The large building sat perched atop the summit of the hill, its slate tiles shimmering in the sunlight. A courtyard sat out by the front of the house, and its other flanks were enclosed by farm buildings constructed by Banner forces during an old war against the gods. Konna walked into the courtyard, and entered the house. She pulled off her boots by the front door, then she noticed that her mother was standing in the hallway.

'Sorry I'm late,' Konna said.

'Don't be silly,' said Aila. 'It's your birthday; this day belongs to you.'

Her mother kissed her on the cheek.

'I wanted to talk to Father,' said Konna.

'I understand. He would have been so proud of you; his eldest girl turning eighteen. I'm proud of you, Konna. A mother couldn't ask for a better daughter. Now, come through to the sitting room; all of your brothers and sisters are here.'

Konna frowned. 'What – even Killop? I thought he was in Plateau City.'

'He was dropped off here less than twenty minutes ago,' said Aila. 'An official with a Quadrant brought him.'

'How did he persuade an official to bring him here?' said Konna.

Aila smiled. 'He asked. You know what they're like in Plateau City – they are always trying to please us, as though by doing us little favours, they think they might be able to make up for... You know what I mean.'

Aila led her through to the large sitting room, and her siblings let out a cheer.

'About time!' cried Cairney. 'We were about to start the party without ye.'

Konna smiled at her brother. Even at sixteen, Cairney was as tall as their father had been, and just as broad-shouldered. Next to him was Killop, a mere inch shorter than Cairney. Among most Kellach, Killop was of an impressive size, but Cairney dominated every room he walked into.

'It's good to see you, sister,' said Killop.

Konna embraced her older brother.

'Careful ye don't catch anything from him,' said Cairney. 'Killop's gone native. Two years at university has fucked with his mind.'

'Language, Cairney,' said Naxor. 'Not in front of your mother, please.'

Konna narrowed her eyes at Killop. 'Is that right, brother? Have ye gone soft?'

'Let's not talk about that,' said Aila. She gestured towards a long table laden with food and drink. 'Sit down, everyone, before the food gets cold.'

Aila went to the head of the table and took her seat. Naxor sat to her right, and Konna took a chair opposite him. Next to her, Killop sat down, then Clova, as Cairney and Carter went to their places by Naxor. The three youngest children – Carron, Ceres and Carla, occupied seats at the other end of the table from their mother, and Aila smiled.

'Today,' she said, 'two of my children are now adults. Happy eighteenth birthday, Konna. Before we eat, we have a few gifts for you.'

Konna smiled. 'I've already opened my gifts, Mother; you gave them to me this morning.'

'I wasn't talking about those gifts,' said Aila. 'You got clothes and new boots – the usual birthday presents we give to the children; but this is a special birthday, and so we have arranged a few special gifts. I have something for you, but I can't tell you what it is just yet – you will have to be patient for a little longer.' She eyed Naxor. 'Why don't you go first, cousin?'

'I would be delighted to do so,' said Naxor. He withdrew two large envelopes from his long robes, and set them down onto the table. 'I'm going to make a little speech,' he went on, and a few of the children groaned. Naxor smiled. 'It will be short; I promise. Konna, you have reached the giddy heights of adulthood but, as an immortal demigod, you are still at the very beginning of a long journey. What you need, as far as I can tell, is a measure of financial independence – a solid foundation from which you can deal with the challenges of living in a mortal world.' He picked up the first envelope. 'This contains the title deeds to a farmstead close to the Kell Pass. Have you heard of a village called Goatcross? No? It happens to be the settlement from where your grandfather Killop originated. His twin sister Keira, the renowned fire mage, also hailed from that place.' He smiled. 'You, Konna, are now the owner of a three-hundred acre farm just to the south of Goatcross. I purchased it for you a while ago, and I am now honoured to present it into your hands. It is farmed by a dozen tenant families and provides a substantial annual income, which now belongs to you.' He picked up the second envelope. 'This contains shares from the Marchbrae companies,' he went on, 'from my own personal stock. They are now yours, to do with as you please. If you hold on to them, they will also provide a substantial yearly income; and if you were to sell them, you would make a small fortune. In short, you are now a wealthy young woman in your own right, Konna, no longer dependent on the family for your income.'

He passed the two envelopes across the table, and Konna took them.

'Thank you, Uncle,' she said. 'I don't know what to say. You are very generous.'

'It is nothing, Konna,' Naxor said; 'merely what you are due. Your mother and I have been growing the Marchbrae businesses for years, and we have some experience of running successful enterprises.' He glanced at the other children. 'Each one of you shall be provided for. We are a family, and we look after each other.'

'I have a present, too,' said Cairney.

Konna eyed him. 'You bought me a gift, brother?'

'Well, I bought the parts, and helped put them together,' said Cairney, 'but I didn't do it on my own. A couple of the blacksmiths on the farm helped me.'

The sixteen-year-old boy got to his feet, then he picked up a box that was lying on the floor, and set it down in front of Konna.

'Open it,' he said.

Konna pulled at the ribbon, and removed the lid from the box. Inside was a steel gauntlet, traced in black Tempest metal. It had been constructed to allow free movement of the fingers on the wearer's right hand, and had two greenhide claws protruding from the reinforced knuckles. Konna slipped her hand into the gauntlet, and lifted it. It was heavy, and she powered a thin thread of battle-vision to cope with the weight. The gauntlet also had a steel and Tempest guard that ran halfway up Konna's right forearm, and she smiled at the intricate swirls and engravings upon it.

Aila raised an eyebrow at the fearsome weapon. 'Is that what you have been doing, Cairney?' she said. 'I wondered.'

Cairney laughed with delight. 'It's called the Clawfist,' he said. 'Like Da's Clawhammer. The greenhide claws are the same age as you, Konna. I found them in the Kell Pass, where they still have great heaps of greenhide bones left over from the war, and Uncle Naxor helped me buy the Tempest that strengthens it. Da probably killed the greenhide the claws come from, and your fingers are free, so that you can still use your death powers when yer wearing it. What do ye think? Do ye like it?'

'Aye,' said Konna, as she hefted the Clawfist over the table. 'I like it, but I don't know when I'll be able to use it.'

'That brings me to my gift,' said Aila. 'We are expecting someone to appear from the Plateau soon, and...'

'Might I give Konna my gift first, Ma?' said Killop.

Aila glanced at her eldest child. 'I didn't know you had brought one, son.'

'Aye,' said Killop, as he dug into a bag by his feet, 'though it's not much, not compared to what Cairney got her.' He pulled a large book from the bag. 'I bought this in the university bookshop in Plateau City for you, Konna. I have my own copy, and I learned a lot from it.'

Naxor arched an eyebrow. 'Which book is that?'

'It's *A History of the Star Continent*,' said Killop, 'by Kelsey Holdfast.'

Cairney and Carter both emitted loud groans.

'Fucksake,' said Cairney. 'Do ye see what I mean now, Konna? Killop's in love with the Colsbury Holdfasts. What are ye doing bringing that pish down to Kell, eh?'

'It's only a book,' said Killop. 'Words can't hurt anyone. No matter what you think of Aunty Kelsey, she is a good writer, and her *History* is worth reading.' He passed the book to Konna.

She took it, unsure what to say. She loathed Kelsey Holdfast, just as she loathed everyone who had been responsible for her father's death on Dragon Eyre. She opened the book at a random page near the beginning, and saw a chapter entitled – *After the Collision*.

'Thank you, Killop,' she said, 'but I don't know if I can read this. Kelsey...'

'Aunty Kelsey didn't kill Father,' Killop said. 'I have spoken to her several times in Plateau City, and she has been nothing but kind to me.'

'The bitch has a guilty conscience,' said Cairney. 'Of course she's been nice to ye. She wants ye to forget who sent our father off to die for nothing.'

'It wasn't for nothing,' said Killop, and the room stilled into silence. 'Da saved the Eastern Rim; he saved the lives of thousands of ordinary folk on Dragon Eyre from the Wystian dragons. He... He died saving Queen Blackrose.'

Aila's eyes darkened, and she stared at her eldest son.

'Yer a fucking eejit, Killop,' said Cairney. 'Ye should have stayed in Plateau City. Kick him out, Ma. Tell him he's not welcome here. And you, Konna, toss that piece-of-shite book onto the fire. Let the flames eat it up.'

Konna glanced down at the book. 'I won't read it,' she said, 'but nor will I destroy it. It was a gift, from my big brother.'

Cairney powered his own battle-vision to snatch it, but Konna pulled it out of his reach.

'Settle down, everyone,' said Naxor. 'Let us respect Konna's intentions, and let us be forgiving as to Killop's rather unfortunate choice of gift. I am sure he meant well.'

'It's only a damn history book, for Pyre's sake,' said Killop. 'Are you frightened of words, Cairney?'

'I'm not frightened,' said Cairney. 'What else have you been learning at university, ya prick? Are ye in love with the Empress, too? Have ye forgotten that yer fucking immortal?'

'I haven't forgotten,' said Killop, 'but it doesn't seem real to me. I can't.... I can't imagine what it will feel like to be hundreds of years old.'

Cairney turned to Aila. 'Ye shouldnae have let him go to university, Ma.'

'It was his decision,' said Aila. 'He chose that path when he was eighteen, just as Konna is now free to choose her own way.'

'Will ye be going to university, Konna?' said Cairney.

Konna shook her head.

'Thank Pyre for that,' said Cairney. 'It's turned Killop's brain to mince.'

'Can we eat now?' said Clova. 'I'm hungry. And I dinnae see what all the fuss is about. It's only a book. If Konna reads it, she doesnae have to believe every word.'

'Thank you, Clova,' said Killop.

'Let's eat,' said Naxor.

The family settled down, and filled their plates with food. Konna kept the large book and the Clawfist close to her while she ate. In a strange way, Cairney's vociferous objections had made her curious about the contents of the book. She had told everyone that she wouldn't read it, but hadn't Clova made a decent point? She didn't have to believe all that she read.

They were starting their second course, when there was a knock at the front door of the farmhouse. Killop got to his feet, then he returned a few moments later with two dark-skinned people. Cole Holdfast was holding a Quadrant in his left hand, while a shorter, Holdings-sized woman was standing next to him.

Aila got to her feet. 'Welcome back to Clackenbaird, Cole.'

Cole bowed his head. 'Thank you for allowing me to make this visit, ma'am.'

Cairney spat out his food. 'What the fuck? Is that Cole Holdfast? What's a Colsbury Holdfast doing here, Ma?'

'I arranged this visit with Kelsey,' said Aila.

'You what?' cried Cairney. He got to his feet, and turned to face the new arrivals, his stature making Cole Holdfast seem short in comparison, while he towered over the Holdings woman.

'You bastards are not welcome here,' Cairney said. 'Use that Quadrant and fuck off.'

'I am here on the invitation of your mother,' said Cole, standing his ground. 'I have a letter for Konna, from the Herald of the Empire.'

'Why is Kelsey playing a role in Konna's birthday?' said Cairney. 'I'm sick of hearing her name.'

'Sit down, son,' said Aila. 'Do you think I never have any contact with the imperial authorities on the Plateau? How do you imagine I arranged Killop's admittance into the university? I might not relish speaking to those who ran the war on Dragon Eyre, but we cannot live in complete isolation.' She turned to Cole, as Cairney took his seat in a sullen silence. 'Please give the letter to Konna.'

'Yes, ma'am,' said Cole. He withdrew a folded and sealed document from his clothes, and leaned over the table to pass it to Konna.

'Happy birthday, cousin,' he said.

Konna eyed him. She took the letter, and broke the seal.

To Konna Holdfast on her eighteenth birthday, from Kelsey Holdfast, Herald of the Empire,

Your mother is a persuasive woman, and I have acceded to her request regarding your future, if you choose to accept it. If you wish, there is a place for you in the City of Salve, helping to defend the new walls being built to protect the settlement of Jezra. Your battle-vision and death powers would be put to good use, and so I have decided to waive the need for you to take any oath to the Empress or to the Empire. If you wish to accept, please inform Cole, and he will return for you in a few days to transport you to the world where your mother and uncle were born. You will report to the Aurelian king and queen, but you will not be beholden to the Empire.

I mourn the situation in which we find ourselves, Konna. I loved your father dearly, and I miss him every day. I long for a time when the Holdfasts of Clackenbaird are reconciled with the other branches of our family. When your father was eighteen, he defended the Great Walls of the City of Salve, and I hope that you take the opportunity to learn more about the world for which he fought so hard.

Yours with all due affection and respect, Kelsey.

'What does it say?' said Killop.

'They want me to fight greenhides in the City of Salve,' said Konna. She eyed her mother. 'Did you ask the Herald to do this? Why?'

'Naxor and I want you to see the City where we both lived for many long centuries,' said Aila. 'I knew that you didn't wish to go to university, and I heard you mention that you would like to travel. Did Kelsey write anything about not having to swear an oath of allegiance to the Empress?'

'Aye,' said Konna. 'They are going to waive that part, if I accept.'

'Ye'd still be working for the Empire, but,' said Cairney.

'No,' said Aila, 'she would be working for the people of the City. The Jezran Walls are only half-built, and they need volunteers to protect the workers. But that will only be a small part of it, Konna – you will be able to see every region of the City; and you can stay for as long as you like.'

'I don't know,' said Konna.

'Why is the Herald waiving the oath of allegiance?' said the short Holdings woman.

All eyes turned to her.

'This is Lieutenant Alva Longhold,' said Cole. 'I'm training her to take over my role as the mage stationed in Rainsby.'

'Can anyone answer my question?' said Alva. 'Everyone who serves the Empire has to take an oath. I took an oath when I joined the army.'

'None of my children wish to serve the woman who posted their father to Dragon Eyre,' said Aila, 'and I can hardly blame them for that, as I would also refuse to swear allegiance to the Sapphire Throne. That is why I asked the Herald to make an exception in Konna's case.'

Alva frowned. 'Is it any wonder that folk think the Holdfasts are above the law?'

Cairney snorted. 'Everyone sitting at this table is a god, ya worthless wee mortal. What makes ye think we need to bow before anyone in Plateau City? We'll still be here when yer long dead.'

'Perhaps,' said Alva, 'but gods and demigods are not exempt from the law.'

'Leave it, Alva,' said Cole. 'We are not here to start a fight.'

Cairney laughed. 'Any fight between us would be over in seconds.'

Cole eyed him. 'Direct your insults towards me rather than Alva Longhold, cousin. She is not a *worthless mortal*, any more than your beloved father was a *worthless mortal*.'

Cairney bristled with anger.

'You deserved that, brother,' said Clova. 'You sounded like an arrogant god.'

'That's enough,' said Naxor. 'Let us conduct ourselves with civility.'

Alva glanced up at Cole. 'Will you tell me all about this when we get back to Rainsby?'

'I am sure he will, young lady,' said Naxor. 'Now, correct me if I am wrong, but Cole requires either an acceptance or a rejection from Konna before he can leave us all in peace.'

The family turned back to Konna.

'If I accept,' she said, 'when would you take me to the City, Cole?'

'I can be flexible, cousin,' said Cole. 'Tell me when you want to go, and I will be here.'

'I'll do it,' she said. 'I want to see the City, and I'll be able to use Cairney's gift against the greenhides. Will you come for me in four days, Cole?'

Cole inclined his head. 'I will be here after dawn on the twenty-fourth of this third, cousin, and then I shall take you to Pella.'

Aila nodded. 'Then it's all settled. Thank you, Cole. We shall see you four days from now.'

Cole glanced at Alva, then he brushed his fingers over the surface of his Quadrant, and the two visitors vanished.

'That fucking prick,' muttered Cairney. He eyed Clova. 'And what were ye thinking, ya wee numpty? I heard ye defend them. Ye called me an arrogant god.'

Clova held her brother's gaze. 'I said ye sounded like an arrogant god. Do ye want every mortal to hate us? What about the hundreds of folk who have jobs in Marchbrae – do ye hate them, too?'

'They work for us,' said Cairney, 'and that's how it should be. The gods rule, and the mortals toil.'

'Did ye learn that from Uncle Naxor?' said Killop.

'Come now,' said Naxor; 'those weren't the exact words I used. Listen, children; is it true that the natural place for gods is to govern? Yes – I think so. But does that mean we should despise every mortal? No – it does not. As gods, we have a responsibility towards the mortals under our care. We should be polite to those less fortunate than ourselves, and we should be patient. Haven't I always stressed the need for patience? As much as I admire your zeal, Cairney, you are but sixteen years of age, and you would do well to conceal your true feelings from the mortals. As for you, Killop, I ask that you be a little more wary of befriending the mortals you meet in Plateau City. Remember that their lives are but leaves in the autumn winds.'

'I don't feel like being patient,' said Cairney. 'I want to smash the bastards who killed Da while they're still alive.'

'Your uncle is correct, Cairney' said Aila. 'As much as most of us sitting here would like to drive a dagger into the heart of Thorn, all we have to do is wait, and the Empire will fall into our laps.'

'I can't believe ye think that, Ma,' said Clova. 'Didn't you fight for the mortals when ye lived in the City? What about Princess Yendra? What would she think if she heard you say those words?'

'Yendra is dead,' said Aila, 'while my grief lives on. Everyone warned me what would happen when Corthie died, but I refused to listen, and my heart has turned to stone. Perhaps in a century or two, my anger will start to fade.'

'My anger will never fade,' said Cairney.

'I hate the Colsbury Holdfasts,' said Carter. 'I will never forgive them.'

Several of the other children joined in, echoing the words of Cairney and Carter. Konna remained silent. To her right, Killop was struggling to keep his mouth closed, while, to her left, Clova was glaring at Cairney with narrow eyes. Out of the eight children, only Killop and Clova didn't seem to loathe their cousins in the Plateau with an undying ferocity. Konna frowned. Where did she place herself among the siblings? She hated the Empire for what it had done to her father, but were people like Cole to blame? As far as she knew, Cole had tried to help her father at the end; he had been there, with Cael and Blackrose, and the two cousins had fought by her father's side.

'I don't hate Cole,' she said, and the others turned to look at her. 'Cole and Cael were sent to Dragon Eyre, just as Father was. How is it their fault? They tried their best. The Empress, though? Her, I do hate. We should be blaming the ones who sent soldiers to Dragon Eyre, not our cousins who stood by our father's side.'

'Maybe Cole isn't too bad,' said Carter, 'but Cael? Cael is the Empress's golden boy; her chosen successor. He's an arse-licking, two-faced wanker, and if he ever comes here, I'll punch him in the face. The same goes for his sister Kyra. That cow nearly killed us when she ran away from Colsbury – have you all forgotten that?'

'I haven't forgotten,' said Cairney. 'Kyra is second on my list, right after the Empress.'

Konna got to her feet as the others continued to argue. She picked up the Clawfist, the two envelopes, and the book.

'Are you leaving us?' said Aila.

'Thank you for the meal, and for the presents,' said Konna. 'I think I might pack some things, so that I'm ready to go to Pella.'

Konna left the room and ascended a flight of stairs. She opened the door to her large bedroom, and stepped inside. She laid her gifts down onto her bed, and reread the letter from Kelsey. She got to the part where the Herald had written about her love for her brother, and Konna's insides coiled with anger and loss. The Herald was a hypocrite. Cole might have been blameless, but Kelsey had possessed the power to remove Corthie from Dragon Eyre at any time of her choosing, and she had neglected to do so.

She sat on the bed, and ripped the letter to pieces, as tears fell down her cheeks.

She would go to the City of Salve. She would fight greenhides, and learn about the world of Amalia and Malik; for were they not also her family? The one thing she would never do, she knew, was bow before the Empress.

Konna cursed the name of Thorn, and began to pack.

CHAPTER 3
POSTMASTER

Plateau City, The Plateau – 22nd Day, Second Third Summer 552

Arrosa gazed at the members of the Imperial Court as they took their seats in the Empress's audience chamber. Her Imperial Majesty had a serene expression on her face, and she gazed down at Kelsey.

'Please begin, my Herald,' said Thorn.

'Thank you, Your Majesty,' said Kelsey. 'With the exception of Secretary Cael, everyone from the Imperial Court is here; thank you all for coming.'

'Where is young Cael?' said Shella.

'He's currently in Sanang,' said Kelsey. 'With any luck, he will have arrested or killed those who tried to assassinate the Matriarch by now.'

'Whom do we suspect?' said Marshal Bedig.

Kelsey glanced at Claudian.

'There are two lines of thought regarding this,' said the Adjutant. 'The first is that some disgruntled criminals have absconded from the Imperial Army, and have decided to revenge themselves upon the Matriarch for having forced them into the military.'

'And the second?' said Bedig.

Claudian frowned. 'As we know, the Matriarch remains firmly opposed to the proposals being formulated by the constitutional convention based on Colsbury. The structure of the government in Sanang does not lend itself to democracy.'

Shella chuckled. 'She's worried that she and her little cronies will lose power.'

'We have a suspicion that some pro-democrats might have tried to kill the Matriarch,' said Kelsey.

The Empress narrowed her eyes.

'However,' Kelsey went on, 'we will reserve judgement until Cael returns. Bedig, have you spoken to Cole this morning?'

'Aye, ma'am,' said the Marshal. 'He has arranged to transport Konna Holdfast to the City of Salve two days from now. To be honest, ma'am, I was concerned about sending him to Kell, knowing what the Holdfasts down there think of us; and I was glad he got out of Clackenbaird unscathed.'

'I am surprised that Konna agreed to go,' said the Empress.

Kelsey gave her a shifty smile. 'I, eh, decided to waive the requirement for her to swear an oath, Your Majesty.'

Brogan shook her head. 'Why am I not surprised? The way you continually try to appease the Holdfasts of Kell never fails to annoy me. They hate us, and we have to accept that.'

'They don't all hate us,' said Kelsey. 'I have been getting along quite well with Killop, and he visits us in the Holdfast townhouse now and again. He was wary of us at first, but I have sensed no ill will from him.'

'I can confirm that,' said Cardova. 'Killop is a likable and reasonable young lad, and he has done well at university. It's the others that concern me.'

Arrosa said nothing. She had spoken to Killop a few times, as she also lived in the Holdfast townhouse. She had found him polite and intelligent, but he was also occasionally evasive with his words. He knew about her Gift of Truth and, like many who possessed that knowledge, he seemed a little uncomfortable in her presence.

'We need to treat them as individuals,' Kelsey went on. 'What worked with Killop might work with Konna. If we allow her a little freedom, then she will be able to explore the Empire. Once she sees that we aren't the monsters that Naxor has no doubt told her we are, then her attitude towards us might soften. If I had insisted upon an oath, she would have refused, and that's the truth.'

'One rule for the Holdfasts, is it?' said Brogan.

'I didn't do it because Konna is a Holdfast,' said Kelsey. 'I did it because she is a powerful god with death powers, battle-vision, and the ability to change her appearance, just as Aila can. There are ten gods living in Kell, nine if we exclude Killop, and all of them either have or will have a wide range of powers. It is essential that we try to build bridges with them.'

The Empress pursed her lips. 'Very well,' she said. 'Konna can work for the Aurelians without having to swear an oath to the imperial crown. Cairney will be the next to reach eighteen; shall we try the same approach with him?'

'According to Cole, Your Majesty,' said Bedig, 'Cairney is the most hostile towards us. He openly threatened Cole and Lieutenant Longhold while they were in Kell. I fear Cairney might never come around to our way of thinking.'

'I thought we were here to discuss the constitutional convention?' said Shella. 'That's the reason I was brought down from Colsbury, not to talk about a few badly-behaved Holdfasts in Kell. You know, I miss the days when you all came to Colsbury for the summer; the place isn't the same without you.'

'The situation is temporary,' said the Empress. 'We shall re-institute that tradition as soon as the convention has completed its work. The humidity down here in Plateau City each summer is reason enough to want to return to Colsbury, but the island is currently overrun with the convention's delegates. Tell me – are they any closer to completing their work? It has been seven years, after all.'

'We are just waiting on the results of the census, Your Majesty,' said

Shella. 'As soon as we have all the figures, we will be ready to present our latest proposals.' She glanced at Brogan. 'Do we have a due date for the completion of the census, Chamberlain?'

'The final tallies should be with us in the next ten days or so,' said Brogan. 'It has been a long hard struggle to conduct the census. We have had to send agents into every remote corner of the Empire, and we have faced more resistance than anticipated. In parts of the Eastern Rim, for example, we had to overcome opposition from several dragons, who objected to us counting the humans under their authority; while conditions in parts of Rakana and Rahain have been appalling. And, I must confess, the Matriarch of Sanang has been less than cooperative, and her officials have hindered us at every step.' She withdrew a letter from a folder. 'I want to bring this to your attention, while I am on the subject,' she went on. 'This document has been signed by a wide variety of provincial leaders, including various Holders in the Holdings, the Matriarch, the human representatives of some dragons of the Eastern Rim, and tribal leaders from among the Gloamers and Sanders of the City of Salve. It was addressed to me, as Chamberlain, and it details their strenuous opposition to the proposed reforms. I won't read it out, but they are demanding a postponement of any changes to the constitution.'

Shella shook her head. 'Every one of those groups you mentioned is frightened of allowing the people to gain any control over how the Empire is run. Their opposition was expected. We aren't going to stop because a few Gloamers, dragons and Holders disagree with us.' She paused for a moment, then she smiled. 'I might not look it, but I am getting along a little in years, and the convention shall be the last piece of work I carry out for the Empire. As soon as my proposals are brought before the Imperial Court, I intend to retire; for good this time. I gave Bridget ten years, and I have given you nearly twenty, Thorn. I am three decades older than anyone else in this room; it is time, I think. You are going to need a new Chancellor, Your Majesty.'

The room fell into silence.

'Is there anything I can do to persuade you to stay, Shella?' said the Empress.

'I'm afraid not,' she said. 'My mind is made up.'

The Empress glanced at Arrosa, who shook her head. There had been no lie.

'Very well,' the Empress went on; 'I accept your retirement with a heavy heart, Shella. You have been a rock for so many years that I can hardly imagine life without you.'

'Hey,' cried Shella. 'I'm not dead; I'm only retiring. You will all be able to see me when you go back to spending each summer on Colsbury. And, who knows? – I might even impart a few nuggets of advice now and again.'

'It appears that we will be needing a new Chancellor and a new Marshal soon,' said Claudian.

'The position of Marshal has been decided upon,' said the Empress. 'Cael Holdfast will be promoted into that role as soon as Bedig moves to the Eastern Rim as Imperial Legate. Cole Holdfast shall then join the Imperial Court as Secretary.'

Bedig half-smiled. 'There is a chance Cole will refuse, Your Majesty.'

'Don't talk shite,' said Kelsey. 'Cole might be reluctant, but he won't refuse. It's time to bring our reclusive hermit back into the fold; he's spent long enough in Rainsby.'

'What about the chancellorship?' said Claudian.

'Are you eying the job?' said Kelsey.

'Certainly not, ma'am,' said Claudian. 'I am a military man.'

'I have a recommendation, if anyone wants to hear it,' said Shella.

'Aye?' said Kelsey.

Shella pointed across the table at Fenu, who occupied the role of Imperial Chief-of-Staff. 'Her.'

'Me, ma'am?' said the Rakanese woman.

'Yeah, you,' said Shella. 'You steered Prime Minister Jazi to three consecutive election victories in Amatskouri, and you handled the purchase of the territories of Adorati.'

'But I have only been a member of the Imperial Court for two years, ma'am.'

'So? We should allocate roles by merit, not time-served.'

'I will take your recommendation under consideration,' said Kelsey.

'Does that mean you're going to ignore it?' said Shella.

'No, smartarse, it doesn't,' said Kelsey. 'I actually think it was a damn good suggestion, and I'm only a little annoyed that I didn't think of it first.' She glanced at the Empress. 'Now seems like a good time to break our news about Arrosa, Your Majesty.'

'I agree,' said the Empress.

Arrosa's eyes widened. 'You have news regarding me, Your Majesty?'

'We do,' said Thorn. 'The Herald, Chamberlain and I have decided to create a new role in the Imperial Court; one that suits your abilities. It will be a junior position, and will rank as equal in authority to that of the Imperial Secretary. For too long, Arrosa, you have sat by my side as my assistant; you deserve more responsibility, I feel.'

'The role we have created shall be that of Imperial Postmaster,' said Kelsey. 'It's a polite way to state that you will be looking after the Empire's network of spies and agents. Of course, that information shall not leave this room. To the outside world, you will be responsible for the postal service, the issuing and registration of Quadrants, and the Calendar Pole portals. You will be getting your own Quadrant – ask Cael to show you how to use it. I'll tell you more about the other aspects of the role when we get home this evening.'

'Do you accept?' said the Empress.

'Yes, Your Majesty,' said Arrosa. 'Thank you.'

'Congratulations, Postmaster,' said Cardova, a smile on his face.

Arrosa smiled back at him.

'You will come under the remit of the Chamberlain,' Kelsey went on, 'so Brogan will be your immediate boss, with me above her.'

Brogan laughed. 'At long last I will have someone to look after the portals and Quadrants for me. The census and the construction of the Blue Palace are taking up all of my time at the moment.'

'How goes the building work, Chamberlain?' said Fenu.

'The exterior is finished,' Brogan said. 'The last blue tile was put in place yesterday, covering the anti-mage protective compound created by clay and stone mages. As for the interior, I estimate that the Imperial Court and the dragons shall be able to move in before the end of summer.'

A wide smile split the Empress' features. 'Well done, Brogan; that is excellent news. We must send word to Frostback and Halfclaw.'

'I will tell them when I return to Colsbury, Your Majesty,' said Shella. 'We will also need to inform Queen Blackrose, as I think she has a dragon ready to live in the Blue Palace as the ambassador from the Eastern Rim.'

'I can do that, ma'am,' said Bedig. 'I was intending to travel to Ulna tomorrow, to speak to the dragons about my new role as legate.'

'Let us end the meeting on that high note,' said the Empress. 'Thank you all for coming. Shella, we will summon you again when the census results have arrived. You are all dismissed.'

Thorn stepped down from her throne, and the others got to their feet. They waited until the Empress had left through a rear door, a small mass of courtiers and officials following her out, then Arrosa smiled again as the others congratulated her on her promotion.

Treasurer Slaeon shook her hand. 'You will be requiring a budget, no doubt,' said the Rahain woman; 'I will make sure it comes out of the Chamberlain's funds.'

'And I will need to speak to you about the placement of operatives based around the Empire,' said Cardova.

'We can do that over a few whiskies tonight,' said Kelsey. 'Come on; let's get out of here.'

They filed out of the chamber, and Arrosa broke away from the others, as they chatted in the hallway. She went into a small side room, where a Kellach courtier had been looking after Arrosa's three dogs. They were short-haired, with black and tan colouring, and each came up to Arrosa's waist. They bounded towards her, nearly knocking Arrosa off her feet as they leapt up to lick her face.

'Down,' she said, and all three dogs sat motionless in front of her.

She glanced at the courtier. 'Thank you, once again. I hope they weren't too much trouble today.'

'No trouble at all, ma'am,' said the courtier, bowing. 'I have dogs of my own, though none are as large as these ones. What is the name of their breed?'

'They are Greenhold Warders,' said Arrosa. 'They were bred for guard duty, but they are very gentle.'

The Kellach courtier laughed. 'I'll take your word for that, ma'am.'

Arrosa took three leads from a shelf and clipped them to the dogs' collars. Having to do so annoyed her, as she knew how well trained they were; but the Empress had insisted. She left the room, and the three dogs walked alongside her. To Arrosa, they seemed like giant versions of Belle, the little black and tan dog that had been Professor Elbannon's pride and joy. As for what she had said about their gentle nature, that had only been half true. With Arrosa, Cael and the others who shared the Holdfast townhouse, all three dogs were affectionate and loving, but their demeanour altered in an instant if strangers came to the front door. Arrosa led the three dogs down to the entrance of the Ministry of the Plateau, where Kelsey and Cardova were waiting for her.

Kelsey smiled down at the dogs, then she scratched them behind their ears.

'Lucius was being rude to me just now,' Kelsey said. 'Will you eat him for me, Maisie? What about you, Millie, or you, Mia? The first one to bite off his head gets a raw steak for dinner this evening.'

Cardova laughed. 'We could have done with a few of these dogs on Dragon Eyre.'

'Shut up about the old days,' said Kelsey. 'No one gives a shit.'

'Charming as always, Miss Holdfast,' he said. He eyed Arrosa. 'With the changes to the Imperial Court, I'm going to be Cael's boss, and Kelsey will be your boss, Arrosa. I pity you, having to endure her attempts at humour.'

Arrosa gave Kelsey and Cardova a slightly-forced smile, and they set off down the street together. As always, several people got out of their way as soon as they saw the three fierce-looking dogs, and Arrosa felt a strange sense of satisfaction whenever it happened. When the dogs were with them, she, Kelsey and Cardova – all members of the Imperial Court – could walk through the centre of Plateau City without any soldiers to guard them or courtiers to accompany them. It felt liberating.

'What did you think of Shella's recommendation?' said Kelsey, as they crossed a busy road.

'Fenu is up to the job, in my opinion,' said Cardova. 'She would make an excellent Chancellor. She would make a pretty good Herald, too; probably a better Herald than you, in fact.'

'Ha ha.'

Mia growled at a Holdings man walking down the street towards them.

'Leave it,' said Arrosa.

The man quickened his pace, then he crossed the road to avoid them.

'Have you trained them to attack on command?' said Kelsey.

'Of course not,' said Arrosa. 'Should I have done so?'

'It would be funny to have them chase Lucius all the way home.'

'Hilarious,' said Cardova.

'Sometimes,' said Arrosa, 'I can't tell if you two dislike each other, or like each other a little too much.'

Kelsey narrowed her eyes. 'What the fuck is that supposed to mean?'

Arrosa shrugged. 'My head hurts now and again when I'm in your company; that's all I'm saying.'

Arrosa looked away as Cardova and Kelsey fell into an uncomfortable silence. With Karalyn absent for long periods of time, Arrosa felt it might be necessary to remind them that Lucius was married. The way Kelsey and Cardova acted together when Karalyn was not present made Arrosa feel a little awkward at times; and their loud proclamations about how much the other annoyed them were nothing but lies that gave Arrosa a headache.

'Lucius is like a brother to me,' said Kelsey, after a long silence.

Arrosa felt a pain in the back of her head. 'If you say so.'

'There's nothing going on,' said Cardova.

That was true, thought Arrosa. It was what might happen that worried her.

'Please remember that I can detect any lie I hear,' Arrosa said.

'I wasn't lying,' said Cardova. 'I am married to Kelsey's sister. We are friends; that's all.'

Arrosa shook her head at the two truths followed by the lie. Once again, her Gift of Truth felt more like a burden than a blessing, and she hoped that Karalyn would return soon. The flirting always stopped when Karalyn was there. No, it wasn't flirting. It was deeper than that, a feeling of ease and joy in each other's company. Cardova had a tendency to shut down his emotions whenever his immortal wife was present, almost as though he feared her; while Kelsey never joked and laughed with him when her sister was there. Was it any of Arrosa's business? Should she have remained silent? She had been living with Kelsey and Cardova for several years, and had tried her best to avoid bringing up anything that would cause the household to descend into awkwardness, but if Cardova was even contemplating a betrayal of his marriage vows, then Arrosa would have to tell Cael about it. And then, it would be up to Cael if he wanted to mention anything to his mother.

They entered the aristocratic district of the city, and walked towards the Holdfast townhouse.

'You've put a right dampener on things,' Kelsey said. 'We were all having a good laugh before you had to open your big mouth, Arrosa. Lucius and I have always been like this. Back in the City, we were forever teasing each other. It didn't mean anything. Was that a lie?'

'No,' she said.

'And now,' Kelsey went on, 'we...'

'Please don't say any more,' said Arrosa. 'I'm sorry I mentioned it. All I was trying to do was warn you about my Gift, as you sometimes appear to forget I possess it.'

They reached the front door, and their butler opened it for them. Arrosa unclipped the leads, and all three dogs bounded into the house.

Cardova went in after them, then Kelsey raised a hand to block Arrosa's progress into the building.

'What do you want?' said Arrosa.

'Has... has Lucius ever said anything that you knew to be a lie?'

'Everyone in this house has lied now and again,' said Arrosa.

Kelsey leaned in closer. 'You know what I'm talking about. I'm not stupid; I know that Lucius and Karalyn's marriage is in trouble. I mean, she's never fucking here, is she? Thirds pass, and we see no sign of the fabled Karalyn Holdfast, so I can understand why Lucius is feeling down about it. Has he ever said anything about me that you knew to be a lie?'

Arrosa held Kelsey's gaze, unsure what to do or say.

Kelsey nodded. 'I see. Listen to me, Arrosa – nothing will ever happen between me and Lucius – do you understand? I would never betray my sister, no matter how I felt. Was that a lie?'

'No.'

'Then that's the end of this little discussion,' said Kelsey.

'Do you like being alone?' she said.

'I'm not going to answer that.'

'You've been divorced for nearly eight years, Aunty. I would understand if you were lonely.'

Kelsey shook her head and walked into the townhouse. Arrosa followed her inside, and hung her coat up on a peg. She handed the dogs' leads to the butler, who closed and locked the door, then Arrosa went into the large drawing room, where four children were sitting by a table. Two adults and an infant were also present – the nursemaid, who was holding on to a two-year-old boy, and Caelius Logos, who was sitting in his favourite armchair with a newspaper on his lap.

Arrosa walked up to the nursemaid, who bowed her head, and placed the boy into Arrosa's hands.

Arrosa kissed her son. 'Hello, my darling Cowie,' she said in Gunstian.

'He was no trouble at all today, ma'am,' said the nursemaid.

'He's a credit to you,' said Caelius.

Cardova and Kelsey came into the room, followed by the three dogs, who ran up to the other children. The hounds jumped up at them, their tails wagging, and the children laughed.

'Down,' said Arrosa, and the dogs obeyed.

Cardova sat by his two children Carden and Caitlyn, while Kelsey gave her own two children a kiss each. Calpurnia and Caelius were sitting at the table doing some schoolwork next to their younger cousins, and Arrosa sat down next to them, Cowie balanced on her lap.

'How was school today?' said Cardova.

The ten-year-old Carden shrugged.

'It was fine,' said Caitlyn, his nine-year-old sister; 'but it's not a real school, is it? There are only four students; us four. I want to go to a proper school.'

'We have talked about this,' said Cardova. 'You and Carden are immortal gods, and your mother is famous all over the Star Continent.'

'But what about us?' said Calpurnia. 'Caelius and I aren't immortal. Apart from our teachers, the only people we meet are the people who live in this house.'

'It would be unfair to allow your two cousins to be taught on their own,' said Kelsey; 'so we decided to put all four of you together, so that you would all have some company.'

'But I am almost sixteen,' said Calpurnia, 'and I have no friends.'

'You have your cousins,' said her mother, 'and you have Frostback, who adores you. I know it's hard to be part of the Holdfast family, and I wish you could lead normal lives; but let's face it – we aren't normal, are we? Carden and Caitlyn are immortal, while you and your brother possess the ability to block all powers.'

'Not all powers,' said Arrosa. 'My Gifts are unaffected.'

Kelsey frowned. 'All right; not all powers. What I meant was that this house is full of gods, mages, and the Gifted; and we have to be careful.'

'I wish we were in Colsbury Castle,' said Caelius. 'It's too hot here.'

Kelsey smiled at her twelve-year-old son. 'I wish we were there, too. As soon as Aunty Shella has finished her work with the convention, then everything will return to normal, and we'll start going back to Colsbury each year. But listen to this – the Blue Palace should be ready by the end of summer, and we'll all be moving in. We'll have a large apartment, high up in one of the towers, and we'll have a great view of the city. Even better – Frostback and Halfclaw will be coming south to join us.'

Calpurnia smiled.

'Will we be able to see the dragons every day?' said Caitlyn.

'That's right,' said Cardova. 'They will be living in their own palace tower, perhaps along with another dragon from the Eastern Rim.'

'I'm not convinced that this is a wise decision,' said Arrosa. 'Should dragons live in the middle of a city? Won't they frighten the citizens?'

Caelius Logos laughed. 'I must say, she might have a point.'

'It will be fine,' said Kelsey.

'It will be better than fine,' said Calpurnia. 'I will get to ride upon Frostback again. Can I fly on her back every day, Mother?'

'That will be up to Frostback,' said Kelsey.

Caelius lowered his gaze. 'I wish Halfclaw would pick me as his rider. It's not fair that Calpurnia has Frostback.'

The butler entered the room and bowed his head. 'Dinner shall be served in ten minutes, ma'am,' he said.

'Thank you,' said Kelsey.

Cardova gestured towards the four children by the table. 'Everyone, get up and washed before dinner.'

The children got to their feet.

'We'll talk about Halfclaw later, son,' Kelsey said to Caelius. 'Don't give up hope just yet.'

The children followed the butler out of the drawing room, and Cardova helped old Caelius get to his feet. The father of Van had been living with them for three years, following his retirement from the Imperial Court as Quartermaster, and he seemed to relish the opportunity to see his two grandchildren every day. Arrosa also stood, her arms clutching on to Cowie. The dogs stared up at her, their ears alert.

'Dinnertime,' she said to them, and all three dogs turned and bounded out of the room.

'Might I feed them this evening?' said Caelius.

'If you like,' said Arrosa.

Caelius smiled, then he took his walking stick and followed the dogs out into the hallway.

'I think he loves those dogs more than he loves us,' said Kelsey.

'They terrified him when he first moved in,' said Cardova.

'They terrify everyone at first,' said Kelsey. 'I don't know why Cael picked such a ferocious-looking breed.'

'The children adore them,' said Arrosa.

'Aye, but they knew them as puppies, before they grew to the size they are now,' said Kelsey.

They walked through to the dining room, where the butler was setting out dishes and jugs. The three dogs had already finished their dinner, and were lying on their large beds by the bay window. Arrosa moved to her seat, just as the air shimmered in the corner of the room. The dogs leapt up, barking loudly, then they realised who had appeared in the room and bounded toward him, their tails wagging as they yelped and whined.

Cael laughed. 'Aye, dogs,' he said; 'it's good to see you, too.'

He patted each one in turn, and they settled down again.

'Bed,' said Arrosa, and they ran back to their baskets. She approached her husband and kissed him.

Cael dropped his bags to the floor and took Cowie from her arms.

'You are back sooner than we had expected,' said Cardova, as he sat down at the table. 'How did it go?'

'I caught the men who had organised the assassination attempt,' Cael said. 'All three are now in the Matriarch's prison.'

'And?' said Kelsey.

Cael sat down, holding Cowie on his knee. 'It's as bad as we imagined. The three men were all pro-democrats, unhappy about the Matriarch's refusal to support the new constitution.'

'I can't believe they turned violent,' said Kelsey.

'The Matriarch has declared that any Sanang who opposes her will on this matter will be treated as a traitor,' said Cael. 'She is determined not to allow any voting to go ahead in her territory. She told me that over eighty per cent of the folk in Sanang are illiterate. If they can't even read a ballot paper, she said, then how can they be trusted to choose their own government? She said she would rather leave the Empire than approve Shella's constitution.'

'But Shella hasn't published the final version of the constitution,' said Kelsey.

'Everyone knows the gist of it, Aunty,' said Cael.

Kelsey sat down next to Cardova, her features displaying her frustration.

'The Matriarch wants a long postponement,' Cael went on. 'She wants time to set up schools throughout Sanang.'

'She's been in power for two fucking decades,' said Kelsey; 'she's had plenty of time to establish schools.'

'She also pointed out that the majority of folk in Sanang live in tiny, isolated villages deep within the forest,' said Cael. 'Many of them have never even heard of the Empress.'

'I've heard these excuses before,' said Kelsey.

'Perhaps we should start listening to the Matriarch,' said Arrosa.

Kelsey glared at her, then the cook's assistant entered the dining room, pushing a large trolley. The four children came in after her, and the Holdfasts took their seats around the table. Arrosa sat next to Cael.

'I'm glad you're home early,' she said.

He smiled at his wife. 'I missed you, and I missed Cowie.'

Arrosa glanced at Kelsey and Cardova. 'Can I tell him?'

Cardova nodded. 'I don't see why not.'

'Tell me what?' said Cael.

Arrosa turned back to Cael. 'You are going to be promoted,' she said. 'When Bedig moves to Dragon Eyre, you will become the new Marshal.'

'Aye?'

'There's more,' she went on. 'The Empress has created a new position within the Imperial Court – for me. I'm the new Imperial Postmaster.'

'Well done,' Cael said, 'but *Postmaster*? What does that entail?'

'She will be running a new department of spies and agents,' said Kelsey; 'but we could hardly call her the Imperial Spymaster, at least, not officially.'

'After dinner,' said Cardova, 'we'll open a bottle of wine and go through the details.'

Kelsey smiled. 'And then we'll put you to work.'

CHAPTER 4
GOD'S CONSORT

Plateau City, The Plateau – 23rd Day, Second Third Summer 552

Lucius Cardova opened his eyes.

The knock upon his door came again. 'It is one hour before dawn, sir,' said the voice of the townhouse butler.

'Thank you,' said Lucius.

He pulled back the thin sheet and swung his legs off the bed. He sat in a stupor for a moment, summoning the will to get up. It had been another hot and humid night in Plateau City, the forty-seventh night since he had last seen his wife. He had stopped wondering where Karalyn might be, or what she might be doing. It was clear that she didn't care enough to let him know why she needed to be away so often, and his anger at her frequent long absences had been replaced by a sour resignation.

He stood, and made his way to the dark bathroom. He lit a single lamp, and washed and shaved in the cool water, then he cleaned his teeth, keeping to the same routine that he carried out each morning. There was no meeting of the Imperial Court due to take place that day, but Carden and Caitlyn needed to be up, fed and dressed for their school lessons. As Kelsey used her rare days off to sleep in until the last possible moment, Lucius decided he would take care of her children that morning, ensuring that they had their breakfast without waking up the entire household. With Cowie passing his second birthday, things had been getting a little easier in the townhouse, and there was no longer a tiny baby to worry about disturbing. If Cael and Arrosa decided to have another child, then Lucius would have to go back to creeping around the house as quietly as possible.

He dressed in his least formal uniform, and pulled a comb through his hair, noticing the few streaks of grey that had appeared by his temples, and the tired lines under his eyes. He tried to recall the last time he had enjoyed a morning off, but soon gave up – it had been a long time, not that he minded.

He left his room and padded downstairs to the second floor of the townhouse. He knocked on the two bedroom doors where his children slept, then he eased them both open.

'Carden,' he whispered through the first door; 'time to get up.'

He went to the second door, and saw Caitlyn pulling a blanket over her head.

'Time for breakfast, Caitlyn,' he said.

'Just a minute, Dad,' she groaned.

He went down another flight of stairs, passing the main bedroom where Kelsey slept, and he remembered what Arrosa had said the day before. The young woman had been making something out of nothing. He and Kelsey had always joked around together, right back from the days when they had first met in the City of Salve. It had never meant anything. They were friends; nothing more.

Arrosa was in the kitchen when Lucius entered the room. She was pacing up and down with Cowie held in her arms, while her three enormous dogs eyed Lucius from their beds. The dogs seemed to have beds in every room of the house, but they followed Arrosa around wherever she went.

'Good morning,' said Arrosa.

'Good morning,' he said.

'The kettle boiled a moment ago,' she said. 'Do you want some coffee?'

'I'll get it,' he said; 'your hands are already full. Did the little one not sleep well?'

'He slept fine,' she said, 'but he woke up early. Listen – I'm sorry about yesterday. I should have kept my big mouth shut.'

'It's all right,' he said. 'You're not the first person to see how Kelsey and I act together and jump to the wrong conclusion. Frostback used to comment on it.'

He walked over to the warm stove and filled a coffee pot with water from the kettle. He spooned in a large amount of coffee, then he began to slice some bread from a loaf while the coffee brewed. He placed some slices into the hottest part of the oven to toast them, then he began preparing the children's lunches.

Arrosa sat down with Cowie on her knee, watching him.

'I've known Kelsey for twenty years,' he said, 'and she's been my best friend for that entire time. I know it's a little weird, to be best friends with my wife's sister, but I knew Kelsey long before I ever met Karalyn.'

Arrosa nodded. 'It's nice to have a best friend.'

'We drifted apart for a while when I was staying on Colsbury, and she was down here, but living together in this house has brought it all back.'

'Do you miss your wife?'

Lucius smiled. 'There's no way I'm going to talk about Karalyn in front of you, Arrosa, not when any lie I say will give you a headache.'

'Why would you need to lie?'

Lucius said nothing as he placed the toast onto two plates. He stirred the contents of the coffee pot with a long wooden spoon, then he filled two cups. He added sugar and milk to both, and passed one to Arrosa.

'Thank you,' she said. 'You didn't answer my question.'

'I'm not going to answer it,' he said. 'Do you mind if I smoke in here?'

'I do, yes.'

'Fair enough,' he said. 'I'll be out by the front of the townhouse for a few minutes. If Carden or Caitlyn make an appearance, please give them the toast I made for them.'

He walked from the room, the eyes of the three dogs following his movements. He went to the front door, unbolted the chain, and stepped outside into the muggy warmth of the predawn light. He pulled out the metal lighter that Sable had given him for his fortieth birthday, and lit a cigarette. He drank his coffee while he smoked, his gaze on the tall townhouses that lined the elegant streets of the aristocratic district of the city.

Did he miss Karalyn? He wasn't sure. He missed the *idea* of Karalyn. He missed the woman he had married, but the new Karalyn was different from the old, and not only in her appearance. She had been immortal for sixteen years, since taking the body of Albany, and she hadn't aged a day in that time, remaining forever twenty-one, while Cardova had entered his mid-forties. Had she tired of him? She had been transformed into the most powerful being in existence, greater than any Ascendant had been; it would be little wonder if a mere middle-aged mortal like himself was no longer enough for her. What surprised him more was her neglect of the two children they had made together. Lucius had been bringing up Carden and Caitlyn on his own for several years; did Karalyn not care about that? The two children were gods, just as she was; did she imagine that she would have millennia to spend with them?

The front door opened again, and Cael stepped outside. He nodded to Lucius, and the older man offered him a cigarette. Cael took it, and Lucius lit it for him.

'Thanks,' said Cael. 'Look at us – thrown out of our own house to smoke on the street.'

Lucius smiled. 'Such is the way of it. If only Kelsey still smoked, then we could sit out on her balcony.'

'Do I have anything on today?'

'No. You can spend the entire day as you choose. We weren't expecting you to get back from Sanang so soon.'

Cael laughed. 'I'm too efficient, that's my problem. The Matriarch is not going to change her mind about Shella's reforms – you should know that.'

'I don't care one way or another, Cael,' he said. 'It's a civil matter, and I don't get involved. Kelsey deals with all that stuff. Leave the armed forces to me.'

'Did you ever imagine that you would become the commander of the military of an entire empire?'

'What kind of question is that, Cael? Of course I never imagined it. I spent the first half of my life as a faithful servant of the Ascendants. I gave my loyalty to the Banner of the Black Crown, then the Banner of the Lostwell Exiles, then the Banner of the Sapphire Throne, and now it's the Imperial Army. To be honest, I have no idea how I ended up in charge of over two hundred thousand men and women in uniform.'

'That's easy to answer,' said Cael. 'You became friends with the Holdfasts. You might also have had a tiny amount of talent as well, I suppose.'

Lucius laughed, then he stubbed out his cigarette. 'I'm heading back inside.'

Cael nodded, and Lucius re-entered the townhouse. He walked back into the kitchen, but there was no sign of his children. He eyed Arrosa.

'They haven't come downstairs yet,' she said.

Lucius climbed the stairs again, and found that both Carden and Caitlyn had remained in bed. He walked into each room in turn, opening the shutters to allow in the pale glow of dawn.

'Up,' he said. 'Get washed and brush your teeth; come on. I want you downstairs in ten minutes.'

He returned to the kitchen. Cael was sitting next to Arrosa, and they quietened when Lucius walked into the room. Lucius pretended he hadn't noticed, then he finished making the children's lunches, putting them into separate bags and placing them onto the table next to the toast.

'I used to do this for you when you were young, Cael,' he said.

'I remember,' he said. 'You were always busy back then, and you're always busy now.'

Calpurnia walked into the kitchen and sat down. 'Is there any spare toast?' she said.

'I'll make you some,' said Lucius.

'Where's Mum?' she said.

'Where do you think?' said Lucius, as he cut through the loaf. 'Your mother rarely rises on her days off before she absolutely has to.'

'She would get up if you didn't do everything for her,' said Arrosa. 'Why do you make breakfast for all the children each day? Why don't you ask one of the servants to do it?'

'I want the children to know that I am here for them,' he said, as he placed the cut bread into the oven. 'They need some structure in their lives.' He eyed Calpurnia. 'When is your father next due to look after you?'

'Caelius and I are meeting him tomorrow after our lessons are over,' said the fifteen-year-old girl, 'and then we'll have to stay over with him and his horrible new wife.'

'She isn't horrible,' said Lucius.

'She is far too young for him.'

'That's what people think when they see me with Karalyn,' said Lucius. 'They think – *what is that old guy doing with that young woman?*'

'Yes, but Aunty Karalyn isn't actually twenty-one, is she? Father's new wife is only twenty-three. She's half his age. It's disgusting.'

Lucius passed her a plate of toast. 'I hope you don't say that in front of them.'

'Of course I don't,' said Calpurnia. 'Is there any jam?'

'Strawberry or raspberry?'

'Is there no blackcurrant? I'll have strawberry.'

Lucius passed her a pot of jam and a knife. He walked to the door, and glanced up the stairs.

'Carden,' he called out. 'Caitlyn. Get down here.'

'Just a minute,' Caitlyn shouted back.

Lucius went back to the stove. He spotted some cheese wrapped in paper on the counter, and cut off three small pieces. The dogs immediately reared up, their eyes on him.

He held out one piece. 'Mia,' he said, and the dog trotted forward. She took the cheese from his palm with the gentlest of movements, as the other two waited their turn.

'Maisie,' he said next. 'Good girl. Millie.'

The dogs stared up at him for more, and he sat down by Cael.

'You spoil them, Lucius,' said Arrosa.

'Do you mind?'

She smiled. 'No. I do need to take them out for a you-know-what, though.'

'A what?' said Calpurnia. 'A walk?'

The dogs jumped up, barking and running around the kitchen. Cowie laughed from his mother's knee.

Calpurnia smiled. 'Sorry.'

Arrosa narrowed her eyes slightly, and got to her feet.

'I'll come with you,' said Cael. 'I could do with a long walk this morning.'

Lucius held out his arms, and Arrosa passed him little Cowie.

'Be careful,' said Arrosa. 'Remember that he can get into your thoughts.'

Lucius smiled.

'He had to deal with me and Kyra when we were young,' said Cael. 'He'll be fine.'

Arrosa and Cael left the kitchen, and the three dogs ran after them, still barking. Carden walked into the room and sat down. Lucius placed a plate of toast in front of his son, then he poured him a glass of milk. Carden yawned.

'At least we can speak freely now,' said Calpurnia. 'Arrosa's Gift always makes things awkward.'

'It's not her fault,' said Lucius. 'Imagine how awful it would have been to grow up like that – having your head hurt whenever anyone lies. You just have to be careful what you say. If in doubt, say nothing.'

'I know how to handle her,' said Calpurnia; 'I'm just saying that it's awkward.' She eyed Carden. 'Have you felt any powers yet?'

Carden shook his head. 'Maybe I haven't got any.'

'Albany was the granddaughter of an Ascendant,' said Lucius, 'and your mother inherited all of her abilities when she took over her body. You will have powers; trust me.'

'Why isn't Carden a dream mage?' said Calpurnia. 'Caitlyn isn't one, either. Why not?'

'Because it was Albany's body that gave birth to them,' said Lucius.

Carden pulled a face. 'My mother is weird.'

'Your mother is the most powerful god to have ever existed,' said Lucius.

'Is that why she's never here?' said Calpurnia.

Caitlyn and Caelius entered the kitchen. Lucius passed Cowie to Calpurnia, then he got up and made breakfast for the two arrivals. He smiled to himself. It could be hard work at times, but he derived a great deal of satisfaction from looking after the children of the townhouse.

'The school carriage will be here for you in ten minutes,' he said, as he laid out more food and drinks onto the table. 'Carden, you have a history test this morning; did you remember?'

'Yes, Dad,' the boy said.

'And Calpurnia,' Lucius went on; 'you are due to hand in your language homework.'

'You watched me do it last night,' said the girl.

'Good job. Remember to tell your teachers that you will need a day off to move into the Blue Palace. I haven't got a date yet, but it won't be long now.'

'I like it here,' said Carden. 'Why do we have to move?'

'There are four members of the Empress's Imperial Court living in this house,' said Lucius, 'and Her Majesty wants us to live close to her. You will all have your own rooms, and remember what we said about the dragons. You will get to see them every day. Even better, you won't have to travel to your little school any more – the teachers will come to us.'

Calpurnia rolled her eyes. 'It sounds as though we'll never leave the Blue Palace.'

Lucius began to tidy away the used cups and plates as the children finished their breakfast, then he shepherded them into the entrance hall. He passed out their coats and school bags, and took Cowie back from Calpurnia's arms.

The butler arrived to open the front door. The school carriage was parked outside the townhouse, and Lucius watched as the children filed past him. Calpurnia led them down the short flight of stairs, and they boarded the carriage. Lucius waved as the carriage pulled away, then the butler closed the door.

'Do you have any plans for this morning, sir?' the butler said.

'This is my day off,' Lucius said, 'but I have one short meeting to get through before I can relax.'

The butler bowed. 'Very good, sir.'

Lucius walked back into the quiet kitchen, and gazed at the mess the children had made. He walked into the drawing room, handed Cowie over to the nursemaid, and returned to the kitchen to start cleaning. When he had finished, he walked back out into the hallway in time to see the butler open the front door to four men in uniform. One of them was Marshal Bedig, while the others were senior staff officers from the army.

Lucius smiled. 'Good morning, gentlemen.'

Bedig inclined his head. 'Have we timed it right, sir? Are the dogs out for their morning walk?'

'They are,' said Lucius. 'Come this way and we can get started.'

Two hours later, after Lucius had signed several dozen documents, and held a discussion on army recruitment and promotion, the four men were led back to the front door and shown out by the butler. With all scheduled business over for the day, Lucius made for the stairs. He paused on the first floor landing outside Kelsey's door, and wondered if he should wake her up. If he didn't, she was liable to sleep for another couple of hours, and then she would be annoyed that he hadn't awoken her. He should make her some coffee and breakfast before waking her, he thought – she would appreciate that; then he remembered what Arrosa had said. He hesitated, and frowned. He should pay no attention to what Arrosa had been insinuating. Kelsey was his friend, and he wasn't going to start acting strangely around her just because Arrosa had jumped to the wrong conclusion. He went back downstairs, prepared a tray with coffee, water and food, and took it up to Kelsey's door.

He knocked.

'Aye?' shouted her voice.

'Are you decent?' he shouted back.

There was a pause. 'I am now.'

Lucius opened the door. Kelsey was sitting on her bed, a dressing gown wrapped round her. She glanced up at him, then at the tray.

'I made you breakfast,' he said.

'Pyre knows what Arrosa will make of that, Lucius.'

'We can't let what she said get to us.'

Kelsey shrugged, and Lucius entered with the tray. He placed it onto her bed, and closed the door. He walked over to her tall balcony doors, and pulled back the heavy curtains, letting the morning light flood the room; then he opened one of the doors and stepped out on to the balcony. He glanced to the left and right, but none of the other balconies along the line of the city's sea walls were occupied. He leaned on the railing, and lit another cigarette.

'Did the children get away all right?' Kelsey called out to him.

'Yes, ma'am,' he said.

'Don't *ma'am* me, ya numpty.'

Lucius said nothing.

Kelsey appeared by the balcony door, a mug of coffee in her hand. 'No witty response this morning?' she said. 'That's a little disappointing.'

'What do you think Karalyn is doing right now?' he said.

Kelsey puffed out her cheeks. 'I haven't the slightest idea, Lucius.'

'It's been forty-seven days since she was last here.'

'Aye?'

'I've been keeping count.' He narrowed his eyes. 'I realise that makes me sound a little pathetic.'

'It isn't pathetic, Lucius; you are entitled to wonder where your wife might be.'

'I am right here,' said a voice.

Lucius and Kelsey started, and they both turned at the same time to see Karalyn standing on the balcony next to them. Lucius's mouth fell open, then he remembered that he should be happy to see her.

'Hello, Lucius,' she said. 'How have you been?'

'Fine,' he said.

'Thank you for looking after the children.'

'Where have you been?'

'The same place I have been whenever I cannot be here,' she said. 'I have been with the Sextant.'

'The Sextant?' said Kelsey.

'Aye,' Karalyn said, a broad smile appearing on her lips. 'I have been making new worlds, beautiful new worlds. One of them has plants and animals, but no humans. The lands are covered in forests, and I can walk there for hours, completely alone. I am going to place the Sextant there, where it will be safe forever. I have also been making a world for the Rakanese, though I still have a lot of work to do. It's difficult to design good freshwater marshlands, and my first few attempts were unsuccessful; but I have been thinking of the future. A few centuries from now, the Rakanese population will be filling the Star Continent, and they will need somewhere else to expand. My new world could support billions of them. I have also moved the Wystians to another world. The place that Cael created has a few structural faults, and it is inherently unstable, so I deemed it unsafe for the long term future of the Wystian dragons. The new world I made for them is small, but it has mountains, rivers, and a few patches of desert, as I know they like warm weather. Its location shall remain a secret, I think.'

Kelsey raised her hands. 'Slow down, sister,' she said. 'Are you saying that you have been communing with the Sextant this entire time?'

Karalyn frowned. 'Did you not hear what I said? I sometimes go walking on my new worlds; I am not always in contact with the Sextant. Anyway, I came to see if the children were all right.'

'They are at school,' said Lucius.

'Ah. Of course. I lose track of the days. I haven't missed Cael's birthday, have I?'

'That's not for another third,' said Kelsey. 'Listen; why don't you and Lucius go downstairs and get some tea, while I get dressed?'

Karalyn glanced at her sister's dressing gown. 'All right.'

Kelsey ushered them off the balcony, then Lucius led Karalyn out of the room and down the stairs. Voices were coming from the drawing room, and they went inside. Cael and Arrosa were sitting on a couch with Cowie, and Caelius Logos was in his usual chair. The three dogs jumped up and started barking, as though they were confused as to how Karalyn had arrived in the house without the front door being knocked.

Karalyn eyed the dogs, and they fell silent. Their tails fell, and they returned to their beds, their heads lowered.

Arrosa frowned.

Cael got to his feet. 'Mother,' he said. 'It's good to see you, but why have you been gone for so long? This absence has been longer than the others. Will you be staying for a while this time?'

'No,' said Karalyn. 'I have too much to do. I just wanted to check that my children were all fine.' She smiled at Cowie. 'And my grandson, of course. I can sense his dream powers from here, but he isn't as strong as you and Kyra were at that age, just as you are not as strong as I am. The dream powers in our family seem to be weakening with every generation, but I always knew that I was an exception. No one will ever be as powerful as me, and that is my curse.'

The butler coughed. 'Would anyone like some tea?'

Lucius eyed him. 'Yes, thank you. Tea for everyone.'

The butler bowed and left the room.

Karalyn turned to her husband. 'I didn't say that I wanted tea.'

'Let's go back a bit,' said Cael, his eyes tight. 'When are you leaving again?'

'In a few minutes, I'd imagine,' said Karalyn. 'I was hoping that Carden and Caitlyn would be here, but it seems that they are at school. How have they been doing?'

'They miss their mother,' said Cael. 'I miss my mother.'

'But they have Lucius,' said Karalyn, 'and you have your own family, son.'

'I don't understand you any more,' Cael went on. 'You fought gods and dragons to be reunited with me and Kyra; don't you care about your other children?'

Anger flashed over Karalyn's features. 'Of course I care, but I have responsibilities. I watch over every world, not just this one. And there is a vital difference between you and Kyra compared to Carden and Caitlyn. They are immortal, son; you and Kyra are not. I have millennia ahead of me to spend time with my younger children.' She glanced at Lucius. 'Has there been any sign of either of them developing any powers yet?'

'No,' said Lucius. 'Carden was only saying this morning that he had no powers but self-healing.'

'They are still young,' said Karalyn. 'When they start to feel their powers emerge, I shall take them both away with me, to begin their training. It will be safer that way.'

Cael took a step forward, his eyes blazing with frustration. 'You are going to *take them away*? They live here, Mother; we are one big family. Why don't you stay here, and then you could spend some time with them while they are still young?'

'I have already told you the reasons,' said Karalyn. 'Why are you getting upset?'

'Immortality has warped your mind, Mother,' her son said. 'Your priorities are...'

'Immortality has broadened my mind,' she snapped back at him. 'I see things more clearly now. I see what is important, and what isn't.'

'And we fall into the second category, I assume?'

Karalyn's eyes widened, as though she couldn't understand why her son might be angry with her.

'You are an adult,' she said. 'You don't need to be mothered. Am I not allowed to have my own life?'

'Forget about me,' he cried. 'I'm not angry because of me; but you have a husband and two young children. What if I were to desert Arrosa and Cowie, because I want to have my *own life*? Would that be fine with you? You talk about being immortal, and having millennia ahead of you – but Carden and Caitlyn need you right now. If you have so much time available, then where is the harm in spending a few years with them?'

Karalyn fell into silence for a moment, her eyes dark. 'Nothing I do will satisfy you,' she said, after a long pause. 'When I spent all of my time with my family, I was continually accused of neglecting my responsibilities. Now, when I am watching over the worlds, I am accused of deserting my children. My brother died because I was caring for Carden and Caitlyn; and now, in his name, I keep the peace between the worlds.' She exhaled. 'Perhaps it was a mistake to return here. Farewell.'

Karalyn vanished, and the three dogs leapt up and began barking again. Kelsey walked into the room at that moment, and glanced around.

'She has gone,' said Arrosa. 'She was here, and now she isn't.'

'Already?' said Kelsey. 'In the time it took me to get dressed?'

'It was my fault,' said Cael. 'I got angry with her.'

'Your anger was justified,' said Arrosa. 'You were pointing out some truths that your mother didn't care to hear.'

Kelsey eyed Lucius, but he remained silent. Arrosa brought the three dogs under control, and the room quietened again.

'Might I offer my opinion?' said old Caelius, from his armchair. 'It seems to me that it might be unwise to anger Karalyn Holdfast. For better or worse, she is no longer the woman we once knew. She looks and acts like a god, because she is a god, and we all know how powerful she can be. Might I recommend a policy of appeasement whenever she arrives?'

Cael shook his head. 'That's how Lucius acts whenever my mother appears. He doesn't want to say anything to annoy her, so he just stands there, saying nothing. Does it do him any good? Does she pay him even the slightest amount of attention? For years, Lucius, you were like a father to me; and now you are sacrificing your own happiness to bring up two children on your own.'

'You're wrong, Cael,' said Lucius. 'Looking after Carden and Caitlyn gives me great happiness.'

'And your marriage?' said Cael. 'How much happiness does that give you?'

'That's enough,' said Kelsey. 'I can see that you're angry, Cael, but don't take it out on Lucius.'

'It's fine,' said Lucius. 'I'm going back upstairs.'

He turned and left the drawing room, just as the cook's assistant was entering with a tea trolley. Lucius made his way to the stairs, and began to climb them. Kelsey caught up with him as he was passing the door to her quarters.

'Hold on a moment, Lucius,' she said. 'Are you all right?'

'What do you think?'

She gazed up at him. 'I think you are angry and fed up,' she said; 'and you have every right to be. You can talk to me, Lucius, if you need someone. Come out on to my balcony. Sit down, and have a cigarette. We can talk.'

She opened her door, and they walked through the bedroom and emerged back on to the balcony. Lucius took a seat, and Kelsey went back into her room. She walked back out a few moments later, as Lucius lit a cigarette. She placed a bottle of whisky and two glasses onto the balcony's small table, and sat down next to him.

Lucius eyed the bottle.

'I've been keeping this,' said Kelsey. 'It's one of Aila's fancy blends.'

'Was it a gift from the Marchbrae Holdfasts?'

Kelsey laughed. 'What makes you think they would ever get me a gift? No, Lucius, I bought it with my own money.'

She opened it, and poured two small measures into the glasses.

'Is my marriage over?' he said.

'No.'

'Is that it?' he said. 'Just a simple *no*?'

'Karalyn is a complicated woman,' she said. 'What she thinks today might not apply tomorrow. Right now, she is obsessed with the Sextant, just as Cael was when he was younger. Her obsession is to the detriment of you and your children; but this will pass.'

'When, in a century or two?'

'But you still love her though, aye?'

'I'm not sure what that means any more. Do I enjoy being in her presence? I don't know. My first instinct upon seeing her appear today was dread. How can I love her if I dread seeing her? It's... it's been three years since we were intimate, Kelsey. Three years, and even then I felt as though she was only doing it to placate me. I have tried to talk to her about this, but you know what she is like when she doesn't want to hear something. She has no desire for me; and she certainly doesn't need me.'

'That's not true. She needs you to look after Carden and Caitlyn.'

'All right; I accept that, but she doesn't need *me*. What am I to her these days? Her children's carer? Is that it?'

'Shut up and drink your whisky.'

Lucius picked up his glass. 'I can't get drunk,' he said. 'Caitlyn and Carden will be home in a few hours, and I told Carden I would help him with his homework.'

'We'll just have the one, then,' said Kelsey.

They clinked their glasses together, then Lucius stretched his legs, and gazed out over the Inner Sea.

CHAPTER 5
THE JEZRAN WALL

Marchside, Kell – 24th Day, Second Third Summer 552

Konna gazed up at the blue sky. Kell had been enjoying a beautiful sunny spell over the previous few days, and she felt the warmth on her face.

'Take a good look,' said Aila. 'You won't see a sky like this in the City.'

Naxor laughed. 'Don't put her off going, cousin.' He held out a large parcel. 'Would you mind taking this with you, Konna? Do you have room in your luggage?'

'What is it, Uncle?' said Konna.

'Whisky, what else?' said Naxor. 'A little gift from Marchbrae for my sisters Lydia and Doria. I would be obliged if you could find time to visit them in Port Sanders.'

'I don't understand why you don't visit them yourself, Uncle. You have a Quadrant.'

'I would rather not return to the City while the current generation of mortals are still in charge; there is too much bad blood between us. Even when I was Imperial Chamberlain, I hesitated to visit the Aurelians. It might also have something to do with the fact that my cousin

Jade wishes to kill me. She has never forgiven me for a few old lapses of judgement.'

'Should I be worried about Jade?' she said, as she took the parcel from Naxor.

'Don't be silly,' said Aila. 'It's only Naxor that she wants to kill; she doesn't hold any grudges against me. Besides, she lives out by the salve mine in the Eastern Mountains.'

'And your powers far outweigh hers,' said Naxor. 'Jade wouldn't stand a chance against you, Konna.'

Konna knelt down by her pile of baggage, and slipped the heavy parcel into a wooden chest.

Cairney emerged from the farmhouse, and laughed at the heap of luggage.

'How much stuff are ye taking?' he said.

'Every item of clothing I own,' she said. 'I am also carrying a lot of presents. I have whisky for Uncle Naxor's sisters, and plenty of books for the Academy in Ooste.'

'Did ye pack the Clawfist?'

Konna smiled as she got back to her feet. 'Of course. Do ye think I would forget it?'

Cairney shrugged. 'Make sure ye kill plenty of greenhides with it.'

'I would rather Konna remained safely on the battlements of the new wall,' said Aila. 'She can kill greenhides from there.'

'That sounds boring,' said Cairney. 'Our father didnae stand on the battlements; he went right out into the middle of those green-skinned bastards. That's what I want to do when I'm eighteen, Ma.'

'I'll bear that in mind, son,' said Aila.

'Do ye think the City remembers what Da did?' said Konna.

'I would be extremely disappointed if they have forgotten,' said Aila. 'It wasn't just the greenhides he fought; he also killed an Ascendant when they invaded. Do you remember his blue armour? He took it from Tamid, the Eighth Ascendant.'

The air in the farmhouse courtyard shimmered, and Cole appeared with Alva Longhold by his side.

'Good morning, ma'am,' said Cole.

'Good morning,' said Aila. 'Thank you for coming to collect Konna.'

Cairney opened his mouth to say something, but Aila silenced him with a look. Cole inclined his head a little, then he glanced at the heap of luggage.

'Are you ready to travel to Pella, cousin?' he said to Konna.

Konna gazed around at the farm buildings, then her eyes were drawn to the neighbouring hilltop where her father's cairn was located. She felt a sudden reluctance to leave Kell but, at the same time, her curiosity was pulling her onwards.

'Aye,' she said. She turned to her mother. 'I will miss you, Ma.'

'You won't be gone forever,' said Aila, as she embraced her eldest daughter.

'I have one more thing to give you,' said Naxor. He plucked an envelope from an inside pocket. 'This is a letter for the branch of the Imperial Bank in Pella. It will allow you to withdraw funds from your accounts here on the Star Continent, in case you need any money.'

Konna took the letter. 'Thank you, Uncle.' She eyed her cousin. 'Where exactly will we be arriving, Cole?'

'Outside Cuidrach Palace,' he said, 'the home of the Aurelians. It will also be Alva's first time in the City of Salve, so I might take her for a quick tour, once I have introduced you to the Royal Court.'

'I would like that,' said Alva.

'And how would I get back,' said Konna, 'if, you know, I needed to get back?'

'You can return to this world via the Calendar Pole portal,' he said. 'Hundreds pass through it every day.'

He took out his Quadrant.

'I love you, Ma,' Konna said. 'And you, Uncle. And even you, Cairney, ya eejit.'

Cairney laughed, then Cole swiped his fingers over the Quadrant. The air shimmered, and they appeared on a long, wide boulevard. On one side was a tree-lined harbour, which was busy with ships of all sizes; while, on the other side was a vast construction site.

Konna and Alva stared up at the red and pink sky at the same time, and Cole smiled.

'It takes some getting used to,' he said. He pointed towards the sun. 'There is no north or south here – that way is called sunward; the other way is iceward. That's about as high as the sun ever gets. This is the height of summer in the City, so it's also the warmest it gets.'

'It's warmer than Kell,' said Konna.

'That wouldn't be hard,' said Alva.

Cole turned to face the east. 'Across the bay are the towns of Tara and Ooste, and through the gap in the cliffs is the Warm Sea, which leads to Jezra.'

'And the massive statue?' said Konna.

'That's Prince Michael, who was your... um, your great-uncle, I think. He ruled for a thousand years.' He turned again, to face the construction site. 'And this is Cuidrach Palace. It was burned down eighteen years ago, then it was left derelict for a while, as the City had no funds to repair it. Now that gold is pouring into the City, the Aurelians decided that it should be rebuilt. About a quarter of it is inhabitable, but the rest won't be finished for a while.'

'I heard that dragons destroyed the palaces of the City,' said Alva.

'Three palaces were destroyed by a single dragon – Dawnflame, who lives in the mountains with Lady Jade,' said Cole, 'but Cuidrach was razed to the ground by Simon, the Tenth Ascendant.' He gestured to the palace gates, where a few soldiers and officials were posted.

One of the officials walked forwards.

'Captain Holdfast,' he said, bowing; 'welcome back to the City.'

'Thank you,' said Cole. 'This is Konna Holdfast. I believe she has an appointment with the Royal Court. She also has some luggage that will need to be brought into the palace.'

The official beckoned two porters, who crossed the road from the palace with a handcart. They began to load the luggage onto the back of the cart, and Cole gestured to Alva.

'And this is Lieutenant Longhold,' he said. 'I am training her to take over my role, so you might be seeing a lot more of her in the future.'

'It is a pleasure to meet you both,' said the official. 'If you would please follow me?'

The official led them to the gates, and they passed through. They entered the palace through a grand entrance hall, and Konna gazed around. The part they were in looked finished, and everything seemed new.

'Are we going to see the king and queen?' Konna whispered to Cole.

He nodded. 'King Daniel and Queen Emily; and their daughter Princess Elspeth will most likely be with them. Don't be surprised at the lack of any ostentatious ceremonies; the Aurelians are very down-to-earth.'

They were taken to a large chamber with tall windows that overlooked the bay. A man and a woman were seated by a long table, but they were dressed informally, and had no crowns upon their heads. Next to them sat a young woman who looked the same age as Konna, while over a dozen officers and courtiers were standing close by.

Cole bowed his head. 'Your Majesties,' he said. 'Might I please introduce Lieutenant Alva Longhold, whom I am training in the service of the Empire?'

Queen Emily smiled. 'How nice to see you again, Cole; and it's lovely to make your acquaintance, Lieutenant Longhold. If you are receiving your training from Cole Holdfast, then you are in the hands of a very fine teacher.'

Cole gestured towards Konna. 'And this, Your Majesties, is Konna Holdfast.'

The queen's gaze settled on her. 'Welcome to Pella, Konna. Any child of Aila and Corthie will always be treated as honoured guests in the City. Indeed, were it not for your father, there would be no City.'

'Thank you, Your Majesty,' said Konna.

'It is we who should be thanking you,' said King Daniel. 'As far as I understand it, you have arrived with exquisite timing, as the Jezran Wall is currently under severe pressure from the greenhides.' He gestured to a courtier. 'Please fetch Lord Maxwell.'

'Yes, Your Majesty,' said the courtier. He bowed and left the hall.

'You will not be the only immortal in Jezra, Miss Holdfast,' Daniel went on. 'Have you heard of Lord Maxwell?'

'Is he the son of God-Queen Amalia, Your Majesty?' said Konna. 'Uncle Naxor has taught us about the demigods who remain in the City.'

Daniel nodded. 'He is Amalia's young son. He has been helping to defend the workforce in Jezra for several months now, and he has proved himself to be a very efficient killer of greenhides.'

'Does he have death powers?'

'He does,' said Daniel.

'And how is his father, Your Majesty?' said Cole. 'Does he remain angry that his only child is fighting greenhides?'

Daniel frowned. 'He does.' He glanced at Konna. 'Lord Kagan has been opposed to his son's involvement in Jezra for several years but, as Maxwell is now an adult, he was unable to stop him.'

'Maxwell has been asking to go to Jezra since he was sixteen,' said Emily. 'It has been a challenge to hold him back.'

The door to the chamber opened, and a handsome young man in battle armour entered. He was as tall as any of Konna's brothers, with the exception of Cairney, and he looked the same age as Konna and Elspeth.

'Lord Maxwell,' said Emily, 'allow me to introduce you to Konna Holdfast.'

Maxwell's gaze went over the two women standing next to Cole, then he stopped in front of Konna. He looked into her eyes and, at once, Konna realised that she was in the presence of another god. The mortals in the audience hall seemed to fade into insignificance, as Konna regarded the immortal man standing a few feet in front of her.

'You are my cousin, I believe?' he said.

'Your mother was my great grandmother,' said Konna.

'I don't remember my mother,' he said. 'She died when I was a baby.'

'I have heard much about the God-Queen from my own mother, and from Uncle Naxor.'

'Those things you heard – were they all terrible?'

'Not all. She was a great ruler, until the very end of her reign, or so I was taught.'

Cole coughed quietly. 'With your permission, Your Majesties,' he said, 'Lieutenant Longhold and I will now take our leave. It was a pleasure to see you all again.'

'We shall talk more the next time you are in Pella, Captain,' said Emily.

Cole activated his Quadrant, then he and Alva vanished.

'We should have asked him to take us to Jezra with his Quadrant,' said Konna.

Maxwell tapped his breastplate. 'I have my own,' he said. 'It has saved me from a greenhide mauling on more than one occasion. Where is your luggage, cousin?'

'It's on a cart by the palace gates.' She frowned, as Maxwell laughed. 'What's so funny?'

'Your accent, Konna,' he said.

'She sounds like her father,' said Emily.

'Everyone sounds like me in Kell,' she said.

'Are you half Kellach?' said Maxwell.

'I'm a quarter Kellach, and a quarter Holdings; that's from my father. And I'm a quarter Pellan, and a quarter god; from my mother's side. What about you?'

'I'm half god, half Shinstran. My father was from Lostwell. Shall we go to Jezra?'

'Now?' said Konna.

'Why not?' said Maxwell. 'We can collect your luggage, and then I will show you the Jezran Wall, and you can see what we are up against.'

Konna turned back to the king and queen.

'You have our leave to go,' said Daniel. 'Please take care over in Jezra, Miss Holdfast; it can be a dangerous place.'

Maxwell inclined his head a fraction, then he placed his hand behind his steel breastplate. The air shimmered, and Konna found herself standing in front of the palace, next to Maxwell and her cart of luggage. The air shimmered again, and the two gods and the cart appeared in the middle of a large open space. To their right was a sheer wall of cliffs, which rose up to a forested plateau, while a redbrick town lay spread out in the other direction. Directly ahead of them, an enormous dark green dragon was standing in the open space, his blue eyes fixed on Konna.

'I've brought her, Seaspan,' said Maxwell.

'I can see that, little Maxwell,' said the dragon. 'So, girl, you are the daughter of the mighty Corthie Holdfast, are you? Can you fight as well as he did?'

'Did you know my father?' said Konna.

'I knew of him, and I saw him on a few rare occasions,' said Seaspan. 'I hail from Throscala in the Eastern Rim, and I have been in this ugly little town for almost a year.'

'I have battle-vision,' said Konna, 'but I am not as good at fighting as my father was. I have other skills. I have death powers, just as Maxwell does, and I can alter my appearance.'

'I see,' said the dragon. 'Do you wish to see the Jezran Wall, Holdfast-demigod?'

'I would,' she said.

'There is space on my harness for three. I will bear you and Maxwell over the battleground of the upper town.'

Konna remembered a piece of advice offered by her mother, and she bowed her head. 'Thank you, dragon; I would be very grateful.'

Maxwell snapped his fingers at a few uniformed workers. 'Take Lady Konna's luggage to her new quarters.'

'Yes, my lord,' said one.

'Am I a *lady* now?' said Konna.

'Of course you are,' said Maxwell; 'just as I am a lord. We are immortal, cousin.'

'Do you ever see Lydia or Doria?'

'Sometimes,' he said, as Konna's luggage was led away by the uniformed workers. 'I like Lydia, but Doria keeps herself hidden away in Tonetti Palace. Neither of them think much of the Aurelian monarchy, but they are all that remains of the old royal family; excepting your mother and Naxor, of course.'

'And Jade.'

Maxwell rolled his eyes. 'The less said about that crazy old witch, the better.'

He gestured towards the flank of the dragon, where several ropes were hanging. Maxwell and Konna climbed the ropes, and pulled themselves into the harness upon Seaspan's broad shoulders.

'Do you have a rider, dragon?' said Konna, as she fastened the buckles round her waist.

'Not at present,' said Seaspan. 'My last rider died of illness over ten years ago, and I have yet to choose another.'

Seaspan stretched out his vast wings and ascended into the air. Konna's eyes widened as the air rushed past her face, and she grinned before she could stop herself.

'Is this your first time upon a dragon?' said Maxwell.

'Aye,' she said.

'It is as good as you imagined it would be, demigod?' said Seaspan.

'It's better,' she said.

Konna gazed at her surroundings as the dragon rose higher. Beyond the redbrick town, she could see a large harbour, where over a dozen ships were tied up, and then the waters of the Warm Sea stretched away to the horizon, where the coast of Tara and Ooste was visible as a grey line. The dragon circled, and Konna's view switched to that of the cliffs. Seaspan rose above them, and Konna saw a second town perched along the top of the ridge. It was protected by a confusing jumble of stone and palisade walls that seemed to go off in all directions. Three large fortresses were being constructed over a mile from the outer limits of the town's perimeter, and a few enormous sections of high stone walls were partly linking the three structures together. There were several large gaps in the stone wall. Some had been blocked by temporary wooden palisades, while others were open, and greenhides were scurrying around, trying to pierce the defences. Another dragon came into view – a large red female. She was soaring down over the gaps in the high walls, burning any greenhide that came close to the hundreds of human workers building the last sections of the wall.

'The upper town and its original walls were built years ago,' said Maxwell, 'but the Aurelians decided to construct their own version of the Great Walls up here, to enclose a far larger amount of territory. When it's finished, Upper Jezra will occupy an area as large as that of the Bulwark, and the three fortresses will protect it.'

Seaspan rose up to join the red dragon, and Konna got a better look at the unfinished Jezran Wall, as the two dragons circled each other. The new defences were made up of three parallel walls – an inner, an outer, and a low wall that ran by a wide moat. The moat was unfilled, and greenhides were crawling all over its steep banks. Lines of ballistae were fixed along the finished sections of battlements upon the inner of the three walls, and they were loosing down at the greenhides, who were there in their thousands.

'There are so many greenhides,' she said.

Maxwell nodded. 'There are none by the Great Walls of the City,' he said, 'but they still flourish on the Western Bank. There are three separate nests in the local area, and the greenhides from each fight each other as much as they fight us.'

'The blame for this situation lies at the feet of Deathfang the Mighty of Lostwell,' said Seaspan. 'He killed the queen of the nest closest to Jezra, but he neglected to destroy her junior queens. Of the twelve that survived, three were able to establish nests. They are a filthy plague upon the Western Bank, and I shall be glad to return to Dragon Eyre once this posting has come to an end.'

'This is the worst it has been for a while,' said Maxwell, his gaze on the swarms of greenhides trying to breach the defences. 'I think the greenhides can sense that summer is coming to an end, and they want to sack Upper Jezra before Sweetmist begins.'

'What does that mean?' said Konna.

'It means two things,' said Maxwell. 'First – you have arrived exactly when we most needed another god with death powers; and second – you will only be fighting for another sixteen days, give or take. As soon as Sweetmist begins, the greenhides will run back into the forest to shelter from the rains.' He glanced at Konna. 'Didn't Aila or Naxor mention Sweetmist to you?'

'I've heard of it,' she said. 'Isn't it two thirds of nothing but rain? I mean – two *months*.'

'There is one month of storms, followed by a month of fog, and then winter begins.'

Seaspan and the red dragon soared down, and both blasted long jets of flame at the area in front of the dry moat, incinerating dozens of greenhides.

'Take us to the Fortress of the Exiles,' said Maxwell. 'I think Konna and I are needed.'

Konna smiled as the dragon soared away towards the central of the three huge, unfinished fortresses.

'Am I to kill greenhides today?' she said.

'You will be doing nothing else for the next sixteen days,' said Maxwell.

Seaspan flew over the outer defences of the fortress, then he circled over a tall, finished keep. He started to descend, as soldiers on the roof of the keep glanced up. The soldiers got out of the dragon's way, and he landed on the roof.

'I will collect you in a few hours,' Seaspan said, 'once the sun sets. Kill well, and kill many.'

Maxwell and Konna unbuckled the straps holding them to the harness, and climbed down to the roof. Seaspan soared back into the air, and began burning more greenhides by one of the gaps in the defensive line. An officer walked towards Maxwell and Konna, and saluted.

'What are your orders, Lord Maxwell?' he said.

'We have a new god with death powers to assist us, Colonel,' said Maxwell; 'the daughter of Corthie Holdfast – Lady Konna. Make sure that word is spread down to every brigade in Jezra.'

The officer smiled. 'Yes, my lord.'

Maxwell gestured to Konna, and they walked towards the edge of the battlements, the soldiers on the roof clearing a path for them. Konna gazed down at the roiling mass of greenhides trying to get through the gaps in the stone and palisade defences. The noise made by the creatures was almost deafening. Dozens of them were attempting to scale a small section of wooden timbers, their rear limbs sliding through the mud, while ballistae and crossbows were loosing an unending stream of bolts into their green flesh.

'You take the left,' said Maxwell, 'and I'll take the right. We'll clear the moat area first, then push back.' He nodded to a soldier, who raised a large red flag over the keep. 'That's to warn the dragons to keep out of our way,' Maxwell said to Konna. 'Are you ready?'

'Aye,' she said. 'I'm ready.'

Amalia's two descendants raised their right hands, and the killing began.

Six hours later, Konna followed Maxwell down a side street that led away from the harbour of Lower Jezra. The buildings on either side had been built over the ruins of the ancient city that had once stood there, and the ground floors and basement levels were built from stone, while their upper storeys were of brick. The sun had set half an hour before, and the lamplit street was busy with civilians and uniformed personnel from the Lostwell Brigades. Half a dozen taverns ran down each flank of the street, and much of the road was taken up by outside tables, where patrons were drinking and eating their evening meals. Konna was keeping a neutral expression on her face, but she was exhausted, and her self-healing was working hard to replace the energy lost by so much use of her powers.

'This is the famous street of taverns,' said Maxwell, 'and your new quarters are close by.'

'My rooms won't be too noisy, will they?' she said.

'Your house is behind this street, so it won't be too bad,' he said.

'Where do you live?' she said.

Maxwell smiled. 'I have a Quadrant, so I have a few choices available to me. If I crave peace and quiet, I can go to my father's villa in the Roser countryside; if I want luxury, I can stay with Lydia and Doria in Tonetti Palace in Port Sanders. If I have an early meeting with the king and queen, I have a room in Cuidrach Palace; but if I want to get drunk, I have a house here in Jezra.'

Konna raised an eyebrow. 'You have four homes?'

'Only one of them belongs to me. What about you? I heard the Holdfasts are so rich they could buy up the entire City.' He paused as they came to a brightly-lit tavern. 'Shall we go in here? I keep a tab running that the crown pays off at the end of each month.'

'All right.'

They descended a set of stairs to a basement level, and entered the tavern through a low doorway, both having to stoop to access the interior. A waiter caught sight of them, then a few others also took notice, and a loud cheer reverberated throughout the tavern.

Maxwell smiled. 'Just another day's work,' he said; 'but now there are two of us!'

The cheer grew louder.

'Is she really Corthie's daughter?' called out one man.

'She is,' said Maxwell.

'Is she related to Kelsey, too?' shouted another.

'Kelsey is her aunt,' said Maxwell. 'Take a bow, Konna Holdfast.'

Konna smiled and shook her head, then she bowed before the customers of the tavern, and they roared out a cheer. The waiter reached them, and led them through the crowds to a quiet booth near the rear of the tavern. Maxwell and Konna sat down.

'Food, ale, brandy,' said Maxwell, 'if you please.'

The waiter bowed, and left them alone in the booth.

Maxwell smiled. 'Where were we? Oh yes, I was asking about the fabled wealth of the Holdfasts.'

'The Holdfasts...' she began; 'well, we... how do I put this? We are divided. The children of Aila and Corthie live thousands of miles from the others, and the two sides don't get along. Both halves have their own sources of wealth, but we aren't as rich as the Holdfasts who live in the imperial capital.'

'What divided you?' said Maxwell.

Konna eyed him. 'I thought you would have known the answer to that question.'

'I have my suspicions,' he said, 'but I would like to hear from someone at the heart of it.'

'It was my father's death,' she said. 'My brothers and sisters hold the other Holdfasts – the Colsbury Holdfasts – responsible for sending our father to die on Dragon Eyre.'

'The other Holdfasts are all mortals, aren't they?'

'Most of them are, but Karalyn's two younger children are gods; and I mean proper gods, like you – not demigods, like me and my siblings. Because of the way my father died, the Marchbrae Holdfasts want nothing to do with the Empress or her government. Tell me – why did someone in the crowd ask about Kelsey?'

'Kelsey Holdfast is probably more popular in Jezra than your father,' said Maxwell. 'Across the Straits in the main part of the City, everyone adores Corthie, but here? Kelsey and her dragon Frostback were based in Jezra for years, right at the beginning of the campaign to re-conquer this land from the greenhides, and the Lostwell Exiles loved them. Is Kelsey one of the Holdfasts that you don't like?'

'Kelsey is one of the worst of them,' Konna said. 'She could have saved my father on Dragon Eyre, but chose not to.'

'And your family is known as the *Marchbrae Holdfasts*? After the whisky?'

Konna laughed. 'We own the Marchbrae distillery. That's why we are independently wealthy; we don't have to rely on the Colsbury Holdfasts for anything.'

'My father says that your whisky is all that gets him through Freshmist each year.'

'I brought some with me. You can take a bottle and give it to your father, if you like. It's the expensive stuff.'

Maxwell smiled. 'Thanks. That will cheer him up. He's not very happy about me fighting in Jezra. He actually avoided the draft when the Lostwell Exiles were first sent here, and he ended up working for my mother as her servant. Because of that, he has never been to Jezra in his life. I think he feels guilty about all of the poor bastards who died here.'

A woman with green skin walked past the entrance to the booth, and Konna narrowed her eyes.

'She is a Fordian,' said Maxwell; 'from Lostwell. Almost every Fordian in the City lives in Jezra, as they face discrimination in the rest of the City on account of being green. They feel safer among the other Exiles. My father says that it's ironic, seeing as how everyone hated them on Lostwell.'

The waiter returned with a large tray filled with drinks. He set down a flagon of water, a flagon of ale, and a small jug of brandy, along with six glasses.

'Your food won't be too much longer, my lord and lady,' he said, bowing.

Konna eyed the waiter as he walked away. 'They seem to hold immortals in a lot of respect here.'

'That wasn't always the case,' said Maxwell, as he filled two glasses with ale. 'As you probably know, most of my mother's family were killed in a succession of wars, and the mortals loathed them.' He lowered his voice. 'They loathed my mother the most. Things have started to change because I risk my life every day on the front line. I have probably killed over ten thousand greenhides since I arrived in Jezra – that's why they respect me. It's also because the people in Jezra have no experience of living under my mother's rule. They've heard the stories, but they don't mean all that much to them. What is it like where you live?'

'My family are the only demigods in the entire region,' she said. 'People respect us because they loved my father. They seem to hate most gods, but they make an exception for us. It's because the Ascendants invaded my world – that poisoned the minds of the mortals against most gods.'

'It's the same here. The Ascendants invaded, three times altogether.

Simon came first, on his own. Then, later, Esher came, followed by Tamid.'

'My father killed Tamid,' said Konna. 'Who killed the others?'

'It took several people and a dragon to put Simon down. My father saw it happen. Kelsey was there, blocking Simon's powers, and the dragon bit his head off.'

'What about Esher?'

Maxwell smiled, but said nothing.

'Who killed Esher?' said Konna.

Maxwell took a long drink of ale. 'I think we are going to work well together, cousin.'

'Don't change the subject,' said Konna.

Maxwell leaned over the table. 'Can you keep a secret?'

'Aye.'

'Esher isn't dead,' he said.

'What?' said Konna. 'One of the Ascendants is still alive?'

'Karalyn Holdfast captured him, and wiped his mind completely clean – his memories, his personality; everything. She also blocked every one of his powers, even his self-healing. He started to age, just like a mortal, and now he looks like a normal, middle-aged man. Imagine that – he has been alive for thirty millennia, and he will die in a few decades from old age. Worse, he has no idea who he really is. He was told that he comes from Lostwell, and that his amnesia was caused by an accident.'

'He thinks he comes from Lostwell?'

'Exactly.'

'Then,' said Konna, 'wouldn't that mean he lives with the other Exiles?'

'You catch on quickly, Konna; he lives among us, here in Jezra. Almost no one knows the truth about him, though, so you mustn't say anything. After all, there's nothing we can do to *fix* him, is there? What Karalyn did to him is permanent, and his memories are lost forever.'

Maxwell raised his glass. 'Let's drink a toast to poor old Esher.'

Konna lifted her glass. 'To Esher, the last Ascendant.'

CHAPTER 6
DISTURBED BY TRANQUILLITY

Rainsby, Southern Plateau – 2nd Day, Last Third Summer 552

Cole gestured towards the Quadrant. 'You touch different areas for different effects,' he said. 'One section deals with direction, another for distance, and so on.'

Alva nodded. 'And what happens if you make a mistake, and your finger goes too far?'

Cole smiled. 'That depends how lucky you are. If you make a mistake with altitude, then you had better hope that you erred on going too high, rather than too low; otherwise, you might appear underground.'

'What if I can't remember how to get back to my starting position?'

'Then you're in trouble. This is one of Elbannon's Quadrants; it doesn't have a *Go back* command, or any of the other commands that require the device to store where it has been in the past. No one has ever been able to work out how to make a Quadrant do that; not since Nathaniel managed to do it millennia ago.'

Alva frowned as she peered at the device sitting on the table between them.

'There are two ways to learn how to use it,' Cole said. 'You can memorise a few sets of instructions about how to travel to certain specific destinations; like the Ministry of the Plateau, or Cuidrach Palace; or you can learn how the device works in principle, and work out each movement in isolation. Most people start with the first approach, and not many make it to the second.'

'What do you do?' she said.

Cole eyed her. 'Neither. My cousin Cael imprinted the knowledge of how to use a Quadrant into my head. It comes naturally to me now.'

Alva's eyes lit up. 'Could you do that to me? It would save me thirds of study, and I wouldn't have to worry about making a mistake.'

'I have never done anything like that before,' he said. 'I'm not sure it would work.'

'You could try.'

'It might hurt.'

'How much?'

'I got a mild headache when Cael did it to me; but he knows what he's doing. I don't.'

'But think how much time we'd save. What's the worst that could happen?'

'I could fry your brain by accident.'

She laughed. 'I'd hope it wouldn't be on purpose.'

'And then Audrey would hunt me down and kill me.'

Alva laughed again.

'Go into my mind,' she said, 'and see if you think you could do it. Could you not copy what Cael did?'

'All right; I'll take a look, but I'm not promising anything.

He gazed into her eyes, and entered her mind. He tried to remain away from her emotions and memories, and concentrated on locating a part of her mind that contained no secrets. He caught a glimpse of her slight anxiety that he was inside her head, then he examined his own mind, sensing the detailed instructions that Cael had placed there. Could he simply transfer the knowledge from his mind to hers? Was it that simple?

'Well?' she said.

'Can you sense me in your mind?' he said.

'Not really,' she said. 'You are being very quiet.'

'It would be safer not to even attempt this.'

'I have faith in you,' she said.

Cole raised an eyebrow. 'Why?'

'You are the calmest person I have ever met,' she said. 'Nothing seems to bother you. Do you ever get angry or annoyed?'

'Rarely, I guess.'

'And I saw you stand up to Cairney Holdfast. Were you scared of him?'

'No.'

'He's a giant.'

'He's a sixteen-year-old boy.'

'Yes, I suppose he is. Are you going to try?'

Cole remained silent. There would be benefits if he was successful, as both of them had found the Quadrant lessons to be a chore. If Alva was able to learn how to use the device quickly, then they would be able to move on to other subjects. On the other hand, he had no desire to hurt her. If the process went wrong, then he might even leave some permanent damage. He could always rush her to Cael if that happened. In fact, perhaps he should ask his cousin to perform the process for him. No. Cael was powerful, but his own abilities weren't nothing. He was over-complicating things; it would be easy.

'All right,' he said. 'Prepare yourself. Relax, and keep your eyes open.'

She smiled. 'I'm ready.'

Cole gathered up the instructions from his own mind, and pushed them into Alva's head with a short and gentle burst of power. Alva screamed. Her eyes rolled up into her head, and she fell from her chair, collapsing onto the wooden floorboards of Cole's office. She began to convulse, and Cole crouched by her.

'Shit,' he cried, taking her hand. 'Alva, can you hear me?'

He went back into her mind, and found it battered and reeling. He soothed her thoughts, and her breathing calmed. She lay still, her eyes staring at the ceiling.

'Sorry,' he said. 'Are you all right?'

'That was... sore,' she said.

'I didn't mean to hurt you.'

'I don't think you have any idea how powerful you are,' she said. 'I could feel the way you stamped the knowledge into my mind; you thought you were being careful, but my head felt as though it was about to explode. Help me sit.'

Cole reached out and pulled her shoulders up. She swayed for a moment, then she rubbed the back of her head.

'Does it still hurt?' he said.

'No,' she said. 'The soreness has faded. It will have been worth a few seconds of pain if it worked.'

'I'm not sure I agree, Alva. It was horrible to watch you suffer like that, even if it was only for a few moments.'

She eyed him, then he helped her get back onto her chair. She glanced at the Quadrant, and picked it up.

'Can you access the information I placed into your head,' he said, 'or is it all mixed up?'

'It's an odd sensation,' she said. 'I can sense what to do, but it feels as though I have a strange new book inside my head, one that wasn't there before. Cael didn't learn how to operate a Quadrant on his own, did he? Someone else placed the information into his head, then he passed it to you, and you passed it to me.'

'You're right,' he said. 'Lord Bailey imprinted the knowledge into my cousin's mind. Shall we test your new skills?'

'How?'

'Have you ever been to Dragon Eyre, or has anyone ever shown you how to get there?'

'No, never.'

'All right. Take us both to a place called Nan Po Tana on the island of Haurn.'

'But how...?'

'Don't think about it,' he said. 'Stand up, and do it.'

'What if I...?'

Cole got to his feet. 'No more doubts. Do it.'

Alva stood, the Quadrant in her left hand. She moved the fingers of her right hand close to the surface of the device, then she closed her eyes and activated it.

The air shimmered, and she and Cole appeared in the middle of a large courtyard, with the sunshine of Dragon Eyre beating down upon them. Palm trees lined the walls of the yard, and several old stone buildings were dotted around amid the orchards and groves. Soldiers from the Imperial Army glanced over at them, and an officer approached, flanked by two men with crossbows.

Cole raised his empty palms into the air. 'Sorry about that, Major,' he said. 'We are conducting lessons on how to use a Quadrant.'

The officer frowned. 'Captain Holdfast?'

'Yes, sir,' said Cole; 'and this is my replacement, Lieutenant Alva Longhold.'

'I heard you were being promoted,' said the major. 'Congratulations. Will you be staying in Nan Po Tana for long?'

'No, sir. We shall be out of your way in a moment.'

The major nodded, then he led the soldiers away.

Cole glanced at Alva, who was having some trouble concealing her emotions.

'That was amazing,' she said. 'I thought about a place I'd barely heard of before, and I knew how to get here. This is a supply depot, isn't it?'

'Among other things,' said Cole. 'It's the westernmost point of the Eastern Rim, and the first place you come to if you sail east from Yearning. Sable Holdfast used to live here.' He pointed at one of the old buildings. 'In there, I believe.'

'Sable used to walk through this courtyard?' she said. 'I'm standing in the same place that she did?'

Cole laughed. 'She isn't dead, you know. She hasn't yet entered the realms of myth.' A thought came to him. 'Would you like to meet her?'

'Are you being serious?' said Alva.

'You talk about her often,' he said. 'She might be too busy to speak to us, or she might not be at home, but we could give it a try.'

Alva puffed out her cheeks.

'Maybe it's a bad idea,' he said. 'Your opinion of my aunt might change if you actually met her.'

'No,' she said. 'I want to see her; even if it's just to say hello.'

'All right then,' he said. 'Take us to the foot of the bridge palace in Udall on Ulna.'

Alva nodded. She took a long breath, then she slid her fingers over the Quadrant. The air shimmered again, and they appeared by the side of the huge palace in Udall. Dragons were circling overhead, and Alva gazed at the town and the harbour. A large new shipyard had been built to the left of the old port facility, and several vessels were in the midst of being constructed.

They stepped aside as a horse-drawn wagon trundled along the road, then Cole led Alva through the busy quayside.

'Welcome to the capital of the Eastern Rim,' Cole said, as they walked. 'What do you think?'

'It's beautiful,' she said, 'and the air seems so clear and fresh. Sable lives on a boat, yes?'

'I think her ship is being refurbished again,' Cole said. 'They don't last too long without having to be repaired. The last time I saw Sable, she was in the new shipyard.'

They took a side street away from the harbour and came to the new ship-building facility. It was flanked by a row of three-storey offices and repair shops, and workers in a succession of dry docks were clambering over the wooden hulls of the vessels under construction. Cole gazed at the people, looking for anyone he recognised. A teenage girl was standing on the gangway of a half-built vessel, and Cole smiled.

'Beth!' he shouted, and the girl turned her head. She saw him, smiled, and walked over.

'Morning, Cole,' she said. 'I hope you aren't here because of an emergency. Is everything all right? Are you here to see my mum?'

'Not this time,' he said. 'I'm training someone to take over my job.'

Beth glanced at Alva. 'Oh,' she said. 'I thought you liked your job.'

'I do,' he said, 'but the Empress has other plans for me. Alva, this is Beth Jackdaw, the daughter of Queen Blackrose's rider. Beth, we were wondering if Sable was close by.'

Beth pointed towards the shipyard's main office. 'She's in there.'

'Thanks,' said Cole.

'I'm coming with you,' said Beth, 'so I can watch the expression on Lara's face. Nothing freaks her out more than one of you Holdfasts arriving here unannounced.'

'Fair enough,' said Cole.

They set off for the large building, and entered through the front door. Beth gestured towards a room, and they went inside. Several people were standing by a long table, examining large drawings of a new ship.

'Look who's here,' Beth cried.

Everyone turned. Cole saw Sable smile, then Lara stepped out in front of her, her eyes narrow.

'What's going on?' said Lara. 'Why are you here, Cole? Has something happened?'

Beth laughed.

'It's just a social visit, ma'am,' said Cole. 'I am showing my replacement how to travel around the Empire.'

'Your replacement?' said Sable, walking forwards. She embraced Cole, then she eyed Alva for a few moments.

'Good morning, ma'am,' said Alva.

Sable raised an eyebrow. 'Good morning, Lieutenant Alva Longhold,' she said. 'Was it worth coming all this way just to see me? Do I meet your expectations?'

Alva's face flushed. 'How do you know my name?' she said. 'Were you in my mind?'

Sable smiled, then she turned to Cole. 'Why are you being replaced, nephew? It can't be for misbehaviour; I know you too well.'

Cole frowned. 'I am being promoted to the Imperial Court.'

'You don't look too pleased about that.'

'I have what I consider to be the perfect job, Aunty,' he said. 'I can keep to myself in Rainsby, but I also get to travel to various exotic places. What's not to like? I don't want any authority or power, and I don't want to have to sit through endless meetings of the court.'

'Yes, but I can see why the Empress would want you based closer to her. Anyway, I am being rude.' She turned back to Alva. 'It's very nice to meet you,' she said. 'Let me do a few introductions. This is Lara,' she went on, gesturing towards the woman. 'And our children are over there, on the couch. Joss and Lindi. Come over here, children.'

Joss got to his feet. The fair-skinned young teenager towered over everyone in the room apart from Cole, and it was obvious that he had Kellach blood in him. His younger sister also stood. Lindi looked more like her mother, and would have passed as someone from the Holdings. She eyed Cole with a smile, her blue eyes lit with mischief.

'Good morning, you two,' said Cole. 'Have you been keeping out of trouble?'

'Yes, Uncle Cole,' said Lindi.

Lara snorted. 'Trouble follows them around wherever they go, Cole,' she said. 'That's why they're in here, so we can keep an eye on them.'

'We were looking at the plans for our new ship,' said Sable.

'What happened to the *Giddy Gull*?' said Cole.

'The poor old *Gull* is just about knackered,' said Lara. 'We've already rebuilt the hull twice, but it's getting too old for the ocean. We want something just as good, but a little less cramped. Joss and Lindi will need their own cabins; Beth, too. We're going to train the girls as middies, and Joss as a master.'

'Joss is already a fine master's mate,' said Topaz.

'Yeah,' said Lara; 'which is just as well, seeing as he's getting too big to be climbing the rigging.'

'We were also thinking about building something much larger than the *Gull*,' said Sable. 'Our own dragon carrier; then we could ferry Blackrose around in style.' She gestured at the plans on the table. 'What do you think, Alva?'

'I don't know much about ships,' she said, 'but a new dragon carrier on this world would be very useful.'

'I agree,' said Sable. 'It doesn't have to be as big as the *Horned God*. Let's get some coffee, and we can look over the plans.'

Several hours later, Cole escorted Alva out of the office after they had said their farewells to Sable and the others. The Holdings mage had a contented smile on her face as they walked towards the harbour, and Cole was pleased that she had enjoyed the visit.

'I can see why you love this job,' she said.

'Remember that you'll be spending most of your time in Rainsby,' he said. 'You won't always be travelling around the most beautiful parts of the Empire meeting Holdfasts.'

'I don't care. Where shall we go next?'

'Home,' he said. 'They will be serving dinner in the mess hall soon.'

She nodded. 'All right.'

'Well?' he said.

'That's right,' she said. 'I have the Quadrant. I almost forgot.'

She withdrew the device, and activated it. The two of them appeared back in Cole's office within Madden's Tower in Rainsby. Alva placed the device onto the desk, while Cole closed the shutters against the fading light.

The door opened, and Audrey peered in. 'Sorry to interrupt, sir,' she said, 'but I was waiting outside the door for you to get back, and then I heard something.'

'Cole has been teaching me how to use a Quadrant,' said Alva. 'We were on Dragon Eyre.'

'Dragon Eyre, eh? Might I come in, sir?'

Cole nodded, then he took his seat by the desk, as Audrey entered the room and closed the door behind her.

'Do you have news?' he said.

'Only personal news, sir,' said Audrey. She eyed her sister. 'One of our instructors is ill, and tomorrow's schedule has been cancelled. In other words, I have a completely free day tomorrow.'

'Do you want to do something?' said Alva.

'Yes,' said her sister. 'I want to go out tonight and get roaring drunk. Me and a few others from my company are going down to the town; do you want to come?'

Alva glanced at Cole.

'Does this mean you'll be hungover in the morning?' he said. 'Unlike you, Audrey, Alva has work tomorrow.'

'But think of all the time we saved with the Quadrant lessons,' said Alva. 'Might I come in an hour late? Please?'

Cole rolled his eyes. 'Fine. One hour, no longer.'

Audrey grinned. 'Thank you, sir.'

Alva eyed her again.

'And, uh…' Audrey went on; 'of course, sir, you are free to join us if you like.'

Cole knew that Audrey was only asking out of politeness. She always asked him, and he always gave the same reply. He thought about eating alone in the mess hall, and made a decision.

'Thank you,' he said. 'I accept.'

Audrey stared at him.

'I have one condition,' Cole went on. 'I want to go somewhere that serves decent food. How many other marines are coming along?'

'Four, sir.'

'All right. I will pay for everyone's dinner, and then I will go home after we eat, leaving you lot free to drink as much as you like. Do we have a deal?'

'That's very generous of you, sir; thank you.'

Cole locked the Quadrant in a desk drawer and got to his feet. 'I'll have a quick shower and meet you downstairs in an hour.'

Audrey and Alva shared a glance, then he ushered them out of his office.

'Make sure you pick somewhere good to eat,' he said, as he locked the door.

'Yes, sir,' said Audrey.

Cole smiled, and left the two sisters standing by the office door.

Two hours later, Cole was seated in one of Rainsby's better taverns with Alva, Audrey and four junior officers from the marines. Waiters and waitresses were placing full bowls and plates onto their table, along with ale and several bottles of wine. Cole had decided that he would have a couple of drinks, though not enough to get drunk in front of the others. He sipped from his mug of ale, as the marines talked loudly about their day's work.

'Do you want some wine?' said Alva, as she held up a bottle.

'No, thanks,' said Cole. 'Wine makes me maudlin.'

'Is that why you don't usually drink?'

'It's more on principle,' he said. 'I don't think it's wise for mages to lose control. I could burn down the whole of Rainsby if I so desired.'

'Like your father did, sir?' said one of the marines.

'Exactly,' said Cole.

They started to eat, and Cole wondered if his presence was making things awkward. He was the highest ranked among them, and he knew that most people didn't relish their superior officers hanging around while they were trying to relax. The food was good, though, better than anything the mess hall served, and he wasn't going to stay for long.

More wine and ale was brought to the table when they had finished eating, then a marine asked for a bottle of whisky.

'We won't ask you to pay for the whisky, sir,' said the marine, 'but we've decided to stay here rather than move on to another tavern.'

'This is the only place in Rainsby that serves Marchbrae whisky,' said another marine. 'Why would we want to drink anywhere else?'

'What did you order?' said Cole.

'A bottle of Lachellan ten-year-old, sir.'

'That's a good choice,' said Cole.

'Do you ever see the Holdfasts down in Kell, sir?'

'We've been to Kell twice since I arrived in Rainsby,' said Alva; 'and we were on Dragon Eyre today. Guess who we saw.'

'Queen Blackrose?' said a marine.

'Guess again.'

'Sable?'

Alva grinned. 'Yes. Sable bloody Holdfast, in the flesh. We also met her two kids.'

Audrey laughed. 'You're mixing with the aristocracy now, sister.'

The whisky arrived, and a marine opened the bottle while another one arranged a line of seven glasses. Cole started to object, then he closed his mouth. One whisky wouldn't hurt. He glanced at the others. They had finished several flagons of ale and bottles of wine between them, and a few were starting to look a little worse for wear.

A marine slid a full glass of Lachellan towards Cole. He took a small sip, and felt the warm spirits slide down his throat.

'Pyre's knackers,' said a marine. 'This stuff is magnificent. How do they do it?'

'It's the brandy casks they use,' said another marine. 'Severton tastes dull compared to this.'

'No, it's the peat,' said a different marine. 'They burn peat instead of coal to malt the barley.'

'Who cares?' said Audrey. 'Just drink it.'

Alva glanced at Cole. 'Why don't you tell the Empress that you don't want to join the Imperial Court?'

A few of the others looked over.

'Is that where you're going, sir?' said one. 'The Imperial Court?'

'I think that was supposed to remain confidential, Alva,' said Cole.

'Was it?' she said. 'Sorry. You told Sable about it.'

'Sable is family.' He nodded at the others. 'It's true. Her Majesty has offered me the position of Imperial Secretary.'

'I thought Cael Holdfast had that job, sir,' said Audrey.

'He is also getting promoted, but you didn't hear that from me,' said Cole.

'Cole would rather stay in Rainsby,' said Alva.

'I'd rather have a quiet life,' said Cole. 'I'm already doing what I want to do; why would I wish to change it?'

One of the marines frowned. 'Excuse me for saying this, sir,' he said, 'but you don't appear to be enjoying yourself in Rainsby. You rarely speak to anyone, and I was shocked when Audrey told us you were coming along tonight.'

'I live the life I want to lead,' he said. 'I don't care if people think I'm unfriendly. I don't bother anyone, and I don't like to be bothered.'

Alva laughed.

'I'm proud of being a Holdfast,' Cole went on, the whisky and ale having loosened his tongue; 'but, at the same time, sometimes I would prefer to be anonymous. There are expectations people have when they learn who I am. They think all Holdfasts are the same. I love my cousin Cael, but I am nothing like him.'

'Didn't you help the Empress when she massacred the Wystian dragons, sir?' said a marine.

'I was there,' he said. 'I didn't kill any of the dragons myself, though. I used my fire abilities to deflect any flames that came near us. That was my role – to defend the Empress. I'm fine with that sort of work – defensive, rather than aggressive. I would prefer to leave the killing to others.'

'You fought off hundreds of dragons,' said Alva. 'It must have been terrifying.'

Cole shrugged. 'It was fine.'

Alva eyed him. 'You are too tranquil, and that disturbs me. What was the last thing that scared you?'

Cole narrowed his eyes. 'I think it might have been upon the world that Cael created. I burned down an entire village. They were trying to kill us, but I unleashed my powers in a way I hadn't done before, and haven't done since. Part of me enjoyed it, and that frightened me.'

'The only thing that scares you is your own powers?' said Alva.

He nodded. 'I fear losing control, and I fear becoming my father. That's why I try not to get angry.'

'Your father was a great hero, sir,' said a marine.

'That might be true,' said Cole. 'I didn't really know him. I saw a lot more of Corthie when I was younger.'

The marines eyed each other.

'You saw Corthie die, didn't you, sir?'

'I was unconscious when he died. I awoke when I was healed by a Sanang hedgewitch; that was when I saw what had happened. I failed my uncle that day. I wasn't strong enough to fight off gods and dragons at the same time. Is it any wonder the Marchbrae Holdfasts hate us?' He paused, realising that he had probably said too much. He gestured to a waiter. 'I would like to settle the bill for all of the food and drink we have had up to this point.'

'Certainly, sir,' said the waiter. He pulled a small notepad from his apron, and flicked through the pages.

'Are you leaving us?' said Alva.

'Yes,' said Cole. 'It's time for me to go home, I think.'

Alva opened her mouth to say something, then seemed to think better of it.

'That will be eighty-one sovereigns altogether, sir,' said the waiter.

Cole passed him a purse of coins. 'There is a hundred in there. Keep the rest as a tip.'

The waiter bowed. 'Thank you, sir.'

Cole got to his feet. 'Have a good evening, all,' he said. 'Alva, I will see you in the morning.'

'Thank you for paying, sir,' said Audrey.

'It was my pleasure.'

Cole walked through the busy tavern and stepped out into the cool night air. He exhaled, and leaned against the wall of the building, his eyes on the seven stars in the sky above him. He had left before he had said anything scandalous or embarrassing, but he had been close to revealing far too much about how he felt. His precepts about remaining quiet and sober had worked for years, and he had almost thrown all of that hard work away in a single evening.

He would have to do better, he told himself. Keeping his distance from others was how he had chosen to navigate the world, and it was time to go back to that approach.

He straightened his back, and set off towards Madden's Tower.

CHAPTER 7
IMPOSTER

Plateau City, The Plateau – 7th Day, Last Third Summer 552

'Mia, to heel,' said Arrosa.

The large dog tore her gaze away from the three spaniels being walked on the opposite side of the road, and resumed her place by Arrosa.

'Good girl,' Arrosa said.

She turned up a narrower lane within the heart of the Old Town, and Mia walked by her side. To her right, the almost-complete Blue Palace towered over the centre of the city. During the long years of its construction, the various departments of the government had been dispersed to different addresses throughout Plateau City. The Ministry of the Plateau held the Imperial Court, but several other buildings had been requisitioned, and it was to one of those that Arrosa was walking. A solitary soldier stood on duty by the back door of an old four-storey block, and he eyed the approach of Mia.

'Good morning,' said Arrosa.

'Good morning, ma'am,' said the soldier. 'Do you have permission to enter the building?'

Arrosa dug into a pocket, as Mia sat on the cobbled road, her gaze on the soldier. Arrosa withdrew a letter with the wax seal of the Adjutant embossed on its front, and the soldier nodded. He opened the door, allowing Arrosa and Mia to walk into the building.

An imperial official eyed her. 'The Adjutant and Chamberlain are awaiting you, ma'am,' he said. 'Come this way.'

Arrosa followed the official into the large front room, as Mia trotted by her side. Adjutant Claudian and Chamberlain Brogan were seated inside, drinking coffee while they spoke together.

'Missus Holdfast has arrived,' said the official, bowing.

'Thank you,' said Claudian.

The official stepped back out of the room and closed the door.

'Please be seated, Arrosa,' said Claudian. 'Coffee?'

'Yes, please,' she said. She took a comfortable chair across from Claudian and Brogan, and Mia sat down on the floor by her legs.

'Just the one dog today?' said Brogan.

'I left the other two in the townhouse,' she said. 'One is usually enough to deter any trouble.'

Claudian poured coffee into a cup, and handed it to her.

'Thank you, sir,' she said.

'The Empress asked us to meet with you,' said Claudian, 'so that you could learn more about your new responsibilities as Postmaster. Have you been briefed by either the Constable or the Herald?'

'They gave me a general overview of what I would be doing, sir,' she said, 'but neither were particularly forthcoming with any details. I understand that I am to take over the running of the Empire's network of agents and spies?'

Brogan smiled. 'Not quite,' she said. 'You are to *establish* a network of agents and spies. At present, the Empire is lacking any overall organisation on this front. As Chamberlain, I have a few agents scattered throughout the provinces, and the Adjutant also has a few under his authority. Others have been controlled directly by the Constable or the Herald.'

'All in all,' said Claudian, 'this approach has led to confusion, and the Empress wishes for a single person to oversee and expand the activities of these agents. That person will be you, Arrosa Holdfast.'

'When my mother was Empress,' said Brogan, 'a woman by the name of Isobel ran an entire department of vision mages, spies and agents. It all fell apart during the wars with Agatha, and no similar network was ever re-established, until now. Part of that was due to the dearth of decent vision mages in the Empire, but their numbers have recovered to a certain extent. Of course, nowadays, we also have Quadrants, which assist greatly with communicating intelligence across the Empire.'

Claudian picked up a box, and opened it. He took out a Quadrant and set it down onto the table.

'This is for you, Arrosa,' he said. He withdrew something else from the box and placed it onto the palm of his hand. 'This is also yours.'

Arrosa gazed down at the ring on Claudian's hand.

'This is your new seal,' said Claudian. 'The seal of the Imperial Postmaster. You will use it on all official documents from now on.'

'Thank you, sir,' she said. She picked up the ring and dropped it into a coat pocket.

'Currently,' Brogan said, 'between the various members of the Imperial Court, we control fourteen different agents across the Empire.'

'I had expected there to be more,' said Arrosa.

'I would imagine that most citizens of the Empire would be surprised to learn how few agents and spies we employ,' said Claudian. 'Four of the fourteen are vision mages. One of them is well known to you – Captain Cole Holdfast. He is under the Marshal's authority at present, but when his position in Rainsby is taken over by Lieutenant Alva Longhold, she will come under your authority.'

'Is my husband considered to be one of the fourteen?' said Arrosa.

'No,' said Brogan. 'Cael sometimes performs commissions as though he were an agent, but he reports to the Herald, and the Herald alone. He will not come under your remit.'

Arrosa smiled. 'That is probably for the best.'

'Eight of the fourteen are based on the Star Continent,' said Claudian, 'and the other six are elsewhere. We have three on Dragon Eyre, two in the City, and one upon the island of Zamata on Athumia.'

'Is Lord Bailey aware of this?'

'He is,' said Claudian. 'The Dominion has also placed their own agents onto the island, and I believe they all know each other. One of your first tasks will be to visit every agent, but we shall not be handing you a written list. You will have to memorise the individual names and locations. Brogan and I shall inform each agent that you will be running a single new department responsible for all of them, and we shall tell them to expect a visit from you. You will also be required to begin the recruitment of new agents, to expand the number of personnel under your control. Use your Gifts to vet any candidates, and put them to work if they measure up.'

'Doing what, sir?' she said. 'What are my department's priorities regarding intelligence gathering?'

'There are two areas upon which to focus,' said Claudian. 'The first relates to external threats, which means keeping an eye on the activities of the Dominion. The peace established by Karalyn Holdfast remains intact, but if anything were to occur, we would wish to be forewarned. You must be cautious, however – give the Dominion no reason to complain to Karalyn regarding the behaviour of your agents. In other words – do not provoke them. The second area to watch involves internal threats to the stability of the Empire. It is well known that a grand coalition of forces opposed to the Empress's proposed constitutional changes is gathering its strength. This coalition spans several worlds, from the Gloamers and Sanders in the City of Salve, to various dragons of the Eastern Rim. Upon the Star Continent, the coalition counts the Matriarch of Sanang as a member, along with several Holders, including Holder Long, the uncle of Alva Longhold. There are also rumours that a group of retired officers from the Banner of the Sapphire Throne are deeply opposed to the proposed changes; we shall have to see if they attempt to make contact with this coalition. If they do, I want to know.'

'We must also be wary of those who are perhaps too enthusiastic about their support for the changes,' said Brogan. 'As you might know, pro-democrats were responsible for trying to assassinate the Matriarch.

All attempts to disrupt the peace of the Empire must be rooted out and crushed, and that applies to both sides of the political argument.'

'I understand,' said Arrosa. 'Do I have a budget?'

'You do,' said Claudian. 'Treasurer Slaeon took some persuading, but we have managed to secure a separate stream of funding for your department.'

Brogan smiled. 'She insisted at first that your budget had to come from my department, but she was overruled by the Empress.'

'As much of your work shall be of the unofficial type,' said Claudian, 'you will have to be careful when filing your receipts with the treasury. Ensure that all expenses are allocated to one of your legitimate responsibilities – the postal service, or the maintenance of the supply of Quadrants. That is your official role, if you recall.'

'I will pass over to you the register of Quadrants, which details where they are located, and their current owners,' said Brogan. 'I will also hand over all spare devices. The university continues to construct new Quadrants at a rate of around three or four per year, and all of these shall be required by law to be handed over into your keeping. Allocate them with care, and confiscate any that have been used irresponsibly. You should be aware that Lord Naxor retained his old Quadrant – the one he held while he was Chamberlain. We also believe that the Dominion has around six or seven devices, while we possess over fifty. If any go missing, it may be a sign that the Dominion is stirring, so keep a close eye on the numbers.'

'And the Calendar Pole portals?'

'There are three portals from Plateau City in daily use,' said Brogan; 'to Na Sun Ka, Ulna, and Ooste in the City of Salve. These are provided as a free service to the citizens of the Empire. There are also porters based in the Ministry of the Plateau who will, for a fee, transport people and their possessions to any part of the Empire. The system works well, and I would advise against altering it, at least for the moment.'

Arrosa nodded, then she glanced at Claudian. 'What authority do I have over the armed forces?'

'You shall be nominally ranked at the level of a major,' said Claudian, 'and the various services have been informed. If you encounter any difficulties, let me know. You might experience some resistance from a few of our older agents, the ones I have been controlling these past years. You are young, after all, and have very little in the way of military experience. How you deal with this shall be up to you, but I recommend that you quickly assert your authority over them.' He paused for a moment. 'I am now going to recite the names and locations of the agents that have been under my control. Lady Brogan will then do the same with her agents.'

'My former agents,' said Brogan.

Claudian smiled. 'Indeed. Let us begin.'

Arrosa and Mia left the building an hour later. Brogan had given her the list of Quadrants and their owners, but that was the only written material Arrosa was carrying – everything else had been committed to memory. Arrosa felt a little like an imposter. Why had she been given so much responsibility at the age of twenty-six? She had no experience of managing a department of agents and spies, and yet the Imperial Court was expecting her to not only run it, but to expand its operations. She thought back to her time on Zamata for inspiration. Leona had been younger when she had assumed control of Colonel Friel's agents on the island, and Arrosa could still remember how well she had handled the responsibility. Then she recalled Leona's fate. She had made several powerful enemies, and one of them had orchestrated her murder.

She led Mia back through the streets of the city to the aristocratic district, and the butler opened the front door of the townhouse for her. Mille and Maisie were barking loudly, and they bounded towards Arrosa as soon as they saw her, jumping up to lick her face.

Arrosa laughed. 'Did you miss me, girls?' she said, as she scratched behind their ears.

'You have a visitor, ma'am,' said the butler.

'Yes?' she said. 'Who?'

'Killop Holdfast, ma'am. He is waiting in the drawing room.'

Arrosa hung up her coat, and the three dogs followed her into the drawing room. Killop got to his feet.

'Hello, Killop,' she said, as she walked into the large room.

'Good afternoon,' he said. 'I'm not interrupting anything, am I?'

'No, I'm free just now,' she said.

Millie went over to Killop, and he rubbed her ears.

'The dogs are getting used to you,' Arrosa said, as she sat.

Killop re-took his seat on a couch. 'Mia still gives me suspicious looks. Would you like some tea? Your butler brought me some while I was waiting.'

'Thank you, yes,' she said.

She eyed her husband's cousin while he filled two cups from a pot.

'How have you been?' she said.

'Fine.'

A slight pain went through Arrosa's mind. 'Is there something bothering you?' she said. 'You can talk to me about it, if you like.'

Killop shrugged.

'Are you going back to university for another year?' she said.

'I'm not sure. I was home for a few days last third.'

'I know,' she said. 'Bedig informed us that Cole had been to Kell a couple of times to pick up Konna.'

'I had a few arguments with my family while I was there. They aren't too happy with some of my choices. They... well, they still blame the Holdfasts up here for the death of my father. The present I got for Konna also caused a bit of an uproar.'

'What did you get her?'

'Aunty Kelsey's *History of the Star Continent*.'

'Was that wise?' she said.

'It's a good book.'

'So you weren't trying to provoke them?'

'Of course not.'

Pain flitted across Arrosa's head again. 'Not even a little bit?'

'Maybe a little bit.'

'They have a right to feel aggrieved.'

'Aye, but it was seven years ago. Some of my brothers and sisters seem to think that Kelsey and Empress Thorn are cackling with delight at my father's death, as if they planned the entire thing. Father's death was a tragedy for the Empire; I know that. If he were still alive, then the Holdfasts would be united. I wish he were here. Naxor did his best, but he will never replace my father.'

'Does Naxor also hate the mortal Holdfasts?'

Killop shrugged. 'At the moment, he is a restraining influence on Cairney and Carter. He keeps advising us to be patient, and he says that we should do nothing rash.'

'Do I need to worry about what any of your siblings might do?'

'Cairney is always angry, so he's difficult to predict. I suspect he has a few trace dream mage powers, as well as death and vision. He's already powerful as a sixteen-year-old; Pyre knows what he'll be like when he's older.'

'The last time you were here,' she said, 'you were talking about how you couldn't imagine being immortal. Have you managed to reconcile yourself to your fate?'

'No. When I look in a mirror, I tell myself that I will look exactly the same for the next few centuries. I'm twenty, and I will continue to appear the same age, while you and every other mortal I know ages around me. I mean, eventually, I might need some salve to stay young-looking, but you get the idea. Naxor told us to avoid making any friends among the mortals. I could see his reasoning, but I'm not that kind of person. I was surrounded by mortals at university, and I made a few friends there. I might regret it when every mortal I know grows old and dies, but I can't change how I feel.'

'I think it's the same for many young gods,' she said. 'They slowly harden their hearts as each generation of mortals comes and goes.'

'Naxor once said something similar. What if I don't want to be like that?'

Arrosa smiled. 'You could always ask Karalyn to block your self-healing powers.'

'Part of me wants to, but the other part is keen to stave off death for as long as possible. I know that sounds selfish, but don't all mortals secretly wish that they could live forever?'

'I don't know if that's true,' she said.

Millie started to cry and whine, setting off Maisie, who rested her head on Arrosa's knee and gazed up at her with pleading eyes.

Arrosa smiled. 'Two of them are jealous that Mia got to go out with me this morning. I should probably take them for a you-know-what. Would you like to come with me, Killop?'

'All right,' he said. 'It's a nice enough day.'

'It's still too humid for me, but it's getting cooler.' She got to her feet, and all three dogs jumped up. 'Shall we go for a walk, girls?' she said.

The barking began.

'Quiet,' Arrosa cried. She picked up a small paper bag of cubed and dried meat, and placed it into a pocket, then she led the dogs to the front door. Killop followed her, and they put their coats on.

'We're just taking the dogs out,' Arrosa said to the butler.

'Very good, ma'am,' he said, as he opened the door for them.

The dogs trotted down the steps next to Arrosa and Killop, and they set off through the aristocratic district.

'I will have to decide about university soon,' said Killop. 'If I don't go back for third year, I will have to give up my room to a new student.'

'You will always be welcome to stay in the townhouse,' said Arrosa. 'Aunty Kelsey has made that clear on more than one occasion.'

'But what would I do?'

'I don't know. Get a job?'

'If I leave university, Mother will probably expect me to go back to Kell. She might ask me to take over the running of some of the Marchbrae businesses, or perhaps the farm itself. If I was mortal, then I might have some purpose to my life, but because I have more time than I'll ever need, I can't seem to decide anything.'

'If you really don't want to go back to Kell, then what else would you like to do?'

Killop looked away, as though he were a little embarrassed. 'I was thinking that, maybe, I could help Aunty Celine on the Hold Fast estate. I keep hearing that she has not been able to find anyone to assist her.'

'Celine would dearly love to retire,' said Arrosa. 'She was hoping that Cole would take over her position as estate manager, but the Empress has other plans for him. Do you know anything about horses?'

Killop gave her a sheepish look. 'Not much.'

She smiled. 'You would have plenty of time to learn.'

'Do you think you might mention this idea to Aunty Kelsey for me?' he said. 'I would need the blessing of Holder Fast.'

'I will bring it up with her.'

'Thank you,' said Killop. 'Now, I don't wish to alarm you, but two men are following us.'

'Are they close?'

'About a dozen yards behind us. My battle-vision noticed them.'

Arrosa turned left at a junction, and they walked down a narrow, tree-lined avenue, where there were no pedestrians or traffic.

'Did they turn with us?' she said.

'Aye. Do you want me to take care of it?'

'I think we'll let the dogs handle this,' she said.

She paused by a tree, then she turned to gaze at the two men. The three dogs stared at them, their hackles rising as the men began to slow.

'Seize them,' said Arrosa.

The three large dogs sped away. Maisie circled round to the left, cutting off the men's escape route, while Mia and Millie approached from the front, growling and baring their teeth. The two men were forced back against an iron fence, their hands raised.

'Good girls,' said Arrosa, as she approached the men. She dipped a hand into her pocket, and threw a cube of meat to each of the dogs in turn, then she smiled at the two men.

'What do you want?' she said. 'Speak, before I order my dogs to tear your throats out.'

'Are you Arrosa of Zamata?' said one, using the Gunstian language.

Arrosa blinked.

'We have spent many long months travelling here to find you, Miss Arrosa,' said the other, also in Gunstian.

'Who sent you?'

'The government of Gunst, ma'am,' said the first man. 'It became known to us that a Gunstian woman was close to the Empress of the Star Continent; and that she had married the son of the Demon Witch. We were following you, ma'am, because we want to speak to you.'

'What are they saying?' said Killop.

'They are speaking in Gunstian,' said Arrosa. 'They want to talk to me.'

'Will you please call off your dogs, ma'am?' said one of the men.

'How do I know that you don't intend to do me any harm?'

'Why would we wish to hurt you, ma'am? Through you, the Gunstian Empire hopes to find itself a new ally against the Dominion – the Empire of the Sapphire Throne.'

'We are at peace with the Dominion.'

'As is Gunst, ma'am; but things can change. Might we sit down and talk?'

'Do you know where I live?'

'We knew only the correct street until you walked out of your front door, ma'am. Why are no soldiers escorting you? We could have been assassins sent by the Dominion.'

'The Demon Witch has pledged to keep the peace between the Empire and the Dominion. There are no assassins in this city.'

'You are being naïve, ma'am. Have your years on the Star Continent made you forget that the Dominion has invaded Gunst three times? And now they have powerful beings as allies – the so-called gods of the Doomed Worlds.'

'And the daughter of the Demon Witch has turned traitor,' said the other man; 'and she now serves the dragons who rule the Dominion. Please, ma'am; might we steal a short portion of your time this day?'

Arrosa narrowed her eyes. 'I would prefer to remain somewhere public.' she said. 'There is a café close by; we can talk there.' She eyed the dogs. 'To heel, girls.'

The three dogs backed away from the men.

'I have one other condition,' Arrosa went on. 'You will speak in Aucterian, so that my cousin here understands you.'

'Very well, ma'am,' said one of the men, switching to the Holdings tongue.

'This is Killop Holdfast,' Arrosa said; 'a nephew of the Demon Witch.'

The two men bowed.

They set off along the avenue, and rejoined the main road. The café that Arrosa had mentioned had several tables and chairs set out in the afternoon sunshine, and they sat down, the dogs keeping their gazes upon the men.

They ordered tea, water and coffee, and sat in silence until the waiter had returned with their drinks.

'How did you find me?' said Arrosa.

'It will not shock you to learn that we have agents planted onto the island of Zamata,' said one of the men. 'President Bauchlie is the nominal leader of that isle, but Lord Bailey is really in charge. One of our agents seduced a member of President Bauchlie's staff, and we have been learning much about the Empire of the Sapphire Throne. One of the names we learned was yours, ma'am. Our government was very surprised to hear that a Gunstian had risen high into the confidence of the Empress; and so my colleague and I were dispatched to Zamata. Our task was to find a way to reach you, but it took far longer than we had hoped. We first had to insinuate ourselves into Zamatan society, and then wait for an opportunity to leave Athumia. In the end, we bribed one of your imperial agents, ma'am – we paid him a fortune to take us to Dragon Eyre.'

The two men shuddered.

'It was a horrifying experience,' said one, 'to see so many flying demons congregating together.'

Killop frowned. 'Demons?'

'They mean dragons,' said Arrosa. 'Gunstians believe dragons to be inherently evil.'

Killop laughed. 'I hope they didn't say that to Blackrose's face.'

'We spoke to none of the demons while we were there,' said one of the men. 'In fact; we were able to leave that world quickly, through a... a...'

'A portal,' said the other man. 'A portal that led us to Plateau City. Once we were here, it was comparatively easy to track you down, ma'am.'

'I will require the name of the agent on Zamata you bribed,' said Arrosa. 'I may have to exchange a few words with him.'

'Certainly, ma'am.'

'Why didn't you approach us officially? You could have simply told Lord Bailey that you wished to speak to someone in the imperial government.'

'Lord Bailey is a vile imposter and a fraud,' snapped one of the men. 'He pretends to be the brother of the Blessed Chadura, and such blasphemies cannot be tolerated. Besides, everyone on Zamata knows that Bailey informs the Dominion of everything that goes on upon that isle. If we had told him our plans, he could have had us arrested.'

'All right,' said Arrosa; 'so what does the government of the Gunstian Empire want from me?'

'We want a treaty,' said one of the men. 'A treaty between our two empires. We will come to your aid if you are attacked by the Dominion, and we would expect your help if we are attacked.'

Arrosa sipped from her cup of tea. The men had uttered no lies, but she wasn't sure if she could trust them. She felt out with her Gift of Kenning, and sensed that one of the men had the Gift of Withering.

'Are either of you Gifted?' she said.

The two men eyed each other.

'I have not been blessed by Chadura in that way,' said one, 'but my colleague has a Gift.'

'Which one?' said Arrosa.

'Withering.'

'What in Pyre's name is the Gift of Withering?' said Killop.

'It means that, if this man touches your skin,' said Arrosa, 'he might be able to kill you.'

'There is no *might* about it, ma'am,' said the second man. 'No one can withstand my Gift.'

'I don't know if that's true,' said Arrosa. 'My friend here is a demigod. He can heal himself.'

'What?' said the man. 'But... didn't you introduce him as a Holdfast? The Holdfasts are mortal; everyone knows that about them. They are mortal killers of gods.'

'And then one of them married a god and had eight immortal children,' said Arrosa. 'I fear your knowledge might be a little out of date.'

'This does not affect our mission here,' said the other man. 'Miss Arrosa, will you approach the Empress regarding our message? Our two empires would be stronger together.'

Arrosa eyed them. 'I don't know what the Empress will say.'

'But will you please try? We can leave you the address of the lodging house where we are staying; it is in the Old Town, in the shadow of the enormous new palace. If you pledge to ask the Empress on our behalf, we will remain there until we hear back from you.'

'I can't see what harm it would do,' said Killop.

'There is a meeting of the full Imperial Court tomorrow,' said Arrosa. 'I cannot promise what the response will be, but I will pass on everything you have told me.'

The two men bowed their heads.

'Praise Chadura,' said one; 'thank you, ma'am.'

CHAPTER 8
NON-BINDING

Plateau City, The Plateau – 8th Day, Last Third Summer 552

'Good morning, sir,' said Rosie Jackdaw, as she walked into the room with a smile on her face and a crate in her arms.

'Good morning, Quartermaster,' said Lucius. 'What do you have for me today?'

Rosie set the crate down onto the table. 'In here, sir, is a Mark Seven Battanara,' she said, as she removed the lid.

Lucius watched as Rosie lifted a metal tube from the crate.

'Now, sir,' she said, 'you might be thinking – *Wait, that looks exactly the same as the Mark Five and the Mark Six*, but there are important differences. It's lighter, for a start, so it sits easier on the shoulder. We also fixed the problem with the trigger mechanism, and added better sights; but the most important difference is invisible from the outside. The outer barrel is still made of steel, but we have added an inner barrel of Tempest. This layer has been cut with spiralling groves; a technique called rifling. In tests, this rifling has greatly improved the accuracy of the weapon. The addition of Tempest also renders the weapon impervious to heat, and makes it just about unbreakable.'

She held it out for him, and he took the Battanara and positioned it on his right shoulder. His hand gripped the handle where the new trigger was located. It had a guard to stop it from being accidentally triggered, and Lucius peered along the sights.

'We've had to redesign the projectile to fit the narrower barrel,' Rosie went on. 'The new one is slimmer, and it has these little fins at the rear, like a fish, or an arrow; and they also help with accuracy. The testers managed to fire off ten rounds in just under a minute.'

'Very impressive, Quartermaster,' Lucius said. 'How quickly can they be put into production?'

'Right away, sir,' she said. 'At the moment we are churning out mortars and Forty-Eighters, but we have a spare production line ready and waiting for the Mark Sevens.' She sat down at the table. 'We have had a few other ideas, sir.'

'I'm listening.'

'Well, sir, what if we reduced the size of the Battanara considerably, and correspondingly reduced the size of the projectiles? We could make a smaller weapon that could fire single anti-personnel projectiles. You know, if we needed to kill one person without obliterating their entire surroundings.'

'What size were you thinking of?'

'A projectile about an inch in length, maybe?' she said. 'And a barrel about a foot and a half long. Imagine if the Imperial Cavalry were equipped with such weapons – they could loose them from horseback.'

'And terrify the horses at the same time?'

Rosie laughed. 'I didn't think of that, sir.'

'It's a good idea, though,' he said. 'Our current output of explosive weapons is perhaps a little too destructive. A small, cheap sidearm could be carried by every soldier in place of a crossbow. They will have more power than a crossbow, yes?'

'Oh yes, sir. And a longer range, and they would be quicker to reload.'

'I assume you will need more money to research this weapon?'

'Yes, sir. The biggest challenge would be to miniaturise everything. We'd probably need a few more steam engines for the factory, too. Only a steam engine has the power needed to press the Tempest sheets and tubing into their required shapes. We could do with a few new lathes, too, sir, and a new mill, and we'll need another engine for that.'

'Write up everything you need, and pass it to me.'

'Yes, sir.' Rosie pursed her lips. 'I worry a little, sir.'

'About what?' he said. 'Are you concerned about the possible deaths these new weapons will cause?'

She narrowed her eyes. 'No, sir. I'm more worried about the amount of smoke and noise our factory is producing. The Dominion is bound to have spies in Plateau City, and I'd bet you a hundred sovereigns that they are desperately trying to discover the secret of the Ectus Powder. If they locate the factory, they then might figure out what we're doing in there.'

Lucius nodded. 'Then perhaps a new approach is required. Maybe we should relocate the entire facility to somewhere sparsely populated, like southern Rahain, or the eastern deserts of the Holdings.'

'Or maybe a small island on Dragon Eyre,' she said, her eyes lighting up. 'I'd be happy to move there. I could see my sister and enjoy the never-ending sunshine.'

'I'm not sure your husband would relish going back to Dragon Eyre,' he said.

'He'd be fine,' she said, waving away his concerns. 'The only places on Dragon Eyre that Nestorian would refuse to go to are Ectus and Na Sun Ka. I mean, he wouldn't refuse if you ordered him to go, of course. To be honest, I wouldn't want to return to Na Sun Ka, either. I know it's been seven years, but I couldn't bear to see the place where Corthie was killed.'

'I know what you mean. I felt that way about Dragon Eyre even before Corthie's death. I often used to wonder how such a beautiful world could be so filled with pain and misery. Regardless, as Quartermaster, you would have to stay in Plateau City, even if the factory is relocated. We need you here, Rosie; your job isn't only about making new experimental weapons.'

'Tell me about it, sir. Only yesterday, I had to sit through a four-hour meeting on boots for the infantry. It wasn't the most scintillating experience.'

Lucius glanced out of the window at the position of the sun. 'It's almost time for the Imperial Court to convene.'

At that moment, the noon bell pealed, and Rosie laughed. 'I don't know how you do that, sir,' she said, as they both got to their feet.

They walked out of Lucius's office, and he locked the door. They went down a flight of stairs, and arrived by the entrance to the main audience chamber, where the Imperial Court met when everyone was present. Kelsey, Arrosa and Cael were already there, and Lucius greeted them.

'Anything new?' said Kelsey.

'Rosie always has something novel to show me,' said Lucius. 'This time, it was a new Battanara.'

'I'd like to have a look at that,' said Cael.

Lucius smiled. 'We won't be handing them out to the city militia any time soon, and, as Marshal, that will be your new responsibility.'

Cael looked a little disappointed.

'Don't worry,' said Kelsey; 'I will still be sending you out on various operations – you won't be confined to a desk just yet.'

'Thank Pyre for that,' said Cael.

The doors to the chamber were opened by a courtier, and those outside filed their way in. The throne was empty, and so the members of the Imperial Court took their seats. To the left of Kelsey, Shella and Brogan were locked in a whispered conversation, and Lucius could see the anxiety on Brogan's face. Lucius took his place opposite Kelsey, and they all waited for the Empress to arrive. As the lowest-ranked members of the Imperial Court, Cael and Arrosa sat the furthest away from the throne, while Kelsey and Lucius were closest.

Thorn walked into the chamber through a rear door, accompanied by guards and courtiers. She smiled at the members of her court, and sat down on her elevated throne.

'Good afternoon to you all,' she said, 'and thank you for coming. I understand that the results of the census are finally with us?'

'Aye, Your Majesty,' said Brogan. 'Should I read them out?'

'Not yet, Chamberlain,' said the Empress. 'I fear that once we start discussing that topic, there will be no time for anything else. Therefore, we shall start the meeting by asking for any other business.'

Kelsey glanced around the table. 'Does anyone have anything to bring up?'

'I have a couple of things, ma'am,' said Arrosa.

'Then speak, Postmaster,' said Kelsey.

'Thank you, ma'am,' said Arrosa. 'The first item won't take long to cover. Killop Holdfast visited me yesterday, and he asked if he could be posted to the Hold Fast estate. He doesn't want to go back to university, and he has no desire to return to Kell.'

Kelsey frowned. 'He wants to help Celine?'

'She is always asking for someone in the family to replace her as estate manager,' said Arrosa, 'and Killop would like the job.'

'I'll think about it,' said Kelsey. 'What else do you have?'

Arrosa glanced around the table. 'Yesterday, while I was with Killop,' she said, 'we were approached in the street by two men working for the government of the Gunstian Empire. They were sent here to talk to me, as they had heard that a fellow Gunstian was in the Imperial Court. They want to discuss the possibility of signing a defensive treaty with the Empire – a treaty that would oblige the two empires to assist each other if either was attacked by the Dominion.'

Kelsey frowned. 'That sounds like the kind of thing we would need to run past Karalyn first.'

'What did you say to these gentlemen, Postmaster?' said the Empress.

'I told them that I would bring it up at today's meeting, Your Majesty. I also told them that we were at peace with the Dominion, but they seemed keen to negotiate. It took them a lot of time and effort to get here.'

'How did they get off Athumia?' said Claudian.

'They bribed one of our agents on Zamata, sir.'

Claudian's eyes tightened.

'I shall deal with it, sir,' Arrosa went on. 'I intend to visit Zamata soon, and I will take the appropriate action.'

'Why didn't they just ask Bailey?' said Kelsey.

Arrosa smiled. 'They believe Lord Bailey to be a blaspheming charlatan, ma'am. They cannot accept that he might be the brother of Chadura.'

Kelsey turned to Thorn. 'What do you think, Your Majesty?'

'I am unsure,' said the Empress. 'Would an alliance be of any practical military benefit?'

'It would come in handy if we were ever invaded by the Dominion, Your Majesty,' said Lucius. 'However, I think it is more probable that we would be drawn into a conflict on Athumia.'

'Is another war between Gunst and the Dominion likely?' said Bedig.

'Not at the moment,' said Lucius. 'The independence of Zamata acts as a hindrance to both sides. However, the Gunstians might wish to reclaim Irlan for their empire, and that might draw the Dominion into a fight. If we sign a treaty with Gunst, they might be emboldened to act.'

'I tend to agree, Constable,' said the Empress; 'but I would be loath to offend the Gunstians after they have made such an effort to reach out to us. Schedule a meeting with them. I shall not attend, but I would like the Constable, Herald, Adjutant and Postmaster to be present. Listen to their suggestions without condemning them, and offer them every hospitality. Also offer to take them directly home, but do not promise any treaty.'

'Understood, Your Majesty,' said Lucius. 'Arrosa, could you please arrange this meeting for us?'

'Yes, sir,' she said.

'As the only Gunstian here,' said Kelsey; 'what is your opinion on this, Arrosa?'

'I think the Constable is correct, ma'am,' she said. 'They did not want the Dominion to know that they were coming here, and I suspect that the Gunstians would use a treaty to feel more confident about reconquering Irlan, and perhaps even Elso.'

'Do you feel any sense of allegiance towards the Gunstians?' said Fenu.

'Absolutely none,' said Arrosa. 'I am a Zamatan Gunstian; I have never been loyal to the Gunstian Empire.'

Kelsey nodded, then she glanced at the others. 'Is there anything else?'

No one spoke.

'All right, Brogan,' said the Herald; 'read out the census figures.'

'Aye, ma'am,' said the Chamberlain. She unfolded a single sheet of paper. 'First of all, the figures have been rounded for clarity. The single most populous province of the Empire is the Holdings, with two million, one hundred thousand inhabitants. Next is Rahain, with one million, six hundred thousand, and Rakana, with one million, two hundred thousand. Nowhere else comes close. Even if we add together the entire population of the City of Salve, that only comes to nine hundred thousand. In other words, under Shella's proposals, the combined voting strength of Rahain and Rakana would amount to an entire third of the assembly, with one hundred and twelve delegates out of three hundred and thirty-six.'

The room fell silent.

'This is a catastrophe,' said Bedig. 'We cannot allow Rahain and Rakana such immense power in the assembly.'

'You're talking as though they would have a majority,' said Shella. 'They will have one third of the votes, not half.'

'For how long?' said Bedig. 'After decades of war and famine, the population of Rakana is growing quickly again. The faster they breed, the more delegates they will have.'

'That is why we shall institute the Provincial Council at the same time as the assembly,' said Shella. 'The council would have to ratify any votes carried by the assembly. It would only take three full provinces to object, and that would act as a veto.'

'None of that makes any difference,' said Bedig. 'All the citizens of the Empire will hear is that the Rahain and Rakanese will be able to hold the rest of us hostage. Have you forgotten that we are roundly loathed by most people in Rahain and Rakana? They hate us, Shella. We shouldn't be including them in the assembly at all.'

'Do you think that would make them like us more, Bedig?' Shella snapped. 'It's not democracy if we exclude two of the biggest provinces.'

'How many people live in Kellach Brigdomin?' said Bedig.

Brogan consulted the document in her hand. 'Three hundred thousand, brother. That would give them twelve delegates.'

'So the Kellach get twelve,' said Bedig, 'while Rahain and Rakana get one hundred and twelve between them?' He snorted. 'This is insanity. The Kellach helped found the Empire, and these proposals will turn them into an insignificant backwater.' He glanced at the Empress. 'I object most strenuously, Your Majesty.'

'Does it matter?' said Shella. 'You have already asked to leave the Imperial Court.'

'Perhaps that allows me to speak my mind more freely,' said Bedig. 'If these census results are made public, there will be an outcry so loud that the Empire will be forced to postpone or cancel the proposals. The Empire is not ready for this extreme form of democracy.'

Shella glared at Bedig, while no one else spoke.

'I need to hear everyone's opinions on this,' said the Empress. 'Let us start with the Herald and work our way down the table. Any vote taken today will be non-binding, but I want to know if, in light of these census results, you are in favour of implementing the constitutional proposals in full, or whether you would prefer a postponement.'

Kelsey glanced up at the Empress. 'I support Shella's proposals, Your Majesty,' she said, 'and I believe they should be implemented. The vetoes held by the Provincial Council will prevent Rahain and Rakana from dominating the legislature.'

Thorn nodded. 'Constable?'

'I remain neutral on this matter, Your Majesty,' said Lucius.

The Empress frowned. 'That answer shall not suffice, Lucius,' she said. 'You must have an opinion, one way or another.'

Lucius narrowed his eyes.

'I do not wish to press you on this,' the Empress said, 'but I will not be satisfied until each one of you has given their opinion; and that includes you, Constable. Speak.'

'In that case, Your Majesty,' he said, 'I would prefer a postponement.'

Kelsey stared across the table at him, her eyes wide.

'As Constable,' Lucius went on, 'my priority is the stability of the Empire, and these reforms carry a risk of disrupting the peace we have fought so hard to achieve. While I admire the principle of allowing the people to vote, I can also see why many would be upset by giving so much influence to the citizens of Rahain and Rakana.'

'Thank you, Lucius,' said the Empress. 'What does my Chamberlain think?'

'I harbour a few doubts about some of the details, Your Majesty,' said Brogan; 'but if pushed, I would choose implementation rather than another delay.'

'I don't think we need to ask Chancellor Shella for her view,' said the Empress. 'I assume you are thoroughly committed to the implementation of your proposals?'

'I am, Your Majesty,' said Shella. 'The vetoes will protect the government from being overly influenced by any rogue provinces.'

'Adjutant?' said the Empress.

'I would have to agree with my commanding officer, if forced into giving an opinion on a civil matter, Your Majesty,' said Claudian. 'There is a serious chance of disorder if these proposals are passed; therefore I vote for postponement.'

'Thank you,' said Thorn. 'Chief of Staff?'

'I am in favour of the reforms, Your Majesty,' said Fenu. 'The Empire deserves democracy, and an imperfect voting system is better than no voting system at all.'

'Treasurer?'

Slaeon glanced up, her eyes dark. Her forked tongue flickered out for a moment, then she shook her head. 'My honest opinion is that these reforms are a colossal waste of time and money. We have already spent a considerable sum feeding and housing the thousands who have been working on these proposals, and yet the results seem to satisfy no one. Let us not throw good money after bad. If cancellation was an option, I would choose it, but, in its absence, I vote for a long postponement.'

Across the table from him, Lucius saw Kelsey and Shella share a glance, their features lit with anger and disappointment.

The Empress glanced at Nardini. 'I assume that my Chief Jurist is as committed to implementation as my Chancellor?'

'Indeed, Your Majesty,' said Nardini. 'As I helped draft the proposals, I am bound to support them.'

'That makes five for implementation, and three for postponement,' said the Empress. 'I shall not ask you, Marshal Bedig, as you have already made your views on this clear. Your vote brings to the total for postponement to four.'

'I plead with you not only to postpone these changes, Your Majesty,' said Bedig, 'but, as the Treasurer suggested, to cancel them altogether. If they go ahead, we will be delivering the Empire into the hands of the Rahain and the Rakanese.'

'Keep your temper, brother,' said Brogan.

'Why?' said Bedig. 'Is this not the perfect time to get angry? What have the people of Rahain or Rakana ever done to build or defend this Empire? Did they help us defeat the Ascendants? Of course they didn't, and now we are supposed to be happy that they will take up a third of the assembly? We are cutting our own throats.'

The Empress glanced down the table at Rosie Jackdaw, who was sitting to Cael's left.

'Quartermaster?' said Thorn.

'I don't know, Your Majesty,' said Rosie. 'I like the idea behind these reforms, but I worry that they will cause protests and riots and so on. That's what happened in the City when King Daniel tried to force through too many reforms at the same time. Is there no way to reduce the power that Rahain and Rakana will have over the smaller provinces?'

'That is why we are also setting up the damn Provincial Council,' snapped Shella. 'Do none of you listen? Rahain and Rakana will not have representatives on this council, as they are not full provinces; and every piece of legislation carried by the assembly will also have to be passed by the council. It will act as a veto, to prevent any large provinces from bullying the smaller ones.'

Rosie frowned. 'It all seems too convoluted. I vote for a postponement.'

'What about you, Secretary?' said the Empress.

Cael chewed his lip for a moment. 'I have a few reservations, Your Majesty, but I think seven years is long enough. If this is the best compromise that has been reached by Shella's team on Colsbury, I would support its implementation.'

'Thank you, Cael,' said the Empress. 'And, finally, what does our Postmaster think?'

'I believe, Your Majesty,' said Arrosa, 'that any reforms of this magnitude require the backing of every province in the Empire. That is not the case. Sanang is bitterly opposed, as are large sections of the Holdings, the Eastern Rim, and the City of Salve. I call for a postponement.'

The Empress nodded. 'So, my court is split down the middle, with six votes apiece? I shall require some time to ponder the way ahead.' She glanced at Brogan. 'Have the census results published in full and disseminated around the Empire; the citizens need to know the truth.'

'It shall be done, Your Majesty,' said Brogan.

'Wait a moment,' said Shella. 'Is that a wise course of action? The enemies of democracy shall use the census figures to stir up trouble.'

'The truth is the truth, Chancellor,' said the Empress. 'I will not hide the results from the people. Most citizens know that a census took place, and they will become even more suspicious if we neglect to reveal our findings.'

Shella frowned, but said nothing.

'This session is ended,' said the Empress. 'I shall withdraw to consider my choices.'

Thorn got to her feet, and the rest of the Imperial Court rose and bowed their heads. Lucius watched as Thorn walked from the audience chamber, then he saw Kelsey's furious expression aimed in his direction.

'What in Pyre's name happened, Lucius?' she cried. 'How could you vote against us? Shella and I have invested everything in these reforms.'

'I didn't want to give my opinion,' he said; 'but the Empress gave an order. Would you have preferred me to lie?'

'You abandoned me, because you think there *might* be a few protests?'

'You and I lived through the riots and disorder in the City when the Aurelians tried to ram through their reforms; just as Rosie reminded us. Do you want the same thing to happen here? Think, Kelsey – how did King Daniel finally get his way? He backed down, and proceeded at a more gradual pace. Maybe we should learn from that, and do the same.'

Kelsey shook her head. 'Was it a coincidence that the three most powerful leaders of the military all voted for a postponement? You don't care if the people have a say – you just want quiet, well-behaved citizens.'

'I understand your disappointment,' said Lucius, as the others in the Imperial Court watched its two highest-ranking members argue; 'but Shella's proposals risk splintering the Empire. Would you be happy if Sanang tried to leave – that's what the Matriarch will threaten if the Empress forces these proposals through.'

'The Matriarch can piss off,' said Kelsey. 'She is frightened of change, because she knows that she and her rich cronies will lose power. I won't forget this, Lucius. When we needed to be bold, you voted to appease those who would keep the people under their heel.'

Kelsey and Shella walked out of the chamber, leaving Lucius standing next to Claudian and Bedig.

'Dinner will be fun tonight,' said Cael. He glanced at Arrosa. 'Are you angry with me for supporting the reforms?'

'No,' said Arrosa. 'I think our marriage is strong enough to survive a few political disagreements. Let's get the dogs and go home.'

Cael took her hand, and they left the chamber, followed by most of the others.

'Kelsey will calm down soon, sir,' said Rosie. 'I thought you did the right thing.'

Lucius eyed her. 'There is a reason why the commanders of the armed forces should stay out of politics,' he said. 'I think today demonstrated how true that is.'

He walked out of the chamber, with Rosie and Claudian by his side.

'What now, sir?' said Claudian.

'We shall have to see what the Empress decides,' Lucius said. 'If she rejects the reforms, there is a chance that several members of the Imperial Court will resign in protest. Shella has already decided to retire, but Kelsey, Fenu and Nardini might be next to go, if they feel that they have been betrayed. The same does not apply if the Empress approves the measures, as Bedig will be leaving shortly. I will not be resigning if the Empress disregards my advice on this subject.'

'Nor I, sir,' said Claudian. 'It is a civilian matter.'

'I will see you both tomorrow,' said Lucius. 'I had best be getting home.'

When he reached the entrance to the Ministry of the Plateau, Lucius was informed by a soldier on duty that Kelsey had already left the building, so he caught up with Cael and Arrosa, who were leading the dogs along the street. Despite having disagreed during the vote, neither Cael nor Arrosa seemed concerned, and they talked all the way home as though nothing had come between them.

Lucius went looking for Kelsey as soon as they returned to the Holdfast townhouse. She wasn't downstairs, so he knocked on the door of her large room.

She opened it. 'What do you want, Lucius?'

'Do you think we should always agree about everything?' he said.

'Of course not, but this is different,' she said. 'Shella and I have been working on these reforms for years, but not once in that time did you ever tell me that you had reservations. All those evenings when I kept you up late so that I could talk and talk about what the convention was doing, and you never made any objections. And all this time, you were opposed? It's as though I don't know who you are, Lucius.'

'You know me better than anyone else, Kelsey,' he said. 'I'm not opposed to the folk of the Empire having a vote, but Arrosa was right – we need the agreement of every province before we try to implement so many changes at once. I hated what I had to say in the audience chamber, because I knew how much it would hurt you. This is why I look after the armed forces, so that I don't get involved in politics.'

Kelsey shook her head, but said nothing.

'What are you going to do now?' he said.

'I don't know,' she said. 'Shella and I anticipated concerns about the high populations of Rahain and Rakana, which is why we created the Provincial Council, so that none of the larger parts of the Empire would be able to bully the smaller ones. But nobody listened. They heard the figures, and jumped to the wrong conclusion. Either that, or they acted out of cowardice.'

'Are you calling me a coward?'

'You are more concerned with keeping order than you are about the rights and freedoms of the people living in the Empire.'

'Don't people have a right to live in peace? How can anyone be free if rioters are burning down their neighbourhood? You know what I'm talking about, Kelsey. You saw what happened in the City of Salve. We both saw it. Even if Simon hadn't arrived, the City was being torn apart by civil strife. It is my job to stop that happening here. Do you want my advice?'

'No,' she said. 'Leave me alone for the rest of the day, while I try to think my way out of this.'

She closed the door, and Lucius lowered his gaze.

'You two fight like a married couple,' said Arrosa.

Lucius turned, and saw Arrosa on the stairs, Cowie held in her arms.

'You shouldn't have been listening,' he said.

'I was going upstairs, Lucius,' she said. 'How could I have avoided hearing you? What were you going to advise?'

'I was going to suggest that she and Shella break their reforms down into several smaller packages, and then try to push them through one at a time. It would take a lot longer, but I think the people need more time to see the effects of each change. I didn't come up with this idea on my own – it's what King Daniel did in the City of Salve. Kelsey doesn't want to hear this, but she needs to be patient.'

Arrosa raised an eyebrow, then she carried on up the stairs with Cowie.

Lucius returned to the ground floor. The children would be getting home from school soon, and he had promised to help them with their homework.

CHAPTER 9
LEAVE

Jezra, The Western Bank – 1st Namen 3441

Konna swung her right hand, and the two talons on the end of the Clawfist ripped through a greenhide's face. Three beasts sprang at her through the forest on her left, and she unleashed a wave of death powers in their direction. Their heads exploded, coating the nearby trees with green gore. Maxwell arrived next to her, Queen Emily's Fated Blade in his right hand. Around them, more greenhides prowled, keeping their distance from the two gods.

Konna laughed out loud, exhilarated, as a dragon soared overhead. Konna charged off into the crowd of greenhides, keeping her death powers back. She wanted to tear them to pieces, and her battle-vision was singing. It would be too easy to fell the creatures with powers alone; she wanted to be close enough to feel the danger. The Clawfist ripped through the chest of a greenhide, then Maxwell's Fated Blade decapitated the beast as it fell. The greenhides began to pull back, then their withdrawal turned into a headlong retreat, as raindrops hit the branches of the forest. Within seconds, the rain was torrential, and every greenhide in the area was fleeing back into the depths of the forest.

'Sweetmist has come,' Maxwell cried, as rain poured down his face and bloody armour. 'It's over; summer is over.'

Konna lowered her right arm, disappointment replacing her lust for death. She reduced her battle-vision, and stared at the backs of the greenhides as they vanished into the thick mist.

'Is that it for two whole months?' she said.

'That's it,' said Maxwell. 'We'll see no sign of the greenhides until winter starts.'

'Pyre's arse,' she muttered. 'I feel as though I was just getting started.'

Maxwell smiled at her, then he sheathed the Fated Blade, and took out his Quadrant. He slid his fingers over the copper surface, and they appeared inside Maxwell's large apartment in the centre of Jezra, from where they had set off that morning.

'You can have the bathroom first,' he said. 'Dry yourself off.'

'Do ye mind if I have a shower?'

'Of course not. There will be plenty of warm water; help yourself to towels and soap.'

Konna picked up the bag she had left there that morning, and walked into Maxwell's tiled bathroom. She undressed and stepped under the shower, washing off the sweat, mud and green gore that had got onto her skin and into her hair. Once clean, she dried herself and dressed in the fresh clothes she had placed in the bag. She had also brought along a brush, and she restored some order to her wet hair, before tying it back. She emerged from the bathroom to find Maxwell reclining on a couch with his feet up on the table.

'We are likely to get another telling off when we report to headquarters,' he said.

'I don't care,' she said. 'We killed hundreds of greenhides today, far more than we could reach when we stayed up on the battlements.'

'True, but we were specifically ordered not to go beyond the walls.'

Konna shrugged as she sat down. 'Tell them it was my idea.'

'It was your idea.'

She smiled at her cousin. 'You worry too much about what the mortals think. They want us to kill greenhides, and that's exactly what we've been doing. They can complain all they like about our methods; I couldnae care less.'

'You're a bad influence on me; that's what they are saying, cousin,' he said. 'I never disobeyed orders before you arrived. You have led me astray.'

'Good,' she said. 'Yer Amalia's son, for fuck's sake; the God-Queen's only living child. You should be able to do whatever the fuck ye like.'

'Have you always cursed so much?'

'You should hear my brothers and sisters,' she said. 'I swear the least out of them. Does it offend ye?'

'Of course not,' he said. 'Your accent suits it. I sound too posh to get away with swearing like that.' He got to his feet. 'My turn for the shower.'

Konna relaxed as Maxwell went into the bathroom. She had been getting along well with her cousin in the seventeen days since she had arrived in the City, and she wondered if the authorities in Pella would send her back to Kell now that summer was over. If not, then what would she do for Sweetmist? She stood and walked over to a window. The sky outside had transformed, and thick dark clouds lay overhead, when only that morning the sun had been shining. The torrential rain was already causing some of the street gutters to overflow, and channels of water were flowing down the slope towards the harbour. The market to the right was being dismantled in a hurry, the stalls and produce taken away before they could be damaged by the Sweetmist deluge. Other than that, the streets were deserted, and most windows had been firmly shuttered.

Maxwell walked out of the bathroom dressed in clean, dry clothes, and he joined Konna by the window.

'We now have thirty days of this to look forward to,' he said, 'followed by thirty days of fog.'

'That's if they decide to keep me here,' she said. 'I'm out of a job.'

'Shall we visit the Brigade commander?'

She shouldered her bag. 'We might as well get it over with.'

Maxwell activated the Quadrant, and they appeared in the reception hall outside the commander's office. Several Brigade workers were standing in the hall, and a few bowed their heads at the arrival of the two immortal warriors. Maxwell knocked on the door of the office, and opened it. Konna followed him into the chamber, where the commander was sitting with a dozen other officers. They were discussing the rapid onset of Sweetmist, and a captain was reading from a list of steps to be taken to close the town down against the coming storms. The ships in the harbour were to be unloaded and made secure, while all major building projects were being postponed until winter.

The commander noticed Maxwell and Konna, and he raised a hand to silence the captain.

'Once again,' the commander said, 'you two flouted orders and left your posts on the battlements of the Fortress of the Exiles. Do you have an explanation for your conduct?'

'Yes, sir,' said Maxwell, a slight smile on his face. 'We ascertained that the most efficient way to destroy the greenhides threatening that section of the defences was to go down and confront them face to face.'

'You disobeyed orders, in other words?' said the commander. 'You thought you knew better than the combined wisdom of the Brigades, who have been toiling in Jezra for nearly twenty years.'

'It was my idea,' said Konna.

'I don't care whose idea it was,' he said; 'you both agreed to it.'

'The greenhides have been moving out of our range, but,' Konna went on. 'They've learned that Maxwell and I can kill them from the battlements, so they avoid that area. Going down there was the only way to kill them.'

The commander shook his head. 'You are both young, and your reckless naivety is clear for all to see. To defend the workers who are constructing the walls, we need to coordinate every aspect of our forces – the soldiers, the ballistae, the dragons, and even our two immortal gods. How can we do that if we have no idea where you are? Where are we supposed to position the dragons, if you might have strayed into their line of fire? Where do we aim the ballistae? Not even an immortal can survive a yard-long bolt going through their head. Regardless, the summer is over, at last, and we can relax a little. I hereby grant you both three days' leave, to spend as you wish. Report back here on the morning of the fifth of Namen.'

'Why?' said Konna. 'What will we be doing?'

'We have a few plans for you this Sweetmist. It's not often that we have two gods with death powers working for us, and there are three greenhide nests out west that need to be located and destroyed. Are you up for it?'

Konna and Maxwell smiled.

'Yes, sir,' said Maxwell.

The commander nodded. 'Dismissed.'

Maxwell and Konna walked out of the room, and Maxwell laughed.

'That was fairly mild,' he said. 'I was expecting far worse.'

Konna paused by the main entrance to the brigade headquarters. Outside, the rain was pouring from the overcast skies.

'What shall we do with three days of leave?' she said.

Maxwell shrugged. 'What would you like to do?'

'Could I visit my family in Kell?'

'I guess so. We would need to go to Ooste first, and pass through the portal to the Star Continent. And then... Is there a way to get from the capital all the way down to Kell?'

'We could hire a porter to take us,' she said, 'or, you could do it; that would be a lot quicker, and cheaper. Use yer Quadrant.'

'I don't know how to make it take us to Kell,' he said. 'I only know how to navigate this world.'

'Could ye take me to Ooste, then? When does the next portal open?'

'At sunset.'

Konna laughed as she gazed out at the leaden clouds. 'And when might that be?'

'Soon, I think,' he said.

Maxwell took out his Quadrant, and activated it. The air shimmered, and they appeared under a long canvas awning next to the derelict Royal Palace in Ooste. A few others were close by, sheltering from the torrential rain next to their luggage.

'You're in luck,' said Maxwell. 'The portal hasn't opened yet.'

Konna eyed him. 'Thanks for bringing me here. What are yer plans for the next few days?'

'I'm not sure,' he said.

'Ye can come back with me, if ye like,' she said. 'Eight of yer cousins are sitting in Clackenbaird farmhouse, and it's still summer in Kell, I think.'

Maxwell glanced up at the tall Calendar Pole. 'Yes, it's still summer where you're from.'

'Well? Do ye fancy it?'

'Would it be all right, do you think? What will your mother say? I don't think she got on very well with my mother.'

'It'll be fine. Come on; we'll give ye a proper Kell welcome.'

Maxwell narrowed his eyes for a moment.

'Is yer father expecting ye home?' Konna said.

'Not particularly.'

'Then what are ye waiting for? I'm trying to be hospitable.'

'I appreciate that,' he said. 'All right; let's do it. My father loved that whisky you gave him. I can pick up another bottle for him. Will we need money to hire a porter in Plateau City?'

Konna patted her bag. 'I have plenty, and we can make sure ye get a decent bottle for yer father; something that ye cannae get in the City.'

At that moment, a woman walked out from a side door of the Royal Palace, escorted by two soldiers, and a courtier holding an umbrella. They hurried through the rain until they reached the shelter of the large awning, then the woman withdrew a Quadrant from her robes. She activated it, and a black swirling mass appeared a few yards away. It grew larger, then the darkness cleared to reveal a sunlit plaza surrounded by tall buildings.

'Is that Plateau City?' said Maxwell.

'I guess so,' said Konna. 'I've never actually been.'

The woman gestured to the queue of people by the Royal Palace, and they picked up their luggage and began to pass through the portal. Konna and Maxwell ran the last few yards, to avoid getting too wet, then they stepped onto the plaza, and Konna felt the warm air against her face. She gazed at the sun, and then at the blue sky, and smiled.

'The sky...' Maxwell murmured.

'Aye, I know,' said Konna.

They got out of the way of the queue that was ready to pass through the portal in the other direction, then Konna spotted a group of officials standing close by. She nodded to Maxwell, and they approached the group.

'We're looking for a porter to take us to Kell,' Konna said.

One of the officials was a Kellach man, and he nodded. 'Whereabouts in Kell?'

'Marchside,' said Konna. 'Clackenbaird Farm, to be exact.'

'That is a restricted area,' said the Kellach man. 'The owners of Clackenbaird only allow close friends and family members to be brought there by a porter. I can take you as far as...'

'I am family, ya numpty,' said Konna. 'I'm a Holdfast. Konna Holdfast.'

'Ah,' said the man. 'I don't suppose you can prove that, miss?'

'How would I prove it?'

'Konna Holdfast has the power to change her appearance,' said another porter. 'If you can do that, we'll believe you.'

'All right. Watch this.'

Konna concentrated. *You see me as Empress Thorn.*

The group of porters gasped, and even Maxwell stepped back in alarm.

You see me as myself.

The Kellach porter laughed. 'That'll do nicely, Miss Holdfast. It's five sovereigns each; eight if you want me to collect you and bring you back later. Is the lad also going?'

'Aye,' said Konna. 'One way will do. I'll get my Uncle Naxor to show us how to get back to the City.'

She reached into her bag and found her purse. She counted out ten sovereigns, and handed them over.

'Your brother used this service a short while back,' the Kellach man said.

'I know,' she said. 'I saw him when I was last home.'

The man nodded to his colleagues, then he pulled out a Quadrant, stared at its surface, and activated the device. The air crackled, and they appeared in the courtyard of Clackenbaird, in front of the farmhouse. The sun was out, but it was low in the western sky, and the air was far cooler than it had been in Plateau City.

'Thanks,' Konna said to the porter, who smiled and vanished. She turned to Maxwell, who was gazing around at the view from the top of the hill.

'The fields go on forever,' he said. 'I didn't know you lived in the middle of the countryside.'

'There's a town a couple of miles away to the south,' said Konna, 'but Kell is mostly empty. If ye walk in any direction, ye'll come across the abandoned ruins of lots of little villages and farms that were destroyed fifty years ago.' She pointed. 'Marchbrae is just over there. That's where we make the whisky. And the ale and the cider and the gin; if that's yer thing.'

'Back already, eh?' came a voice from their right. 'Did the greenhides kick yer arse, sister?'

Konna smiled as she turned. Cairney, Carter and Clova were walking towards her and Maxwell.

'The rains started,' she said, 'and the greenhides ran away.'

'So ye claim,' said Cairney. He eyed Maxwell. 'And who's this?'

'This is our cousin Maxwell,' Konna said. 'The God-Queen's son.'

'So he's a proper god?' said Carter. 'Not a demigod?'

'That's right,' said Maxwell. 'My mother was your great grandmother, I believe.'

Cairney laughed. 'Listen to him speak; like a right posh wee boy.'

'He's older than you, Cairney,' said Konna; 'and he's not bad in a fight. Maxwell has slaughtered thousands of greenhides over the summer.'

Cairney nodded. 'Battle-vision?'

Maxwell shook his head. 'Death powers.'

'We have a few days of leave,' said Konna, 'so I thought I'd bring Maxwell here to introduce him to everybody.'

'We should go indoors,' said Clova. 'It's nice to meet ye, Maxwell, but I'm starving.'

They walked to the front door of the farmhouse and entered the warm hallway.

'Take yer boots off, Maxwell,' said Konna. 'My mother goes mental if ye drag mud into the house.'

All five pulled off their boots and coats by the front door, then Aila appeared round a corner in the hall's passageway. Her eyes lit up at the sight of her eldest daughter.

Konna walked forward and embraced her mother.

'Why are you back so soon?' Aila said.

'Sweetmist, Ma,' said Konna. 'We got a few days' leave. This is Maxwell.'

Maxwell bowed. 'It is an honour to meet you, Lady Aila of Pella.'

'I haven't been called that in a while,' said Aila.

'Is it all right if he stays over with us for a couple of days, Ma?' said Konna. 'I thought it was time he met the Marchbrae Holdfasts.'

'Of course it's all right,' said Aila. 'Maxwell is family. Come into the kitchen, and we'll sit down while dinner is prepared.'

Aila led the others through the farmhouse and into the large kitchen, where a Kellach woman was chopping vegetables by a sink.

'Two more places for dinner, please,' Aila said.

'No problem, ma'am,' said the woman.

Konna and Maxwell sat by a table, while Cairney helped himself to an apple from a bowl. Aila also sat, as Naxor appeared by the doorway.

'I thought I heard your voice, Konna,' he said. 'Welcome back.' His gaze fell on to Maxwell. 'Ah. We have a guest, I see – our grandmother's son, Aila.'

'I know who he is,' said Aila.

Maxwell got back to his feet and bowed again. 'Lord Naxor of Port Sanders,' he said. 'I am honoured to meet you.'

Naxor laughed. 'We are all gods here, Maxwell,' he said. 'There is no need to call me *lord*.'

'My father wishes to thank you for the whisky,' Maxwell went on. 'It was a most generous gift.'

Naxor frowned. 'It was a gift that was supposed to go to my sisters in Tonetti Palace.'

Konna smiled. 'I've not had a chance to visit Lydia or Doria yet, so I decided the whisky should go to Maxwell's father.'

'I was unaware of that,' said Maxwell, his features flushing.

'Pay Naxor no attention, Maxwell,' said Aila. 'The one thing we have here is plenty of whisky. When you go back, you can take some for Lydia and Doria, and some more for your father as well.' She raised an eyebrow. 'Now, where is your luggage?'

Maxwell and Konna eyed each other.

'We were in a rush,' said Konna; 'we didn't bring any. Maybe Maxwell can wear some of Killop's old clothes – they are around the same size.'

'Never mind that,' said Cairney. 'Sister, have ye used the Clawfist?'

'Aye,' said Konna. 'I was using it this morning. It rips right through the greenhides.'

'I thought you were supposed to stay up on the battlements, daughter?' said Aila.

'That only worked for the first few days, Ma,' she said, 'then the greenhides learned to stay away from us. We had to go down to find them.'

'But I left strict instructions that you were not to be allowed to fight beyond the walls.'

Konna laughed. 'We might have disobeyed a few orders. Apparently, I'm a bad influence on Maxwell.'

Cairney laughed. 'I wish I could be there,' he said. 'It sounds like fun.'

'You have two more years to wait, son,' said Aila. 'You can go as soon as you turn eighteen.'

Maxwell eyed Cairney. 'Are you only sixteen? But...'

'Aye; that's right, wee man,' said Cairney. 'I know I look older, but.'

'You look a lot older.'

'I take after my father,' said Cairney. 'Do ye know who I'm talking about?'

'Yes, of course,' he said. 'Corthie Holdfast is renowned throughout the City; the mortals adore him.'

'As they should,' said Cairney. 'My father was the greatest mortal who ever lived. I have battle-vision, like him, but I also have death powers, thanks to yer mother.'

'Just like Konna,' said Maxwell.

'My battle-vision's better than hers,' said Cairney. 'As for my father, didn't he once cut off yer mother's arm after she opened the gates to the greenhides? That's true, aye? Yer mother slaughtered hundreds of thousands of mortals.'

'That's enough, son,' said Aila. 'None of that is Maxwell's fault.'

'I didnae say it was, Ma,' he said. 'It was his mother's doing.'

'You're right,' said Maxwell. 'My mother did all those things, and more; but she also saved the City in the first place, and she fought greenhides for over a thousand years. The memories of mortals are short, and they only talk about some of the bad things she did in her last days as the God-Queen.'

'She was indeed a mighty ruler,' said Naxor, 'but I fear you are right. The mortals of the City never recall any of the good that she did.'

Aila glanced away.

'I know that you rebelled against my mother, Lady Aila,' said Maxwell, 'but I hope we can put all that behind us.'

'My ire against your mother has long since faded, Maxwell,' said Aila.

Cairney nodded. 'Ma only hates the other Holdfasts now.'

'Not all of them,' said Aila. 'I have no issue with Sable, for instance. I know that Sable would have remained by Corthie's side, right until the end, had Kyra not blocked her powers. And how can I blame Cole? He tried his best to help your father on the day he was killed.'

'Cael helped, too,' said Clova; 'and he rescued me from that desert world.'

'Maybe,' said Aila, 'but then Cael fell straight back into the cloying embrace of the Empress, dragging Arrosa with him. All Cael wants now is to become the next Emperor – his heart is full of nothing but ambition.'

'Which other Holdfasts do you oppose?' said Maxwell.

'The Empress,' said Aila, 'Kelsey, Lucius Cardova – all those who forced Corthie to fight upon Dragon Eyre. I also loathe Kyra Holdfast, for hurting my children when she fled from Colsbury, and for what she did to Sable. More than that, though, I hold Karalyn Holdfast responsible. She could have ended that war any time she chose; instead, she looked away, claiming it wasn't her duty to intervene. She only became angry *after* Corthie's death. If she had shown even an ounce of concern before that, my husband would still be alive.'

The kitchen fell into silence. Clova looked as though she wanted to say something, but then lowered her head and kept her mouth closed.

'Let us move through to the dining room,' said Naxor. 'My stomach is starting to rumble.'

'We're going to play a wee drinking game,' said Cairney, as he sat in the small drawing room with Konna and Maxwell.

'What are the rules?' said Maxwell.

'No self-healing allowed,' said Cairney. 'If one of us uses their powers to sober up, the other two get to stop their heart for a minute as a punishment. Last one to take a drink is the winner.'

'My brother likes this game,' said Konna; 'because he always wins. You don't have to play, Maxwell.'

'Of course ye dinnae have to play,' said Cairney. 'I understand if yer too scared.'

'I'll play,' said Maxwell.

Konna frowned. 'How well can ye handle a drink?'

'I guess we'll find out,' he said.

Cairney grinned, then he filled three glasses with whisky. 'This is only Pitburn, but. The cheap stuff.'

'I've never heard of it,' said Maxwell.

'We usually only stick it in blends,' said Cairney.

'We also sell it to the poorer end of the market,' said Konna. 'The Reapers and Evaders drink it in the City.'

'I didn't know that,' said Maxwell.

Cairney picked up his glass. 'In one.'

He downed the whisky, and slammed the glass back down onto the table. Konna laughed, and did the same. She coughed, and laughed again, as the spirits burnt her throat. Maxwell frowned, looking a little anxious, then he lifted the glass to his lips and drank. He started to struggle when he was halfway through the whisky, but he persevered, much to Cairney's amusement.

'Good lad,' Cairney cried, as Maxwell gasped and grimaced. 'Now, remember that Konna and I can tell if ye use self-healing, Maxwell, so don't be getting any funny ideas.'

He refilled their glasses from the bottle of Pitburn.

'I have to say,' Cairney went on, 'I'm a wee bit jealous that you two will get to go back to the City to kill greenhides. I wish I was going with ye.'

'If you turned up in Jezra,' said Maxwell, 'none of the mortals would believe that you're only sixteen.' He pointed at Cairney. 'Do you know who you remind me of? I've been thinking about it for a while, and I've just realised – you look like Prince Michael. There are two enormous statues of him in the City, and you have the same face. He was also a giant of a man.'

'Prince Michael, eh?' said Cairney. 'Should I be flattered?'

Maxwell laughed. 'It depends who you asked. Many mortals feared Michael, but he was a strong leader. He ruled the City for a thousand years, right through its golden age.'

Cairney nodded. 'I'll take that as a compliment. Drink up.'

They downed their second glasses, and Konna started to feel sick. She resisted the temptation to power her self-healing, as Cairney would immediately sense it, and she had no desire to have her heart stopped for a minute. Maxwell's face turned pale, and he swayed in his chair, as Cairney laughed.

'How many gods have the Holdfasts killed?' said Maxwell, as Cairney filled their glasses again.

'Hundreds,' said Konna. 'Maybe thousands.'

'Would they kill me if they could?'

'Things have changed,' said Cairney. 'We're Holdfasts and gods. We won't allow the mortal Holdfasts to slaughter our people any longer. Those days are over.'

'Didn't your father kill several gods?'

'Aye, but only the bad ones,' said Cairney. 'You know, the Ascendants.'

Maxwell eyed Konna, and smiled. 'Konna and I know a secret about the Ascendants.'

'Aye?' said Cairney.

'One of them is still alive, and he lives in the City.'

'Yer fucking kidding me,' said Cairney. 'A real Ascendant?'

'Yes.'

'It's Esher,' said Konna; 'the one that Karalyn captured. She wiped his mind and blocked his powers. The poor guy now lives as a middle-aged mortal in Jezra. He has no idea who he really is.'

'I'd forgotten about him,' said Cairney. 'Have his memories gone for good? Is there no way to bring them back?'

'None,' said Maxwell. 'Karalyn fried his head. Apparently, it took a few years before he could speak properly, and then he had to learn how to read and write again. He has a job as a draughtsman, drawing up plans for the Jezran Wall. I see him every now and again. He's a big guy – not as big as you, Cairney, but he almost looks like he could be a god, if he wasn't so old. I'm half-tempted to tell him, just to see the look on his face.'

'What would happen if ye did that?' said Cairney.

'I'd get in trouble with the Aurelians,' he said. 'I'm not supposed to tell anyone, least of all him.'

Cairney looked deep in thought for a moment. 'Who else knows?'

'The Aurelians and their closest advisors in the City government,' said Maxwell, 'and I'm guessing that the Empress probably knows. And Karalyn Holdfast, of course.'

'I wonder why they didnae kill him.'

'Queen Emily told me that Karalyn forbade them from executing him. If he had no memories, how could he be held responsible for what he had done?'

'And his powers are all blocked?'

'That's right.'

'You'll have to keep this a secret, brother,' said Konna. 'If the Aurelians discover that I know about this, they might not let me go back to killing greenhides.'

Cairney smiled. 'You can trust me, sister,' he said. 'Right – drink up; down in one.'

CHAPTER 10
ON THE SPOT

Rainsby, Southern Plateau – 21st Day, Last Third Summer 552

Cole's vision flew over the waters of the Inner Sea. He was following the vision Alva had sent out, tracking her progress as she tried to reach the settlement of Bannerton. The town of retired Banner veterans was located along the coast, south-east of Westport, and Alva had yet to reach that far with her powers, despite numerous attempts.

You are close, he said in her mind. *Keep going; just another eighty miles to go.*

I can't, she said. *My head is aching; I can't go on.*

Cole sensed her vision powers slowing and fading, then they ceased completely. Cole severed his own connection, and glanced at Alva. The young Holdings mage was gripping on to her stomach, then she got up and ran to the bathroom. Moments later, the sound of her vomiting reached Cole's ears. He got to his feet and stood by the bathroom door. Alva was shaking as she leaned over the toilet.

'I'll get you a glass of water,' he said.

'Water won't cure the pain in my head,' she groaned. 'Have you got any salve?'

'The marines keep a small supply; but it's for serious injuries. They won't hand it out because you are suffering from a mage-induced headache.'

She vomited again, then she sat by the toilet, sweat on her brow.

'Why are you all right?' she said.

'I am supposed to have a few residual dream mage abilities,' he said. 'I guess this is one of them.'

'You lucky bastard. I feel as though I am about to die.'

'The good news is that you ranged well over two hundred miles today; that's double what you could do when you arrived here.'

'But it's still not good enough. What will happen if I can't reach Plateau City?'

'I don't know.'

She eyed him from the bathroom floor. 'Are you secretly hoping that I fail, so that you get to keep your job?'

'I would rather stay in Rainsby, but not at your expense,' he said. 'I don't want you to fail, but we are running out of time. We were given two thirds, and we are well past the halfway stage.'

'Keenweed might help.'

'Keenweed would definitely help, but I don't think we should go down that route.'

'Why not?'

'What if you become addicted?'

'It's not dullweed, Cole; I'll be fine. Do you know where I can get some?'

'Maybe.'

'Will you please try?'

Cole narrowed his eyes. 'Fine. Wait here.'

He walked to the front of his apartment, and left by the main door. He made his way downstairs to the large mess hall, and saw the marine corporal who supervised mealtimes. Cole walked up to him.

'Good morning, Captain,' said the corporal. 'You are a little early for lunch.'

'It wasn't lunch I was after,' said Cole. 'Can you be discreet?'

'Of course, sir,' he said. 'What are you after?'

Cole glanced around the mess hall. Keenweed wasn't illegal in the Empire, but its use by the armed forces was frowned upon.

'A little keenweed,' he said. 'Maybe an ounce?'

The corporal hesitated.

'I have the money on me,' Cole went on. 'There is a mage-related emergency I need to deal with.'

The corporal glanced over his shoulder, then he gestured towards the kitchen. 'This way, sir. I trust that you can also be discreet?'

'I have no desire for either of us to get into trouble, Corporal.'

They walked into the kitchen, and the corporal led Cole to a storeroom. Once inside, he closed the door, then he reached up onto a high shelf and took down a tin of flour. He opened it. All of the flour had gone, and the tin was full of small bags and pre-rolled weedsticks.

'An ounce, did you say, sir?' he said. 'Can you roll your own?'

'It's been a while, but yes.'

'I get the feeling this isn't for you, sir,' he said, as he removed a paper bag from the tin.

'I wouldn't like to say.'

The corporal handed over the bag. 'That's one ounce of the finest keenweed, grown in the Holdings. That will be twelve sovereigns, sir.'

Cole dug into a pocket and passed over the money. 'Thanks.'

'No problem, sir. If you need any more, let me know.'

Cole walked out of the kitchen, and climbed the stairs to his apartment. He entered, and found that Alva was lying on a couch in the sitting room with a blanket over her head.

'Your weed dealer has returned,' he said.

Alva pulled the blanket down. 'Already? That was quick.'

'If you know, you know, I suppose. I'll make a weedstick for you. I'll need your tobacco.'

Alva turned so that she was lying on her side. She reached into her uniform and threw over her cigarette case. Cole caught it, and sat down. It had been years since Cael had last badgered him into making a weedstick, and Alva watched him as he got to work.

'How's the head?' he said.

'Pounding.'

'And the stomach?'

'Empty.'

'Are you well enough to make us some tea?'

She nodded, and got to her feet. She disappeared into his small kitchen, and by the time she returned with two mugs, Cole had finished. He passed her the weedstick, and she sat down and lit it.

Her pained expression vanished, and she exhaled. 'That feels better. Thank you. My headache has gone.'

'You'll pay for it tomorrow,' he said.

'Don't you want the money now?'

'What? No, I meant... never mind. And don't worry about the money; I took care of it.'

'Thanks, Cole.' She stretched her arms and smiled. 'My sister and I used to smoke this on the Hold Long estate,' she went on; 'we also smoked dreamweed now and again. Have you ever smoked it?'

'Only when my cousin was around,' he said. 'Cael has always been more of a risk-taker than me.'

'Perhaps your approach to life is too cautious,' she said. 'You don't drink, you don't smoke, and you hardly ever go out.'

'That's all true, but it's what I want. I don't feel the need to escape into oblivion. Shall we try to reach Bannerton again?'

She nodded. 'Yes. Definitely. I can do it this time, and then you will have to admit that keenweed has its uses.'

She looked around for an ashtray, and Cole passed her a saucer. She set the weedstick down, and they both relaxed. Cole sent his powers out, and waited for Alva to do the same.

Are you ready? he said, as soon as her powers had lifted clear of her body.

I've been meaning to ask you, she said; *how are you able to do that? You can sense my powers and talk to me when I am ranging. That shouldn't be possible. Is it another dream mage trait?*

I think so, he said. *There are other Holdfasts who can do it. Can you not sense my powers in the same way?*

No; well, only if you talk to me first. Shall we?

Her vision raced out of the window at high speed, and he followed her. She soared over Rainsby, then turned towards the west and shot off, racing above the Inner Sea. She increased her speed, and Cole chased after her. Within minutes, they had passed the point she had reached earlier that day, and then, before much longer, they saw Bannerton in the distance. They raced towards the town, and soared over the large harbour.

I did it! Alva cried. *See?*

Well done, he said.

They cut their powers, and glanced at each other in his sitting room. Alva grinned.

'Not bad,' he said, 'even if it was aided by narcotics.'

'I feel like having a drink now,' she said.

'Yes, well, that's keenweed for you.'

'Maybe I should go to the mess hall and buy some wine. Would you like some? I reached Bannerton, so we don't really have anything else to do today. Maybe we should drink to celebrate my success.'

'Are you going to talk all afternoon?'

'Am I talking too much? My sister always says that I talk too much. Do you like her?'

'Your sister?'

'Yes.'

'I, uh, haven't really thought about it.'

'What do you think, then? Yes or no? Should I get wine?'

The air shimmered in the corner of the room, and Cael appeared.

'Would you look at that?' said Alva. 'Cael Holdfast is standing in your sitting room, Cole.'

Cael glanced at Cole, then he sniffed the air. 'Is that keenweed I can smell?'

'Cole bought me some,' said Alva.

Cael laughed, then he sat down. 'Did he, eh? What's this, cousin – are you trying to get this young lady intoxicated?'

'She needed it for her vision powers,' Cole said. 'Was there a specific reason for this visit, or are you just being sociable?'

'We were going to get some wine,' said Alva. 'Do you want some, Cael? Can I call you Cael, or do you prefer Secretary Holdfast?'

'You can call me Cael,' he said. 'I assume you must be Alva Longhold?'

'I am, yes.'

'We were not going to get wine,' said Cole. 'At least, I wasn't.'

'Has Cole always been so reserved?' said Alva.

'He likes his privacy, and his peace and quiet,' said Cael, 'but there is no one in the Empire apart from my wife that I trust more; no one upon whom I can rely. Cole is the best man I know. I would crawl over broken glass for him. In answer to your previous question, cousin – I am here to ask for your help. Could I have some of that keenweed first? – then I'll explain.'

Alva passed him the saucer. Cael picked up the half-smoked weedstick and lit it. He sat back on the chair, and eyed Cole.

'It's dragons again, I'm afraid,' he said. 'I need you to help me with the transport of a particular dragon from the Dominion to Dragon Eyre.'

'A defector?' said Cole.

'No, an emissary. An unofficial emissary. If asked, the Dominion government will deny all knowledge of this dragon's whereabouts and objectives. Likewise, Queen Blackrose also requires a level of deniability.'

'Does this break the treaty?'

Cael shook his head. 'Do you think we want to bring my mother's wrath down upon us?'

'Then why all the secrecy?'

'The two queens – Blackrose and Famula Min Gahad – have, on their own, come to the conclusion that they wish to commence negotiations. This is specifically allowed by the treaty, but the majority of dragons on both sides would be outraged if they knew that any talks were taking place. My job is to ensure that the Dominion's emissary reaches Dragon Eyre safely. I need you because you're good with dragons.'

Alva frowned. 'In what way is Cole good with dragons?'

'He means I can deflect dragon fire,' said Cole; 'and that means he suspects that he could be walking into a trap.'

'It's possible,' said Cael. 'The Empire heard of this through Lord Bailey, who heard about it from an unnamed source in Inopei, who might be trying to lure an imperial agent to Nom Karta in order to claim that we have broken the treaty, or for interrogation. Or both. Most dragons and pretty much every god on Athumia hates the Empire, even after seven years of peace. In the Dominion, though, at the very highest levels, there are a few signs of them wanting to reach out to us. The first stage of that would be to travel to Inopei, and then move their dragon to somewhere in the Western Rim, where one of Blackrose's friends will be waiting to talk to them.'

'Not the Eastern Rim?'

'Queen Blackrose does not want any Dominion dragon to enter her territory – that's part of her need for deniability.'

'Should you be saying all this in front of me?' said Alva. 'I am a very junior agent.'

Cael passed her the weedstick. 'I intend to alter your memories as soon as this conversation is over, Lieutenant Longhold.'

'Couldn't I come along?' she said. 'I might be able to help you.'

Cael smiled. 'No. I am sure that you are a very capable agent, but I need a veteran for this operation.'

Alva glanced at Cole, her eyes pleading.

'I agree with Cael,' he said. 'No offence, but you would get in the way.'

Alva glared at him. Cael raised his hand, and Alva blinked, then her eyes closed and she slumped back onto the couch.

'She'll wake up in ten minutes or so,' Cael said. 'I have removed all of the specifics of what we'll be doing, but left her with the knowledge that you shall be accompanying me on some reckless and brave operation in service of the Empire. That way, she won't wonder where you are when she opens her eyes.'

They got to their feet.

'If we're facing dragons,' said Cole, 'then I think I'm probably better off without a sword.'

Cael nodded. 'We'll go as we are. I have the location, the date, and the time of the meeting. The dragon we shall be visiting is one Raddon Mon Konran, the son of Lord Konran Mon Gahad, who is one of Queen Famula's closest supporters.'

'I'm ready,' said Cole.

Cael activated his Quadrant, and the air crackled as they appeared on Athumia.

Cael smiled at his cousin. 'We are now technically in breach of the treaty.'

Cole glanced up, and saw a massive castle that stretched between the cliff walls of a high gorge in the mountains. The castle had clearly been built to accommodate dragons, but only two were visible – a huge black and white male, and a slightly smaller grey male with yellow flashes on his wings. Both were standing before the castle gates, their eyes on the two arrivals.

Cael raised his arms to show that he was empty-handed. 'Greetings, dragons of the Dominion,' he called out. 'Might we approach in safety?'

'You may step forward, agents of the Sapphire Throne,' said the black and white dragon.

Cael and Cole moved closer to the two dragons. Cole kept his fire powers ready, his gaze never leaving the enormous creatures a few yards in front of him.

'My name is Cael Holdfast,' said Cael.

The black and white dragon's eyes flashed with fury. 'How dare the Empress send a son of the Demon Witch to parley with me? Has she no shame?'

'I am under the command of my sovereign,' said Cael, 'as I suspect you might also be. I am here to assist your companion to travel to another location, not to argue over old wrongs.'

The black and white dragon stared down at the two men. 'I am anxious to get this over with as soon as possible,' he said, 'as I abhor your presence so close to my ancestral home. I am Lord Raddon Mon Konran, son of Lord Konran Mon Gahad; and the dragon by my side is Lord Limnan Mon Limonen, a trusted retainer from my household. I do not wish you to tell me where you will be taking Lord Limnan, but if any harm comes to him, I shall be avenged.'

'Like you, my lord,' said Cael, 'I am wary of a trap; and like you, I shall have to accept the wisdom of those who have arranged this exchange. Might I now transport Lord Limnan from Athumia?'

Limnan turned to Raddon. 'I do not wish to leave your side, my lord, but if you command me to go with these humans, I shall do so.'

'You know the queen's orders, my friend,' said Raddon. 'Do not commit any act of aggression against the Sapphire Empire; but if they betray you, fight to the end. If you fall by their treachery, be assured that I shall never rest until I taste bitter revenge for your loss. Go. Behave honourably, and fulfil the desires of our rightful monarch.'

The grey and yellow dragon inclined his head, then he stepped forward, and stood by Cael and Cole.

Cael bowed. 'Thank you, Lord Raddon Mon Konran,' he said. 'Let us hope that this exchange bears fruit, and that a greater understanding can develop between our two realms.'

'Leave in peace, son of the Demon Witch,' said Raddon.

Cael eyed Cole, then he triggered the Quadrant. The air crackled loudly, and the two men and the grey and yellow dragon appeared on a broad stretch of sand beneath the sunshine of Dragon Eyre. Ocean waves were rolling up against the shore, and a thick row of palm trees flanked the landward side of the beach.

'Is this the world known as Dragon Eyre, humans?' said Limnan.

'It is,' said Cael. 'We are on the island chain of Alef, to the far north of the Western Rim.'

'Then we are not within the territory of Queen Blackrose?'

'That is correct. We are on neutral ground.'

The palm trees rustled, and two dragons emerged on to the golden sands. Limnan tensed. He adopted a defensive stance, and sparks flashed over his jaws.

'Come no closer, wild dragons!' he cried.

'Wild, you say?' said an older dragon with scales of burnished iron. 'We are the original dragons, and all dragons come from us. Yes, even those duplicitous specimens who dwell upon the benighted lands of Athumia are descended from my kin. I am Greysteel, advisor to Queen Blackrose. Who might you be?'

'I am Lord Limnan Mon Limonen,' said the grey and yellow dragon. 'Am I to be torn to pieces?'

'You are not,' said Greysteel. 'You are to be left alone here upon this island with my companion, Honeytail of Throscala.'

'What foolish names you dragons bear.'

'These are the names by which we are known to the humans, Limnan,' said Greysteel. 'We have other names, learnt only by those we trust and hold dear; and you are not one of those.'

'Greetings, Limnan of Athumia,' said Honeytail, his blue eyes gleaming bright. He had a dark, almost black body but, as his name suggested, his tail was of a golden hue. 'I have been chosen to speak with you these coming days, to discover if there is a way for the dragons of our two realms to be better acquainted.'

Limnan said nothing.

Greysteel turned to Cael and Cole. 'Thank you for escorting our visitor to these shores, Holdfasts. Your part in this is over. You may go.'

Cael and Cole bowed, then Cael activated the Quadrant and the air shimmered.

Cole had expected to be taken back to Rainsby but, instead, he found himself standing next to Cael in a small chamber with the Empress seated opposite him.

'Your Majesty,' Cole said, bowing.

'Good afternoon, Cole,' said the Empress. 'You have my thanks, Cael, for bringing your cousin into my presence. It has come to my attention, Cole, that you have neglected to either accept or decline the offer that was made to you by Marshal Bedig – that of a place upon my Imperial Court. Is there a reason for this silence?'

Cole eyed Cael, who smiled and shrugged, then he faced the Empress.

'I have not yet trained my replacement to an adequate level, Your Majesty,' Cole said. 'There remains the possibility that she will be unable to take up the role as the resident agent in Rainsby. If that were the case, then I expect that I would have to remain in place. I was delaying my response until I knew if this were true or not.'

The Empress smiled. 'Let me be clear, Cole – I want you as a member of my court. Your considerable abilities are sadly underutilised at present, and I shall not let the skills of one Holdings mage stand in the way of your promotion. I now ask you directly – will you become my Imperial Secretary once Cael assumes the role of Marshal? Do not prevaricate – give me a yes or no answer.'

Cole cursed under his breath. 'I would be honoured to accept, Your Majesty.'

'Excellent,' said Thorn. 'There shall be rooms set aside for you in the Blue Palace. Cael, please return Cole to Rainsby.'

'Aye, Your Majesty,' said Cael, bowing.

The air shimmered, and they appeared back in Cole's office in Rainsby. Alva glanced up from the couch.

'Sorry about that, cousin,' said Cael.

'You might have told me where we were going,' said Cole.

'I was ordered to keep it quiet,' he said, 'but I can see why the Empress wanted to talk to you. Her Majesty has been patiently waiting for your answer for some time; was it not your duty to let her know?'

'What are you talking about?' said Alva. 'I thought you were both on a secret operation for the Empire.'

'We were,' said Cole, sitting in an armchair, 'and then, after it was over, Cael dragged me into the presence of the Empress. It's official – I'll be joining the Imperial Court.'

Alva smiled. 'Congratulations.'

Cole frowned at her.

'The Empress put him on the spot,' said Cael. 'Cole had to either accept or decline Her Majesty's offer.'

'Oh,' said Alva. 'Well, I think you did the right thing, Cole. It would have been foolish to decline.'

'I couldn't agree more,' said Cael. 'I'll be off now; thanks for helping me today, cousin.'

'Might I ask you something before you leave?' said Alva. 'I heard a rumour that the proposals to implement a democratic constitution are in some difficulties; and that the Imperial Court is evenly split on whether or not to proceed. Is that true?'

Cael sat down. 'Where did you hear that? Don't make me read your mind, Lieutenant Longhold.'

'I heard it from my sister,' she said.

'Audrey?' he said. 'I have fond memories of her from my brief time in the marines. From where did she glean this information?'

Alva's features flushed. 'I think it was from our uncle.'

'Holder Long?' said Cael. 'I wonder how he came to hear of such a scurrilous rumour.'

'Then it isn't true?' said Alva.

'I'm not going to confirm or deny something that took place behind the closed doors of the Imperial Court, Lieutenant Longhold. Have you seen the published census results?'

'Yes, of course,' she said. 'They made for sober reading.'

'What is everyone here saying about it?'

Alva reached into a pocket of her uniform and withdrew a crumpled slip of paper. She smoothed it out.

'These have been distributed all over the town,' she said, holding it out.

Cole took it from her, and held it where both he and Cael could read the words that had been printed onto the paper.

Betrayal! ran the large headline.

Her Imperial Majesty plans to give overwhelming power to the rogue and untrustworthy nations of Rahain and Rakana, in a misguided attempt to implement mob rule over our beloved Empire. Together, the free peoples of the

Allied Worlds need to make a stand against this proposal, which would see the smaller nations controlled by the thugs and criminals inhabiting Rahain and Rakana. We demand that these two nations be removed from the proposed assembly, else a campaign of peaceful disobedience shall be initiated. We further demand a delay to the entire proposals, to allow time for the Empress to reflect upon her actions before she makes a catastrophic error.

Below was a summary of the census results, with the populations of Rahain and Rakana highlighted in red ink. At the bottom was a further line:

While we remain forever Her Majesty's loyal subjects, we must resist this attempt to destroy the peace and harmony of the Empire.

'Hundreds of these leaflets have appeared in Rainsby,' said Alva.

'Holder Long's friends have purchased several steam-powered printing presses,' said Cael. 'They can produce thousands of leaflets every day.'

'But is any of it true?'

'Like all good propaganda, much of it is based upon the truth,' said Cael. 'The census results are accurate, for example. But there is no mention of the Provincial Council anywhere to be seen. This council will prevent Rahain and Rakana from dominating, by giving all of the smaller provinces a veto over legislation. The truth is here, but it is being wilfully distorted. Ask yourself why that might be the case. Ask yourself who would benefit if the reforms were to be stopped.'

Alva remained silent.

Cael got back to his feet, the scrap of paper in his hand. 'Might I keep this?'

Alva nodded.

'Thank you,' he said. He nodded to Cole, and vanished.

Cole sat back in his chair. 'Have you recovered from the keenweed and the sickness?'

'I'm feeling fine, thank you,' she said. 'Which way would you have voted, had you been in the Imperial Court?'

'I have no idea,' he said. 'I haven't read anything about the proposed reforms.'

'Trouble is coming; I can sense it. The opposition to the Empress is only going to increase if she doesn't postpone these changes.'

'Is that what your uncle thinks?'

'My uncle has always loathed the limited democracy implemented by Daphne Holdfast in the Holdings,' she said. 'He hates that peasants in the River Holdings are able to influence decisions taken by the government. It was no surprise to me that he would also be against these new changes.'

'Do you agree with him?'

'Partly. Why should Rahain and Rakana get so many votes? It doesn't seem fair. We had to force those nations into the Empire against their will, and they hate us for it. Why should they get a bigger voice than, say, Kellach Brigdomin?'

Cole lowered his gaze. 'I am going to have to study the proposals; the Empress will expect me to be knowledgeable about them when I join the Imperial Court. It seems that my life of peace and quiet is about to be taken from me.'

'Your duty to the Empire outweighs your feelings, Cole.'

'Which is why I accepted Her Majesty's offer,' he said.

He picked up Alva's cigarette case and the bag of keenweed.

'What are you doing?' she said.

'I'm making you another weedstick,' he said. 'It's time you tried to reach Plateau City.'

CHAPTER 11
CASTING A SHADOW

Plateau City, The Plateau – 24th Day, Last Third Summer 552

'They are late,' said Claudian, as he gazed out of the third-storey window of the nondescript tenement block. 'Are we certain that they received our message?'

'I delivered it myself, sir,' said Arrosa.

'That seems a little risky,' said Cardova. 'You shouldn't be placing yourself in danger like that.'

'I thought it best to limit the number of people who knew that two Gunstian agents were in the city, sir,' she said; 'and I had my dogs with me.'

'I am grateful that you haven't brought them along today, Postmaster,' said Claudian.

'Cael is at home,' she said, 'and he volunteered to watch Cowie and the dogs. He was telling me that Cole has accepted the offer of becoming Imperial Secretary.'

'Aye, that's right,' said Kelsey. 'The Empress forced Cole to come to a decision; she was getting tired of waiting for his response.'

Arrosa glanced at the Herald, who was sitting at a table nursing a mug of coffee. Both Lucius and Kelsey were speaking, Arrosa had noticed, but not to each other.

'Wait; I see them,' said Claudian. 'Or I see who I think might be them. Two men are approaching from the direction of the Old Town, and they appear to be a little wary of their surroundings.'

Arrosa rose to her feet and joined the Adjutant by the window.

'It's them,' she said, recognising the two men down on the street. 'Do you recall the signals I will use to notify you if they speak a lie?'

Claudian nodded. 'I do. How is their grasp of the Divine Tongue?'

'Adequate,' said Arrosa, 'although they know it as the language of the Aucterians.'

'I've always called it the Holdings language,' said Kelsey. 'We should all call it that, to be consistent.'

Claudian smiled. 'It was the Divine Tongue long before your world was even created, ma'am.'

'I don't care,' said Kelsey. 'I'm the Herald, and you are obliged to humour me.'

'The Gunstians are at the front door of the building,' said Arrosa. 'The soldiers are letting them in.'

'We should take our seats,' said Cardova.

Arrosa, Cardova and the Adjutant moved round the table to where Kelsey was sitting, and took their places.

'Remember that one of them has a Gift that could kill us,' said Cardova. 'What was it called, Arrosa?'

'The Gift of Withering, sir.'

Kelsey snorted. 'That sounds particularly unpleasant. Is it like death powers?'

'The Gift extracts all water from any living creature,' Arrosa went on, 'but the end result is the same. It requires physical contact to work. I am sure that they will not try to kill us, but if they do, I shall use my own Gift to destroy them.'

'You'll turn them into glass, you mean?' said Kelsey.

Arrosa nodded. 'Yes, ma'am.'

'While we are on the topic of Gifts,' Kelsey went on; 'remember not to mention that Lahnos Laimos lives within the bounds of the Empire. I don't think the Gunstians would look too kindly upon us if they knew we were friends with one of their enemies.'

'Lahnos and Sigum once annihilated the entire Gunstian Fleet,' said Arrosa. 'They believe him to be an extremely dangerous demon. The Gunstians are unaware that I knew him on Zamata, and I think we should keep it that way.'

The door to the room opened, and two soldiers entered.

'Our guests have arrived,' said an officer.

'Show them in,' said Kelsey.

'Aye, ma'am,' he said.

The door opened wider, and the two Gunstian agents entered the room, along with six soldiers armed with swords and crossbows.

Claudian got to his feet. 'Greetings, he said. 'I am the Adjutant of the Empire. To my left is the Imperial Constable, who is the highest-ranked military official in the Empire; and then, to his left is the Herald, second only to Her Majesty. At the end of the table is Arrosa, the Imperial Postmaster, whom I believe you have already met. Please be seated.'

The two Gunstians frowned deeply, then they sat down opposite the four representatives of the Empire.

'Tell us what you want,' said Kelsey.

'Thank you, my lady,' said one. 'You have our sincere gratitude for agreeing to meet with us. As Arrosa may have told you, we have travelled a great distance to reach the heart of the Empire of the Sapphire Throne. We were sent by the honourable government of the Gunstian Empire to request a treaty and a defensive alliance between our two peoples. I admit that we have little in common, but we share the same enemy – the Dragon Dominion. We believe that an alliance would protect us both from the aggression of the Dominion – a realm that seeks suzerainty over all of Athumia. For centuries, the Dominion's ambitions have troubled my world, for it was the stated policy of King Gahad and his successors to never rest until they had conquered Gunst. We may currently be at peace with the Dominion, but we have learned through painful experience never to trust the promises made by the wicked demons who govern that realm. They lie; they steal, and they have invaded Gunst three times. Furthermore, they are now in league with the so-called gods of the Doomed Worlds; who are also your enemies, I believe. Tell me, Herald – what could or should stand in the way of our two peoples coming to a mutually beneficial agreement?'

'I can think of a few problems,' said Kelsey, 'but first I want to thank you for coming here. You risked much to deliver the request of your government, and I applaud your courage and resourcefulness. You shall be treated as honoured guests and emissaries of a nation against whom we bear no ill will.'

'What problems do you speak of, Herald?' said one of the Gunstians.

'Let us say that we were to agree to a full defensive alliance with the Gunstian Empire,' said Kelsey. 'Would you also pledge not to invade or trouble any of your neighbours in the western half of Athumia?'

'Are you referring to Irlan and Elso, Herald?'

'I am.'

'Those lands were historically ours,' said the Gunstian, 'before the Dominion invaded and colonised them. With the Dominion no longer able or willing to occupy these lands, why should Gunst hesitate to act?'

'But you have already hesitated,' said Cardova. 'You could have attempted to re-conquer those territories at any time over the last two decades, but you haven't. Are you hoping to leverage any alliance with us in order to initiate military action against Irlan?'

The Gunstians remained silent.

'Let me paint a picture for you,' said Kelsey. 'Say we sign a treaty, and then you invade Irlan. The Dominion then responds to a plea for assistance from the Irlanians, and sends troops across the ocean. Would you expect us to come to your aid?'

'The Empire does not wish to become entangled in a war over Irlan,' said Cardova; 'and any such treaty between us would first have to be approved by Karalyn Holdfast, who is the guarantor of peace.'

The two Gunstians eyed each other.

'Without wishing to cause offence,' said one, 'can we trust the Demon Witch? Everyone in Gunst is grateful that she killed the infamous beast known as King Gahad; but she has otherwise proved herself to be... unreliable.'

'What do you mean?' said Arrosa.

'You may not be aware of this,' said the Gunstian, 'but Bailey the blasphemer once tried to infiltrate Great Gunst. He preached openly in the city's plazas, repeating his sacrilegious claim to be the brother of the blessed Chadura. He also healed hundreds of the sick, and his presence caused several riots among the populace. Did you know that he had a companion with him? His companion was none other than the Demon Witch. Tell me – why was Karalyn Holdfast trying to undermine the religion of Gunst?'

'I was unaware of any of this,' said Kelsey. She glanced at Arrosa. 'Did you know?'

'Lord Bailey took Karalyn against her will,' said Arrosa. 'She was Lyla back then, and she had very few powers, and Bailey abducted her. He claimed it was to save her from Albany and Arden, who wanted to kill her, but I always suspected that he was keeping Karalyn as a hostage.'

'I can confirm that,' said Cardova. 'I was on Athumia at the time with Sable. I knew that Bailey had Karalyn, but I didn't know that he had tried to insert himself into the Gunstian religion.'

Kelsey nodded, then she eyed the Gunstians. 'We know of Chadura here as Theodora.'

'We are aware of that name,' said one of the Gunstians.

'Theodora was one of twelve Ascendants.'

The Gunstians frowned.

'Now you are merely repeating the claims of the false religion of the Aucterians,' said one. 'We utterly reject this twisted theology. Chadura is the sole god, unequalled and alone in her divinity. She is not one among twelve. She is the first and the last, the only, the creator.'

'Theodora was slain by another Ascendant many millennia ago,' said Kelsey, 'and her remains are now buried on Zamata. Lord Bailey himself dug the grave for his sister.'

Arrosa frowned. 'Let us not offend our guests,' she said, earning a glare from Kelsey. 'Let us instead imagine that Chadura and Theodora were different people – one being the sole divine authority of Athumia, and the other merely one among twelve powerful beings. Could we use that as a compromise to avoid arguing over religious differences?'

'That is indeed what we believe, Arrosa,' said one of the Gunstians. 'Let the Aucterians worship this false god Theodora. They understand nothing of the truth.'

'I would be interested in hearing what the Gunstians might have to offer as part of any treaty,' said Claudian. 'The Empire already has a military strong enough to repel any attack by the Dominion. Why should we ally ourselves with you?'

'The Dominion has thousands of winged, fire-breathing demons,' said a Gunstian. 'Without our assistance, they could raze your cities to the ground.'

'If you were invaded by our common enemy,' said the other man, 'Gunst would be able to send hundreds of Gifted warriors to help you. Are you familiar with the Gifts of Chadura? Has Arrosa told you about them?'

'She has mentioned them,' said Kelsey. 'What types of Gifts would be available to come to our assistance?'

'The Gifts of Pain, Immolation, Poison, Famine... these would all be of great use in a conflict with the Dominion. Dragons are not immune to the Gifts, as they have learned to their cost whenever they have invaded our territory. Similarly, if we were attacked for a fourth time by the Dominion, we would expect you to send forces to aid us. Your vision mages would be especially useful.'

'How do you know about them?' said Kelsey.

One of the Gunstians smiled. 'We were on Zamata for a considerable amount of time before we were able to travel to Dragon Eyre,' he said. 'We learned many things about the Empire.'

'Can we return to the subject of Irlan?' said Cardova. 'Can you give us an assurance that Gunst will not initiate hostilities against that nation if we were to agree to a treaty?'

'We lack the authority to make any such promise, Constable,' said a Gunstian. 'We would need to speak to our government first.'

'Then maybe we should do that,' said Kelsey. 'It might have taken you a long time to get here, but we could be in Gunst within a few moments.'

'We are aware of your travelling devices, Herald. We watched them being used when we were taken from Athumia to Dragon Eyre, and from there to this city.'

'Then you know I am telling the truth,' she said.

'If you were to visit Great Gunst, Herald, it should be in an official capacity. We do have the power to invite representatives from the Sapphire Empire to Gunst; in fact, our government would be honoured to host any such visit.'

'Let's end this meeting now,' said Kelsey, 'as the assurances we require will have to come from your superiors in Gunst. Go back to your quarters, and we shall be in touch, after we have discussed the possibility of conducting a state visit to the Gunstian Empire with Her Majesty.'

The two Gunstians got to their feet and bowed low.

'It was a privilege to meet with you,' said one, 'and we look forward to our next conversation.'

The others remained silent as the soldiers led the two men out of the room.

'Were there any lies, Arrosa?' said Claudian.

'None,' she said.

Kelsey narrowed her eyes. 'I had no idea that the Gunstians mistrusted Karalyn. I thought they all loved the Demon Witch. Perhaps we should speak to Bailey, to ask him what in Pyre's name he thought he was doing, trying to subvert their religion like that.'

'You were doing a fine job of trying to subvert their religion, ma'am,' said Arrosa. 'You didn't require Bailey's help.'

Kelsey laughed. 'I was merely trying to educate them about Chadura.'

'I thought they were going to walk out,' said Arrosa.

'You did the right thing, Arrosa,' said Cardova. 'You smoothed away their concerns.'

'Why do I feel as though everyone is ganging up on me?' said Kelsey. 'I prefer the truth, even if it offends people. Chadura is dead, and that's all there is to it. I saw her body being taken out of the Palace of the Almighty, along with Nathaniel's. No amount of prayer and wishful thinking is going to alter that fact.'

'It took me a long time to reconcile myself to the reality that Chadura and Theodora were one and the same,' said Arrosa. 'We won't win over any Gunstians if we start off by telling them that their entire religion is a sham.'

'It occurs to me,' said Claudian, 'that if we were to accede to their desire for a state visit to Gunst, then perhaps you, Herald, should not be part of the delegation. The two agents will no doubt report your words to their superiors.'

Kelsey rolled her eyes. 'Fine. I didn't want to go to Gunst anyway.' She eyed Claudian. 'Let's report all this to the Empress.'

Thorn gazed down from her throne. 'A state visit?'

'That's what they want, Your Majesty,' said Kelsey. 'We asked them for guarantees that they would not use any treaty to invade Irlan, but they claimed to lack the authority to do so. To get round this, they invited us to Great Gunst.'

'Do we know how to get there?'

'Lord Bailey knows, Your Majesty,' said Kelsey. 'He has been there, though he didn't make himself very popular in the process.'

'That means Cael will also know,' said Arrosa; 'as Lord Bailey imprinted everything he knew about Quadrants into his mind.'

'And then Cael did the same to Cole,' said Claudian. 'In theory, both should know how to get to Gunst.'

'That is good,' said the Empress, 'as I would rather not have to ask Bailey for help. I suspect that everything we tell him is quickly passed on to Lord Edgar in Inopei.'

'But maybe we should allow the Dominion to find out what we are planning, Your Majesty,' said Kelsey. 'We don't want them complaining to Karalyn that we went behind their backs to forge a treaty with their enemy.'

'I suppose that is a good point,' said Thorn, 'though I still deem the likelihood of us agreeing to any treaty to be slight. All the same, it would be discourteous to refuse their invitation. Our two Empires might never become close friends, but I see no use in making a new enemy. In your opinion, who should travel to Gunst as part of an official delegation?'

'I would like to rule myself out, Your Majesty,' said Kelsey.

'Why?'

Kelsey frowned. 'I might have made a few disparaging remarks about their religion.'

The Empress laughed.

'I couldn't help myself,' Kelsey went on. 'Their almighty god has been dead for millennia.'

'Very well, Herald; you will remain here,' said the Empress. 'Postmaster, I would imagine that you are the most suitable delegate, as you understand their language and their culture. Are you willing to go?'

'I am, Your Majesty,' said Arrosa, 'but I would need to ensure that Cowie and my dogs are cared for in my absence.'

'I am sure that Cael will manage,' said the Empress. 'I will keep him in Plateau City until you return.'

'I was hoping that Cael might come with me, Your Majesty, as he also understands Gunstian. Bailey imprinted the language into his head at the same time as he taught my husband how to operate a Quadrant.'

'Kelsey and I can look after Cowie and the dogs,' said Cardova, 'if Cael were to accompany you.'

'Let me think on it,' said the Empress. 'Adjutant, you shall go with Arrosa; and... and Brogan, I think. A state visit falls under the remit of the Chamberlain. Yes. The Chamberlain, the Adjutant, and the Postmaster – that shall be the core of the delegation. If I allow Cael to also travel, I suspect his role might be of the unofficial variety, to allow him a free hand if necessary.'

'Do you suspect a trap, Your Majesty?' said Claudian.

'Not particularly,' said the Empress, 'but we should nevertheless proceed with caution. Once you are in Gunst, I imagine that you will be followed, watched and spied upon; and every word you say will be recorded and discussed. Go to Zamata first, and inform Lord Bailey of our plans, as the Herald suggested. Be clear that we expect word of this to reach Edgar's ears, but assure Bailey that we have no intention of breaching the treaty. And do not ask him for any help; I do not wish to feel obliged to him. The Chamberlain shall lead the delegation. Herald, please brief Brogan on all that shall be required of her.'

'Aye, Your Majesty,' said Kelsey.

'Postmaster,' Thorn went on, 'inform the two Gunstians that we accept their kind offer, and tell them that we are making the necessary arrangements. Let us schedule the visit for early autumn. Dismissed.'

The dogs bounded up the hallway as soon as Arrosa stepped into the Holdfast townhouse. She allowed them to jump up on her for a moment, and all three licked her face.

'Down,' she said, and they dropped onto their haunches, their tails wagging. 'Good girls.'

They followed her as she walked into the drawing room. Cael was sitting with Cowie, while old Caelius Logos was in his armchair.

'How did it go?' said Cael, as the dogs settled down into their beds.

'It looks as though I might be going to Gunst for a while,' she said.

Cael frowned.

Arrosa leaned down to kiss him. 'For a state visit. You might also be going.' She sat down, and took Cowie from him. 'Have Lucius and Kelsey arrived home?'

'Aye, though not at the same time.'

'I hate this,' she said. 'They haven't spoken to each other since the last full meeting of the Imperial Court. The house feels tense. It can't be doing the children any good.'

'What do you suggest?' he said. 'Lucius is open to mending their friendship, but Aunty Kelsey has dug her heels in; not that I'm blaming her for that. She's been working on those plans for seven years.'

'I think Kelsey should be grateful that he spoke honestly. There are serious problems with the proposals that she is ignoring. A postponement would be in the interests of everyone.'

Cael smiled. 'I'm not sure I agree.'

'This is the proper first argument I have witnessed between them,' said Caelius Logos. 'Kelsey used to have blazing rows with Van almost every day, and I knew long before they did that their marriage wouldn't last. Kelsey and my son are as stubborn as each other; but Lucius always seemed more easy-going.'

'Are you talking about me again?' said Kelsey from the door.

Arrosa turned. 'We were hoping that you and Lucius would be able to fix whatever has broken.'

Kelsey walked over to a side table and poured herself a cup of tea. 'I don't know if it can be fixed,' she said. 'I feel as though my oldest friend has betrayed me. I've known Lucius for twenty-one years. Maybe I took him for granted, but I never expected him to turn on me in the Imperial Court.'

Arrosa shook her head. 'He didn't turn on you. The Empress ordered him to give his honest opinion; that's all he was doing. You're upset because his opinion didn't align with yours.'

'Have you always believed that you are right about everything, Arrosa?' she said.

'I don't think that's very fair, Aunty,' said Cael.

'It's all right,' said Arrosa; 'I can stand up for myself. If Kelsey wishes to be rude, that's her business.'

Kelsey laughed. 'I can't believe that you might actually be Empress one day.'

'I don't want to be Empress,' said Arrosa. 'If a time ever comes when

Cael is selected to succeed Empress Thorn, then I will do my duty. It is not something I desire.'

Kelsey sat down with her cup of tea.

'Let's not argue,' said Arrosa.

'Why not?' said Kelsey. 'Let's get it all out into the open. I understand that my recent problems with Lucius have cast a shadow over the townhouse, but am I not allowed to be angry? Lucius has had seven years in which to voice his objections to Shella's proposals; and yet he saved it all for the Imperial Court. I feel humiliated. If the proposals are rejected, I will have to resign. Is it too much to expect that my best friend might want to support me?'

'I understand, Aunty,' said Cael, 'but could you not separate the politics from your personal feelings? If Lucius is your best friend, then does that mean you have to agree on every topic? Arrosa and I disagree on a few things, but we don't fall out over them.'

'Cael is right,' said Caelius. 'Don't throw away what you have with Lucius over one disagreement.'

'You lot are out of your minds,' said Kelsey. 'You're talking as though Lucius and I were an old married couple. We're not. Lucius is married to my sister, in case you had forgotten.'

'Then why are you so upset?' said Arrosa. 'Lucius isn't your husband; he is the commander of the Empire's armed forces. You have no hold over him, and he has no hold over you. Is that the problem? Do you wish that he was your husband?'

'Fuck off,' muttered Kelsey. 'I'm sick of hearing you say shit like that.'

Cael narrowed his eyes. 'Don't say that to my wife.'

'Or what?'

'Or Arrosa, Cowie and I will find somewhere else to live,' he said.

'Then tell your wife to stop insinuating that there's something going on between me and Lucius.'

'All right,' said Arrosa. 'For the sake of harmony, I won't mention it again. My Gift of Truth has already told me all I need to know.'

Kelsey got to her feet and walked out of the room.

'You went too far,' said Cael.

'Did I?' said Arrosa.

'Aye. She shouldn't have told you to *fuck off*, but you shouldn't keep bringing up your suspicions about her and Lucius.'

'What if my suspicions are true?'

'Do you have any proof?'

'I have lots of proof,' she said. 'Every lie they have spoken about it is stored in my mind. I believe them when they say that nothing has happened, but they both wish something could happen.'

Caelius frowned. 'That can't be right.'

'I know that no one wishes to hear this,' she said, 'but Kelsey and Lucius are in love with each other. And it's not just an infatuation or a crush – they are deeply in love. Only Karalyn is holding them back; but what would she do if she found out? They need to come to their senses before that can happen.'

'What would Karalyn do?' said Caelius.

'I don't know,' said Cael. 'My mother's response could range from apathy to extreme violence. If she's currently obsessed with the Sextant, then I would imagine that she isn't giving any of us a second thought right now. I still have my doubts, though. Might those lies simply be evidence of harmless flirtation?'

'I'll give you some examples,' said Arrosa. 'Kelsey is fond of saying that she loves Lucius like a brother. The *love* part is true, but the *brother* part is a lie. When Lucius says that he's not interested in Kelsey – a lie. When he says that he wants to make his marriage work – a lie. When Kelsey says that she is happy with Lucius just being a friend – a lie. When she says that she has no interest in being with anyone – a lie. When Lucius says that...'

'All right,' said Cael. 'We get the picture.'

'I hate having the Gift of Truth,' she said, 'because it tells me things that I don't want to know, and the lies hang over my head like a thick shadow. I wish I could turn it off, but I can't. And if I say nothing about it, then everyone soon forgets, and they start telling lies again. I have tried to remind Lucius and Kelsey on multiple occasions to be more careful, but they never listen.'

Cael and Caelius eyed each other, but said nothing.

'I'm looking forward to going to Gunst,' Arrosa said, 'because then, for a while at least, I won't have to endure all the headaches I get from the lies I hear in this house.'

CHAPTER 12
THE DECISION

Plateau City, The Plateau – Autumn's Day 552

'Here they are,' cried Kelsey.

Lucius and the others in the imperial party halted on the wide steps leading up to the main entrance on the southern flank of the Blue Palace. Above them, two dragons were circling over the city.

'What a sight,' said Claudian.

Frostback and Halfclaw soared down, then they flew between the two massive towers of the palace. Three bridges arced across the gap. The highest and lowest were slender, and fit only for humans to cross, while the central bridge was strong, wide and robust enough to bear the weight of several dragons at once. The Eastern Tower had been constructed to house four dragons, with space for visiting guests, and it was crowned by a flat platform, which would serve as an eyrie. Frostback and Halfclaw both alighted onto the platform, their necks craning out so that they could gaze at the panoramic view of the city and its surroundings.

Lucius lowered his gaze. The base of the new palace took up a large area within the heart of the city, covering the ground where the Great Fortress had once stood. It also encroached into parts of the Old Town, the New Town and the Old Peasants' District, where several streets had been demolished to make way for the colossal building. Apart from two large sections, every inch of the exterior surface of the palace had been coated in foot-long ceramic tiles, each a subtly differing shade of blue. They had been produced by the renowned clay mages of Amatskouri, and the effect was staggering. The exceptions were two large areas on the Western Tower – one near the top, the other halfway down. For those sections, reinforced and tinted glass had been used to cover the exterior instead of blue tiles, to allow a great deal of sunlight to penetrate the interior. The towers were visible from miles around, and sailors had reported that the new landmark was being used to guide ships into the harbour of Plateau City. Aside from the Implacatus-built Palace of the Almighty in Holdings territory, the Blue Palace was the largest single structure upon the Star Continent, relegating the half-ruined Senate building in the Rahain Capital into third place.

Lucius noticed the Empress smiling as she gazed up at her new home. For years, Thorn had been living inside the Ministry of the Plateau, as they had waited for the Blue Palace to be constructed, and she looked relieved and happy to be finally moving in.

The two dragons swooped down from the eyrie, their wings casting fleeting shadows over the streets below, then they landed on the wide steps next to the imperial party.

'Greetings, Empress,' said Halfclaw. 'Did you have a pleasant summer in the city?'

'It was rather humid, Halfclaw,' said Thorn. 'I am looking forward to resuming our tradition of spending each summer on Colsbury.'

'Colsbury remains overrun with Shella's people,' said Frostback, 'and my mate and I are rarely there.' Her red eyes gazed out over the Old Town. 'So this is to be our new home? It goes a little against the nature of a Lostwell dragon to dwell in such close proximity to so many humans.'

'That wasn't always the case,' said Lucius. 'Before Implacatus invaded, many dragons lived in Dun Khatar, as welcome guests of King Nathaniel and Queen Belinda.'

'My father used to talk of such times,' said Frostback; 'but all Halfclaw and I knew were the Catacombs, where we were taught that human cities were filthy and dangerous places.'

Lucius smiled. 'I hope you regard Plateau City with more fondness than you did Alea Tanton.'

Frostback tilted her head. 'Indeed we do, Lucius.' The silver dragon hesitated, then she eyed Kelsey. 'My rider,' she went on, 'is there anger between you and Lucius? I am sensing conflict.'

'Kelsey and I disagreed over a political decision,' said Lucius.

'I was not asking you,' said Frostback. 'Answer me, rider? Has this man caused you pain?'

The others on the steps remained silent, as Kelsey averted her eyes.

'It's nothing,' said Kelsey. 'Forget about it.'

'Whatever it is,' said the silver dragon, 'it is not *nothing*. Lucius is one of my favourite humans, but I will kill him if he has given you insult.'

'Please don't do that,' said Kelsey.

Frostback turned her fiery gaze towards Lucius. 'I shall be watching you closely,' she said. 'For twenty years, you have been close to my rider, and you have become dear to my heart; but I will always choose her over you.'

Lucius inclined his head, but said nothing.

'Might we inspect the interior of our new home, Empress?' said Halfclaw.

'Please do,' said Thorn.

'There are three main ways for dragons to enter the Eastern Tower of the palace,' said Brogan. 'You can descend via a ramp from the eyrie; you can enter through the tall arch by the middle bridge; and you can get in through a large opening halfway up the tower on the eastern side. There is also a hidden entrance on the ground floor, which is linked to pulleys that can raise a wounded dragon up to the accommodation levels.'

The two dragons took a moment to gaze up at their tower.

'This pleases me greatly,' said Halfclaw. 'It is clear that you have given much thought to the design of our new home, and I thank you for it.'

Brogan beamed with pride. 'We took some inspiration from Queen Blackrose's palace on Ulna; except there, the humans live on the lower floors, while the dragons take those above them. Here, we have placed the two side by side – with each occupying their own tower. The ground levels, before the towers begin, shall house the offices of the imperial government, while the Empress shall live at the top of the Western Tower.'

Halfclaw tilted his head. 'There must be thousands of steps for a human to climb between the ground floor and the highest part of the palace. Is the Empress to become a prisoner in her own home?'

Brogan pointed to a large stone outbuilding attached to the base of the palace at its western flank.

'Do you see the smoke rising from those chimneys?' she said. 'That building houses several new steam engines, which power a series of platforms that can be raised or lowered. The Empress will be able to use them to ascend and descend the many floors of the palace.'

Cael tapped a pocket. 'I will probably use my Quadrant to get around inside.'

Brogan smiled at him. 'You will not be able to use that device to appear directly within the Empress's new quarters, Cael,' she said. 'We have taken note of how the interior of the Palace of the Almighty was constructed, and the upper floors of the Western Tower are exceedingly difficult to penetrate with vision powers or Quadrants.' She glanced at Kelsey. 'This was the Herald's idea.'

'The doors have no key holes or any other way to allow vision to move around,' said Kelsey, 'and the windows have a fine mesh over them for the same reason. Of course, with practice, and once you have learned the layout, it will be possible to use a Quadrant to get inside, but it should be enough to deter any strangers.'

'Let us ascend,' said Frostback. 'Empress, shall we meet you on the middle bridge?'

'Indeed we shall,' said Thorn.

The two dragons took off. They circled slowly as they ascended, then they approached the middle bridge, and entered the Eastern Tower of the palace. The imperial party got underway again, and they climbed the wide steps towards the grand doorway.

'The palace reminds me of Lahnos,' said Arrosa. 'The towers look like horns.'

Lucius laughed. 'Maybe if we tell him that it was done deliberately, he might be persuaded to come and live with us again. There is room for Sigum, too.'

'I have long given up hoping that Lahnos will re-enter my service,' said the Empress. 'He craves a quiet life.'

'Where does he live, Your Majesty?' said Arrosa.

'He asked that it remain a secret,' said the Empress, 'and I shall respect that.'

Soldiers from the Imperial Guard came to attention by the main entrance, and the Empress led her party through the open doors into a large marble-lined foyer. To the left were the offices where the various branches of the government would operate, once they had moved out of their existing facilities, while storerooms and guard posts were on the right. Brogan gestured to a row of bronze-rimmed doors, and a porter opened one, revealing a square platform with handrails set into a shaft that rose upwards through the building.

'Which floor, Your Majesty?' said the porter.

'We wish to go to the middle bridge,' said the Empress.

'Each platform can take up to ten people, Your Majesty; 'not all of your party will be able to ascend together.'

The Empress strode through the doorway, and stood on the platform. Others from the Imperial Court walked in next to her, but Lucius hesitated when he saw Kelsey stand back.

'I'll take another platform,' Kelsey said.

The porter closed the bronze-rimmed door, and pulled on a metal lever until the arrow pointed towards the twentieth floor, where the middle bridge was located. A bell sounded, followed by the noise of gears and shafts turning. The porter opened another door, and gestured for the rest of the party to enter. Lucius followed Kelsey onto the platform, and made sure he was standing next to her as it filled up.

The door closed, the noise began again, and the platform started to ascend the square shaft.

'Might we talk?' Lucius said, his voice low.

Kelsey ignored him.

'I have a few suggestions for today's meeting of the Imperial Court,' Lucius went on.

'I'm not interested,' said Kelsey. 'You have made your opinions known.'

'But I may have found a possible compromise.'

'You've had seven years to offer advice,' she said.

Lucius nodded. He hated what he had done in the previous meeting of the full Imperial Court, and he felt nothing but regret that he hadn't voiced his reservations to Kelsey while she had been working hard on the proposals. He had told himself at the time that it was none of his business – it was a civil matter, and had nothing to do with the armed forces. He had been treating the issue in a professional manner, forgetting about the personal aspect of his friendship with the Herald. Would she ever forgive him? He hadn't realised how much he depended upon seeing and speaking to Kelsey every day, and he already missed being close to her. Arrosa would no doubt infer something sordid, and Lucius again questioned his feelings towards Kelsey. Might Arrosa have had a point? Lucius loved Kelsey, but not in the way that Arrosa had insinuated. That was right – wasn't it?

The platform juddered to a halt, and Kelsey pulled the bronze-rimmed door aside. Their half of the imperial party stepped off the platform, then Lucius came to a halt, his eyes widening as he gazed upwards. He had been expecting to arrive in a hall, but what he saw seemed more like a cavern. On one side, a huge portion of the tower's outer wall was constructed of long glass panels, and sunlight was flooding the vast interior space. Dozens of trees had been planted amid sprawling beds of flowering bushes, neat lawns and ornate fountains; and small waterfalls were tumbling down from the upper storeys, creating streams that wound their way into small pools. Trellises of vines and ivy were draped over long rows of balconies, which were stepped up in terraces opposite the glass exterior of the tower. On the level where Lucius was standing, to his right was an arched opening, where the western end of the middle bridge began. The Empress and her half of the party were standing by the edge of the bridge, and Lucius and the others joined them.

'This place is amazing,' said Rosie. 'I had expected the inside to look like a block of tenements; this is more like what I imagine the great cities of Rahain to have been like.'

The Empress smiled. 'I wanted it to seem as though we were in the midst of a beautiful, cavernous forest. We are calling this hall the Teal Garden, and many of you will have apartments with balconies that overlook it.'

'We decided that having balconies on the outside of the building would make it too easy for enemies to breach the palace,' said Brogan; 'so we put the balconies on the inside. The same steam engines that drive the platforms also pump water to the top of the tower, to supply the waterfalls and fountains, as well as the kitchens and bathrooms. The Empress has her own private gardens on the upper floors; they are a slightly smaller version of this.'

'It truly is a marvel,' said Claudian. 'Well done, Brogan; you kept this secret well hidden from us.'

'I helped implement it,' said Brogan, 'but I was following Her Majesty's design. Everything you see here was the idea of the Empress.'

'It's beautiful,' said Lucius.

'I would love to see the engineering plans for those steam engines,' said Rosie.

'The engines power long steel shafts that go under the palace,' said Brogan. 'Some of them are attached to the pulleys and gears that operate the platforms; while others control the water pumps.'

'It is all very impressive,' said Claudian.

'This is only the beginning,' said Kelsey. 'You should see what the engineers in Adorati are doing with steam. They have pumps to drain the swamps of their new territory, and digging machines to cut canals. We all know how quickly the Rakanese can build, and steam has accelerated their progress. They even have an idea to mount an engine on the front of a long carriage, which will be able to pull other carriages along behind it.'

'They plan to connect their new cities with these steam carriages,' said Fenu. 'If they work, someone will be able to travel overland from Amatskouri to Stretton Sands in a few days, rather than taking over a third.'

'I'd still rather have a Quadrant,' said Cael.

'Yes, but what about the ordinary folk?' said Shella. 'Not everyone has a Quadrant.'

Kelsey smiled as Frostback appeared through an opening on the far side of the bridge, followed by Halfclaw. The two dragons walked over to the central point, and gazed around.

'Shall we move onto the bridge?' said the Empress. 'The dragons are waiting for us.'

She gestured to the imperial party, and they set off along the wide bridge towards the dragons.

'I hope no one is frightened of heights,' the Empress went on. 'We are only halfway up the Western Tower, but we are still higher than any other building in Plateau City.'

They reached the middle of the bridge, and Lucius's eyes narrowed as he looked down at the streets of the Old Town. He remembered the many enormous buildings he had seen upon the mountainous heights of the city of Cumulus on Implacatus, and the scale of the Blue Palace reminded him of such structures. It was as if Empress Thorn had built a home worthy of an Ascendant, though he felt it would be better if he kept that opinion to himself.

Lucius moved closer to the Empress.

'Your Majesty,' he whispered, 'might I have a few moments of your time?'

'Of course, Constable,' said Thorn.

They walked a little away from the others.

'I have a few suggestions about a possible compromise regarding the constitutional changes, Your Majesty.'

'Shouldn't you be speaking to my Herald about this?' she said.

'I have tried, Your Majesty. She refuses to listen to anything I have to say.'

The Empress eyed him. 'You hurt her deeply, Lucius.'

'I am aware of that, Your Majesty.'

'It is strange, is it not, that she does not seem to be very upset with the others who voted to postpone the reforms? Kelsey's ire and disappointment has been aimed at you, and you alone. Why is that, do you think?'

Lucius said nothing.

'Might it be because, unlike the others, Kelsey holds you in such high esteem?' she said. 'She would not be so upset if you meant little to her, Lucius. You must see this, yes?'

'I made a mistake, Your Majesty. For years, I have kept my mouth closed about the reforms, thinking that it would have been wrong for me to interfere in a civil matter. I should have realised that Kelsey was looking for some constructive criticism.'

Thorn eyed him. 'Let me hear your suggestions, Constable.'

Three hours later, every member of the Imperial Court was seated in an open area amid the trees, grass and fountains of the Teal Garden. The space had been designed so that several dragons could observe and take part in the discussions, and Frostback and Halfclaw were standing next to the arched opening by the western end of the bridge.

Shella leaned on her walking stick and got to her feet.

'I have decided to speak first,' she said, 'for what will be my final appearance in the Imperial Court. No matter what the Empress decides to do regarding the constitutional proposals, my retirement begins the moment this session is over, and I shall disappear into obscurity. Well, not complete obscurity – I will still be living in my home on Colsbury with Olo'osso, so I expect to see you all each summer. Olo'osso and I plan to spend my retirement disgracefully, which should come as no surprise to anyone.'

She turned to the Empress. 'Your Majesty, it has been a privilege to serve in your government. I have enjoyed most of my time as Chancellor, but the high point for me will always be the tough times we endured in Clackenbaird, when all seemed lost. We dug deep, and somehow managed to rebuild the Empire from the ruins left by the Ascendants. The lowest point came soon afterwards, when we lost Daphne. I don't think I've ever been the same since. I look at all you young folk, and I wonder – why did I survive? Why me? At least Daphne managed to go out in a fine fashion. If you had asked her – how do you want to die? – she would have said *defending my family*, and that's what happened. But I still wish she was here. It always seems harder for those left behind. The dead take on a light of their own, a bright memory in which they are forever frozen; while the rest of us get wrinkles and sore knees. Anyway, that's enough from me. I'll bow out, knowing that I am leaving the Imperial Court in capable hands. Whatever is decided today, that won't change. Thank you, Your Majesty, for allowing me to serve the Empire.'

Shella sat down.

'Shella, my beloved friend,' said the Empress, 'I wish you were not leaving, but I respect your decision. No one has done more than you to build this Empire; and no one but you could have brought us back from the brink of annihilation in Clackenbaird. I am sure that the rest of the Imperial Court will join me in wishing you a peaceful and happy retirement; and I am already looking forward to seeing you in Colsbury Castle next summer. Go with my love and my blessings, and never forget how valued you are by all who sit in this court.'

The Empress paused for a long moment, then she turned her gaze to Kelsey.

'I have come to a decision regarding the constitutional proposals,' Thorn said. 'It seems clear to me that while the convention has done a noble and diligent job, there remain many in the Empire who are bitterly opposed to so much change happening at the same time.

Therefore, I decree the following – the Provincial Council shall be established as planned, with two delegates from each of the six full provinces of the Empire – the Holdings, Kellach Brigdomin, Adorati, Sanang, the Eastern Rim, and the City of Salve. The casting vote shall be held by the Herald of the Empire, as my representative. For imperial legislation to pass, nine votes out of thirteen shall be required. Therefore, if three or more provinces object, their votes shall qualify as a veto, just as the convention has suggested. Brogan shall have the task of setting up this council. Secondly, the Plateau shall become a new, full province, and will elect its own government according to the convention's democratic criteria. Once its administration has been established, it will send two delegates to the Provincial Council, raising its membership to fifteen. Cael will be responsible for delivering these changes, once he has taken up his role as Marshal.'

The Empress paused again. 'All other aspects of the proposals are hereby postponed indefinitely.'

There was an audible gasp from the members of the court. Kelsey lowered her gaze, her fists clenched. Next to her, Shella put an arm over the Herald's shoulder.

Lucius said nothing. The Empress had accepted his suggestions in their entirety, and she had also respected his request to keep his name out of the discussion.

'Might I speak, Your Majesty?' said Fenu.

The Empress tilted her head.

'What is to be done about the rest of the proposals?' Fenu said. 'Are we to consider them as dead? Is this postponement a cancellation?'

'Nothing has been cancelled,' said Thorn. 'Instead, we must find a way to reach a compromise with those who object to the reforms. In particular, an agreement must be reached over the inclusion of Rakana and Rahain within the proposed assembly. Until a consensus can be agreed, there shall be no progress on these other changes. It is my hope that the populace will see the work of the Provincial Council and be reassured. Patience is required if we are to bring the entirety of the Empire with us. I understand that many here will be disappointed with this decision, but I feel a gradual approach best serves the interests of the people I rule. Step by step, we shall change this Empire, but we must not run too fast, lest we stumble. That is all; those of you who are not part of the upcoming state visit to Gunst are dismissed.'

Most of the court rose to their feet, with only Brogan, Claudian and Arrosa remaining in their seats.

Kelsey led the others towards the bridge, where Frostback and Halfclaw were watching.

'Come with us, humans,' said Halfclaw. 'We wish to show you our new dwelling place.'

Lucius remained near the back of the group as they walked across the bridge. Kelsey stayed close to Frostback, and Lucius watched as the silver dragon whispered to her. They passed through a tall archway into the Eastern Tower, and entered a vast chamber, which was large enough to accommodate six dragons. While Halfclaw began to give a tour of their surroundings, Kelsey remained by Frostback's side, along with Shella, Fenu and Nardini, the other ardent supporters of the reforms. Lucius listened to Halfclaw talk about the spacious dragon quarters within the Eastern Tower, then he walked over to the silver dragon.

Kelsey glared at him. 'Are you happy now?' she said. 'I am so fucking angry I could scream.'

'I am sorry you feel that way,' Lucius said, 'but we got through two of the most important reforms – the Provincial Council, and the Plateau's transition to democracy. I know it wasn't everything you wanted, but it's a start.'

'You betrayed my rider, Lucius,' said Frostback.

'I was wrong not to tell you about my reservations,' said Lucius. 'I'm sorry, Kelsey; I should have spoken up. I didn't want to interfere, but it was a mistake.'

'It was a mistake that has led to the end of my career,' she said. 'I have no choice but to resign. For seven years, I have been advocating these reforms – I staked my whole political capital on them – and they are in ruins. The Empress will have to find a new Herald.'

'And a new Chancellor,' said Fenu, 'for if you resign, Kelsey, then I will also step down.'

'And I,' said Nardini. 'I was appointed as Chief Jurist precisely because I had helped draft the constitutional proposals. If they go, then I go, too.'

Cael joined them. 'What did I just hear?' he said. 'You can't be serious; three resignations, on top of Shella's retirement and Bedig's transfer to Dragon Eyre? That amounts to almost half of the Imperial Court.'

'If you were to resign, too,' said Nardini, 'then we could force the Empress to think again.'

Cael shook his head. 'I will not be resigning.'

'But you supported the reforms,' cried Nardini.

'And I now have the job of bringing democracy to the Plateau. This isn't all that we wanted, but it's a decent start, aye? We get the council, and the Plateau will become a proper province, at last. We didn't win everything, but I'm not going to throw away what we managed to gain from this. I can live with this compromise. It gives us something to build on. When history looks back, it will consider this day to be one of the most significant in the Empire.'

'Without an assembly, it's meaningless,' said Kelsey. 'Decisions will still be taken by a tiny minority, where power will remain, leaving millions of citizens without a voice. It's over. We lost.'

Shella laughed. 'That was a little melodramatic, Kelsey,' she said. 'We suffered a setback, not a catastrophe. Listen to Cael. He might be young, but he's speaking sense. Build upon what we achieved today, and keep fighting.'

Kelsey glared at her. 'How can you say that? And why are you so calm? You've just wasted seven years of your life.'

'Don't be ridiculous,' said Shella. 'Do you imagine that these things always run smoothly? We gained two important concessions today, and you will need to entrench them before asking for more. Do you think I faced no opposition when I tried to implement democracy in Akhanawarah City? I also had a hand in the Holdings constitution. I was unable to persuade Laodoc and Daphne to push for full democracy, and so I had to accept their compromise – was that a failure? Life is full of obstacles, yet there are also small victories. The key is to accumulate the victories, while not being disheartened by the defeats. I am too old to see these reforms through, Kelsey, and so it is to you that I pass on this responsibility. You will be the one to do it. It will take time, and you will face many more obstacles before you succeed. But one thing is certain – you will never bring democracy to the Empire if you resign.'

'It's too difficult,' said Kelsey.

'I know,' said Shella, placing a hand onto Kelsey's shoulder, 'but I have faith in you. You must draw upon your inner strength, and stay resolute. It might take decades, and you may have to deal with many more setbacks, but you will do it.'

Kelsey lowered her gaze, and said nothing.

'I would like to know how the Empress came to her decision,' said Nardini. 'Was she advised? Why did she choose those two particular reforms?'

'I have no idea,' said Shella.

'It was me,' said Lucius.

All eyes turned to him.

'I advised the Empress,' Lucius said. 'I know that I should keep to military matters, but I wanted Her Majesty to listen to my suggestions. I had little faith that she would act upon them, but she did. If you wish to blame someone, blame me.'

Kelsey stared at him. 'You fucking arsehole.'

'I did it for the good of the Empire,' he said. 'I wanted you to present these suggestions, Kelsey, so that we could all come together, but you refused to listen to me. The Provincial Council will show everyone that the smaller nations will be able to veto legislation, just as the convention intended. Let everyone see how it works, and then they might be more prepared to move to democracy. The same goes for the Plateau. If the reforms there are successful, and the Plateau prospers, then more people will be convinced that the entire Empire should be governed by the same rules. It's a start, not the end.'

'It's the end of our fucking friendship, that's what it is,' said Kelsey. She eyed Shella. 'This hurts, but I'll take your advice and stay on as Herald.'

'Then I will also remain in the Imperial Court,' said Fenu. 'You will require support, Herald, and, as the new Chancellor, I will be there to see that you get it.' She eyed Nardini.

The Chief Jurist frowned, then he nodded. 'I begrudgingly agree. I, too, will remain in office.'

Cael smiled. 'Thank Pyre for that. I am going to need help and advice about transforming the Plateau. For decades, it has been governed as the personal fiefdom of the Emperor or Empress, and I'm not sure where to begin.'

'We will help you, nephew,' said Kelsey.

Cael nodded. 'You could also help me by forgiving Lucius, Aunty,' he said. 'You might not agree with what he did, but I sincerely believe his motives were sound. His suggestions have avoided a complete collapse of the reforms, and have given us something to build on. Can you imagine the alternative? The Empress might have cancelled the entire programme.'

Kelsey said nothing for a while, then she shook her head.

'No,' she said. 'I don't think I will ever be able to trust him again.'

'Do you wish me to slay him, rider?' said Frostback. 'I will make it quick.'

A fleeting smile passed over the Herald's lips. 'That won't be necessary, Frostback,' she said. 'I never intend to speak to him again, and I will make sure that my new apartment in the Blue Palace is as far away as possible from his. He's dead to me.'

Lucius bowed his head and walked away. Cael caught up with him as he reached the edge of the middle bridge.

'Let me talk to her again, Lucius,' Cael said. 'My aunt is too wrapped up in her own anger to see the sense in your suggestions.'

'The damage was already done before I spoke to the Empress,' Lucius said. 'It breaks my heart, but I will respect her wishes, and stay clear of her. It's the children I feel sorry for. Caitlyn and Carden love being with Calpurnia and Caelius, and I don't know how I'm going to break the news to them.'

Cael opened his mouth to say something else, then he seemed to think better of it.

'I know what Arrosa has been saying,' said Lucius; 'but it's not true. Nothing was ever going to happen between me and Kelsey.'

'You and my mother,' Cael said; 'are you...? I mean, if it's not working out, then...?' He shook his head. 'I don't know what I'm trying to say.'

'Your mother is an incredible woman,' Lucius said, 'and she is my wife.'

'Then where is she, Lucius? She's never here. I used to be so close to her, and now... You know she's changed, and I'm not just talking about her appearance. What I mean is this – if you are so unhappy that you want to end your marriage to my mother, don't imagine for one moment that I will think any less of you. You have been like a father to me for years. That will never change.'

Lucius tried to smile. 'Thank you, Cael. That means a lot to me.'

He walked on to the bridge, and gazed down at the city. For much of his life, he had been close to the two daughters of Daphne Holdfast – one his wife, and the other his closest friend. With both turning their backs on him, he wondered what was left for him. He had Carden and Caitlyn, and he had Cael, his adopted son. It would be for them that he would strive, and for them that he would continue to get up each morning to serve the Empress. He doubted Karalyn still loved him; she had moved beyond the mortals in her life, and he had almost managed to make his peace with that. He closed his eyes. What did he want? An image of Kelsey appeared in his mind, and he at once knew the crushing truth.

Arrosa was right. It was Kelsey he loved; perhaps it had been Kelsey he had always loved. If Van had not been so besotted with the Holdfast woman, then Lucius knew that he would have told Kelsey how he felt many years before.

And now it was too late; much too late.

CHAPTER 13
DRAUGHTSMAN REECE

Jezra, The Western Bank – 24th Namen 3441

'Load the Battanaras,' cried the Brigade officer; 'then form a defensive perimeter.'

Forty Brigade soldiers slid the slim projectiles into their metal tubes, and primed the fuses. They moved into a tight circle, surrounding the sixty other members of the Brigades who would be accompanying Konna and Maxwell to the first of the three greenhides nests. All the while, the rains of Sweetmist poured down from the ashen sky, creating hundreds of rivulets that streamed down from the foundations of the ancient palace onto the deserted streets of Jezra.

'The rest of the City thinks we're insane for being out in this weather,' said Maxwell, 'but the Brigades are used to working in these conditions.'

Konna smiled. 'It's only a bit of rain. I've repaired sheep enclosures in Kell in worse weather than this.'

The officer eyed them, rain spilling down his face and armour. 'The detachment is ready to leave, my lord.'

A great mound of munitions and equipment lay covered by sheets of tarpaulin in the centre of the defensive circle, and Maxwell and Konna walked through the lines of Brigade soldiers until they were standing next to it. Maxwell withdrew his Quadrant from his drenched uniform.

'Prepare to loose as soon as we arrive in the forest,' the officer shouted above the noise of the rain. 'The greenhide nest is located beneath the high earthen banks of a ridge, close to a stream. Lady Konna and Lord Maxwell will kill all greenhides that get too close to us, and our job will be to entice the young queen from her lair. She will have no junior queens with her, as she remains too small to have produced any, so the queen herself is the sole target. Unleash everything we have at her as soon as she has been sighted. If our perimeter is breached, Lord Maxwell will bring us all back here.'

The soldiers from the Lostwell Brigades remained silent, and the officer nodded towards Maxwell. The young god eyed Konna, then he slid his fingers over the surface of the Quadrant. Konna and the others appeared in the midst of the dark forest. The area seemed deserted, but evidence of the greenhides was all around. The tracks they had made through the woods had been turned to mud by the incessant rain, and many of the trees were withered and dying, their branches bare. Ahead of them lay the steep banks of the high ridge, its slopes muddy and devoid of life, though a few trees still existed upon its long summit.

The Brigade officer pointed at a row of dark entrances in the earthen bank. 'Destroy the tunnels,' he cried; 'leave only the entrance on the far left.'

The soldiers formed up into a thick line fifty yards from the dark tunnels, their Battanaras pointed at the entrances.

'Loose!' shouted the officer.

Forty Mark Seven Battanaras fired at once, their projectiles exploding into the earthen bank. Behind them, forty others from the Brigades were waiting, and they helped reload the weapons. Konna and Maxwell stood to the left of the soldiers as volley after volley struck the ridge, collapsing the entrances beneath tons of earth and stone. The roar of the Battanaras competed with the smoke rising from the metal tubes, as dozens, then hundreds of projectiles were fired. By the left-hand entrance, which had remained intact, several greenhides appeared, their cries echoing off the ridge, and their claws clacking.

'Wait for them to emerge,' said Maxwell, as Konna raised her right hand. 'We don't want their dead to block the queen's only escape route.'

More greenhides gathered by the tunnel entrance, then they charged forward, racing down the muddy slope towards the hundred humans.

Konna unleashed her death powers when the first greenhides were only a few yards from the line of soldiers. Next to her, Maxwell did the same, and the greenhides fell, their heads exploding in a crescendo of noise amid the torrential rain. Bodies toppled and slid down from the side of the ridge, and they piled up at the bottom in front of the Brigade soldiers. Greenhides continued to pour out from the sole remaining tunnel, and the pile grew larger.

The officer raised a hand, and the Battanaras ceased firing, their barrels sizzling from the heavy raindrops. Along the ridge, there was no sign that the tunnel entrances had ever been there, and the entire stretch was churned up and smoking.

'Prepare the mortar,' the officer cried.

A dozen brigade soldiers pulled the tarpaulin covering from the large mortar. It loosed projectiles that were the same size as a beer barrel, and the device was adjusted until it was pointing at the remaining entrance. The projectile was lowered using a mobile crane, while the long fuse was prepared.

'Wait for my command,' said the officer, and the soldiers kept their gazes on the last entrance, from where greenhides were still emerging.

'It's not working,' said Konna, as the pile of dead grew even higher. 'Where is the damn queen?'

Maxwell swept his arm from left to right, and another twenty greenhides fell to their deaths.

Konna pulled her Clawfist onto her right hand, and fastened the straps. 'I'm going in. I'll lure her out.'

Maxwell stared at her. 'You have to be joking, Konna.'

Konna shrugged, as the rain pelted against her face. 'We came here to get the queen; I'm not leaving without her. Keep using yer death powers – I'm immune.'

Konna set off. She skirted the left flank of the great heap of dead greenhides, and scrambled up the muddy slope. Four greenhides veered to their right to attack her, and she raised her hand, killing them. She powered her battle-vision, then charged up the ridge and into the mass of greenhides by the tunnel entrance. She swung her right hand, and the Clawfist slashed through hide and bones. Konna ducked and dodged the talons lashing out at her, then she stood by the entrance. She felt for her death powers, and unleashed a great blast down the tunnel, killing everything that stood there for a distance of a hundred yards. The cries and noise faded in the downpour. Konna glanced back at Maxwell, then she entered the tunnel. Bodies were littering the ground, and she climbed over them, heading deeper into the side of the ridge.

She passed a large cavern to her left, where pale-skinned worker greenhides were sheltering. She raised her hand, and they cowered back. Konna carried on, heading downwards into the near darkness. A greenhide flashed out before her from a side entrance, and Konna drove the Clawfist into its skull, then she wondered why she wasn't frightened. If anything, she was having fun, and the thought unsettled her a little. Had she inherited her father's love of death and destruction, or had it come down from her mother's side of the family? Perhaps it was from both. A greenhide appeared behind her, slashing out with its claws. Konna sprang forward, but a trailing claw ripped down her back, and she cursed her lapse in concentration. She rolled to the tunnel floor, her self-healing getting to work, then she lifted a hand, and the greenhide's head exploded. She needed to spend less time thinking about her family, and more on what she was doing.

Before she could get to her feet, an enormous creature began to climb up the tunnel ahead of her, its bulk barely fitting through the confined space. Konna had been briefed that morning, and she knew that she was looking at the young greenhide queen. It was still underdeveloped, and had not yet become permanently immobile, but it was as large as a fully-grown dragon. Konna began to retreat, her feet retracing the path through the nest. Warrior greenhides were clustering beneath and behind the lumbering queen for protection as it made its way up the tunnel.

Konna sent a short blast of death powers into its head, and the young queen roared in pain, the thick hide melting from the side of its face. Enraged, the queen increased its speed, and Konna turned. She sprinted up the long tunnel, heading towards the small circle of grey light at the top. More greenhides emerged from side tunnels to block her retreat, but her death powers cut them down.

Konna charged out of the tunnel entrance, then tripped and fell down the slope, her clothes and hair coated with thick mud and green blood. She glanced up, and saw the queen begin to follow her, its insect-like eyes blazing with agony and fury.

'Loose the mortar!' shouted the Brigade officer.

There was a whoomp, then, two seconds later, the huge projectile landed on top of the queen, and the entire hillside exploded. Greenhide body parts went flying through the air, along with tons of mud and rock. Konna went flying with the rest of the debris. For a second, she managed to retain consciousness, then everything went black.

When Konna awoke, they were in the comfortable caves next to the foundations of the ancient palace in Jezra. The two resident dragons from the Eastern Rim were staring down at her, while dozens of Brigade soldiers and workers were watching from the side of the cave.

Konna sat up, and the Brigades cheered.

'Did we get it?' she said.

Maxwell knelt by her, a smile on his face. 'Yes, Konna,' he said. 'We got it.'

'I hear tell of your recklessness, demigod,' said Seaspan, his dragon eyes glowing. 'It seems that you are indeed a true Holdfast.'

'If I had been a mortal Holdfast,' she said, 'I'd be dead.'

'Well done,' said the Brigade officer. 'One nest down – two to go. Best of all, there were no casualties; not one.'

Konna got to her feet. Her wounds had healed, and she felt fit; no, she felt exhilarated. She glanced at her clothes. They were torn and covered in mud, and her hair and face were also plastered.

'I need a bath,' she said.

Maxwell joined her, his Quadrant in his hands.

'That will be all for now,' he said to the watching crowd. 'I'll take Lady Konna to get cleaned up, and then we'll report to Brigade headquarters. The drinks are on us tonight, if any of you care to join us in the town's taverns.'

The crowd cheered again, then Maxwell activated the Quadrant. The air shimmered, and they appeared in Maxwell's apartment in the centre of Jezra.

'You are going to get another telling off,' he said. 'We were ordered not to enter the nest.'

'I couldn't give a shit,' said Konna. 'That was the most fun I've had since Sweetmist began.'

Maxwell eyed her. 'Fun? Is there something wrong with you? It was pouring with rain, and we were surrounded by blood, death and mud.'

'Aye,' she said. 'I enjoyed it. I reckon the commanding officers won't care about our tactics. We did what they wanted – we killed the queen. That only leaves two of the bastards. Do you think we can get them both before the end of Sweetmist?'

'Probably not,' he said.

'But we still have a few days of Namen left.'

'Yes, but the seasons hardly ever change on the exact date. The Fog of Balian could start tomorrow, for all we know, and the greenhides will emerge from their nests again. We might have to wait until Freshmist. Do you think you will still be here five months from now?'

Konna shrugged. 'Who knows?'

She went to sit down on one of Maxwell's low couches, and he raised a hand in alarm.

'You're covered in mud,' he cried. 'Stay standing, and I'll run your bath.'

Maxwell hurried into the bathroom. Moments later, Konna heard the sound of water hitting the bottom of the large bathtub. She walked to the window and gazed out at the rain. Jezra looked miserable in the grey light, but no worse than Kell on a dreary autumn's day. Would she still be in Jezra when Freshmist began? She had yet to see most of the City, having restricted her movements to Jezra, Pella, and a single trip to Port Sanders to deliver her uncle's gifts to Lydia and Doria. Perhaps she should take a look at the Great Walls of the Bulwark, but that seemed dull when she considered that there were no longer any greenhides there to slaughter. The Circuit, too, seemed unappealing, as did Dalrig. It was all so *small*, she thought, as she wondered how her mother and Uncle Naxor had lived for so long in the City. Perhaps it would be more attractive in the summertime, or maybe even in winter, when the rain and fog had cleared up.

It was almost evening when Konna emerged from the bathroom, clean and wearing a dress instead of her usual fighting clothes. Maxwell was reading a book about the Ascendants that he had borrowed from Naxor while in Kell, and he glanced up at her.

'Dinnae say anything,' she said. 'I'm allowed to wear a damn dress now and again. I stuck all my dirty clothes into yer laundry basket – can ye take care of them for me?'

'Of course, cousin,' he said. 'Are you hungry?'

'Ravenous.'

'Well, we can either eat here, in relative peace and quiet, or we can eat in a tavern, where we will no doubt be mobbed by grateful mortals. The town will be singing our praises tonight.'

'The mortals who came with us did a good enough job,' she said, as she sat down.

'They did,' he said, 'but how much courage does it take to fire an explosive at a greenhide? You were the one who lured the queen out. By nightfall, the entire town will know what you did.'

'If that mortar had landed on my head,' she said, 'I would be dead, aye? I mean, my self-healing wouldnae have been much use if my body was torn into a thousand pieces.'

'I suppose so.'

'Should we allow these weapons to be developed? Is it sensible to let mortals possess weapons that could easily kill us?'

'Our powers were still necessary to destroy the nest.'

'Aye, but for how long? The mortals are forever improving their weapons, while our powers don't get any stronger over time. At some point, even a mortal child would be able to kill us, if they have the right weapon.'

'I hadn't thought about it like that.'

'I'd heard of these weapons,' she went on, 'but down in Kell we never saw them. Today was my first real experience of seeing the Battanaras in action. And that fucking mortar? It worries me. What if the mortals decide to get rid of us?'

'Why would they do that? The mortals and the immortals of the Empire are getting along well enough. There are gods from the Doomed Worlds on Athumia who probably long to slaughter the mortals of the Empire, but isn't Karalyn keeping the peace between the two sides? We should be safe enough.'

'Aye, but if we wait and do nothing because things are fine at the moment, then what about in a century from now? What if the mortals make even more powerful weapons, and then they start to take a dislike to us? By then, it'll be too late.'

'I'll order food,' he said, getting to his feet and placing the book onto a table. 'We can continue this discussion later.'

Maxwell walked towards the door but, before he could get there, the air shimmered in the corner of the room, and Cairney appeared with a large trunk next to his feet.

Konna's eyes widened. 'Brother?'

Cairney hurried over to Maxwell. 'Yer Quadrant – I need it. Quickly.'

Maxwell blinked. 'What?'

'Yer Quadrant, Maxwell. I'll bring it back in a moment.'

Maxwell took out his Quadrant. Cairney snatched it from his hand and vanished.

'I, uh...' Maxwell stammered.

Cairney reappeared, then he laughed and handed the Quadrant back to Maxwell.

'What are ye doing?' said Konna.

'I needed to put Uncle Naxor's Quadrant back before he realised I'd taken it,' said Cairney.

'You stole his Quadrant?' she said.

'I borrowed it for a minute,' he said. 'How else do ye think I got here, ya dozy cow?'

Cairney sat, as Konna and Maxwell stared at him.

'Carry on with what ye were doing,' said Cairney.

'I was... well, I was just about to order dinner,' said Maxwell.

'That's a great idea,' said Cairney. 'I could eat a manky greenhide.'

Maxwell frowned, then he walked to the front door of the apartment and slipped outside.

'Well?' said Konna.

'Later on tonight,' said Cairney, 'Ma and Uncle Naxor will realise that I've gone. I left a note, but. A vague note. I didnae tell them where I was going, but they might be able to guess.'

'If yer here to slaughter greenhides, brother,' she said, 'then ye've come at the wrong time. Look outside; it's pishing down.'

'I'm not here for greenhides, sis,' he said. 'My plans are bigger than that.'

Konna laughed. 'You have a plan?'

'Aye; and a fucking beautiful plan it is, too. I've been thinking about it ever since ye were last in Kell. Do ye not yearn for revenge, sis? It eats me up. Uncle Naxor is always telling us to be patient, but if we're too patient, then everybody responsible for Da's death will be feeding the worms by the time we act.'

Cairney closed his mouth as Maxwell re-entered the room.

'Dinner for three has been ordered,' he said.

'Did ye remember to ask for ale?' said Cairney. 'I cannae eat without decent ale. What else do they drink here?'

'Wine, mostly,' said Maxwell, as he sat down.

Cairney pulled a face. 'Who drinks that shite?'

'I'm growing to like it,' said Konna.

'Then it seems that I have arrived just in time, sis,' he said.

'I did order three ales,' said Maxwell. 'Is that enough?'

'For me, maybe,' said Cairney. 'I don't know what the rest of ye are gonnae drink. Maxwell, tell me – do ye like the Empire?'

Maxwell's eyes narrowed. 'I'm not sure what you mean.'

'It was a simple enough question, Maxi-boy,' said Cairney. 'Eight years ago, the City was pretty much blackmailed into joining the Empire, aye? Does that not rankle? Before that, your family used to rule the City. Now, mortals control everything. Is the son of God-Queen Amalia content to take his orders from mortals?'

Maxwell smiled. 'If I tried to take power, the Holdfasts would arrive in numbers to kill me.'

'Yer sitting next to two Holdfasts right now,' said Cairney.

'All right; let me be clearer. If I rebelled against the Empire, Karalyn Holdfast would come here to kill me.'

'No, she wouldnae. Naxor keeps track of what's going on in the Empire; and did ye know that Karalyn is never around? Not any more. She's barely ever seen on the Star Continent. Anyway, I'm getting ahead of myself. I'm not asking ye to lead a rebellion, Maxwell – I was merely pointing out that, if we follow my plan, then the City might be yours without provoking Karalyn. What we need to do, right, is stir up a war between the Empire and the Dominion. Then, when things are kicking off, Karalyn will swoop down to punish the leaders of both sides. There will be opportunities amid the confusion; that's what I'm saying. Are ye in?'

Konna shook her head. 'Don't answer that, Maxwell,' she said. 'My wee brother seems to have forgotten something; something that rips his stupid plan to pieces.'

Cairney laughed. 'And what's that?'

'Karalyn can read our minds, ya twat. So can Cael. Our thoughts might be protected from most gods and mages with vision powers, but we cannae stop those two from getting into our heads. What's to stop them from finding out that it was us who provoked the trouble in the first place?'

'I like yer thinking, sis,' said Cairney. 'Yer objections are based on practicalities, rather than principle. What yer saying is this – that if I could find a way to make sure no blame lands on our shoulders, then ye'd be up for it?'

Konna narrowed her eyes.

'I have a principled objection,' said Maxwell. 'I don't want power. What if I'm happy as I am? I don't want to have to sit in a palace and make decisions; I don't want the responsibility. I might change my mind later, after a few centuries, maybe; but, fundamentally, I don't see the problem with the Empire as it is.'

Cairney nodded, then he stared into Maxwell's eyes. 'You hate the Empress,' he said.

Maxwell blinked.

'Ye want to see the mortals removed from power,' Cairney went on. 'Ye want to help me.'

Maxwell's eyes tightened, then he looked confused for a moment.

'What are ye doing?' said Konna.

'I might have been keeping a secret from ye, sis,' said Cairney. 'Now, Maxwell, do ye like Empress Thorn?'

Maxwell shook his head. 'No. I hate her.'

'Good lad,' said Cairney. 'That's more like it.'

Konna got to her feet and took a step back, her eyes wide.

Cairney laughed.

'But...' said Konna. 'You...'

'Spit it out, sister,' he said.

'You can't read minds,' she said. 'How are ye doing that?'

'Through the power of my voice,' said Cairney. 'Relax – it doesnae work on you. It doesnae work on any of our brothers or sisters. Believe me – I've tried. Now, watch this.' He turned back to Maxwell. 'Forget the last ten minutes,' he said. 'Forget what we've just been talking about.'

Maxwell's face contorted with confusion. He glanced around, as though he was emerging from a daze.

'I ordered food for us,' he said. 'It should be here soon.'

'Thanks, Maxi-boy,' said Cairney. 'Now, I was wondering if, after we've eaten, ye might want to take us to where Esher the Ascendant lives and works. I'd like to see him.'

'I'm not sure about that,' said Maxwell. 'I wouldn't want us to get into trouble.'

'It'll be fine,' said Cairney. 'I only want to see him; nothing more. I'm curious. We'll take a wee peek, and then we'll come back here and have a few ales. Or, ye could take us out to a couple of taverns – it's up to you.'

Maxwell frowned. 'You only want to look at him?'

'Of course,' said Cairney. He stared into Maxwell's eyes again. 'It'll be fine.'

Cairney didn't seem to mind the weather as the three of them hurried up the rainswept alleyway. Konna's boots were splashing through the deep channels of water flowing down from the gutters, and her hair and clothes were drenched.

They stopped before a large brick building.

'He lives in here,' said Maxwell. 'He has rooms above the floor where the planners work. He might even still be at his desk.'

Cairney nodded. 'Remember, if anyone asks, I'm only in Jezra for a wee visit.'

Maxwell approached the main entrance of the building.

'I don't like this,' whispered Konna.

'I couldnae give a shite,' said Cairney. 'Are ye still angry with me for keeping secrets?'

'What do you think? How long have ye known that ye can... persuade folk?'

'Only a year or two,' he said.

'Does it work on Ma?'

Cairney shrugged.

They followed Maxwell into the building and stood in the hallway for a moment, letting the water drip from their clothes. Oil lamps were burning from wall sconces, illuminating the slightly shabby interior of the office block. Maxwell led the way up two flights of stairs, passing a noisy common room, where dozens of Brigade workers from the planning department were eating their evening meal.

Cairney glanced into the large room, as Maxwell headed for the next flight of stairs.

'Might he be in there?' he said.

Maxwell shook his head. 'He keeps to himself,' he said. 'He doesn't have any friends.'

'Why not?' said Konna.

'It might be because he's a bit awkward around people,' said Maxwell. 'He had a hard time when he was trying to relearn how to speak and write, and he has a reputation for being odd.'

Konna frowned, and she began to feel a little pity for Esher. He had been one of the mightiest beings in existence, and now he was being shunned by ignorant mortals for not conforming? She and Cairney followed Maxwell up to the next floor, and they came to a large office, which was lined with wooden desks. Plans of the Jezran Wall and its three fortresses were pinned to every wall of the chamber, but it was in silence, with only a single lamp lighting up one corner, where a man sat alone, working on a set of drawings.

'That's him,' said Maxwell. 'That's Esher. But, that's not his name anymore. He's known as Reece now. Draughtsman Reece.'

Konna stared over into the corner. The man was tall and well-built, but he was sitting hunched over his desk, his features knotted in concentration. He looked as though he was in his mid-forties, and he had aged well. In fact, she thought, he was an extremely handsome man, and she found it easy to picture him as a god.

'Right; you've seen him,' said Maxwell. 'Should we go to one of the taverns now?'

Cairney eyed Maxwell, then he began walking towards the corner of the room.

'What's he doing?' said Maxwell.

'My brother does whatever he pleases,' said Konna. 'We should go with him, to stop him doing anything too stupid.'

They went after Cairney, who had walked up to Reece's desk.

The draughtsman glanced up. 'What do you want? I am busy.'

Cairney grinned at him. 'I just came to see if you needed anything.'

Reece frowned. 'I am busy.'

'So ye said.'

Reece's frown deepened as he noticed Konna and Maxwell stand next to Cairney.

'What are you working on?' said Konna.

Reece glanced down at the detailed plans he had been drafting. 'The turrets for the gatehouse on the Fortress of the Exiles. The specifications state that they have to be twenty yards apart, but the section of wall is fifty yards long.'

'An interesting conundrum,' said Cairney.

'The instructions are contradictory,' said Reece. 'It isn't interesting; it's infuriating.'

'Ye don't seem very furious,' said Cairney.

'I want to go back to work,' he said. 'Leave me alone.'

'Are ye happy?' said Cairney.

Reece eyed him with disdain, and started working on the drawings again.

'Tell me if yer happy,' Cairney repeated. 'Tell us how ye feel about yer life.'

Reece blinked, then he put his pencil down and lowered his eyes.

'I hate it,' he whispered. 'No one likes me, and the only satisfaction I get is from my work, which you are disturbing. I feel out of place, as though I don't belong here. I am not happy. I have no memories of ever being happy. My colleagues have husbands and wives, but no woman will talk to me. I met a Reaper girl once, and I thought she liked me, then, one day, with no warning, she was transferred to the Bulwark, and I never saw her again. Every other woman thinks I am strange, and some of them think I might hurt them. I am so lonely I sometimes wish I was dead.'

'That's enough,' said Cairney. 'Forget what we have been talking about. We are going to leave you now. You will forget we were ever here as soon as we've gone.'

He nodded to Maxwell and Konna, and they turned and walked away from Reece, who went back to work as though nothing had happened.

Maxwell stopped when they came to the stairs. 'That was... weird,' he said. 'I've never heard him open up like that to anyone before.'

'I feel sorry for him,' said Konna. 'Imagine being so lonely.'

'What was done to him was a terrible crime,' said Cairney; 'and I'm not just talking about Karalyn wiping his mind. The City should have taken better care of him; they should have made him feel welcome; instead, they dumped him out here, friendless and unwanted.'

'I think the Aurelians want to forget that he exists,' said Maxwell.

'I want to help him,' said Konna; 'but how?'

Cairney smiled. 'Fear not, sis – my plan will take care of everything.'

CHAPTER 14
OLD ENMITIES

Rainsby, Southern Plateau – 5th Day, First Third Autumn 552

'You can do it,' said Cole; 'you are so close. One more try.'

Alva said nothing, her features exhausted.

'We have ten days left,' he said, 'and then it will be two thirds since you arrived in Rainsby. Two thirds was our deadline.'

'I know,' she said, 'but I am so tired.'

Cole eyed her. 'I can't give you any more keenweed, Alva. You've already had far too much in recent days, and I'm worried about your health.'

'You must think I'm so useless.'

'Useless? Of course not. You are a very fine vision mage,' he said; 'one of the best to come out of the Holdings in years. The mage based in Tahrana City can barely reach the Great Tunnel; while you are being expected to cover three times that distance. And you are still improving. At this rate, if you practise hard, you will be able to reach any point along the Inner Sea, as well as the Great Tunnel.'

'Say I manage to stretch my vision as far as Plateau City,' she said, 'what's the use of that if I am too drained to talk to anyone there?'

Cole refilled their mugs with fresh coffee. 'This is unlike you, Alva.

When you arrived here, you were full of confidence. Am I a terrible teacher; is that it? Have I sapped your spirit?'

'No,' she said. 'You are a very patient teacher; it's not your fault. It's... I have never worked as hard as I have since I got here. Every day for fifty days in a row, I have been exercising my vision powers, and I sometimes feel as though my head is about to explode.'

'I have been pushing you too hard.'

'That's what I don't understand,' she said. 'You clearly don't want to leave Rainsby, and you could have easily allowed me to fail.'

'I am to join the Imperial Court regardless of whether or not you fail to reach Plateau City,' he said. 'The Empress made that clear. I am trying to prepare you for when you will be the sole mage in Rainsby. I'm pushing you now, to make it easier for you in the future. Let's try one more time and then, win or lose, I'll let you sleep for the rest of the day.'

'You'll let me sleep? For the whole day?'

'For the whole day.'

She glanced at her mug. 'But I've already drunk too much coffee,' she said. 'I don't think I'll be able to sleep.'

'I'll help you,' he said. 'I will calm your thoughts and let you get some proper rest.'

She nodded. 'All right.'

'North by north-west,' he said. 'Let's attempt a straight line over the Inner Sea. I will entangle our powers, and you will follow me. Agreed?'

They turned to face the open window, and Cole pushed his powers out into the sunshine. He gazed down at the streets of Rainsby for a moment while he waited for Alva to reach him, and noticed that there were more people outside than usual. Many of them were heading towards the area around the large, commercial harbour, and he wondered if something was happening.

He sensed Alva's vision powers, and entwined them with his own.

Are you ready? he said.

Yes.

Cole orientated himself to face the direction of Plateau City, then he pushed his vision out. Alva kept pace with him, and they passed over

Rainsby and started to cross the waters of the Inner Sea. Cole increased his speed in stages, while always ensuring that Alva was able to stay close, and the sea passed under them in a blur of grey. Cole increased his pace again, reaching the current limits of what Alva was capable of. He knew that she was getting better, and had witnessed her rapid improvements over the time he had known her. At some point, she would reach her real limit, but she still had far to go.

He began to feel her tiring, but she didn't complain, and he was proud of her resolve. That was odd, he thought – he was *proud* of her? She had been right before; it didn't matter to the Empress if Alva was ready when Cole had to leave to join the Imperial Court, so why was he so determined to see her succeed? He suppressed his thoughts, and focussed on escorting her vision as it surged north.

At length, just when Cole could sense that Alva's mind was about to close down from exhaustion, he saw the two towers of the Blue Palace appear on the horizon.

Do you see that? he said. *The towers of the Empress's grand new palace – do you see them?*

I see them, she said.

A few more miles, and we shall be there.

He pushed onwards. Alva was flagging, but she persisted, and they sped over the sea walls that marked the boundary of the New Town of Plateau City. They soared together over the tall spires of the university, then banked by the shimmering blue tiles of the new palace. Halfclaw was circling overhead, his green and blue wings resplendent in the autumnal sunlight.

You did it, Alva; you did it, Cole said. *Now, ease off.*

Alva's vision thread collapsed, and Cole cut off his own powers. In an instant, his consciousness was back in his office in Madden's Tower. He got up from his seat as Alva began to topple over, and he caught her in his arms before she could fall to the floor.

She groaned, her gaze upon him.

He smiled down at her, then helped her back into her chair. She was shaking, and sweat was coating her forehead.

'Well done,' he said, his hands still round her shoulders. 'You reached Plateau City; I knew you could do it. '

She retched, her hands trembling, and he held her for a few moments.

'I feel terrible,' she gasped.

'I know. Do you want me to help you sleep?'

She nodded.

He pulled back from her, and entered her mind. He could feel her pain and exhaustion, and he felt a sudden pang of sympathy for her.

He soothed her mind. *Sleep.*

She closed her eyes. Cole picked her up, and lay her down onto the low couch. He set a cushion under her head, and covered her in a blanket, then he got to his feet, his gaze on her face. He was going to miss her. For fifty days, they had been in each other's company, and he had said more to her in that time than he had said to anyone else in the years since he had been posted to Rainsby.

He sat down, and picked up his mug of coffee, annoyed with himself that he had allowed someone to get close to him. Alva had seen him at his best and worst, and he had lowered the walls that usually surrounded him. He had done it to help her, he told himself, not because he liked her. Rainsby needed a good mage to channel messages to and from the imperial capital, and by helping her, he had been doing his duty to the Empire. That was it; nothing more. He wondered if she saw him as a friend. It would be nice to have a friend. Perhaps he had been isolated for long enough. It was true that he had been content to be alone, with nothing but the occasional visit from Cael to punctuate the long periods of keeping himself apart from others; but what if there was a cost to living like a hermit? Did he always want to be alone?

The Empress had no concern for any of his objections. Her Majesty knew what she wanted for Cole, and it most certainly wasn't a life of isolation. It was a little ironic, he thought, that the person who would be replacing him in Rainsby was the one person he was interested in getting to know better, the one person he might actually miss when he moved to Plateau City.

There was a knock on his door, and it opened. A marine lieutenant entered the room. He glanced down at Alva for a moment, then he saluted.

'Mage Cole,' he said; 'your presence is required down at the military harbour, sir.'

'Why?' said Cole. 'I'm not scheduled for any work down there today.'

'The marine colonel is requesting that you join him, sir,' said the lieutenant. 'A disturbance has broken out by the commercial harbour. Holdings and Kellach citizens are protesting against the new constitution, and we are about to move squads into the streets to protect lives and property.'

Cole got to his feet. 'Who are the protesters targeting?'

'Rahain businesses, sir. You will see the smoke if you look out of your window.'

Cole walked over to the window and gazed out. Two plumes of dark smoke were billowing up from the harbour.

'Let me check in with the Imperial Court,' said Cole, 'then I will join the colonel in the military harbour as soon as I have spoken to someone in the capital.'

'Aye, sir,' said the marine.

Cole took out his Quadrant as the marine left the room and closed the door. It would be far quicker to visit Plateau City directly, though the thought irritated him, as it proved once again that his vision powers were becoming less valuable over time. Battle-vision, fire and death powers were being replaced by high explosives, and vision by Quadrants. He locked the door of his office, leaving the key in the lock in case Alva awoke and needed to leave, then he slid his fingers over the copper device. The air sparkled, and he appeared in the internal courtyard of the Ministry of the Plateau.

A courtier saw him and bowed.

'Where can I find Marshal Bedig?' said Cole.

'The Imperial Court is in the process of moving into the Blue Palace, my lord,' said the courtier. 'We who remain here have been assigned the task of transporting the archives and all office personnel.'

Cole nodded, then he turned to face the colossal towers of the new palace, which were visible over the rooftops of the New Town.

'You won't be able to use a Quadrant to access the upper floors, my lord,' said the courtier; 'not unless you are already familiar with the internal layout. I suggest that you select a lower floor, and someone there will guide you to Marshal Bedig.'

'Thank you,' said Cole, then he triggered the Quadrant again. He appeared on the grand steps leading to the main entrance of the new palace, and hurried up them. The soldiers by the doors stopped him, and he realised that none of them knew his face.

'Do you have permission to enter the palace, Captain?' said one.

'My name is Cole Holdfast,' he said. 'A riot is breaking out in Rainsby and I need to speak to Marshal Bedig.'

Halfclaw swooped down and landed next to him.

'Cole,' said the dragon, 'it has been too long since I saw you, though I hear that you are soon to be living with us in the palace.'

The soldiers by the main doors bowed.

'Apologies, my lord,' said one. 'You may enter.'

'Who are you looking for?' said Halfclaw.

'Bedig, or anyone from the Imperial Court,' said Cole.

'Then use your device to appear upon the middle of the three bridges,' said the dragon. 'Some of the Imperial Court are meeting in the gardens by its western edge.'

'The *gardens*?' said Cole.

'You will see,' said the dragon.

'Thank you, Halfclaw,' said Cole. He triggered the Quadrant again, wishing he had used his vision powers to reach Plateau City.

The air shimmered, and he found himself standing on the wide, robust bridge, halfway up the palace. He glanced up at the Western Tower, and saw that a large section of the exterior wall was made of glass. He hurried towards the tower, where he was again stopped by armed soldiers. He saw Lucius Cardova over the shoulders of the soldiers, and called out to him. The Imperial Constable approached.

'Cole Holdfast has permission to enter the Western Tower,' Cardova said.

The soldiers parted.

'Thank you, sir,' said Cole. 'A riot has broken out in Rainsby over the constitutional changes. It appears that Holdings and Kellach civilians are burning down any Rahain businesses they can find. The marines are about to move in to restore order.'

Cardova frowned. 'Come this way.'

Cole followed Cardova through a tall, arched opening, then he paused to take in his surroundings. It was as though he had entered a vast cavernous garden. Trees, flowers and waterfalls each competed for his attention, then he saw the tiered rows of balconies that lay against the opposite wall of the large space.

'This, uh... was not what I was expecting,' he said.

'You will be seeing a lot more of it soon enough,' said Cardova. 'Follow me.'

Cardova led him along a path that ran by a stream, then they walked through a doorway in the side of the cavern and entered a large oak-lined chamber, where dozens of officials were working, along with several members of the Imperial Court. He looked around for Bedig or Cael, but saw neither. Cardova walked over to a desk, where clerks were sitting, and he picked up a document.

'Take this back to Rainsby with you,' he said to Cole. 'The majority of the constitutional reforms have been indefinitely postponed. Ensure that the populace of Rainsby is given this information with all speed. That should quell the riots.'

Cole narrowed his eyes. 'The reforms have been postponed, sir?'

'By order of Her Majesty,' said Cardova. 'The details are in the document, which was due to be sent to Rainsby this evening. Have the news proclaimed throughout the streets. If the riots continue, use all reasonable force to restore calm.'

'Yes, sir.'

He took the document from Cardova, saluted, and triggered the Quadrant. The air shimmered, and he appeared on the long quayside of the military harbour in Rainsby. Dozens of marines were being kitted out in armour, their swords and maces replaced by short batons. Cole walked towards the commanding colonel, who was overseeing the mobilisation.

Cole saluted again, and handed the colonel the document.

The colonel frowned. 'What have you brought me, Captain?'

'I have just been to Plateau City, sir,' said Cole. 'The reforms have been postponed. Constable Cardova wishes this proclamation to be issued across the town.'

The Kellach colonel's gaze scanned the text, then he gestured for the other officers to gather round.

'Captain Holdfast has been of great service,' he said to them, holding up the document. 'The reason behind the riots is now officially out of date. The constitutional reforms have been cancelled. Have criers announce the news immediately, throughout every part of the town. Tell the rioters that the Empress has listened to their objections; then order them to return to their homes.'

The officers dispersed.

The colonel eyed Cole. 'I still require you to enter the streets, Captain,' he said. 'I believe that you have the ability to quell fires? Is that correct?'

'Yes, sir.'

The colonel gestured towards a row of small, coastal ships tied up by the quayside. 'Those vessels shall be taking two hundred marines directly to the commercial harbour. Your job shall be to extinguish every fire currently blazing in Rainsby, so you may travel with them, or go by Quadrant – the choice is yours. However, if you decide to use a Quadrant, I strongly recommend that you take a couple of squads with you.'

'I will go by ship, sir,' said Cole.

'Then you had better hurry up, Captain, as they are about to depart.'

Cole ran off towards the row of vessels, and bounded over the gangway onto the first one. He spoke to the officer in charge of the marine detachment on board, then he stood by the bow as the ship cast off. Its two sails had been raised, and it slipped away from the shore, leading the other four vessels out past the long breakwaters that protected the military harbour.

Cole wondered why he had chosen to go by ship, but he knew the reason. His father had burned Rainsby to the ground from a ship while he and the garrison had been evacuating, rather than leave the town in the hands of the Rahain army. Despite having lived in Rainsby for years, Cole had never entered the town via the harbour, and he decided he would test the limits of his powers.

His vessel turned to the west as soon as it had left the military harbour, and Cole saw the mighty sea defences of Rainsby approach. At least six thick plumes of smoke were now rising over the town, and Cole flexed his fingers. Could he undo what his father had done? Rather than burn the town, could he save it from the flames?

A few marines joined him by the bow as their ship neared the narrow entrance to the commercial harbour. Two small forts sat upon the ends of the overlapping breakwaters, leaving a single channel by which all vessels had to enter and leave. With the southern Plateau enjoying decades of peace, the defences looked too powerful for what was needed, but they remained as a legacy of Empress Bridget's plan to repel Agatha and her horde of gods.

Cole raised his hands.

'What are you doing, Captain?' said a marine lieutenant.

'I am going to extinguish the fires from here,' said Cole.

A few of the marines laughed.

'But we can't even see the fires from out here, sir,' said one.

'If my father could start fires from a ship,' he said, 'then I can put them out.'

He had made sure that his voice had seemed confident, but he knew he had never tried to do what he was about to attempt. He would need to combine his vision skills with his fire abilities, but to save lives rather than take them.

He sent his vision out, as over a dozen marines watched him. He looked down on the commercial harbour. Several warehouses along the quayside were ablaze, and all of them, as far as Cole knew, belonged to Rahain merchants dwelling in Rainsby. Those owned by the Rakanese had been untouched, but there was a good reason for that – the merchants were from the new nation of Adorati, not the Republic of Rakana. Adorati was reputedly inhabited by *good* Rakanese, as far as the local Holdings and Kellach Brigdomin saw matters.

Cole's vision approached the first of the conflagrations lighting up the horizon. He moved closer to the flames, then felt for his fire powers. Nothing happened at first, then he sensed it – a faint, almost welcoming feeling, as though the flames wanted him to take them under his control. He tried to move the flames, and they responded.

His vessel entered the narrows of the harbour entrance at that point, and it passed between the forts. Cole summoned his strength, and began to quell the first fire, just as the quayside came into view for the marines on board. The flames dampened down, spluttered, and went out. The rioters on the quayside stared at the sight. Some of them gazed up, as though they felt that it had to be raining, but the skies were clear. Cole moved on to the second fire, which was raging along a street of Rahain-owned shops and businesses. Again, he took control of the flames, and extinguished them.

'Pyre's arse,' cried a marine.

Cole severed his vision connection. He could see the town with his own eyes, and no longer needed to search for the fires. He pointed towards the flames that were enveloping the upper deck of a large merchant vessel and, in seconds, the fire died away. Those on the deck who had been fighting the flames stepped back and stared around. By this time, almost every marine on board Cole's vessel had gathered close to the bow, to watch him in action.

Cole continued to work as the ship pulled ever closer to the quayside of the commercial harbour, until every fire in the town had been extinguished. Crowds of bewildered rioters were standing in groups, staring at the scorched buildings, unable to understand what had happened.

Cole's vessel bumped against the quay, and the marines piled off the deck, pushing their way through the crowds to occupy the area. Cole lowered his hands and followed them.

'The harbour is now under the authority of the Imperial Marines,' shouted an officer. 'Disperse, or you shall be arrested.'

Many in the crowd booed and jeered.

'Traitors!' cried a Holdings man armed with an axe. 'We will not give this Empire to the Rahain bastards.'

Cole joined the other marines at the front. He was unarmed, but he didn't care.

'The reforms have been cancelled!' he shouted. 'You have won. The Empress has postponed all constitutional changes. There will be no assembly.'

The crowds facing the marines fell silent for a moment, then a great roar of victory arose from them, as the rioters slapped each other on the back and cheered.

Cole felt sick watching them. The people who had set fire to much of the town were the same people as Cole – for he was descended from both the Holdings and the Kellach. A group of Rahain merchants who had been held hostage was released, and the marines moved along the quayside to shield them. Many of the merchants had been beaten, and they aimed curses at the jubilant rioters.

The other marine vessels also berthed by the quay, and their squads took control of the rest of the harbour, pushing the celebrating rioters back into the streets of the town. More Rahain emerged from where they had been hiding, along with a few Rakanese who had been keeping their heads down amid the violence.

Cole saw a few scraps of paper fluttering along the ground, and he stooped down to gather one up. It was a similar diatribe to the one Alva had shown him, and accused the Empress of selling the Empire to a horde of illiterate and ungrateful barbarians from Rahain. A Rahain merchant saw him read it, and spat onto the quay.

'Those lies nearly killed us,' he cried. 'We have lived in this town for years, in peace.'

Cole said nothing.

'Your army slaughtered tens of thousands of our people in Rahain,' another merchant shouted. 'You forced us into your wretched Empire, and now you plan to silence us? Shame on you!'

A few of them edged closer to Cole, and two marines stepped out with their batons.

'Stay back,' one shouted.

'Or what, you filthy Kellach dog?' cried a Rahain.

Many of the marines bristled.

'You want to be careful,' shouted a Holdings officer, 'or my Kellach friends might take that the wrong way.'

Rocks were thrown, as the Rahain in the harbour confronted the marines.

'Disperse, or we will respond!' shouted a marine sergeant.

A rock struck Cole on the side of his head, and he went down, as pain swept through him. He held his head as he lay on the ground, while marines formed a thick line to protect him. Cole took a hand away from his head, and saw blood.

'You fucking idiots,' shouted a marine officer. 'Cole Holdfast put out the fires. You just wounded the man who saved your businesses, your ships and your damn lives.'

Cole staggered to his feet, blood streaming down the side of his face. The crowd of Rahain moved back, their eyes on him, then the marines began herding them away from the quayside.

'That's a nasty cut, sir,' said a marine sergeant.

'I think I'll live,' said Cole. 'If nothing else is required of me, I think I might go back to Madden's Tower.'

The officer in charge of the operation nodded. 'You do that, Captain,' he said. 'Thank you for your help this evening; we shall send word to Plateau City commending your actions here today.'

Cole took out his Quadrant, and swiped his fingers over it. He appeared back in his office, and walked over to his desk. He opened a drawer, withdrew a bottle of brandy and a glass, and sat down on a couch. He glanced over at the couch opposite him. Alva Longhold was still sleeping with the blanket over her. Cole wanted to wake her. Instead, he dipped his hand back into the desk drawer and removed a tiny vial of salve. He removed the stopper, and took a small dose.

At once, the pain in his head vanished. He put a hand to the injury, but it had healed.

He heard a gasp from the couch, and turned to see that Alva had awoken.

'What happened, Cole?' she said. 'Did you fall?'

'You're supposed to be sleeping,' he said.

She stared at the blood coating the left side of his face.

He held up the vial. 'I'm fine.'

'You have salve?'

'I do. Before you ask – I won't give you any for vision-related exhaustion. The only way to improve is to fight through it. If you took salve, you'd never get any better. I know it sounds cruel, but...'

'It doesn't matter,' she said. 'What happened to your head?'

'There was a riot.'

'A rioter did that?'

'No, the ones the marines saved from the riot did it. Angry Rahain. The reforms have been cancelled.'

Alva walked into the bathroom and re-emerged with a damp cloth. She began to clean the side of Cole's face, and he took another glass from the drawer. He filled both with brandy, and passed her one.

'I'm going to get drunk,' he said. 'Right now, I feel as though I've had enough of this place. The Holdings and Kellach were behaving like savages, and as soon as we rescued the Rahain from the harbour, they turned on us as well. I thought those days were behind us.'

'They were,' she said, as she dabbed at his cheek; 'right up until we invaded Rahain. We killed an awful lot of them, and maybe the Empress thought that they deserved a say in the assembly as a way to make up for their suffering.' She stepped back and peered at her handiwork. 'That's most of it cleaned up, but you'll need to wash your hair.'

'Thanks, Alva,' he said. 'Sit down, and drink with me.'

'How could I say no to such a charming invitation?' she said, as she took a seat on the couch next to him.

'Are we friends?' he said.

'I certainly hope so,' she said. 'Why? Do you doubt it?'

'I have tried not to make any friends. I think I might have failed.'

'In ten days,' she said, 'you will be going to Plateau City.'

'I know.'

'Ten days. At the risk of making a fool of myself, I am going to miss you, Cole Holdfast.'

'I'll miss you, too.'

She raised an eyebrow. 'Really? I thought you didn't need anyone.'

'I was wrong. Maybe it took a rock on the head to wake me up, but I'm a little tired of being alone. I like you, Alva. I admire the way you never give up, despite the headaches and nausea; and I know I've been pushing you hard. I want you to succeed. I wasn't lying when I said that you were one of the best vision mages to come out of the Holdings in many years.'

'Thank you,' she said. 'You could always visit me when you go to Plateau City. You have a Quadrant, and I would like to stay in touch.' She smiled. 'Then I can tell everyone that I have a Holdfast as a friend.'

'You know,' he said, as he put his feet up onto the low table; 'I might just do that.'

CHAPTER 15
THE DELEGATES

Plateau City, The Plateau – 7th Day, First Third Autumn 552

Arrosa stood, her two-year-old son held in her arms.

'That's everything, ma'am,' said one of the men. 'Do you need us to unpack the crates?'

'No, thank you,' she said; 'I can take care of that.'

The men bowed and left the large apartment. Arrosa weaved her way through the boxes, crates and trunks that were piled up on the floor, and walked out on to the apartment's long balcony. Her new home had an excellent view. It was on the twenty-second floor of the Blue Palace, and she could look down onto the Teal Garden, all the way to the middle bridge, or the Dragon Bridge, as people were calling it. Through the large glass panes of the exterior wall, she could see the Old Peasant District, and then the large military base on the far side of the river. Beyond that stretched suburbs, and then the fields to the south of the city.

She and Cael had ensured that they were living close to several other members of the Imperial Court. Lucius Cardova had the apartment directly below theirs, where he was going to be living with Caitlyn, Carden and old Caelius Logos; while Rosie Jackdaw and her husband Nestorian were moving into the rooms above. The apartment next door to Arrosa's was empty, but it had been put aside for Cole, and she was looking forward to living close to Cael's cousin.

The rest of the Imperial Court would be living many floors above them, clustering around the Empress's spacious quarters on the upper floors of the Western Tower. A smaller, more private version of the Teal Gardens had been constructed there, complete with trees, waterfalls and flowerbeds, and it ran up the side of all three floors where the Empress lived. There were hundreds of stairs between Arrosa and the Empress, and hundreds more to reach the ground levels, but the steam-powered platforms worked day and night. Arrosa and Cael also had their own Quadrants, and they had learned how to access the Dragon Bridge, as well as the main audience chambers where the Empress liked to meet her court.

It was very different from living in the Holdfast townhouse, Arrosa thought, as she gazed out at the panoramic view to the south. Thousands of people could fit inside the Blue Palace, and the floors were beginning to fill up with courtiers, officials, clerks and soldiers, not to mention the servants and the maintenance staff that kept the palace running.

Halfclaw soared past the Western Tower. The blue and green dragon was out most days, circling and swooping over the city and the Inner Sea, while Frostback regularly took Calpurnia for long flights over the Plateau. Each dragon had been assigned a multitude of staff to see to their needs, and they seemed happy with their quarters, though not as happy as the Empress, who was clearly delighted to be living in her new home.

The air shimmered behind her, and Cael appeared. He joined his wife and son on the balcony.

'I don't know when I'll find time to unpack,' Arrosa said. 'Our first full day in the new palace, and it's the day I'm leaving to travel to Athumia.'

'I have news about that,' he said.

'Yes?'

'Aye. Lucius has agreed to look after Cowie and the dogs for us. I'll be coming with you to Zamata, and then I'll be scouting Gunst, but not as part of the official delegation. Once I've ensured that the arrangements for the delegation's visit are in place, I'll be returning to Plateau City.'

'That's a pity,' she said, 'but Cowie will be glad to have you back.'

'The Empress wants me to get started on the Plateau's transition to democracy. The Ministry of the Plateau is to become the home of the province's new government, once elections have taken place.'

'That could be years away,' she said.

'Aye.'

'Have you checked in on Cole?'

'He's fine,' said Cael. 'He took a blow to the head during the riot, but he had some salve in his office. The people of Rainsby are hailing him as a hero, for putting out the fires in the harbour district.'

'Has his replacement been trained?'

'She has. I spoke to her when I visioned there this morning. She can reach Plateau City, and Cole reckons she's ready to take over.'

'Then he has no excuses to linger in Rainsby,' she said. 'I half-wondered if he would try to drag out his time there.'

'He still might,' he said. 'I saw something in his mind. I didn't mean to; I wasn't poking around or anything – but it was too clear to miss.'

Arrosa eyed him. 'What did you see?'

Cael gazed out over the Teal Garden. 'This is between us.'

'Of course.'

'Cole has developed feelings towards his replacement. I would be happy for him, if he wasn't about to leave her behind in Rainsby. I mean, it's about time he looked beyond himself.'

'Does she feel the same?'

'I don't know for certain, as I wasn't in her mind, but I would guess that she does.'

'How did you come to that conclusion?'

'From the way they were talking together, and from the way she was looking at him. I might be wrong.'

'What should we do about it?'

'What can we do? He has a Quadrant. He can still see her, if he wants to.'

The sound of barking arose from the hallway outside the apartment, and Arrosa smiled. Their door was opened, and a servant led in the three dogs. He unclipped their leads, and they ran at Arrosa and Cael, jumping up and wagging their tails in their excitement.

'Welcome to your new home,' Arrosa said to them.

Cael thanked the servant, who bowed and left, closing the door behind him. The dogs began to explore, sniffing the crates and furniture, and venturing into the other rooms.

'One benefit of having the dogs is that they will force us to leave the palace every day,' said Arrosa. 'Otherwise, we could stay in here forever, and forget what the outside feels like.'

'For their first walk,' said Cael, 'I was thinking of taking them over the bridge into the Eastern Tower, to introduce them to Frostback and Halfclaw.'

Arrosa smiled. 'That could be amusing.'

'For now, though, we'll have to take them downstairs to Lucius's apartment.'

'Which I notice is as far away from Kelsey's quarters as physically possible.'

'That was her decision,' he said. 'She needs to be next to the Empress, and she didn't want Lucius living anywhere near her.'

'For all her wisdom,' said Arrosa, 'your aunt can be a fool at times.'

'I thought you wanted them to be apart, to reduce temptation.'

'I am beginning to doubt if Lucius and your mother have a future together. But maybe you're right. At least my headaches will start to reduce.'

Cael picked up the luggage containing Cowie's things, then he called on the dogs. All three came bounding towards them, then they sat calmly, waiting.

'We are going to see Lucius,' Cael said to them. 'Come on.'

Cael and Arrosa set off, the dogs walking by their side as they left the apartment. They descended one flight of stairs, and came to the open front door leading to Lucius's new quarters. Old Caelius was sitting by the balcony, his old armchair having been transported from the townhouse, and the dogs ran up to him.

'Good girls,' Caelius said, as he scratched each one behind their ears. 'It's nice to see you, Mia, and you, Maisie; and yes, you, too, Millie.'

'Thanks for looking after them,' said Arrosa.

'It's no problem,' said Caelius. 'It'll get me out of this chair. How long do you think you'll be?'

'I will be away for ten days or so,' Arrosa said, 'but Cael should be back sooner.'

'I'll take Cowie and the dogs off your hands as soon as I return,' said Cael.

Caelius gestured to his live-in maid, and she walked forward. Arrosa kissed Cowie, then she placed her son into the woman's arms.

'I'm going to miss you,' Arrosa said, kissing the boy again.

Cael placed the large bag onto the floor. 'This has all of Cowie's things in it.'

'Thank you, sir,' said the maid.

Lucius walked into the room. 'How are you finding your new apartment?' he said.

'It's massive,' said Cael. 'I could get lost in it. I like that we're close to you, though, and to Rosie and Nestorian.'

'And Cole will be joining us soon,' said Arrosa. 'We can have our own little community overlooking the gardens and the Dragon Bridge.'

'Are you coming to see us off?' said Cael.

'I have too many things to do today,' said Lucius.

Arrosa felt an ache in the back of her head, but said nothing.

'We'd best leave you to it, then,' said Cael. 'I'll see you when I get back from Zamata.'

Arrosa kissed her dogs, then she kissed Cowie once more, before she and Cael left the apartment. Arrosa felt a tear spring from her eyes, and she wiped it away.

'Are you all right?' said Cael, as they made their way back upstairs to their quarters.

'Yes,' she said. 'This will be by far the longest time I'll have been away from Cowie. I wish I didn't have to go to Gunst.'

'It'll be over before you know it,' he said. 'And we have Zamata to visit first.'

Arrosa nodded. She decided to ignore the tightening knot in her stomach at the thought of visiting the island that had once been her home. It would be fine, she told herself.

An hour later, the delegation leaving for Athumia had gathered in one of the new audience chambers. It was smaller than the others, and had an excellent view over the waterfalls and trees of the private, upper gardens of the Empress. Brogan and Claudian were standing next to a great heap of luggage, and Cael and Arrosa joined them. Two dozen courtiers would be travelling with the party, and they had also assembled in the room. Some were genuine officials, while others were soldiers masquerading as courtiers, there to provide discreet protection to the delegates.

'I wish you all the best of luck,' said the Empress, who was seated upon a low platform, with Kelsey standing by her side; 'and I hope that your visit to Gunst bears fruit.'

'Not too much fruit, but,' said Kelsey. 'Don't be tempted to sign any treaty.'

'And pass on our regards to Lord Bailey,' said the Empress, 'and to President Bauchlie.'

'We shall represent the Empire to the best of our ability, Your Majesty,' said Brogan.

'How many Quadrants are you taking?' said Kelsey.

'Four, ma'am,' said Claudian; 'though that will be reduced to three once Cael returns here.'

'That should be enough,' said Kelsey. 'Don't hesitate to come back if you need to ask us anything, or if the food in Gunst happens to be terrible. Keep us updated, and bring us back some presents.'

'Yes, ma'am,' said Brogan. She glanced at Claudian, and nodded.

The Adjutant took out his Quadrant, then the delegates bowed before the Empress. Claudian activated the device, and the air crackled and spat. Arrosa prepared herself, then she gazed around. They were standing on the large lawn in front of the Dragon Palace in Igatz, the capital of Zamata. Claudian had already travelled there that morning to forewarn the government of their arrival, and a party of Zamatans was waiting for them, along with President Bauchlie.

'Welcome to Zamata,' said a courtier.

Bauchlie eyed Arrosa. 'Perhaps we should be saying *Welcome back*. It has been a long time, Arrosa.'

'It has,' she said. 'Might I introduce Chamberlain Brogan? I think she is the only one of our party you might not know.'

Bauchlie smiled. 'It is a pleasure to meet you again, Brogan.'

'I was last here during my short spell as Herald,' said Brogan.

'You were delivering imperial gold to pay for four new frigates, if I recall correctly,' said Bauchlie. He laughed. 'Those were the good old days, when the Empire showered this island with money. Your treasury has been a little more parsimonious of late, but we are forever grateful for all that you have done for us.'

'The independence and security of Zamata remains a vital part of our treaty with the Dominion, my lord,' said Claudian.

'And long may that continue,' said Bauchlie. 'If you like, I can put on a tour of all of the facilities that the Empire has paid for over the years, from the refurbished dockyards at Handshore Naval Base, to the new Chain Castles. Or perhaps you would like to visit the training academy for the Zamatan Army? You deserve to see where your gold was spent.'

'Perhaps tomorrow, my lord?' said Claudian. 'We have an appointment with Lord Bailey this afternoon.'

Bauchlie inclined his head. 'Tomorrow it is. Please come with me. I hope you are all hungry, as we have a feast prepared for you.'

Courtiers loaded the luggage onto carts, and the party followed Bauchlie and his officials into the white, marble-lined Dragon Palace.

'Is it the same as you remember?' Cael whispered to Arrosa.

'Yes,' she said.

'Does it feel like coming home?'

She shook her head. 'Zamata is not my home,' she said. 'I have too many bad memories of the island. Less than a mile from here, Dominion dragons slaughtered almost every Gunstian who lived on Zamata. I was glad to leave.'

They came to the vast, circular hall in the centre of the palace, and were shown to their seats by a long table. Bauchlie allowed Brogan to take the place of honour, as the highest-ranked imperial delegate, while Cael and Arrosa sat down next to Cisca, who embraced Arrosa tightly.

'I've been looking forward to this,' said Cisca, as she gazed at Arrosa. 'Sixteen years. You are looking very well, Arrosa. I hear that you have a son.'

'Yes,' said Arrosa. 'Cowie. He's two.'

Cisca smiled. 'Tell me; how is Lahnos? I still worry a little about him, and I still think of Leona.'

'Lahnos has withdrawn from public life,' said Arrosa, 'and we don't see much of him. He is with Lord Sigum, of course, and Ora'lya; and he has his own son to look after, when the boy's mother is away on duty with the army.'

'When did you last see him?'

Arrosa lowered her gaze. 'About six years ago. The death of his Bullan friends hit him hard.'

Cisca shook her head. 'Poor Lahnos has lived through more tragedy than anyone deserves. I am glad he has Lord Sigum. What is Ora'lya like?'

'She's from Dragon Eyre,' said Arrosa. 'I like her, but, you know. Lahnos is immortal now, and she isn't. His son is also mortal. There will be more pain in Lahnos's future – that's for certain.'

'He is always welcome to return here,' said Cisca.

Arrosa nodded, but she knew that Lahnos would rather jump off a cliff than return to Zamata.

The food arrived, delivered on a series of trolleys. Arrosa gazed at what was on offer, and began to wish she had stayed on the Star Continent.

. . .

Bailey was lurking in the shadows waiting for them when the feast was over. President Bauchlie wished the imperial party well for their state visit to Gunst, though Arrosa noticed that he barely glanced in Bailey's direction. Cisca embraced Arrosa again, then Bailey triggered his Quadrant, and the delegates and their luggage arrived by the main door of the monastery of Zamata Gataza.

'You have all been here before, I think,' said Bailey. He eyed Arrosa. 'Though, for some, it has been longer than others.'

Arrosa gazed up at the tall structure, and she frowned when she noticed the presence of dozens of black-clad monks.

'Yes, they're back,' said Bailey. 'I came to an agreement with the local religious order, and have allowed them to re-occupy much of the monastery. It was only fair. I kept the upper floors, though – they remain mine. And, of course, the remaining Serpent Eyes are under my control.'

'How many are left, my lord?' said Claudian.

'The mine beneath the monastery contains sufficient amounts for your needs, Claudian; you can be assured of that.' He smiled. 'Are you hungry?'

'You watched us eat the feast that Bauchlie provided for us,' said Cael.

'I know, but it was only polite to ask,' said Bailey. 'I haven't actually prepared anything for you.'

'Why are you wearing eye-guards?' Cael went on.

'Why do you think?' said Bailey. 'I knew you were coming, Mister Cael Holdfast, and I did not wish my thoughts to be disturbed.' He glanced at Arrosa. 'Was that a lie?'

'It was not,' she said, her gaze still on the monks.

'I haven't told them that a Gunstian would be calling round,' Bailey said, 'but they know where you are intending to visit next. How long will you be staying upon Athumia?'

'We are not entirely sure,' said Claudian. 'We are awaiting word from Great Gunst that they are ready to receive us, so we could be here for a few days. We hope that is all right with you, my lord; we wouldn't wish to inconvenience you.'

'It will be fine,' said Bailey. 'You can stay in the monastery for as long as you like. Do you have anything planned for your time on Zamata?'

'Chamberlain Brogan and I have agreed to tour the island's defensive facilities tomorrow.'

'Bauchlie can be quite persuasive, can't he?' said Bailey. 'I am sure you will have a wonderful time inspecting the new dockyards. Shall we move upstairs? I will find rooms for you and your staff.'

Brogan nodded her approval, and Bailey triggered his Quadrant. They arrived within the upper floors of the monastery along with their luggage. Bailey spoke to a few monks, who led the courtiers to their rooms, then the god gestured for Cael and the three imperial delegates to follow him. They came into a large, palatial chamber that looked fit for a king, and sat by the open balcony doors.

'I've had the place redecorated,' Bailey said, as he lifted a bottle of wine from an ice bucket. 'Now it reminds me of my old quarters on Implacatus – the ones I lived in before my sister created an entire world for me to rule. How times change. Wine?'

'Yes, please,' said Brogan. 'Shall we discuss our impending visit to Gunst? I would like to make it clear that we are not trying to keep this a secret from the Dominion. Furthermore, we intend to keep strictly to the terms of the treaty.'

'Save your breath, Chamberlain,' said Bailey, as he filled eight glasses, emptying the bottle. 'The Dominion already knows about your plans. In fact, if I am not mistaken…' He gestured toward the centre of the room with a flourish, but nothing happened. 'Damn,' he muttered. 'I was hoping that I had timed it correctly. Now I feel a little foolish.'

The air shimmered before anyone could speak, and three figures appeared in the middle of the room.

Bailey laughed as he got to his feet. 'You are ten seconds late, my friends.'

Everyone stood, as Edgar, Kyra and Elmhirst approached.

'Sister?' said Cael, his eyes wide.

Kyra smiled at him, then Cael hurried forward and threw his arms around her.

'I missed you, brother,' she said.

'Apologies for the unexpected visit,' said Edgar. 'I felt it best to greet you all in person.'

Claudian and Brogan eyed the arrivals with wary expressions. Lord Elmhirst glared back at them, and the room fell into an uncomfortable silence.

'Perhaps we should all sit,' said Bailey. 'I have poured wine for everyone.'

'Thank you for your hospitality, old friend,' said Edgar. 'Let me be clear – we are not here to cause any strife between us. Our intentions are honourable.'

They sat down, the imperial delegates sitting opposite Kyra and the three gods.

'This is cosy,' said Bailey. 'Please recall that Karalyn Holdfast herself appointed me as the arbiter of the peace; therefore, this will count as an official meeting between the Empire and the Dominion.'

'You have caught us off guard, Bailey,' said Brogan. 'You should have warned us.'

'The Imperial Chamberlain is correct, old friend,' said Edgar. 'You should have told them we were coming.'

'I love seeing both sides agree about something,' said Bailey; 'and I am delighted to have been the one to unite you. Before we get down to business, we should remember that Cael and Kyra have not seen each other in several years, not since the treaty was signed in Colsbury Castle.'

'Will you be staying in Zamata Gataza for long, brother?' said Kyra.

'For at least a few nights, it seems,' said Cael. 'We can't go to Gunst until we know they are ready to receive us.'

'Then might I also stay here, Bailey?' she said.

'Of course,' he said. 'Feel free. Did you know that Arrosa and Cael have a son?'

'I heard,' she said. She eyed Arrosa. 'Cowie, I believe?'

Arrosa nodded.

'He's two,' said Cael.

'I have two sons of my own,' said Kyra. She smiled. 'And yes, they are immortal.'

'Two immortal boys?' said Cael.

'It is wonderful to be a father again,' said Edgar.

'What are their names?' said Cael.

'Edward and Alfred,' said Kyra.

Cael frowned. 'I assume Edgar named them? They don't sound like Holdfast names.'

'I don't particularly see myself as a Holdfast any more,' she said, 'and I didn't see the point of continuing Granny Daphne's tradition of making their names sound as though they might be from Kell. Is that all right with you, brother?'

'Aye. Of course.'

Arrosa's head ached, but Cael was doing a good job of looking as though he was fine with his sister's decision.

'Did you use a Quadrant to get here?' said Arrosa.

'I have one,' said Edgar, patting his pocket, 'but Kyra brought us all to Zamata.'

'I have improved my ability to travel without a device,' said Kyra, 'and I don't need to steal anyone's powers to do so anymore.'

'Aila and her children will be happy about that,' said Arrosa.

Kyra narrowed her eyes.

Bailey chuckled. 'Now that we have caught up with family gossip, shall we move on?'

'I would like to discuss the proposed state visit to Gunst by members of the Imperial Court,' said Edgar.

'I thought you might,' said Brogan. 'We weren't attempting to keep it a secret from the Dominion. Her Majesty the Empress has made it clear that we are to conduct our business with Gunst with your full knowledge.'

'We appreciate that,' said Edgar, 'but might I ask – what does the Empire hope to achieve with this visit? You must be aware of the troubled history between Gunst and the Dominion.'

'We are aware that the Dominion has invaded Gunst three times,' said Brogan. 'We are also aware that the neutrality of Zamata acts as a safeguard to prevent any further aggression from the Dominion.'

'What once applied in the past is no longer the case, my lady,' said Elmhirst. 'We have our own Quadrants; we do not require Zamata as a staging post. If we wished to invade Gunst, we could open portals and send gods, dragons and whole armies of soldiers through.'

'But we have no intention of doing any such thing,' said Edgar. 'The Dominion is content at present with Inopei and Aucteran. I ask again – what does the Empire hope to achieve by visiting Great Gunst?'

'The establishment of a cordial relationship,' said Claudian. 'Surely, the Dominion cannot object to that.'

'And a defensive treaty?' said Edgar. 'Should the Dominion be concerned?'

'We do not intend to sign a defensive pact with Gunst, at present,' said Brogan. 'Would the Dominion complain to Karalyn if we did so?'

'The Dominion would not,' said Edgar. 'We have scrutinised the treaty agreed on Colsbury seven years ago. There is nothing in it to prevent either party from forging alliances with foreign entities. We would, however, be perturbed about where any such pact with Gunst may lead.'

'Please be more specific,' said Brogan. 'Do not dance around the subject.'

'Very well, Chamberlain,' said Edgar. 'Let me make this clear for you. If the Empire of the Sapphire Throne enters a defensive alliance with Gunst, and then Gunst decides to move its forces towards Irlan or Elso, the Dominion's response shall be robust.'

'You no longer have any claims to those lands,' said Claudian.

'True, but they remain our friends. Representatives from Irlan have already contacted Queen Famula in Nom Karta regarding this matter. Be in no doubt that the Dominion shall lend aid to its friends if Gunst attacks. Does the Empress wish to go to war over the Gunstian Empire's aggressive ambitions in Irlan?'

'Her Majesty desires peace,' said Brogan.

Edgar smiled. 'I am sure she does.'

Elmhirst snorted. 'This sounds like an attempt to encircle the Dominion.'

'Look at it from our point of view,' said Cael. 'The Gunstians approached us, not the other way around; and we are perfectly aware of the situation in Irlan. Nevertheless, we did not wish to insult the Gunstians by refusing to visit them. There are many things we could do to improve our relationship with Gunst that fall short of an alliance. Embassies, for example, or a Quadrant link to allow people and goods to flow between the two empires. None of this would adversely affect the Dominion.'

'Say that this is true,' said Edgar. 'Trade links sound reasonable, but would the Empire permit Gunst to purchase your advanced weaponry? We are aware of what your munitions factories are producing these days; would you allow the Gunstians to access this technology?'

Brogan's eyes tightened. 'Let us imagine that we would, for a moment. How would the Dominion respond?'

'Her Majesty Queen Famula would be disheartened, to say the least,' said Edgar. 'Seven years ago, the Holdfasts used explosives to attack the royal residences in Nom Karta, so the court there has some experience of the Empire's destructive capabilities. Your new Mark Seven Battanaras and your new mortars represent a considerable improvement on the weapons used that day. If the Dominion discovers that Gunst is in receipt of these weapons, we will take action to neutralise this threat.'

'How? Through the declaration of war?' said Brogan.

'Not at all, Chamberlain,' said Edgar. 'Instead, we would deploy gods with Quadrants to destroy any such weapons as soon as they arrive in Gunst. And then, you can complain to Karalyn, if you so desire.'

'Thank you for your honesty,' said Claudian. 'The imperial delegation shall take your words under advisement.'

'You are on a dangerous path,' said Edgar. 'Let us hope that sensible heads prevail. Kyra, my beloved, Lord Elmhirst and I shall now return to Nom Karta. I hope you enjoy your stay here.'

She kissed him. 'I shall be back in a few days, Edgar.'

Edgar and Elmhirst rose to their feet.

'It was a pleasure, Bailey, as always,' said Edgar. 'Keep us informed of any developments.'

Bailey stood, and he embraced his old friend. Edgar took out his Quadrant, and nodded to Elmhirst, who was gazing at the delegates with contempt.

Edgar triggered his device, and the two gods vanished.

'I hope that answered some of your questions,' said Bailey. 'Now you won't be able to say that you weren't warned.'

'The gods fear our new weapons,' said Cael.

'Of course we do,' said Bailey. 'I am old enough to recall a similar time in the past, when mortals invented machines and weapons that killed untold thousands of gods. We do not wish history to repeat itself.'

Kyra stood. 'Walk with me, brother. There's so much I want to tell you.'

Cael smiled and got to his feet. 'I would like that.' He glanced at Arrosa. 'I will see you a little later.'

Arrosa nodded, keeping her feelings to herself. She watched as Cael and Kyra left the room, then she picked up her glass of wine.

'I assume Lord Edgar was not lying about his threats,' said Claudian.

Arrosa sipped her wine. 'Every word he spoke was the truth.'

CHAPTER 16
LUCIUS CARDOVA'S DAY OFF

Plateau City, The Plateau – 9th Day, First Third Autumn 552

'Have a good day at school, children,' said Lucius. 'Study hard, and I will see you this evening.'

Caitlyn and Carden waved at him, then they allowed the tutor to lead them off to their new classrooms, which were located several levels above Lucius's apartment on the twenty-first floor.

Lucius stood by his front door, Arrosa's three dogs sitting quietly by his side. He and old Caelius had been out with them for their morning walk, just after sunrise, and they had taken the dogs across the middle bridge to visit the cavernous quarters of Frostback and Halfclaw. It had not gone well. Mia had barked until she was delirious, Maisie had whimpered with her tail between her legs, and only Millie had seemed unperturbed by the sight and smell of the two enormous dragons.

'Good morning, sir,' called a voice from the stairs.

Lucius turned, and saw Rosie and Nestorian coming down the steps.

'Good morning,' said Lucius. 'Have you both got a moment? I couldn't sleep last night, so I worked. I have something I want to discuss with you.'

Rosie smiled. 'As long as those big brutes don't eat us, sir.'

Nestorian crouched by the dogs. They approached him, and he scratched behind their ears.

'I think they are starting to get used to us,' said the former Banner sergeant.

'You should have seen them earlier, when I took them to visit Frost-back,' said Lucius. He gestured towards the door.

'I thought this was your day off, sir,' said Rosie.

'It is, but I still have a list of things to get through.'

They went into the apartment, the dogs trotting along behind them. Lucius led them into his new study, where crates of books sat amid the empty shelves.

'Excuse the mess,' he said. 'Take a seat.'

'I was wondering if you could settle an argument, sir,' said Rosie, as she and Nestorian sat down next to Lucius's desk.

'Go on,' said Lucius.

'When the Ascendants invaded Dragon Eyre,' she went on, 'they discovered that the natives were using explosive devices, yes?'

'That's right.'

'Why hadn't the technology spread to other worlds?'

'No one on Dragon Eyre had a Quadrant back then,' said Lucius.

'Then how did dragons get to other worlds, sir? There were dragons on Lostwell, and others on Athumia.'

'Gods would sometimes visit Dragon Eyre,' said Lucius, 'and rustle up volunteers to colonise different places. Dragon Eyre was known about, but most gods ignored it. As for explosives, no god wanted the knowledge of them to seep out to other worlds. When they invaded, they did their best to contain the secret from spreading. They concentrated every expert they could find on Ectus, and sealed them up inside the specialist facilities they had built there. Then, they tried to kill every native who knew how to produce the black powder. They didn't manage to do so, of course. The Unk Tannic retreated into their mountain caves, and they were still manufacturing their primitive devices right up to the end of the war.'

Rosie eyed her husband. 'Fine. You were right.'

Nestorian shrugged and smiled.

Rosie rolled her eyes. 'Don't let it happen again.'

'Coffee?' said Lucius.

'Thank you, sir,' said Nestorian. 'Was there something you wanted to ask us?'

Lucius filled three cups from a pot. 'Yes. Rosie and I have spoken about this before, briefly; it was about an idea she had come up with for a new weapon.'

Rosie raised an eyebrow. 'Is this about the miniaturised, handheld Battanaras, sir?'

Lucius nodded, then he set the coffees down in front of his guests. 'What does Director Ravi think of the idea?'

'He is in favour of it,' said Rosie, 'but, like us, he is aware that we don't currently have the facilities to build such a device.'

'I read through the list of requirements that you handed in,' said Lucius. 'New steam engines, new lathes, new mills, and a large quantity of steel and Tempest – this is going to be an expensive project.'

'Too expensive?' said Nestorian. 'Are we to cancel the work?'

'On the contrary,' said Lucius; 'Let Ravi know that I am approving the entire budget.'

'You are?' said Rosie, a big smile on her face. 'Thank you, sir.'

'Just so our ideas are aligned, sir,' said Nestorian, 'could you specify what it is that you need?'

'I want the research facility to build the Imperial Army a weapon that will replace the crossbow,' Lucius said; 'something that can be carried and reloaded by an individual soldier; something small and light enough not to be an encumbrance. The weapon needs to be less destructive than usual, designed to eliminate enemy personnel, rather than take down entire buildings or dragons. It needs to be accurate and reliable, with a longer range than a crossbow. Ideally, it should also be quicker to reload than a crossbow. And, naturally, the army would need a large quantity of these weapons – perhaps a hundred thousand of them. Is such a thing possible?'

'It is certainly possible,' said Rosie, 'but we have made little progress so far, beyond a few plans and designs. '

'How would it work?' said Lucius.

'We were thinking of using Ectus Powder to propel a small metal projectile out of a thin, rifled barrel,' said Nestorian.

'Do you remember we talked about a device with a barrel a foot-and-a-half long, sir?' said Rosie. 'It would be a scaled-down version of the Battanara. You would hold it in one hand, aim, and fire.'

'I must warn you, sir,' said Nestorian, 'that it won't be easy, and it might take a considerable amount of time to develop something safe and reliable. If we were free to liaise with the metalworkers of Adorati, then we might be able to make quicker progress. The Rakanese are moving ahead of us when it comes to all kinds of steel-making techniques.'

'But they aren't producing any weapons.'

'That is correct, sir; Adorati has no armaments industry to speak of, but we would need their expertise to be able to produce the parts we require for a handheld weapon.'

'I will make a few enquiries about involving experts from Adorati,' said Lucius. 'It doesn't matter if it takes a decade to produce something that the infantry can carry into battle – we must push onwards while we still possess an advantage over the Dominion.'

'We can get started on building a few prototypes as soon as the new equipment arrives,' said Nestorian. 'Once we have a working model that fits the specifications, we will then need somewhere to manufacture these weapons. Our current facilities are tied up with making Forty-Eighters, mortars and Mark Seven Battanaras.'

'I was thinking of Rainsby as a suitable location for a new facility,' said Lucius. 'The land there is cheap, it has an excellent harbour, and it would draw less attention compared to building a brand new factory in Plateau City.'

A servant knocked and entered the study.

'My Lord Constable,' he said, 'you have a visitor.'

'Yes?' said Lucius. 'Who?'

'One Killop Holdfast, my lord.'

'Send him in.'

The servant bowed and departed.

'We shall continue this discussion later,' Lucius said to Rosie and Nestorian; 'in fact, tell Director Ravi that I want to arrange a meeting with him to go over the details.'

'Yes, sir,' said Rosie.

Killop walked into the room, and Lucius got to his feet.

'It is good to see you, Killop,' he said. 'Please take a seat. 'Do you know Rosie and Nestorian?'

'I don't,' said Killop, as he sat.

'Rosie is Imperial Quartermaster, and her husband Nestorian also works for the government,' said Lucius, as he retook his own seat. 'Killop is the eldest child of Aila and Corthie.'

'It is nice to meet you,' said Nestorian.

Killop eyed them. 'Your names are familiar to me,' he said. 'You were both on Na Sun Ka when my father was killed. Aye?'

Rosie nodded. 'We were there.'

'Your father was a great man,' said Nestorian.

Killop's eyes darkened, then he nodded. 'Aye.'

'Was there something I could do for you, Killop?' said Lucius.

'Maybe; I don't know,' he said. 'I spoke to Arrosa a while ago about an idea I had, but I haven't heard anything about it.'

'What idea was this?' said Lucius.

'I don't want to go back to university for another year, but I would rather not return to Kell. I think I might need a break from my family. I love them, but we don't seem to agree on much.'

'Are you looking for a job?' said Lucius.

'Aye, but not with the imperial government,' said Killop. 'If I worked for the Empress, then my mother might never speak to me again. What I want... well, I want to get away from things for a while. Everyone at university knows who I am, and I want to find something different.'

'Wait – I remember this,' said Lucius. 'Arrosa brought it up during a session of the Imperial Court. You want to work on the Hold Fast estate; is that right?'

'Aye, that's right,' he said. 'Arrosa brought it up, did she? What happened after that? Did Holder Fast say anything about it?'

'She said she would think about it, but I don't know if it's been taken any further,' said Lucius. 'That particular meeting of the court had a lot to talk about, and your request might have been overlooked. So, you want to help Celine? Do you know anything about horses, or running an estate?'

'I helped out in Clackenbaird Farm for years. Arrosa said that Celine needs help.'

'She does,' said Lucius. 'She's had a run of bad luck when it comes to finding a suitable manager to replace her, and I believe the Holdfasts wish to keep it in the family. However, I would have to remind Holder Fast about it, as she owns the estate, and it would be up to her. Are you sure about this? Have you ever been to the Holdings?'

'No.'

'It's very different from Kell,' he said. 'There are no mountains anywhere near the Hold Fast estate, and the summers are extremely hot. Would you be there for long?'

'Not too long,' he said. 'A few decades, perhaps? No longer than a century.'

'Celine would certainly appreciate the assistance,' said Lucius.

'I would work hard, and I'm a quick learner,' said Killop.

'Might I ask – why did you approach me and not Kelsey about this? It will be her decision.'

Killop lowered his gaze. 'My family would be unhappy if I spoke to Kelsey,' he said. 'They blame her for my father's death. They blame you, too, but not as much; and they don't bear any ill will towards Celine.'

'Where are you staying at the moment?'

'I'm still in university accommodation, but I'll have to leave in a few days. They want my room for other students.'

'I understand,' said Lucius. 'I will speak to Kelsey today, and then someone will let you know.'

Killop stood. 'Thank you. I appreciate this.'

'I'm happy to help,' said Lucius.

Killop inclined his head, then he left the room, a servant accompanying him.

Rosie narrowed her eyes. 'Did he say *a century*?'

'He did,' said Lucius.

'He has young-god syndrome,' said Nestorian. 'Well, that's what I think. He knows he is immortal, but he can't quite accept it yet.'

'He seems nice, though,' said Rosie.

'Of all his siblings,' said Lucius, 'Killop is the most similar to his father, but without the confidence and bravado. Some of his brothers and sisters may be a little trickier to handle. Anyway, I'd better go upstairs to ask Kelsey about the Hold Fast estate.'

Rosie eyed him. 'Is she still... angry with you, sir?'

'She is.'

'She'll come round in time,' she said.

Lucius said nothing.

Nestorian got to his feet. 'I think that's our cue, Rosie. I had better get to work.'

The dogs stirred from their beds as Rosie and Nestorian left the room. Lucius remained where he was, preparing himself to venture up to the highest floors of the Western Tower of the palace. He wanted to see Kelsey, but their recent meetings had left him with a bitter taste in his mouth. For years, he had watched her unleash her acerbic tongue on others, but he had never imagined that he would be the target of her ire. He could take it, he told himself; his skin was thicker than most.

He stood, and the three dogs got to their feet, watching him expectantly.

'Come on, girls,' he said, and they followed him out of the apartment.

He walked to one of the steam platforms, and pulled on a rope. A bell sounded, and he waited. After a few moments, there was a grinding noise, and the door to the platform opened. A courtier was inside, and he bowed his head. Lucius led the dogs onto the platform, and the courtier slid the door shut.

'To where, my lord?' the courtier said.

'The Empress's private garden,' said Lucius.

The courtier nodded, then he pulled on a long lever, setting it for the upper floors. The platform began to move. The dogs had reacted badly the first time they had been on a moving platform, but they had grown used to it, and they sat patiently as they were lifted through the building.

The bell sounded again when the platform came to a halt, and the courtier slid the door open. Lucius thanked him, and led the dogs out into the upper gardens. They were on the lowest of the three floors taken up by the Empress's private quarters, and Lucius walked along a path by a fishpond until he came to Kelsey's rooms. He stopped by her office, and was about to knock when the door opened. Three Rahain in dark robes walked out of the room, tilting their heads to Lucius as they passed, and staying well clear of the dogs.

Lucius tapped the door with his knuckles, and entered.

Kelsey glanced up, and her expression soured.

'Oh. It's you,' she said. 'What do you want?'

'Could I have a minute?' he said.

'Make it quick.'

Lucius and the dogs went into the room, and he took a seat.

'Did I say you could sit?' said Kelsey.

'No,' said Lucius. 'I need to ask you about Killop.'

Kelsey frowned. 'What about him?'

'He visited me earlier, and he wanted to remind us about his desire to work on the Hold Fast estate.'

'I had forgotten about that,' said Kelsey. 'Why in Pyre's name would he want to live on the edge of a desert? It'll be too hot for a lad from Kell.'

'He doesn't want to go back to university. He wants a job away from both Kell and Plateau City.'

'What did you tell him?'

'That I would have to speak to you.'

Kelsey frowned, then she nodded. 'I will send word to Celine, and see what she thinks. If my aunt agrees, then I will work out the details.'

'Thank you. Killop is due to be evicted from his rooms in the university a few days from now, and...'

'I said I would take care of it.'

Lucius got to his feet.

'Wait,' she said. 'As you're here, there's something I need to tell you. It's probably nothing to worry about. Cole was in contact with Threeways yesterday; apparently Aila is looking for Cairney. The lad has gone missing.'

'Where was he last seen?'

'In Clackenbaird, obviously. He hasn't got a Quadrant, so he probably hasn't gone far. However, he is a demigod with death powers and battle-vision, so we'll need to keep an eye out for him. That was it. You can go now.'

'We could send Cael to look for him as soon as he's back from Zamata.'

'I will deal with it,' said Kelsey. 'The Empress asked me to let you know.'

'I made a mistake,' said Lucius.

'I'm not interested in hearing your excuses.'

'I thought it would be wrong for me to interfere with the plans that you and Shella were working on.'

Kelsey shrugged. 'Yet you still went behind my back to offer your suggestions to the Empress.'

'I spoke to her after I had tried to get you to listen to me.'

'You're a duplicitous, treacherous numpty, Lucius.'

'And you are a pig-headed, stubborn cow, Kelsey. Do you have any more names you want to throw at me?'

'I can think of a few. Arsehole, for instance.'

Lucius laughed.

'Is this funny to you?' she said. 'You were my best friend, Lucius, and you threw it all away.'

'The Empress ordered me to give my opinion.'

'And you couldn't wait to piss all over my plans,' she said. 'Admit it – you just don't want the ordinary folk to have a say in the running of the Empire.'

Lucius shook his head. 'Is that what you think? I support your plans, Kelsey; I was advising caution. If I was opposed to democracy, then why would I suggest giving the vote to everyone who lives in the Plateau? And why would I recommend setting up the Provincial Council? Have you learned nothing from the experiences of the City of Salve? One step at a time, not all at once.'

'You humiliated me.'

'Yes, and I am sorry about that. That was my fault. I wish I had spoken to you about this before it ever came to a vote in the Imperial Court. But, I didn't, and I would be angry with you if it was the other way around.'

He glanced down at the dogs, who were watching the exchange, the tension in the air making them wary.

'I am sorry I hurt you, Kelsey,' he said. 'Come on, girls; let's go.'

He turned to leave. He saw something move from the corner of his eye, and ducked as a heavy book flew past his head. The dogs started to bark.

'Fuck off and leave me alone!' Kelsey shouted, her eyes red.

Lucius gazed at the book she had thrown, then he ushered the dogs out of the room. A door opened by a cluster of beech trees, and the Empress emerged, flanked by Bedig and a few courtiers. Thorn's eyes widened in fear at the sight of the barking dogs. Lucius pulled a set of leads from a pocket, and clipped them to the collars of Arrosa's dogs, then he shortened the leashes, keeping them close to him.

'I have them under control, Your Majesty,' Lucius said.

The Empress eyed him. 'I think it is time that I had a little chat with you and my Herald, Lucius,' she said. 'Bedig, please take the dogs for a moment.'

'Yes, ma'am,' said Bedig.

Lucius handed the leashes to the Marshal, then he followed the

Empress back into Kelsey's office. Kelsey glanced up, then she got to her feet when she saw the expression on Thorn's face.

'This has to end, now,' said the Empress. 'I am growing tired of seeing the two of you constantly argue.'

Kelsey frowned. 'But...'

'Do you think I am deaf?' cried Thorn. 'I could hear you trading insults. This cannot continue. I rely upon my Herald and my Constable – my two most senior advisors and ministers, and if you cannot get along, then one of you will have to be replaced.'

'I apologise, Your Majesty,' said Lucius.

'Yes,' said the Empress, 'and I heard you say sorry several times to my Herald. However, it appears that Kelsey is not yet ready to forgive you.'

'I will step down from my post if I have become a hindrance,' said Lucius.

The Empress folded her arms over her chest. 'Is this what it has come to? I don't expect you to always agree with each other, but I do require a certain level of civility and decorum. I also realise that I am partly to blame. Had I not insisted upon hearing the opinions of everyone in the Imperial Court, then you two would still be friends.'

Lucius said nothing, and Kelsey averted her gaze.

'I am going to be painfully frank with you both,' the Empress went on. 'Kelsey – it is clear to me that you are not upset with the others who voted to postpone the reforms. You are still getting along well with Claudian and Slaeon, for example. Why are you treating Lucius differently? Don't answer – I already know the reason. And Lucius – why would you imagine that Kelsey would not wish to hear your advice? You have been close for twenty years – so close that I have occasionally found myself getting a little jealous of your relationship. Can you not admit how much you care for each other? It is obvious to everyone else. Kelsey – I want you to accept Lucius's apology; and Lucius – do better. Kelsey deserves more from you.'

The Empress fell silent, her eyes blazing as she stared at Lucius and Kelsey.

'Think on that,' she said. 'The next time I see you together in the Imperial Court, I will expect a more cordial approach to matters.'

The Empress turned, and left the room.

'Well,' said Kelsey; 'that's us told.'

'You are more essential to the running of the Empire than I am,' said Lucius. 'I will resign if you can no longer work with me. Claudian would make a good Constable, and there are plenty of decent officers who could take over his role as Adjutant.'

'Shut up, Lucius,' she said. 'I don't want you to resign.'

'What do you want?'

'For you to understand how I feel.'

'Say I did understand; then what? How can I make this up to you?'

'I don't know.'

Lucius held her gaze. He wanted to tell her how much she meant to him, that he loved her, but he forced the words to remain unsaid. Telling her something like that would likely result in another raging argument, in which Kelsey would accuse him of betraying Karalyn.

'I miss being your friend,' he said instead.

She nodded. 'I need to go back to work. Those Rahain who left my office before you arrived – they are the stone mages who helped build the new palace, and I need to look at a list of potential improvements they've drawn up.'

'All right. I will see you later. I'm meeting Van this afternoon; do you have a message you want to pass on?'

'Aye – tell him he's a dickhead. Wait; will his new wife be there?'

'I don't think so.'

'Good. I have a message for her, too, but I probably shouldn't say it out loud.'

Lucius left her office and closed the door. Bedig was waiting for him in the hallway, the three dogs sitting patiently next to him.

'Is everything all right, sir?' said the Marshal.

'It is what it is,' said Lucius, taking hold of the three leads. 'I will be out for the rest of the afternoon, so I will see you tomorrow.' He glanced down at the dogs. 'Let's go, girls.'

. . .

Two hours later, Lucius was sitting at an outside table of a tavern in the Kellach Quarter. The weather was still mild, the summer's heat lingering into autumn, and the dogs were lazing by his feet, their wary eyes on the other customers. He was looking forward to seeing Van, though the one topic he wanted to talk about was the one he most needed to avoid. How would Van react if he discovered that his oldest friend had feelings for his ex-wife? For that matter, how would Karalyn react? As far as he knew, Karalyn had not been in his mind for several years, but he wasn't sure if that meant she trusted him, or that she was no longer interested in what he thought about anything.

'Sorry I'm late,' said Van, as he entered the tavern's walled garden. 'Have you ordered?'

'I was waiting for you,' said Lucius.

Van sat, and gestured to a waitress.

'A bottle of red, and the lunch menu,' Van said to her.

The waitress narrowed her eyes.

'Are you forgetting where we are?' said Lucius. He eyed the Kellach waitress. 'Two ales, please.'

'Bloody Kellach,' muttered Van, as she walked away. 'You would think they would serve wine by now. So, how have you been?'

'Well.'

'I'm a little annoyed with your government at the moment,' said Van. 'I was perfectly happy with being the City's ambassador, and now I hear that the post is being abolished, to make way for some manner of Provincial Council. I think I am supposed to have to apply for a position on it, even though I have been ambassador for seven years. I suppose this was Kelsey's doing? I imagine she has done it to spite me.'

'I don't think she bears any grudge towards you.'

Van snorted. 'Did you tell her you were meeting me? How did she respond?'

'She called you a dickhead.'

'She can be a nasty piece of work,' said Van. 'Do you have any idea how much I regret my entire relationship with her? And all because of her blasted prophecy. That knocked my life off course for far too many years.'

'Come on,' said Lucius; 'I'm sure you don't regret having Calpurnia and Caelius. It wasn't all bad.'

Van fell silent as the waitress returned with two large mugs of ale, and a paper menu. Van picked up the menu, and started reading.

'How is Kate?' said Lucius.

Van eyed him from over the top of the menu. 'She wants to start a family.'

'Have you spoken to Calpurnia or Caelius about this?'

'Not yet, because I haven't decided if I want any more children.'

'Did you not discuss this before you got married?'

'We talked about it, but I didn't make any promises. The polite thing to do now would be to enquire about your own wife, Lucius, but I don't suppose you have seen her for some time.'

'Karalyn visited back in summer,' said Lucius.

'She *visited*? She visited her husband, children, and her own home? That doesn't sound very promising, Lucius.' He signalled to the waitress. 'I'll have the ribs.'

'The same for me, please,' said Lucius.

Van put the menu down. 'Do you ever think it was a mistake for us to get involved with two Holdfasts?'

'I don't dwell upon the past.'

'What about the future? Do you have a future with Karalyn?'

'She's distracted just now,' said Lucius. 'She's busy making new worlds with the Sextant, and she has no time for anything else.'

'Do you not feel abandoned? You have good grounds to divorce her, Lucius.'

'Did Kelsey abandon you when you were addicted to salve?'

Van stared at him.

'I apologise for that comment,' said Lucius. 'I'm a little touchy about my marriage to Karalyn at the moment. When I met her, she was powerful, but she was also mortal. Now?'

'Her immortality must have resulted in a few benefits,' said Van. 'Karalyn is our age, but she looks as young as Kate. When you're seventy, she will still be young and beautiful. She's the spitting image of Arete.'

'I preferred her before she became a god,' said Lucius. 'Shit – forget I said that. It's not her immortality or her new body that's the problem, it's that she doesn't seem to care about me any more. I can live with everything else, but how can I get past that?'

Van leaned across the table. 'Are you too frightened to divorce her? Are you afraid that she might lash out? She could reduce your brains to mush with a click of her fingers, or she could turn her death powers on you. Is that it?'

Lucius laughed. 'I'm not frightened of her.'

'Perhaps you should be.'

'Since when does Karalyn act violently towards anyone? She has the power to do so, but she never does. The last time she intervened, it was to stop Sable, Cael and the Empress from annihilating the leadership of the Dominion.'

'But wouldn't you feel better if you could move on with your life? I'm happier now than I have been in years. You've already admitted that you don't think she loves you. Maybe you should think about your own life, instead of hoping that Karalyn will return to the way she was. Did you know that a small sect in Plateau City has started to worship your wife? There are only a hundred of them or so, but they actually believe that Karalyn is a real god; a proper, all-powerful god, and they pray to her, asking her to watch over them. They've bought a building in the Rakanese Quarter, and are converting it into a shrine. A shrine, Lucius, to your wife. Where does that leave you?'

'I have Carden and Caitlyn to think about.'

'Of course – you are their father. You have taken on the job of looking after them on your own, and that is commendable; admirable, even. You will still be their father, no matter what happens between you and Karalyn. Tell me – what does Kelsey have to say about this? I don't particularly care about my former wife's opinion, but Kelsey is your friend, as well as Karalyn's sister. I would imagine that she has a few strong views on the subject.'

Lucius hesitated, reluctant to tell Van that he and Kelsey had fallen out over her political reforms. It was none of Van's business. He frowned. He had been fine with discussing Karalyn, but drew the line when it came to his relationship with Kelsey.

'She doesn't talk about it,' he said.

'I find that hard to believe,' said Van. 'She usually has an opinion about everything.'

The waitress returned, bearing two enormous plates of food.

'Thank you,' said Van, as she placed them onto the table.

The dogs looked up, attracted by the aroma of food.

'Be good girls, and I'll save you some,' Lucius said to them.

'They can't understand you,' said Van.

Lucius laughed. 'I know.'

'Do you know your problem, Lucius?' Van went on. 'You're too nice. Karalyn leaves you with the children, and you don't complain. Kelsey gets you to look after Caelius and Calpurnia, and you say nothing; and now Cael and Arrosa dump their dogs on you, and yet you don't raise any objections. I assume that you are also looking after Cowie?'

Lucius nodded. 'He's with his nursemaid today, but yes.'

'Do you ever think that you are being taken for granted?' said Van. 'Who looks after you, Lucius? Don't let the Holdfasts walk all over you. They will, if you let them.'

'Don't worry about me,' said Lucius, as he picked up his fork. 'I can look after myself.'

CHAPTER 17
FIRST OUTING

Jezra, The Western Bank – 1st Balian 3441

Fog had flooded the landscape, drowning the forest in a thick grey murk. Only the upper branches of the tallest trees were breaking through, along with the finished towers of the Fortress of the Exiles. Konna stared out at the view in silence from one of its turrets, adrift in a sea of swirling greys. Kell had periods of fog, but nothing that compared to what had descended upon the land of the City that morning.

'It's right on time this year,' said Maxwell. 'It turns out that we might have been able to attack another nest after all.'

Konna said nothing.

Maxwell eyed her. 'Will your brother be returning today?'

'I don't know.'

'He has been away for four days this time,' Maxwell went on; 'and he was gone for two days the time before that. I need my Quadrant back.'

'Then you shouldn't have given it to him.'

'You speak less like a Kellach when he's not here – did you know that?'

Konna narrowed her eyes.

'I'll have to ask one of the dragons to carry us back to Lower Jezra,' Maxwell said. 'Have you any idea how good they are at rooting out lies? What if they ask me where my Quadrant is? What am I supposed to say?'

'You'll think of something.'

'Your brother has been taking liberties.'

Konna laughed. 'You are two years older than Cairney, and yet you allow him to push you around. If you didn't want to lend him your Quadrant, you should have said so, to his face. There's little use complaining to me about it.'

Maxwell closed his mouth and looked away. Konna shook her head, savouring the return of silence. She knew that Maxwell wouldn't admit it, but he was scared of Cairney. There was something about Konna's sixteen-year-old brother that scared a lot of folk; something slightly unhinged in his eyes that acted as a warning.

'I suppose we could stay over in the fortress again,' said Maxwell.

'There's no hot water out here,' said Konna, 'and I've run out of clean clothes. I need a bath, and a warm meal. What are the chances that the greenhides will attack in the fog?'

'They've done it before,' he said. 'I wasn't here this time last year, but I heard that they probe the defences, looking for gaps.'

'Then we'll be fine if we go back to Lower Jezra for a while; the defences are solid. There's no way through, not until the Brigades resume work in winter. I also want to ask the officers about the new plan to drop explosives onto a nest from a dragon.'

'It'll never work,' said Maxwell. 'The dragons won't be able to find the exact locations of the nest in this, and no explosives will be able to penetrate deep enough to harm a queen.'

'I still want to go back, but.'

'Fine,' said Maxwell, his eyes tight.

'Shall we see if Seaspan is still down in the castle forecourt?'

'Where else would he be?' said Maxwell. 'He hasn't flown past us.'

'Don't be a prick about it,' said Konna. 'You'll get yer Quadrant back.'

Maxwell said nothing as they picked up their bags and descended the stone steps that ran down the inner wall of the high battlements. They entered the thick fog, and Konna felt the temperature drop. The rains of the first month of Sweetmist had been humid and warm, but the arrival of Balian had seen a chill sweep over Jezra; a chill that reminded her of home.

Seaspan was resting in the large forecourt, his head on his massive forelimbs. Work was still going on within the interior of the fortress, and the rear gatehouse was cloaked in scaffolding, as Brigade workers swarmed over it.

'Are there any greenhides to kill, immortal ones?' the dragon said, as Konna and Maxwell approached him. 'Have they emerged from the gloom?'

'If they have, then we couldn't see them,' said Konna. 'Listen, dragon – we were hoping that you might take us to Lower Jezra. We would be very grateful.'

The dragon eyed them. 'Why don't you use your Quadrant?'

'If I used a Quadrant every time,' said Maxwell, 'then I would never get to fly over Jezra.'

'But you will not see Jezra through the fog,' said Seaspan.

'Please?' said Konna. 'I would like to look down on the fog from above.'

'Very well,' said the dragon, lifting his head; 'since you asked so politely. Climb up.'

Konna smiled. 'Thanks.'

They walked round to the dragon's flank, and pulled themselves up onto the leather harness. They buckled the straps, as Seaspan stretched his wings.

'Are you ready, little godlings?' said the dragon.

'We are,' said Konna.

Seaspan launched himself into the air, and they were above the fog in seconds. The dragon circled as he ascended, and Konna looked down at the ocean of thick, grey mist. The high lines of completed outer wall were visible, along with the towers of the fort, but all else was lost.

Above them, the sky was clear and the air cold, and Seaspan circled one last time before speeding off to the west. They covered the open ground between the old defences and the half-built new ones, then the land fell away, dropping two hundred feet to the large town nestled at the bottom of the cliffs. Down in Lower Jezra, the tops of several brick buildings could be seen, while the streets were a grid of thick grey.

'Will the top of the Brigade Common Rooms be acceptable, godlings?' said the dragon.

'That would be great, thank you,' said Konna.

The dragon smiled. 'Such a courteous girl.'

Seaspan swooped down over Lower Jezra and alighted onto the flat roof of a large, square building. He turned his long neck to watch as Konna and Maxwell unbuckled the harness straps.

'I shall come back for you if the greenhides stage an attack,' he said to them.

'We'll be ready, dragon,' said Maxwell.

Seaspan stared at him.

Maxwell rolled his eyes. 'And thank you for bringing us here.'

'It was nothing,' said Seaspan.

Konna and Maxwell stepped down to the roof, and the dragon soared away.

'What's wrong with you?' said Konna. 'You should always remember to say please and thank you to a dragon. There are only two rules – don't lie to them, and be polite.'

Maxwell frowned as they went to the stairwell. They made their way through the building, and emerged into a street, where the fog lay thick and dense. They almost got lost trying to find their way to Maxwell's apartment, and they had to feel their way along a wall to locate the front door. They climbed the stairs to the right floor, and Maxwell took out his keys. He unlocked the apartment door and they stepped inside, to see Cairney sitting on a long couch. He had his boots up on a low table, and he was drinking from a tall glass.

'About time,' Cairney said. 'I was getting bored.'

Konna put her bag down. 'When did ye get here?'

'A couple of hours ago,' he said. 'We have shit to do.'

'I need a bath before I do anything else,' she said.

Cairney glared at her. 'But I have a whole fucking plan worked out.'

'Tough shit,' she said. 'Bath, coffee and food, and then I'll be ready.'

She walked off to the bathroom before her brother could make any further objections. She turned the taps of the bath, and held her hand under the stream of water as it heated up. She pushed in the plug, lit a lamp, and closed the door. She stared at her reflection for a few moments. Four days in the fortress had left her looking bedraggled, and she was grateful for some peace and quiet. She wondered what her brother was intending to do. It would be something stupid, no doubt; and she would have to stand up to him if it turned out to be foolish and reckless. People forgot how young he was; they looked at him and thought they were talking to an adult, rather than a sixteen-year-old boy.

She shook her head. For a while, she would be able to sink into her hot bath and forget about anything else. Cairney could wait.

An hour and a half later, Konna emerged from the bathroom, wearing a fresh set of clothes, with her damp hair tied back. Cairney narrowed his eyes as he saw her, while Maxwell was sitting across from him, his features despondent.

'Do I have yer permission to go over the plan now, sister?' Cairney said. 'Is that all right with you?'

Konna walked to a side table. Maxwell had either made or ordered coffee, and she filled a mug.

'I can't wait to hear it, brother,' she said. 'I'm giddy with anticipation.'

'Cow.'

'Prick.'

'Can we talk like civilised people?' said Maxwell. 'Where have you been for four days, Cairney? I need my Quadrant back.'

'Shut yer face, Maxi-boy,' said Cairney. 'Ye'll get it back when I don't need it. And I've been to loads of places. I was looking for the perfect target, and I've found it. But first, we'll need to collect Esher.'

'That's not a good idea,' said Maxwell. 'People will notice if he goes missing.'

'We'll put him back when we're finished with him,' said Cairney. 'Nobody will notice.' He got to his feet and pulled out the Quadrant. 'Let's go.'

Maxwell stood, and Cairney activated the device. The air shimmered, and they appeared in the building where Draughtsman Reece worked, Konna still holding on to her mug of coffee. Unlike their previous visit, the large chamber was full of others all working on the plans for the Jezran Walls. A few glanced up, but they recognised Maxwell, and no one seemed concerned by their sudden appearance. Esher was at his usual desk in the corner, keeping his head down as he worked.

'Hey, Konna,' said Cairney. 'Go up to Reece and tell him you want to talk to him for a minute.'

'Why me?' she said.

'Cause yer a girl,' he said. 'It'll look less suspicious.'

She raised an eyebrow.

'Lead him out into the hallway,' Cairney went on. 'We cannae make him vanish in front of everyone else, can we?'

'Fucksake,' Konna muttered. 'Fine.'

She walked into the large room, making her way between the rows of desks until she reached Esher. She stood next to him for a moment, but he ignored her presence.

'Good morning,' she said.

'I'm busy.'

'Can I talk to you alone, please?'

'Why?'

'I'll tell you if you come with me.'

Esher sighed and put down his pencil. 'Is it important?'

'Aye.'

'Make it quick,' he said, as he stood.

He followed her out of the large room, then he frowned as he caught sight of Maxwell and Cairney. He opened his mouth to speak, then Cairney grinned and swiped his fingers over the Quadrant. The air around them crackled, and they appeared amid palm trees, a hot sun blazing down from a clear blue sky.

Esher's eyes widened, and he took a step back.

'Have a wee nap,' said Cairney, staring at him.

Esher stumbled on the sand, and collapsed, his eyes closed.

'Where are we?' cried Maxwell.

'Have a guess, Maxi-boy,' said Cairney, as he knelt by Esher's unconscious body. He prised open one eye, and gazed into it.

Konna eyed her brother. 'What are ye doing now?'

'Ye'll see,' said Cairney. 'I've never actually tried this before, but it should work.' He stared into Esher's open eye. 'Your powers are unblocked.'

'What are you doing?' Maxwell shouted. 'Are you insane?'

'I'm getting a wee bit tired of yer whinging,' said Cairney. He raised a fist, and punched Esher on the nose, breaking it. Blood streamed from his nostrils, then his face healed again. Cairney laughed. 'I am a fucking genius. I knew it'd work.'

Konna knelt next to him. 'Are ye telling me that his self-healing is working again?'

'All of his powers should be working,' said Cairney. 'Did ye not hear what I said to him?'

'That cannae be right,' she said; 'not through yer voice alone.'

'Karalyn can do it.'

'What?'

'Karalyn's voice can command folk,' Cairney went on; 'and she's supposed to have every dream mage power. This is the only one I've inherited; but it's a fucking beauty.' He reached into a pocket and withdrew a small glass vial. 'Now for some of this.'

'Is that salve?' said Maxwell.

'Aye,' said Cairney. He opened Esher's mouth, then he pulled the stopper from the vial.

'Stop,' cried Maxwell. 'You can't give him salve. He'll...'

'Shut yer gob,' said Cairney, then he tipped the contents of the vial into Esher's mouth.

Konna watched as Esher shuddered on the sand. Nothing else happened for a moment, then his appearance began to alter. The grey streaks in his hair vanished, then the tired lines around his eyes smoothed themselves.

'I hope I didnae give him too much,' said Cairney; 'I dinnae want him looking like a twelve-year-old.'

Konna stared as Esher continued to look younger. His handsome looks became more boyish, and she found herself agreeing with Cairney.

'It's stopped,' said Maxwell. 'Shit – now he looks the same age as me. What have you done?'

'I've restored him to his prime,' said Cairney.

'I thought he looked better as he was,' said Konna.

'You two are missing the point,' said Maxwell. 'Salve's ability to de-age someone is irreversible. How can we put him back if he looks twenty years younger?'

Cairney blinked, as though he hadn't considered that.

'Malik's ass,' groaned Maxwell. 'We'll get blamed for this. People in his office saw us lead him away; well, they saw Konna lead him away.'

'Then we don't go back to Jezra,' said Cairney. 'We'll keep moving.'

Konna sat on the sand. She felt guilty for having tricked Esher into following her, and she was reluctant to give her brother free rein over the last Ascendant.

'You should block his powers again,' she said. 'For now, at any rate. He might freak out when he wakes up; who knows what he'll do? Where are we, exactly?'

'We're on a tiny island near Olkis,' said Cairney. 'It has a spring with fresh water, but there's no food. Anyway, I'm not about to seal up his powers again; not yet. Esher has something to do for us first.' He prised open one of Esher's eyes again, and stared into it. 'I am going to wake you up soon,' he said. 'When ye awaken, you will not panic, or try to run away, and ye'll not try to hurt us. We are yer friends. Wake up.'

Esher groaned and opened his eyes. He glanced up at Konna and Cairney, then he saw where he was.

'Stay calm,' said Cairney. 'Your name is Esher.'

'What? No. That's not my name. Where am I?' He sat up and rubbed his head, then he looked at his hands. 'Something's changed about me.'

'Ye feel healthy, aye?' said Cairney. 'No aches and pains?'

'How did you know that?' said Esher. 'What have you done to me?'

Cairney smiled. 'We have restored ye to the way yer supposed to be. It was the jealous mortals in the City who stole yer powers and yer youth. We couldnae stand by and watch ye suffer like that.'

Esher said nothing.

'Do ye remember telling us that ye didnae fit in? That ye felt ye were in the wrong place?' Cairney went on. 'Ye were right. The mortals destroyed yer memories, and then they turned off yer god powers.'

'God powers? I'm not a god.'

'My brother's right,' said Konna. 'You are a powerful immortal. We are also immortal. We want to help you.'

'Have ye heard of the Ascendants?' said Cairney.

Esher frowned.

'You're one of them,' said Konna. 'You are Esher, the Ninth Ascendant.'

Esher started to laugh. 'You three are starting to worry me. Take me back to Jezra; I have work to do. I don't want to play these games.'

'It's no game,' said Cairney. 'There's a wee stream just past those trees, and there's a pool. Go and look at yer reflection.'

Esher seemed confused, but he got to his feet. He eyed Maxwell, who gave him a shrug; then he walked towards the stream. The others followed him, and they stopped by the banks of a pool next to a tumbling waterfall. Esher gazed down into the waters, and his mouth opened.

'I'm... I'm young again.'

'Ask yerself,' said Cairney: 'how could that be possible? What's the only way to look young again?'

'No.'

'It's true,' said Konna. 'Eighteen years ago, you invaded the City of Salve with a Banner army. You were captured, and Karalyn Holdfast destroyed yer memories. For eighteen years, you have believed yourself to be a mortal from Lostwell, but it's not true.'

'Have you drugged me?' said Esher, his composure starting to crack.

'Stay calm,' Cairney repeated. 'I know this is a shock, but don't panic. Don't get agitated.'

Esher turned to Maxwell. 'I don't know these other two, but I've seen you dozens of times before. Are they lying to me?'

Maxwell shook his head. 'It's all true.'

'I'll prove it to ye,' said Cairney, then he pulled out a small knife and stabbed Esher in the face with it.

Esher cried out, then he staggered backwards, his hands going to his face. He came to a halt, his fingers going over the place where the wound had already healed.

'I feel no pain,' he said. 'Am I hallucinating?'

'It's all real,' said Cairney. 'Try to use yer powers – ye have them all: death, fire, vision, stone and flow. Hold out yer hand and make a spark; or try to read Maxwell's mind.'

'Why my mind?' said Maxwell.

'Cause me and Konna's minds are shielded, ya daft twat,' said Cairney. 'We're Holdfasts.'

Esher looked at Maxwell. 'How do I do it?'

Maxwell frowned, then he put his hands to his head and screamed. He fell to his knees, then onto the ground, and convulsed.

'Stop it,' Konna shouted. 'Esher – stop it.'

'I'm sorry,' cried Esher.

They all stared down at Maxwell, who was trembling next to the pool.

'My thoughts have been battered,' Maxwell whispered.

'I didn't mean to hurt you,' said Esher. 'This can't be happening.'

'Oh, it's happening,' said Cairney. 'This is the first day of your new life, Esher; and there's no going back.'

Esher sank to his knees by Maxwell, and wept. Cairney frowned.

Konna put a hand onto Esher's shoulder. 'You're going to be all right,' she said. 'Don't be frightened.'

'I want to go home,' he sobbed. 'I want to go back to Jezra.'

'Fucking pansy,' muttered Cairney.

'Shut up, brother,' said Konna. 'Try to imagine what he's going through. Everything he knows about himself is a lie.'

'The Ascendants were evil,' said Esher. 'Everyone knows that.'

'Some of them were terrible and cruel,' said Konna. 'You don't have to be like that. You can be whoever you want.'

'I want to be Reece,' he whispered.

'You hated being Reece,' shouted Cairney. 'Ye hated yer life – ye told us so. How many friends does Reece have, eh? Esher has three friends – us three standing here. An hour ago, ye were sad old Reece, lonely and miserable. Now, yer the Ninth fucking Ascendant, the most powerful god in existence. A wee bit of gratitude wouldnae go amiss.'

Maxwell got back to his feet. 'What do we do now?'

Cairney smiled. 'Esher is going to carry out a wee task for us,' he said, 'by way of a thank you.'

'What task?' said Esher.

Cairney stared into his eyes. 'Say nothing and listen. There are two dragons on an island that you are going to kill for us. One of them is from the Eastern Rim, and the other is from Athumia. They're on Dragon Eyre to talk about an agreement between the dragons of both worlds; and you're going to put a stop to it.' He held out the Quadrant. 'Watch my fingers,' he went on, as he moved his hand over the surface. 'Copy what I just did, then do this to get back here. Did ye get all that? The dragons are alone on the island. Kill them both, and make sure of it. Do you understand?'

Esher nodded.

'Leave no clues behind,' Cairney went on, 'and say nothing while yer there, just in case anyone is listening. Come back here as soon as they're dead.'

'I understand,' said Esher, his eyes hazy.

Cairney gave him the Quadrant. Esher stared at it for a few moments, then he swiped his fingers over it, and vanished.

'Pyre's arse, brother,' said Konna; 'what have ye done?'

Cairney shrugged. 'It's just the first step in my plan. The Dominion will blame Dragon Eyre, and Dragon Eyre will blame the Dominion.'

'What two dragons were you talking about?' said Maxwell.

'The dragon from Athumia is called Lord Limnan Mon Limonen,' said Cairney. 'He was sent in secret by the Dominion to start talks with Honeytail of Throscala. If the talks succeeded, then the dragons of the two worlds would come closer together.

'And how is that a bad thing?' said Maxwell.

'I couldnae give a shit if it's good or bad,' said Cairney. 'The point is to stir up trouble between the Dominion and the Empire, so that Karalyn comes down and punishes both sides. That's why we're here. Do ye never fucking listen to anything I say?'

Konna turned and walked away, leaving Maxwell and her brother standing by the pool. She went past the little clearing where they had arrived, and walked through the line of palm trees and onto the long, golden beach. She folded her arms across her chest and stared out at the waves crashing against the shore.

Part of her was disgusted by what Cairney had done. He hadn't freed Esher, he had turned him into a weapon, one he could manipulate into killing two dragons. Konna had seen the fear and confusion in Esher's eyes, and she felt pity for him. As for Cairney's plan, it went against all of the advice Uncle Naxor had given them. He had told them over and over again to be patient; to wait for an opportunity, and not to do anything rash that might provoke the anger of the other Holdfasts.

'What's the matter with you?' said Cairney.

'No wonder you didnae tell Ma or Uncle Naxor what ye were thinking of doing,' she said.

'They would have tried to stop me.'

'Karalyn is going to kick our arses for this.'

Cairney laughed. 'No, sister, she won't, because she'll have no idea that we were behind it. Just wait and see. Queen Famula and Edgar of the Dominion will be raging when they find out that their dragon emissary has been murdered on Alef. Queen Blackrose will also be furious – ye know what dragons are like. Each side will demand revenge, and by the time Karalyn gets involved, no one will care how it all started.'

'Yer plan is full of holes, but,' she said. 'We cannae take Esher back to Jezra, because we gave him salve, and folk are going to ask questions. I was the last person anyone saw him with. What am I supposed to say?'

'Ye don't have to go back to Jezra.'

'Then they'll definitely suspect us. Maxwell and I will have to go back, or someone will raise the alarm, and everyone will be hunting us. Ye don't think things through, Cairney; ye never have.'

'At least I'm trying to do something!' he shouted. 'I'm the only one trying to get revenge for Da; does nobody else care?'

'If ye wanted my help, ye should have told me yer plan. We could have talked it through, and worked out any problems; but no. Ye had to do it all yerself. If ye hadnae given him salve, then we could have put him back, wiped his memories, and no one would have known a thing.'

'Aye, all right; I fucked up with the salve – but we can fix it. I know – tell them that ye spoke to Esher and told him who he was, and he ran away. Ye'll get into a wee bit of trouble, but then they'll be looking for Esher, not us. And I'll make sure no one finds him.'

'He's back!' cried Maxwell, from the trees. 'Esher's back.'

Konna and Cairney hurried into the clearing. Esher was staring at his bloody hands, the Quadrant lying on the sand by his feet. Cairney swooped down and picked up the device, and wiped the blood from it with a sleeve.

Konna walked up to Esher. 'What happened?'

'I have battle-vision,' he whispered.

'Of course ye do,' said Cairney. 'Is that how ye killed them?'

'I broke their minds first,' said Esher. 'I went into their heads, just like I did with Maxwell, and I hurt them both. They were thrashing about on the ground, screaming in agony. I tried to use death powers, but I don't know how, so I… I picked up a long branch, from a tree they had knocked down, and I rammed it into the eye of one. I pushed it in so far… until it snapped. For the other one, I lifted a great boulder, and smashed in its skull.'

'And both dragons are definitely dead?' said Cairney. 'There's no doubt?'

'They are dead,' said Esher. 'I murdered them.'

'Did anyone else see ye?'

'No. They were alone, on a beach, lying out in the sun. There was so much blood.' He walked to the pool, knelt, and lowered his bloody hands into the water. 'Why did I do it? I don't understand.'

Konna stared at him, feeling nothing but guilt and shame for her part in what had happened. She tried to harden her heart. Esher would recover, and perhaps Cairney's plan would work. Didn't she yearn for revenge against Kelsey and the Empress? If Karalyn had to stop another war between the Empire and the Dominion, then wouldn't she be likely to remove Thorn from power? To see Thorn and Kelsey humbled would justify a few deaths. Besides, mortals came and went, and their lives didn't hold as much meaning as… She stopped herself. Did she really believe that the life of a god was worth more than that of a mortal? Uncle Naxor had told her that many times – he believed it, and Cairney also seemed to believe it. Did she?

'Nap time,' said Cairney, and Esher toppled over, landing on the ground next to the pool. Cairney glanced at Konna and Maxwell. 'I'll take ye both back to Jezra now, and then I'll come for ye when it's time for Esher's next wee adventure.'

'Where will you and Esher be?' said Maxwell.

'I'm not going to tell ye that,' said Cairney. 'If ye don't know, then ye won't be able to tell anyone else.'

He activated the Quadrant, and they appeared in the sitting room of Maxwell's apartment in Jezra.

'Mind and behave yerselves,' said Cairney, then he vanished.

Maxwell sat down and put his head in his hands. 'Your brother is insane.'

'He's angry,' said Konna; 'he's always been angry.'

'He's going to get us locked up, or worse.'

'Not if you remain calm,' said Konna. 'Let me deal with Reece's disappearance, and we say nothing about Cairney. Agreed?'

Maxwell turned to gaze at her. 'I'm too frightened of your brother to say anything.'

'I know,' said Konna. 'That fear will keep us safe.'

'Aren't you scared of him?'

Konna snorted. 'I'm frightened of a few things, but my wee brother isnae one of them.'

CHAPTER 18
SECRETARIAL DUTIES

Rainsby, Southern Plateau – 12th Day, First Third Autumn 552

'The happiest time of my life?' said Cole, as he sipped from his mug of tea. 'I'm not sure.'

'Try to remember,' said Alva.

She was sitting next to him on the roof of Madden's Tower, and she had been asking him all kinds of personal questions. Some he had refused to answer, while he had enjoyed talking about others with her. She was easy to talk to.

'All right,' he said. 'This is a difficult one, because it came right before the saddest time of my life.'

'Go on.'

'My mother, my Aunty Celine and I had been on the run from soldiers and gods sent by the Ascendants. They were combing the Holdings looking for mages to kill, and I was on their list of targets.'

'That doesn't sound very happy, Cole.'

'I'm getting to it,' he said. 'Remember that I had spent almost all of my life up to then in the Holdings. Anyway, we were found and rescued, and taken all the way down to Kell. My cousins Cael and Kyra were there. I hadn't seen all that much of them over the years, and the adults were busy with the war, so the three of us were left to our own devices.'

He smiled. 'We had a great time, playing on the farm, and running through the fields. Clackenbaird was full of soldiers, and they used to wave at us and say hello. The farmhouse was overcrowded, but we didn't mind.' His smile faded. 'And then... Everyone knows what happened after that.'

'Your parents were killed?'

Cole stared out at the view of Rainsby. The sun was setting, and the waters of the Inner Sea were streaked with reds.

'It sounds terrible,' he said, 'but I hardly mourned my father. I didn't know him. He left when my mother was pregnant with me, and she brought me up until I was nine. That's how old I was when they were killed. I went back to the Holdings with Aunty Celine, but all I could think about was the last time I had seen my mother. A god killed her in front of me, for nothing. He was angry because Kyra had used her Quadrant, and he wanted to lash out at someone. He chose my mother. She was holding on to my cousin Konna at the time – she was just a baby. My Aunty Celine tried her best to look after me on the Hold Fast estate, but she was also grieving, and the next few years were the worst I have lived through.' He eyed Alva. 'Sorry. You asked me about a happy time, and I've piled misery upon you.'

She took his hand. 'I can't begin to imagine what you went through, Cole. Did you stay on the Hold Fast estate for long after that?'

'For another ten years,' he said. 'Aunty Celine wanted me to take over as estate manger, but the place holds too many memories. I went to university, and then I joined the army. I still feel bad about leaving Aunty Celine on her own up there. I mean, she's not on her own, but she has no family around her.'

'Doesn't she have any children?'

'No. She was married to my grandmother's brother, but he died a long time ago. The Holdfasts adopted her after that. I thought you knew all about my family.'

'I'm not sure I even mentioned Celine in my class project about the Holdfasts,' she said.

'That's a pity,' he said. 'She's one of the nicest people you'll ever meet. But, of course, she doesn't have any mage powers, and she isn't immortal, so people tend to forget about her.'

'Maybe you could take me to visit her. We still have three days before I am due to take over your role here in Rainsby, and I can reach Plateau City with my vision powers. What else should we do with our time?'

Cole could think of something, but he wasn't about to say it out loud. They were friends, he told himself; and he mustn't ruin it.

'You have a strange look in your eyes,' she said; 'one that's far from harmless.'

Cole frowned.

'Do you recall what I called you on the first day we met?' she said. 'I told you that you were known as the *harmless* Holdfast. I wish I'd never said that.'

'I had forgotten.'

'Well, I take it back.'

He shrugged. 'It's probably accurate.'

'No. You don't like causing harm, but that's not the same as being harmless. You fight, when you need to.'

He glanced away. He wasn't fighting for her, even though he wanted to. He was dreading the coming days, when he would have to leave to go to Plateau City, and they would be separated, but he had done nothing to try to change that outcome.

He stood, and extended his arm.

'Are we going somewhere?' she said.

He took out his Quadrant, then he pulled her up with his free hand, and she smiled.

He moved his thumb over the copper surface, and they appeared by the rear porch of the Hold Fast mansion on the estate. The sun was beating down onto the rolling plains, the grass a dull brown after the unremitting weather of the summer that had just passed. Cole filled his lungs with warm Holdings air, then he turned and saw Celine sitting out on the porch. By her was a young man, and Cole narrowed his eyes.

Celine got to her feet. 'Cole!' she cried, as she came down the steps. She eyed Alva. 'And who is this young lady?'

It was then he realised that he and Alva were still holding hands.

'This is Miss Alva Longhold, Aunty,' he said.

Should he remove his hand from hers? Alva was making no move to separate their fingers, and he didn't want to embarrass her by yanking his hand away.

'One of the Longholds?' said Celine. 'Are you related to the Holder?'

Alva curtsied, and in the process, her hand came apart from Cole's. 'He is my uncle, ma'am.'

'Ah, your uncle,' said Celine. 'Come up onto the porch and sit. I was just welcoming Killop to the estate.'

They went up the stairs and under the shade of the porch. Killop was sitting in a chair, and he stood.

'Cole,' he said, inclining his head slightly.

'Cousin,' said Cole. 'What brings you here?'

'Sit first,' said Celine. She beamed as they all took seats. 'Killop is looking for a job on the estate,' she went on. 'He's left university, and he's keen to try something new. So, Cole, tell me about you and Miss Longhold.'

'I've been training her to replace me in Rainsby,' he said.

'Yes, and?'

Alva eyed him. 'Cole's a little shy about it, ma'am,' she said, 'but we've been seeing each other for a little while. He wanted to come here to tell you.'

Celine dabbed her eyes with a handkerchief.

'Please excuse an old woman's tears,' she said. 'This makes me very happy. Tea?'

Alva smiled. 'That would be lovely, ma'am. Thank you.'

An hour later, Cole and Alva appeared in his office in Rainsby. They glanced at each other, and laughed.

'Did I do the right thing?' Alva said. 'I couldn't think of any other reason why we might have been holding hands. *We're just friends* would have sounded awkward.'

'I don't think I've ever seen her so happy,' he said, as he sat by his desk.

'She wants the best for you,' Alva said. 'She looked after you for ten years, Cole. If I were her, I might have been a little worried about you – all alone in Rainsby, cut off from the rest of your family. You were right, though; she seems very nice. Your cousin looked... how do I put this? He looked as though he didn't want us to be there.'

'I guess he wanted to make an impression on Aunty Celine, and then we arrived to steal all of the attention. Still, I have no idea why he would want to live on the estate.'

'Then you're not angry with me for what I said?'

He eyed her. 'Why were we holding hands?'

'That is a very good question, Cole,' she said. She looked hesitant, then she exhaled. 'All right; I'm going to say it. I figure that if this goes horribly wrong, then we'll only have three days to get through before you leave. Audrey will kill me for telling you this, but here goes – I like you, Cole. Yes, I know I'm being unprofessional, and I didn't mean or want it to happen, but you... I like being with you, and I had to tell you. Will you visit me when you go to Plateau City?'

Cole stared at her.

Alva's shoulders sagged. 'I had to try,' she said. 'The first time I have been forward with a man, and I've made a complete fool of myself. Can I leave work early today? And please don't tell my sister what I said.'

Cole stood. 'Wait, Alva. Did you mean that?'

'Of course I meant it. I decided I had to tell you when we were sitting on the porch of your family mansion. It felt right. Clearly, I was wrong, and now I feel...'

He took her hand. 'You weren't wrong. I feel the same, except...'

'Except what?'

'I was worried about ruining our friendship.'

She gazed up at him.

'Let's not be friends,' he said. 'Let's be more than that.'

She closed her eyes, and he leaned down to kiss her. As their lips were about to touch, a man appeared in the room next to them.

'Oops,' said Bedig. 'I may have arrived at an inopportune moment.' He laughed. 'Don't you two work together? Cole, you old rogue; is this the kind of thing that goes on down here when I'm not paying attention?'

Cole and Alva eyed him.

'Lord Marshal,' said Cole; 'might I explain?'

Bedig waved his hand. 'I don't care what you do, Cole; you know me. And I'm not the Lord Marshal, not any more. Today's the day, Cole. As of this moment, you are the new Imperial Secretary, and Cael is the new Lord Marshal. Fenu has replaced Shella as Chancellor, but they haven't found a new Chief of Staff yet.' He sat. 'Do you have any whisky?'

'I have some brandy, I think, sir,' said Cole.

'Don't call me sir. I am now the Imperial Legate to the Eastern Rim and, technically, you outrank me. I should be calling you sir.' He smiled at Alva. 'I hear you're ready to take over in Rainsby. You will be reporting directly to Arrosa Holdfast from now on. She will be in contact at some point over the next third or so.'

'I thought we had three days left,' said Cole. 'You're three days early.'

'The Empress felt no need to wait, not if Alva is ready to assume your old role. She wants you in the capital, Cole. Coming here to collect you is my last official act as Marshal. Have you packed?'

'Not yet.'

'How long do you need?' said Bedig. 'The Empress has something she wants you to do right away.'

Cole frowned. 'Might I ask what that is?'

Bedig glanced at Alva. 'I suppose I'd better confirm you in your position as well, Lieutenant Longhold. Officially, you are now an imperial agent. Well done. That means you can stay in the room while I brief Cole. Take a seat, both of you.'

Cole and Alva sat.

'People get the wrong impression when they hear the title *Imperial Secretary*,' Bedig went on. 'Some might imagine that the job entails taking down notes at meetings and so on; but I don't think Cael has ever done that. Do you happen to know the kinds of things that Cael has been doing for the Empire?'

'I have a rough idea, sir,' said Cole.

'Good. Your first job is to travel directly to Athumia to meet with Queen Famula and Lord Edgar. Kyra will likely be there, so prepare to have your mind read. You are to inform the leadership of the Dominion that the Empire had nothing to do with the murder of one of their dragons on Alef.'

'Lord Limnan?' said Cole.

Bedig blinked. 'How in Pyre's name did you know that? Aye – that's the dragon's name. One of Queen Blackrose's friends was also killed. Honeytail of Throscala. Do you know what they were doing on Alef?'

'Yes.'

'That makes this a lot simpler to explain. Yesterday, the bodies of the two dragons were found butchered on a beach. As of this moment, we have no idea who was responsible, but the Dominion needs to hear the news from us. Queen Blackrose is furious, as you can imagine; the Dominion is also likely to take this very badly. Get your arse out of there if things look like turning violent. Your next job depends upon whether or not Bailey knew about the secret meetings on Alef. If he did, then go to Zamata. Cael will be there, along with Arrosa and the other delegates for the state visit to Gunst; but it's Bailey you need to speak to first. Tell him that the Empire will do everything in its power to find those responsible for the murders; then tell Cael that the Empress needs to talk to him, immediately. Have you got all that?'

'I do, sir.'

'Don't call me that. Go and get packed. Miss Longhold, do not repeat a word of what you've just heard to anyone – is that clear?'

'Yes... what do I call you?'

He smiled. 'Bedig.'

Cole got to his feet. 'Alva, would you help me pack?'

She stood. 'Yes, Imperial Secretary.'

'You've got ten minutes,' said Bedig. 'I'll be waiting here for you.'

'The brandy is in a desk drawer,' said Cole; 'help yourself.'

Cole and Alva left the office, and made their way up a flight of stairs towards Cole's quarters inside Madden's Tower. Cole glanced at Alva as they walked, but she remained silent. He unlocked his door, and they went into his rooms.

Alva turned to him as soon as he closed the door behind them.

'Athumia?' she cried. 'They're sending you to Athumia on your first day? Alone? Are they trying to get you killed?'

'I have been inside Queen Famula's palace before,' he said. 'And Kyra will be there; she won't let anything happen to me.'

'Why are you so bloody calm about it?' she said. 'Is this the kind of thing you'll be doing from now on? I was one of those idiots Bedig was talking about – I thought you would be taking the minutes at the meetings of the Imperial Court.'

Cole laughed as he pulled an empty bag from a cupboard. 'I already knew what Cael got up to. The Imperial Secretary reports to the Chief of Staff, who reports to the Lord Constable. It's a military position.'

'You knew, and you didn't tell me?'

'But you were here when Cael came to ask for my help.'

'I thought that was just bravado; I didn't think you were actually going to do anything dangerous.'

Cole tossed some of his clothes into the bag. He glanced around his rooms, but saw little he wanted to take with him.

'You'll be getting these quarters,' he said. 'You can keep everything, or throw it out.'

'You will not leave me like this,' she said. 'Talk to me. Will you be coming back? Where do we go from here? Is it over before it started?'

He faced her. 'I don't want it to be over. Will you be happy knowing what I'll be doing each day? I won't always be travelling to the capital city of our greatest enemy, but there will be other times when I will have to do things that might be considered dangerous. You know that I wanted a quiet life, but I also need to do what the Empress commands. This is your chance to walk away, Alva. I don't want you to, but if you would rather end it, then end it now.'

She stared at him. 'I don't want you to go.'

They embraced, and Cole held her close.

'I'll visit after I've been to Zamata,' he said.

He put a hand to her face, and they kissed. Cole closed his eyes, and wished he had more time with her.

'Be safe,' she said, looking up at him.

'I will.'

He picked up his bag, then he threw her a set of keys for the rooms, and left his old quarters. He hurried down the stairs, and walked back into the office.

'Do you have your Quadrant?' said Bedig.

Cole patted a pocket.

'I don't want to ask this, but I have to,' Bedig went on. 'Whatever is going on between you and Lieutenant Longhold, will you both be able to carry out your responsibilities?'

'We will.'

'I hope you know what you're doing, Cole,' he said.

'Cael and Arrosa both work for the Empress, and they don't seem to have a problem.'

'They've been married for years. How long have you been seeing Miss Longhold?'

'About twenty minutes.'

'Oh. Well, all right. It's no longer any concern of mine, but I would let Constable Cardova know, as he is your direct superior, at least until we get a new Chief of Staff. You will also have to tell Postmaster Arrosa, as Lieutenant Longhold now works for her.' He took out his Quadrant. 'Shall we?'

Cole nodded.

Bedig activated his Quadrant, and they appeared in a large unfurnished room with plain white walls.

'This is your new apartment,' said Bedig. 'We are on the twenty-second floor of the Blue Palace. Leave your bag here and go directly to Nom Karta. I will inform the Constable that you are on your way to Athumia.'

Cole dropped his bag onto the polished wooden floor. He took out his own Quadrant.

'It was a pleasure to work with you, Cole,' said Bedig. 'Be careful.'

'Enjoy the beaches of Dragon Eyre,' said Cole, then he swept his fingers over his Quadrant.

The air crackled, and he appeared on a wide boulevard, outside the enormous palace in Nom Karta where Queen Famula lived with her court of dragons and gods. An armed patrol of Bullan soldiers saw him, and they approached, their crossbows levelled at his chest.

Cole slipped his Quadrant back into his pocket and raised his empty hands.

'I am here on behalf of Her Majesty the Empress of the Sapphire Throne,' Cole said, 'and I request permission to speak with the government of the Dominion. I bear a message from the Empire.'

The Bullan moved in to surround him. Their officer gestured to one, and he raced off in the direction of the steps leading up to the great palace.

'Name?' said the officer.

'Cole Holdfast,' he said; 'Secretary to the Imperial Court.'

The officer nodded to his men, and Cole was searched. He was carrying no weapons, but one of the soldiers plucked the Quadrant from his pocket and handed it to the officer. Cole listened as the Bullan talked among themselves in their own language. He made out the word *Holdfast*, but nothing else was intelligible.

The soldier sent to the palace returned, bringing reinforcements. Following them out into the bright sunshine was a pale green dragon, his eyes gleaming.

Cole remained still as the dragon approached, his hands still raised.

'He claims to be a Holdfast, my lord,' said the Bullan officer. 'We have confiscated his Quadrant.'

The dragon stared down at Cole. 'A Holdfast? What do you want, insect?'

'I bear a message from Her Majesty the Empress of the Sapphire Throne,' he said.

'What message?'

'Might I deliver it to Her Majesty Queen Famula Min Gahad, my lord?'

'We are not in the habit of allowing Holdfasts to enter the palace; not since the last time your kind was here.'

'I could have used my Quadrant to appear directly before the queen,' said Cole. 'I chose to arrive here, to show that I am no threat.'

'Had you appeared inside the palace, you would already be dead, insect,' said the dragon. He turned to the Bullan. 'Bind his wrists and hood him.'

The soldiers pulled Cole's arms behind his back, and secured them with a cord. The soldiers had no hood, so they wrapped a thick scarf round Cole's head, covering his face. Cole relaxed, confident that the Dominion would not brazenly breach the treaty by having him summarily executed simply for wanting to talk. Hands gripped his arms, and he was led up the steps and into the dark interior of the palace. Unlike his cousin Cael, Cole had no dream vision, and the scarf was blinding him to his surroundings. He was walked along a corridor for a few minutes, then he heard the sound of other humans and dragons talking. The voices hushed as Cole was brought to a halt.

'Remove the scarf,' said Edgar, 'and free his hands.'

A Bullan did so, and Cole gazed out at the dozen huge dragons watching him from the audience chamber. By the feet of the queen stood several humans, including Edgar and Lord Elmhirst of the Doomed Worlds.

'Why has a filthy Holdfast come here?' said a dragon. 'Has he been searched?'

'He has, my lady,' said the Bullan officer.

'We should pluck out his eyes,' said another dragon, 'lest he uses his powers to bewitch us.'

'That will not be necessary,' said Edgar. 'Tell me, Cole, why have you come here? The treaty clearly states that you are to relay messages from the Empire to the Dominion through Lord Bailey. Why are you not upon Zamata?'

'The news I bear was to be delivered directly to this royal court, my lord,' said Cole; 'for the ears of only the leadership of the Dominion.'

Queen Famula narrowed her great eyes. 'Is he using his mind powers on us?'

'He is not, my queen,' said Edgar. 'Cole's powers are impressive, but they are not as dangerous as those possessed by his cousin Cael.'

Cole smiled.

'Does that amuse you?' said Edgar.

'I was recalling, my lord, that I have been referred to as the harmless Holdfast.'

'You are far from harmless, Cole,' said Edgar. 'You were part of the small team that annihilated the Wystians on Na Sun Ka, were you not?'

'I was there, my lord.'

'Where is your Quadrant?'

The Bullan officer stepped forward, the device in his hands. 'We confiscated it, my lord.'

Edgar reached out and took it. 'You did well, Captain.'

'Let the Holdfast insect deliver his message,' said Famula.

Cole inclined his head. 'Thank you, Your Majesty,' he said. 'However, the news I bear is not for everyone. It concerns a matter arranged by Lord Raddon Mon Konran, son of Lord Konran Mon Gahad. I see that Lord Konran is present here today; perhaps he discerns my meaning.'

Konran's eyes gleamed, then he glanced at the queen, who glanced back at him.

'Clear the hall,' said the queen. 'Let only the two gods and those belonging to the royal line remain.'

Cole kept still as the other dragons departed the large chamber. The Bullan soldiers bowed and followed them out, leaving only Famula, Konran, Abda and Saphben standing before Cole, along with Edgar and Elmhirst.

'Speak,' said Edgar.

Cole inclined his head again. 'Yesterday, my lord, the bodies of two dragons were found upon an island on Dragon Eyre. Both had been murdered. One of the dragons was a close aide to Queen Blackrose of the Eastern Rim; the other was Lord Limnan Mon Limonen.'

'Treachery!' cried Abda. 'Did I not warn this court that the vile dragons of the Eastern Rim would betray us?'

'Hold, Abda,' said Famula. 'Did the Holdfast insect not also say that one of Blackrose's aides was murdered along with Limnan?'

'Have you seen the bodies, insect?' said Lord Konran.

'I have not, my lord,' said Cole. 'I was briefed by my superior officer on the matter, but I have not visited the scene. The Empire wishes the Dominion to know that we had nothing to do with these murders, and we join you in utterly condemning them. An investigation has been established to ascertain who is responsible for this crime.'

'It is a trick,' said Abda. 'They lured poor Limnan to his death. Who could have slain two dragons but the perfidious Holdfasts?'

'The Empire was encouraging the secret negotiations, my lady,' said Cole. 'We had no desire to see them fail. If Kyra Holdfast is here, she will be able to read my thoughts. I will allow it.'

'Kyra remains on Zamata with her brother,' said Edgar.

'Then I shall permit you to enter my mind, Lord Edgar. I will lower my defences to prove I am speaking the truth.'

Elmhirst rolled his eyes. 'This sounds like another trick. Are the Holdfasts not capable of distorting their own minds, to allow us to see whatever they wish us to see? Sable Holdfast used to play this game with us.'

Cole frowned. 'Yes, that is true. I have not done so in this case, but I understand your suspicion.'

'When will Limnan's body be returned to us?' said Konran.

'That can be arranged through Lord Bailey,' said Cole, 'if I am permitted to discuss this matter with him. I am unsure if Bailey knew about the negotiations.'

'He knew,' said Edgar. 'Who among the Empire also knew? I suspect that the news has been leaked to a third party, one who does not wish to see peace flourish between the dragons of Athumia and those of the Eastern Rim.'

'I am not privy to that knowledge, my lord,' said Cole, 'but the Dominion can be assured that we shall investigate every possible avenue. The Empire deems it to be of the utmost importance that the Dominion does not rush to any premature judgements regarding these murders. The treaty has served us well for seven years, and we wish it to continue. Am I free to leave Nom Karta? I am due to visit Lord Bailey, now that I know I am able to speak to him about this matter.'

'Perhaps we should hold him as a hostage, my lord,' said Elmhirst, 'until those responsible for Lord Limnan's death are brought to justice.'

'I am inclined to treat Cole Holdfast as an official emissary,' said Edgar. 'Cole, I want you to ask Bailey to arrange the transport of the body of Lord Limnan to Inopei; and then I wish you to pass on a message to the Empress. Tell Her Majesty that we shall not rest until Limnan's murderer is found and executed. Tell her that the Dominion is greatly angered by this news. Also, ensure that your next messages are relayed through Lord Bailey.' He handed Cole the Quadrant. 'Do not return to Nom Karta without our permission.'

Cole bowed his head. 'I will pass on your words, my lord. Thank you for hearing me, Queen Famula Min Gahad; may your reign shine through the ages.'

Cole smiled to himself, then he activated the Quadrant and vanished.

CHAPTER 19
REMAINING FAITHFUL

Kaugatz, Serpent Isle – 22nd Luddinch 1605

Arrosa kept her head down as she walked through the streets of Kaugatz. She knew that no one would recognise her, and she had long before shed the last traces of her Gunstian accent, but she was taking no chances. She passed through a crowd of Zamatan labourers, then she took a wide road leading towards the west. She had taken three ferries to reach her location, and had set off from Zamata Gataza at dawn that morning. The first ferry had been to cross the Hansarta, but she had not wished to walk the entire length of Kaugatz, so she had taken another ferry to Igatz, before re-crossing the Cyasarta to the ferry terminal close to the monastery of Tsallon Anura, where she had once lived with Lahnos and Leona.

She walked down a street in what had previously been a Gunstian area. The houses and shops now echoed to the sound of the Aucterian language, or the Holdings tongue as Kelsey called it. Arrosa wondered how many Gunstians remained on the island. If there were any, then they were probably agents sent from Gunst, rather than true natives of Zamata.

She took a side road, and entered a large public square in the eastern district of Kaugatz. She came to a halt in the shade of a tree, and lowered her gaze. There should be bloodstains, but there were none. The cobbles had been scrubbed clean, washing away any sign of the massacre that had taken place in the square, the massacre of her people carried out by Lord Malum and Lady Macsin, when they had decided to eradicate the Gunstians from the island. Arrosa had not been in the square that day. She had fled, jumping down from a wagon and bolting through the back alleyways of Kaugatz; but she had heard the screams. There was a bench next to the tree, and Arrosa sat down to watch the local Zamatans going about their business. Did any of them remember what had occurred? Were some secretly pleased that the Gunstian presence on Zamata had been extinguished? The Gunstians of the Serpent Isle had never conformed to Zamatan culture; they had continued to speak their own language, and had kept to their own community, shunning those they had perceived as being no better than demon-worshippers.

Despite her preoccupation, she noticed that the shabbily-dressed man entering the square to her right was the same man who had been among the passengers on her third ferry that day; and she knew immediately what it meant. She watched the man from the corner of her eye as he pretended to browse through the contents of a small market. He was middle-aged, and there was something about his posture that she recognised. She scoured her memory, but part of her had actively suppressed much of her early years on the island, and she couldn't put a name to his face. She decided to see what he would do if she continued to sit on the bench. The man made his way along the line of market stalls, and she caught him glancing over in her direction.

She smiled and waved.

The man frowned, then he gave up his pretence and walked over to where she was sitting.

'Can I help you?' said Arrosa.

The man said nothing.

'Were you following me for a reason?' she went on.

'I think I have made a mistake, ma'am,' he said, inclining his head. 'I thought perhaps that I recognised you, but I was wrong. Pardon my presumption.'

'Your voice,' she said. 'I know it. Perhaps you weren't wrong. Tell me who you think I might be, and I will answer.'

'May I sit?'

She inclined her head, and the man sat down two feet from her on the bench.

'Forgive me, ma'am,' he said, 'but are you Arrosa?'

'I am,' she said.

The man shook his head and smiled.

'And you?' she said.

'My name is Saewa, ma'am,' he said. 'I used to work for...' He glanced around, as though wary.

'For Leona?' she said.

'Yes, and then for Lahnos.'

'But not for Bauchlie?'

'No, ma'am, not for Bauchlie. It was I who employed Athyro, who turned out to be a Gifted Gunstian agent. President Bauchlie was understandably reluctant to continue my employment in the Dragon Palace following that. I am a humble shopkeeper these days.'

'And yet you trailed me through Igatz, and then into Kaugatz?'

'My old ways took over for a while, ma'am. I saw you close to where Leona once lived in Igatz. My house is still there. I had to find out if it was really you. When did you first notice me?'

'On the ferry.'

Saewa smiled. 'Then I haven't lost all of my old skills. Is... is Lahnos also on Zamata?'

'No. He leads a quiet life these days, with Lord Sigum. He has a son.'

'Does he? Has the lad got horns?'

Arrosa smiled back at him. 'Not yet.'

'What brings you to Kaugatz?'

'Do you remember what happened in this square?'

Saewa's features darkened. 'I do. I also remember the day you appeared, just after the... slaughter. I tried to look after you, but Farakai and I thought it best to take you to Leona. You were a bit of a handful, and we didn't know what else to do with you.'

'You could have thrown me out onto the street.'

'You were found raking through piles of rubbish, looking for food. You were cold and bedraggled, and starving. You were also one of the last Gunstians on the island, and we felt responsible. And look at you now – a beautiful young woman. Where do you live?'

'On the Star Continent,' she said. 'In the imperial capital, with my husband and our son.'

'I am glad you found yourself, Arrosa,' he said.

She glanced at his thread worn clothes, and at the cheap shoes that were falling apart.

'I wasn't on Zamata when Leona was killed,' she said. 'How was Lahnos able to rule after her murder?'

Saewa lowered his gaze. 'At first, he was incapable of doing anything,' he said. 'For a short while, the island was governed by myself and a Bullan sergeant; though we issued our orders in the name of Lahnos. Then Athyro arrived in the Dragon Palace. We already knew her, from when she had worked for Typan. After that, Lahnos changed, almost immediately. He started to work again; he toiled from dawn to midnight.'

'Did you not consider this to be suspicious?'

'We certainly thought it was odd. His brother Karl had been spending time with him, and I gave him the credit for Lahnos's transformation. It was only later that I understood that Athyro had been manipulating him; she had been manipulating many of us.'

'What did she do to you?'

'She filled me with a desire to trust her; nothing more than that. I was lucky – she did far worse to others.'

'I can remember where you live. Is your front door still painted red?'

'It is.'

'Saewa, would you like a job? Would you consider moving to the Star Continent? I have a need for people with your... particular skills.'

He eyed her. 'Would I be working for you, miss?'

'Yes.'

'And what is it that you do?'

'I am a member of the Empress's Imperial Court. I deal with the postal service, among other, more sensitive areas of policy. Some of the work is similar to what Leona used to do, but I cannot tell you any more, not unless you agree. I assume you would need to speak to your wife, so I don't expect an answer just yet. The pay would be considerable, and I would ensure you were provided with comfortable quarters. You served Leona and Lahnos well, and I don't hold you to blame for employing Athyro. You were up against an agent with formidable Gifts, and I think Bauchlie may have acted unwisely when he let you go.'

Saewa nodded, but wouldn't meet her gaze. 'My wife left me some time ago, when things got too difficult for us. She never forgave me for being so loyal to Leona.'

'And your children?'

'All grown up. If you are serious, then I might take you up on your offer. I would miss my sons, but they have their own lives, and I barely see them.'

Arrosa got to her feet, and Saewa gazed up at her.

'It was good to see you again,' Arrosa said. 'Sort out your affairs on the island, and my husband will be in touch about the job. You should know that he is the son of the Demon Witch, and he has the power to read your mind.'

Saewa's eyes widened, but he said nothing. Arrosa tilted her head, and walked away, leaving the large square behind.

'He is exactly what I have been looking for, ma'am,' said Arrosa.

Brogan narrowed her eyes.

'He used to run Leona's network of agents on Zamata, and then he helped Lahnos govern the island,' Arrosa went on. 'I need people like that to get me started in my new role as Imperial Postmaster.'

'And you just happened to bump into him?'

Arrosa smiled. 'He followed me. Even after all this time, he recognised my face; and he wanted to see if it was really me.'

'He can't be very good if you noticed him.'

'I was unaware of his presence for most of the time; and perhaps you are forgetting that I'm not so bad at this sort of thing myself. I want him. When Cael returns from Gunst, I'm going to ask him to collect Saewa on his way back to Plateau City. Cael can read his mind to ensure that his motives are sound. I detected no lies coming from him, but we need to be sure.'

Brogan gazed at the view from the balcony of Zamata Gataza. 'It's your decision,' she said, 'but his salary and expenses will have to come out of your budget.'

Arrosa smiled. 'Thank you, ma'am.'

Brogan glanced up at the position of the sun. 'Your husband is late,' she said. 'We've been waiting out here for twenty minutes.'

'Sorry to have kept you, ma'am,' said a voice from behind them.

Arrosa got to her feet and embraced her husband. 'How was Gunst?'

'Their capital is larger than anything on the Star Continent,' said Cael, 'but I didn't introduce myself to anyone; I remained invisible for most of the time.' He glanced at Brogan. 'The Gunstians are ready, ma'am. The two agents have reported the Empire's plans to the government, and they have agreed to host a state visit. I have the location. They expect you to arrive later today.'

'At last,' said Brogan. 'I thought we were going to be stranded on this island for thirds.' She got to her feet. 'I will let Claudian and Bailey know, and we shall prepare to depart. Good work, Cael.'

Cael sat down in the seat that had been occupied by Brogan, and Arrosa sat down next to him.

'Read my mind,' she said.

Cael gazed into her eyes. 'A house with a red door?' he said. 'Southern Igatz?'

'I want you to go there, and I want you to take a man called Saewa back to Plateau City. I have found my new spymaster.'

'Do you need me to vet his thoughts?'

'Please. I think I can trust him, but there's no harm in being sure.'

'It'll probably be tomorrow,' said Cael. 'If today's your last day on Zamata, then Kyra will also be leaving soon.'

'I'm glad that you've had an opportunity to catch up with her.'

Cael smiled. 'It's good of you to say that, especially since I know you don't like her.'

'She walked out on the Holdfasts when the family needed her.'

'I had fun telling her that I will be responsible for introducing democracy to the Plateau. It could have been her if she'd stayed.'

'I'm sure you'll do a good job, brother,' said Kyra.

Arrosa and Cael turned. Kyra was standing by the balcony doors.

'Look who's here,' Kyra went on. 'I found him talking to Bailey.'

Cole walked out from behind her, then he and Kyra stepped on to the balcony.

'This is like old times,' said Cael; 'the four of us together.'

Cole and Kyra sat, and Cael lit a cigarette.

'I have just come from Nom Karta,' said Cole. 'I was delivering a message from the Empress.'

Cael raised an eyebrow. 'And they let you leave with your life? We're supposed to send messages through Bailey, not travel to Inopei ourselves.'

'It was Bedig's last order as Marshal,' said Cole. 'You're the new Marshal, as of today. The Empress wants you back in Plateau City immediately; but wait until I tell you why I was in Nom Karta.'

'I'm listening,' said Cael.

'Two dragons were murdered on Alef yesterday,' said Cole. 'We don't know who did it, but we weren't sure if Bailey was part of the secret, so I had to go directly to Famula and Edgar.'

'How did they take the news?' said Kyra.

'As well as you'd expect. I was hoping you would be there, so you could read my mind to confirm that I wasn't lying to them. I've spoken to Bailey about it. He's going to arrange the collection of the body.'

Arrosa kept her mouth closed, unsure if she should reveal that Cael had told her all about the two dragons who were negotiating on a small island off Alef. It might be better to allow Kyra to think that she was ignorant, she decided.

'I'd better go back to Inopei,' said Kyra. 'Edgar will want to take action, and he'll need me.' She smiled at Cael. 'I've enjoyed these last few days, brother. It's been too long. Take care, Cole. And you, too, Arrosa.'

They got to their feet, and Kyra embraced each in turn. Arrosa put on a smile, then Kyra stepped back from them and vanished.

Cael lowered his gaze, and Arrosa took his hand.

'I'll pick up Saewa now,' he said, 'and go back to Plateau City,' he said. 'Are you coming with me, Cole?'

'I have something to do in Rainsby first,' Cole said.

Cael nodded, then he gazed into Arrosa's eyes, and she felt him push a location within Great Gunst into her mind.

'Did you get that?' he said.

'And I thought you just wanted to look into my eyes, Cael.'

He laughed. 'I could have just told you the location. I'm going to miss you.'

'I'll miss you, too.'

He kissed her. 'Take care in Gunst. I'll check in when I can. Use your Quadrant to leave if you don't like how things are going.'

Arrosa nodded. 'Give Cowie a hug from me, and remember to walk the dogs.'

They kissed again, then Cael moved away. The two cousins took out their Quadrants, then the air shimmered and they vanished, leaving Arrosa alone on the balcony. Cael had left his cigarette burning in the ashtray, and she stubbed it out.

She thought about the two dead dragons on Alef. Was someone trying to sabotage an attempt to bring the Dominion and the Empire closer together? Who would benefit from a new conflict? Whoever it was, they had been clumsy. If their intent had been to divide the two sides, then killing one of the dragons and leaving the other alive would have been the cleverer choice. Killing both looked sloppy. Her thoughts moved to Saewa, and her plans for him. She would first ask him to teach her all he knew about organising agents, and then she would be able to pass some of her responsibilities onto his shoulders. He could train new agents, and recruit others; and Arrosa would build up her parallel empire of spies and informants. If it ever came to pass that Cael was selected to replace Thorn upon the throne, then Arrosa would be in a powerful position.

She smiled to herself. Leona had managed to run her network of agents at a younger age than she was. Leona would be her model, she decided; as long as she could avoid Leona's fate.

Two hours later, the delegates and their aides were gathered in Bailey's grand reception room, their luggage piled high next to them.

'Thank you for allowing us to stay here,' Brogan said. 'I hope we weren't too much trouble.'

'It was no trouble at all, Chamberlain,' said Bailey.

'And thank you for imprinting the Gunstian language into our minds,' Claudian went on. 'It will come in very useful.'

'Yes, well, please remember that I have given you the version of Gunstian that I originally took from the mind of Lyla, who took it from Lahnos, so you will all sound as though you come from Zamata. Some of the terminology differs a little, and you may get a few strange looks.'

Brogan rolled her eyes. 'Now he tells us.'

Bailey laughed. 'Have a joyous time in Great Gunst; at least, have a better time than I had when I visited. Remember not to emphasise that you know me. The Gunstians believe me to be a scoundrel of the highest order.'

'That's what happens if you try to undermine their religion,' said Brogan.

'Undermine? My good lady, I merely saw myself as a supplemental addition to the religion of Gunst. A living, breathing brother of their one true god. I thought they were going to welcome me with open arms. Needless to say, I was mistaken. Now, who shall be operating the Quadrant that takes you to Gunst?'

'I will do it,' said Arrosa. 'Cael has given me the location where they shall be expecting us to arrive.'

'And do you all know how to get back here?' said Bailey.

'We do,' said Claudian.

Bailey nodded. 'I would be much obliged if you did all you could to prevent any possible conflict between Gunst and the Dominion. Farewell, my friends.'

Arrosa took out her Quadrant. She gazed at the engraved surface, and eyed the others. Brogan tilted her head, and Arrosa swept her fingers over the device. The air around them shimmered, and they arrived in a great open plaza in the midst of a city. Towers and steeples rose into the sky, along with golden domes that shone in the sunlight. At one end of the plaza was an enormous building of yellow stone, with arches stacked upon arches, and buttresses that extended outwards on every side.

A group of soldiers and courtiers were sitting together under a large awning. They looked as though they had been waiting there for some time, and most got to their feet as soon as they saw the party from Zamata arrive. Soldiers formed up into lines, and several courtiers approached. In their midst were the two agents that Arrosa had met in Plateau City. The agents whispered to the courtiers as they walked across the plaza, then the courtiers took the lead. They stopped before Brogan, Claudian and Arrosa, and bowed their heads.

'Welcome to Great Gunst,' said one, using the Gunstian language. 'May the blessed Chadura witness this meeting between the two great empires of our times, and may she shower her gifts upon us.'

'May this meeting strike fear into the hearts of the demons of Aucteran,' said another courtier; 'may their spirits shrivel into the dust from whence they came.'

Another official moved forward, ready to translate what they had said into Holdings.

Brogan bowed. 'Thank you for the gracious welcome,' she said in Gunstian. 'We bring greetings from Her Majesty Empress Thorn of the Sapphire Empire. May our two peoples be united in friendship.'

The eyes of Gunstian courtiers widened. 'We had not realised that you understood our language, Chamberlain of the Empire.'

'It was taught to us by Lady Arrosa Holdfast,' said Brogan, making Arrosa's head ache.

'That explains the Zamatan inflections in your accent,' said the courtier. 'My name is Lakai, chief minister to the high guardians of Gunst. We have no emperor or empress, despite being a great empire. Instead, our people are governed by those who have received their Gifts from the blessed Chadura.'

Arrosa felt out with her Gift of Kenning. She found one among the courtiers with the same Gift, one with the Gift of Truth, and another with the Gift of Pain. She would need to warn Brogan. The Chamberlain had already lied once to the officials, when she had claimed that Arrosa had taught them the Gunstian language. She noticed the courtier with the Gift of Kenning glance at her. Their eyes met, and the Gunstian tilted his head.

'A banquet has been prepared in your honour,' Lakai went on. He gestured towards the enormous building at the end of the plaza. 'It is a short walk to the Temple of the Great Mother, and we would be privileged to escort you.'

The soldiers turned to flank the party, and they set off towards the building. Arrosa tried to get closer to Brogan, but several courtiers moved between them. Brogan was still talking to Lakai, and Arrosa began to worry about what she might be saying to the Gunstian minister.

'Is this your first time in Gunst, Lady Arrosa?' said the courtier with the Gift of Truth.

'It is,' said Arrosa.

'Then may I bid you welcome to your spiritual home?' he said. 'I understand that we have you to thank for this state visit. I hear you have risen high in the government of the Sapphire Empire.' He smiled. 'Did you use your Gifts to reach such heights?'

'Only one of them,' said Arrosa. 'There isn't much need for Kenning on the Star Continent.'

The man laughed, though Arrosa felt it was a little forced.

'Of course,' he said. 'Are you the only one in the Empire with Gifts?'

'As far as I know,' she said, before she realised that she had unwittingly lied. For a brief moment, she had forgotten about Lahnos. Did that count as a lie? She wasn't sure.

'You must tell me how a Gifted girl from Zamata was able to attain the ear of your Empress,' he said. 'I am sure it would make a most fascinating tale. You would have been on the island when the wicked demons slaughtered the Gunstian population – is that correct?'

'It is,' she said. 'I visited the site this morning, out of respect.'

'How did you survive that dreadful day?'

'I ran away and hid. I was very young, and I was very fortunate.'

'Chadura was clearly watching over you,' he said. 'She must have foreseen your future, and she spared your life, praise be her name, so that you could become her evangelist in the Sapphire Empire. Is it difficult to dwell among so many unbelievers?'

'I was adopted into a rich and powerful family,' she said. 'They ensured that I was fed, housed and educated, and then I married one of them.'

'Your marriage will not be valid here, my lady,' he said. 'Only marriages performed by priests of the blessed Chadura are recognised within the bounds of our empire.'

Arrosa knew she should hold her tongue, but couldn't help herself.

'My marriage *was* carried out by a Gunstian priest,' she said, watching as the smirk vanished from his lips. 'It was a beautiful and moving ceremony.'

'But, my lady, I was under the impression that this family you speak of includes the infamous Demon Witch as its matriarch; and that you were wedded to her son. Is that not so? Or, tell me – has the son of the Demon Witch converted to our religion?'

Arrosa cursed under her breath.

'Let us find a time to discuss this at length,' she said. 'I am looking forward to seeing the interior of the Temple of the Great Mother. There is no temple like it upon the Star Continent.'

'Is that not because the Star Continent is a godless place? I hear rumours that the people there believe in nothing; that we came from nothing, and to nothing shall we return.'

'It is true that most religions have died out,' she said. 'The Kellach Brigdomin, for example, once believed in a fire god called Pyre, but their faith fell away when their neighbour destroyed their holy mountain.'

The man laughed. 'A fire god? Are all the peoples of the Star Continent so backward? And how will the Empress deal with the Empire's annexation of Dragon Eyre? How does she plan to tame the vile hordes of demons inhabiting that blighted land?'

'The Empire does not view dragons as demons.'

'How then, my lady, are you able to serve this Empire? It seems that you have pledged yourself to a people who treat demons as friends. Is this not incompatible with your religion?'

'Were you sent to test me?' she said.

He smiled. 'I am merely making polite enquiries, my lady.'

Arrosa was saved from any further conversation by the party's arrival at the gates of the Temple of the Great Mother. They were escorted inside, and taken to a grand dining room, where dozens of Gunstian priests mingled with officials, uniform-wearing army officers, and government ministers. Brogan beamed as the delegates were led to seats of honour in the heart of the hall, and the Gunstians stood and applauded. Arrosa made sure she had a seat between Brogan and a courtier from Plateau City, and everyone sat.

Brogan leaned over to Arrosa. 'This is going well so far,' she said. 'I had a good talk with Minister Lakai on the way here, and I think we might be able to make some decent progress while we're here.'

'There was someone with the Gift of Truth in the group that welcomed us, ma'am,' Arrosa whispered. 'Please be careful.'

Brogan nodded, though her features had paled a little.

Arrosa's gaze scanned the hall. She saw Minister Lakai sitting among a row of high priests. Two of the Gifted men from the welcoming party were standing by Lakai's shoulders, whispering in his ear. Arrosa watched as all three glanced over at where she was sitting next to Brogan. Lakai smiled, then he turned to the high priest sitting to his right, and they exchanged a few words.

The high priest nodded and got to his feet, a heavy set of black robes over his shoulders.

He raised a hand, and the hall fell into silence.

'Praise be to Chadura,' he said.

'Praise be unto her,' chanted the Gunstians in the hall.

The old priest smiled. 'This is an auspicious day in the history of the Gunstian Empire. For the first time, we have sitting with us representatives of an Empire that spans three different worlds.' he gestured over to the imperial delegates, and there was loud applause from the Gunstians.

'If it is the will of the blessed Chadura,' the high priest went on, 'we shall unite with the peoples of this Empire – we shall forge an unbreakable alliance that will serve as a shield against another invasion by the wicked Dominion, for the demons of Inopei are the Empire's enemies as well as our own. Credit must go to our brave agents, who travelled across the ocean of stars to find the capital city of the Empire of the Sapphire Throne.' He smiled. 'And who did they find there? None other than a fellow Gunstian – Lady Arrosa of Zamata. Yes, for Arrosa has climbed high in the favour of the Sapphire Empress, and serves upon her inner council. With her are Chamberlain Brogan and Adjutant Claudian, two of the highest-ranking ministers in the government of the Sapphire Empire. Let us make them feel welcome while they stay with us in Great Gunst, for they are our honoured guests. Before we eat, we shall say the customary prayers and, on this occasion, I call upon Lady Arrosa to recite them for us. She deserves this honour, as it was she who bridged the gap between our cultures and traditions. Without Arrosa, this great day would not be happening; so, come, Arrosa, say the prayer to cleanse us before we feast.'

He sat, to another round of loud applause. Arrosa calmed her nerves, as hundreds watched her. Most were smiling in welcome, and she could discern no ill will coming from the majority of the Gunstians, but she had no doubt about why she had been chosen – they were testing her faith, to see if she remained true to Chadura.

Arrosa knew what she had to do. She plunged into her memories, and raked up the old prayers that had been spoken by her mother or father before each meal. She got to her feet, her palms upturned, and the hall hushed. Her version of the prayer was probably local to Zamata, and it might sound a little rustic in the midst of Great Gunst; but the Gunstians would forgive that. Godless apostates, on the other hand, they never forgave.

'Great Mother Chadura, provider of all,' she began, her voice clear and steady; 'bless the food and the drink that your faithful gathered here shall partake. Bless the hands that till the generous soil, and the hands that pull in the fish-heavy nets; and cleanse our hearts of bitterness, that we might always praise your name with pure spirits. Let it be so.'

'Let it be so,' the crowd chanted back at her.

Arrosa sat, and the crowd of dignitaries began to talk among themselves again. Arrosa caught the glance of Lakai. He eyed her for a long moment, then a servant passed between them, and Arrosa looked away. She stared at her food, picked up a fork, and began to eat.

CHAPTER 20
A DRAGON'S SYMPATHY

Alef, Western Rim – 2nd Luddinch 5273 (18th Gylean Year 24)

Lucius Cardova suppressed all feelings of nausea as he and Bedig walked onto the long, curving beach. The bodies of the two murdered dragons were still lying prostrate on the churned-up sand, and pools and streaks of coagulated blood had gathered along the high tide line. One of the dragons had a stout tree limb embedded into his left eye, while the other's skull had been split open by a large, blood-stained boulder that lay close by. A small crowd of soldiers was guarding the beach, while Blackrose and a few others were standing by the bodies of the slain.

'Which one is which?' said Bedig.

'The one with the branch in his eye is Honeytail,' said Lucius. 'The other is Limnan.'

Bailey walked up to them, his eyes dark. 'We are looking at the handiwork of a being with battle-vision,' the god said. 'No dragon would use a branch or a boulder to kill, and no human lacking battle-vision would have been able to wield either as weapons. We can also rule out a powerful god, since we can assume that they would have used death powers. Who do we know that has battle-vision but no death powers?'

Bedig eyed him. 'Do you know the answer to that?'

'There are a few refugee gods and demigods on Athumia that fit that description,' said Bailey, 'but Edgar has vouched for their whereabouts. The Dominion possesses very few Quadrants, and all are closely monitored. Can you say the same about the Quadrants in the Empire?'

'What are you implying?' said Bedig. 'The Empire wasn't responsible for this.'

'I wasn't insinuating anything, Lord Marshal,' said Bailey; 'but could it be at all possible that one of your Quadrants has fallen into the wrong hands? Who looks after the register of devices these days?'

'That has traditionally been the responsibility of the Imperial Chamberlain,' said Lucius; 'but the new role of Postmaster will be taking over.'

Bailey nodded. 'And Brogan and Arrosa both happen to be in Gunst. That seems a little inconvenient.'

'That is why I have come in person,' said Lucius. 'And you should know that Bedig is no longer the Lord Marshal.'

'This is my first day as legate to the Eastern Rim,' said Bedig. 'My first day, and this is what I have to deal with.'

'I am sure that the two murdered dragons are terribly sorry for causing you such an inconvenience,' said Bailey. 'I need an assurance from the Empire that you will thoroughly check the locations and owners of every Quadrant under your authority. Someone, somewhere, has used one of your devices to come here to wreak bloody havoc. The Empire might not have killed these poor beasts; but it was a lapse in imperial security that made their deaths possible.'

'We will look into every Quadrant, Bailey,' said Lucius. 'Ensure that Edgar is informed of this. If one of ours has gone missing, we will track it down.'

'No one in the Empire has a motive for this,' said Bedig.

'That was a rather sweeping statement,' said Bailey. 'Are you sure? *No one*? There is no one living in the Empire who would like to see the Dominion and the Empire come to blows?'

'You know what I meant,' said Bedig. 'The gods of the Doomed

Worlds are the likeliest suspects. They are the ones who long for revenge against the mortal Empire; and, as you said, several of them fit the description – battle-vision was used here, and self-healing was probably also required.'

'According to the first witnesses on the scene,' said Lucius, 'there were footprints in the sand around the bodies, but the tide has washed them away. The footprints did not lead off the beach; therefore, the murderer used a Quadrant to appear directly onto the sand. We need to know how the location leaked out. Has the Dominion compiled a list of everyone who knew about the secret negotiations?'

'Edgar and Kyra were in the process of doing so when I visited them,' said Bailey. 'Kyra intends to discreetly read their minds to discover if they let the secret slip. Naturally, if she discovers anyone's complicity in this crime, we will inform you.'

'Cael will do the same with those from the Empire who were aware of the meetings,' said Lucius.

'Have you placed Cael in charge of the investigation?'

'We have,' said Lucius. 'He was here yesterday evening, scouring the scene. My presence here today is to publicly reassure everyone that we are taking this very seriously.'

Bailey gazed at the bodies. 'Do we have any obvious suspects?'

Lucius shook his head.

'What about Lord Elmhirst?' said Bedig. 'He has never been happy with the treaty, he has a Quadrant, and he possesses battle-vision.'

'Elmhirst has already voluntarily subjected himself to having his mind examined by Kyra,' said Bailey. 'She found nothing to connect him in any way to this crime.' He frowned. 'Naxor?'

Bedig raised an eyebrow. 'He has no battle-vision of any note, and he lacks the valour needed to take on two dragons.'

'He might have sub-contracted the job to someone else,' said Bailey.

'I will ask him if he knows anything,' said Lucius, 'but Naxor has been keeping his head very close to the ground for the last few years. As far as we know, he has been focussed on building up Aila's Marchbrae business empire. They are amassing a fortune down in Kell. If I had to guess, he is playing a very long game. With eight young immortal Holdfasts in Clackenbaird, he can afford to be patient.'

'What about Sable?' said Bailey. 'She has the cunning and the ruthlessness required to carry this out. Two dragons wouldn't present much of a problem for her.'

Blackrose lifted her head. 'Do not insult my friend,' she said. 'Sable has not left Ulna in the last month; nor would she be inclined to sabotage any negotiations that might have led to peace between the two tribes of dragons.'

'Apologies, my queen,' said Bailey, as he bowed low. 'I was not aware that you were listening to our conversation.'

'If you do not wish a dragon to hear your every word,' said Blackrose, 'then do not speak in their company.'

'I learned that the hard way a long time ago,' said Maddie, who was standing by her dragon's forelimbs. 'Nothing escapes Blackrose's ears. What are we going to do with Honeytail's body?'

'His family has instructed me to burn it with all due honour,' said Blackrose. 'I will do so when these humans have finished looking for evidence.'

'You may do so now, Your Majesty,' said Lucius. 'Cael has already been over the site in great detail.'

'Then I shall take my leave,' said Bailey. 'Lord Raddon Mon Konran awaits the return of the body of his faithful retainer. If there is nothing else to be done here, I will bear Limnan to Inopei.'

'Go in peace, Bailey,' said Blackrose. 'Whoever did this is a fool if they believe that it will further divide my people from the dragons of Athumia. Tell Queen Famula that I mourn the loss of Limnan as I do that of Honeytail. Neither deserved to die.'

Bailey bowed again. 'I will pass on your words, Your Majesty.'

He took out his Quadrant, swiped his fingers over the copper surface, and then he and the body of Limnan vanished from the beach. Lucius and the others walked over to the deep indentation in the sand where the body had been, to see if Limnan had been covering anything of note, but only blood was staining the sand.

'I shall also leave you,' said Lucius. 'Bedig shall remain with you, Your Majesty, as your new imperial legate. If you need anything, Bedig will relay your messages to us.'

'Farewell, Lucius,' said Blackrose. 'Find who did this, and bring their miserable lives to a violent end.'

'And say hello to Greysteel from me if you see him,' said Maddie. 'He has something he wants to ask you.'

'Indeed he does,' said Blackrose.

Lucius inclined his head, then he touched the *Go back* command on his Quadrant. The air crackled, and he appeared in the Teal Garden next to the Dragon Bridge in the Blue Palace. Cael and Cole were sitting in one of the deep alcoves positioned along the southern wall of the cavernous chamber, and Arrosa's three dogs were lying on the grass by their feet. Lucius approached them.

The two young men got to their feet. The dogs glanced up, then they relaxed when they saw who it was.

'Commander,' said Cael.

'At ease,' said Lucius.

They sat down again, and Lucius took a seat next to them. A silver coffee pot was on the table in the alcove, and Lucius poured himself a cup.

'How did it go, sir?' said Cael.

'It was a brutal scene,' said Lucius, 'but then you already know that. It was as though someone had gone into a bloodlust, using anything close to hand to kill the two dragons. I don't understand that aspect. If someone desired to murder a pair of adult dragons, why wouldn't they bring weapons with them? There were no signs of sword cuts or bolt wounds. They used sticks and stones.'

'We can rule out a professional assassin,' said Cael, 'but it must have been planned in advance.'

'Your sister is reading the minds of everyone in the Dominion who knew the location.'

'No one in the Dominion knew the exact location, sir,' said Cael. 'When I transported Lord Limnan to Dragon Eyre, neither he nor Lord

Raddon knew the destination. They knew the purpose of the meeting, but not the location; I was careful about that.'

'Then the leak must have come from our side,' said Lucius. He glanced at Cole. 'This has overshadowed your first couple of days as the new Imperial Secretary,' he said, 'and I haven't had a chance to officially congratulate you on your elevation to the Imperial Court.'

Cole inclined his head, but said nothing.

'With no Chief of Staff,' Lucius went on, 'you will be reporting directly to me for a while. I want Cael to continue to lead the investigation into the murders, and so I will need you to carry out some other tasks.'

'Do you have anything for me to do today, sir?' said Cole.

'I was going to give you a day off to settle into your new apartment.'

'I haven't got any furniture, sir,' he said, 'and the apartment is ten times bigger than my old quarters in Rainsby. I'd rather be kept busy than stare at all those empty rooms.'

'All right,' said Lucius. 'You are familiar with travelling to Kell, so you can come with me when I leave the palace for a second time this morning.'

'Kell, sir?' said Cole. 'Why are we going to Kell?'

'I told Bailey that I would ask Naxor a few questions, to rule him out of our investigation.'

Cael looked sceptical. 'Can you imagine Naxor trying to kill two dragons with his bare hands?'

'I know it sounds implausible,' said Lucius, 'but Bailey wants to be sure. He also suggested that Sable might have done it, but Blackrose was quick to come to her defence.' He turned back to Cole. 'We'll leave as soon as I've finished this coffee.'

Cole nodded, then his eyes narrowed, as though he wanted to say something.

'What is it, Cole?'

'Lord Bedig told me that I needed to report something to you, sir,' said Cole.

Cael laughed.

Cole shot his cousin a glance. 'It's not an urgent matter, but...'

Lucius sipped his coffee, waiting for Cole to continue.

'It involves Lieutenant Alva Longhold,' Cole went on. 'She and I... well, we might be...'

'Bedig already told me,' said Lucius.

Cole frowned.

'As long as it doesn't interfere with your duties,' Lucius said, 'then you can do what you like in your private life. Is it serious?'

'It has barely begun, sir.'

'It's about bloody time you got yourself a woman,' said Cael.

Lucius smiled at the annoyed expression on Cole's face, then his own features flattened as he noticed Kelsey approach. The dogs looked up, but settled down again.

'Good morning, dogs,' said Kelsey. 'Good morning, boys. What are you talking about?'

'Cole's new girlfriend,' said Cael. 'Didn't you interview Alva for the job? Were you trying to set him up with someone, Aunty?'

'It never crossed my mind,' said Kelsey. 'Alva Longhold's the best young Holdings vision mage we have at the moment.' She shook her head at Cole. 'You were supposed to train her, not seduce her.'

'I'm not rising to the bait, Aunty,' said Cole.

Kelsey smiled. 'You're going to have to get used to a long-distance relationship, because I'm not transferring Lieutenant Alva up to Plateau City, not after you went to the trouble of making sure she could reach the capital with her vision powers.'

'Won't that be up to Arrosa, Aunty?' said Cael. 'She'll be Alva's boss when she gets back from Gunst.'

'Have you checked in on your wife today?' she said.

'I'm going to do it now,' said Cael; 'as soon as Cole and Lucius leave for Kell.'

Kelsey raised an eyebrow. 'Kell?'

'We're going to ask Naxor if he knew anything about Alef,' said Lucius. 'Bailey insisted.'

'Bailey's a twat,' said Kelsey. 'If and when Naxor ever turns on us, he'll do something far more cunning and sly than butchering two dragons on a beach.'

Lucius nodded. 'That's what I said to Bailey, but I've decided to humour him. We shouldn't be long.'

'I heard that Killop arrived on the Hold Fast estate,' Kelsey went on. 'Thanks for taking him up there.'

Lucius almost hesitated. Was Kelsey being friendly towards him? She had yet to unleash a barbed comment in his direction, and she had her old crooked smile on her face.

'I saw Killop there a couple of days ago,' said Cole.

'Aye?' said Kelsey 'What were you doing on the estate?'

Cole lowered his gaze. 'I was... uh, Alva wanted to meet Aunty Celine, and...'

Kelsey and Cael started to laugh, and Lucius smiled. Lucius glanced down at his cup of coffee, but it was empty. Cole noticed, and got to his feet.

'Shall we go?' he said.

Lucius nodded. He crouched down by the three dogs and gave each one some attention, then he straightened his back.

Kelsey's expression became more sombre. 'Pass on my regards to Aila and her family.'

'I will,' said Lucius.

'Oh, and can you get me a bottle of Lachellan Fourteen Year Old while you're there?'

Lucius smiled. 'No problem.'

He and Cole stood apart from the others, then Lucius took out his Quadrant and activated it. They appeared in Clackenbaird, outside the front door of the farmhouse. It was raining, and a cold autumnal wind was gusting over the brow of the hill.

'The last time I was in contact with Threeways,' said Cole, 'they told me that Aila had reported Cairney as missing.'

'Kelsey told me about that,' said Lucius. 'She was going to take care of it.'

They approached the farmhouse, and Lucius knocked on the front door.

Moments later, Carter opened the door. He looked out, and scowled when he saw who it was.

'Might we speak to your mother, please?' said Lucius to the boy.

Carter glanced over his shoulder. 'Ma!' he shouted. 'A couple of Colsbury Holdfasts are at the door.'

'Which ones?' came Aila's voice.

'Cole and Lucius Cardova,' the boy called back.

'Let them in.'

Carter frowned at the two men, then he stood aside.

'Make sure ye take yer boots off,' he said.

Lucius and Cole loosened their boots and left them by the door, then Carter closed it, and they followed him into the kitchen. Several of the other children were there, along with Aila and their cook, and they were in the midst of preparing a vast amount of food.

Aila wiped her hands on a cloth, and eyed Lucius. 'Yes?'

'Sorry to interrupt you, ma'am,' said Lucius.

'If you're here about Cairney,' she said, 'it was a false alarm. I admit that I almost panicked when I came home and found that he had gone, but he's been back a few times since, to pick up some supplies of food. He's camping in the hills south of Marchside, and exploring Kell. He seems to be enjoying himself, so I left him to it.'

'That's good to hear, ma'am,' said Lucius. 'However, we wanted to talk to Lord Naxor if he is available.'

'Naxor's working in the Marchbrae warehouses today,' said Aila; 'in the office, overseeing the arrival of more stock from Severton.'

'Cole and I will walk there,' Lucius said. 'Kelsey passes on her regards.'

Aila rolled her eyes. 'You know, considering today's date, I had foolishly imagined that you were here for a different reason. Do you know why we're making a mountain of food?'

Lucius frowned.

Cole coughed. 'It's Carter's fourteenth birthday tomorrow, ma'am.'

'That's right; thank you, Cole,' said Aila. 'At least one of the Colsbury Holdfasts remembers. Could you see yourselves out? As you can gather, we're a little busy.'

Lucius inclined his head, then he and Cole walked back to the main entrance. They paused to pull on their boots, then they left the farmhouse.

'That never gets any easier,' said Lucius, as they took the road leading to Marchbrae Distillery.

'Aren't they allowed to grieve?' said Cole.

'That's not what I said – of course they can grieve; but I don't like the way they blame Kelsey for what happened. Do they think that she doesn't mourn her brother? Kelsey tried her best to persuade Corthie to leave Na Sun Ka, but he was determined to stay. His death wasn't in vain, Cole. If Corthie had pulled out of Na Sun Ka, then Blackrose would be dead, and the Wystians would have conquered the Eastern Rim. Kelsey knows this, but she can't say it out loud, in case the Marchbrae Holdfasts take offence. Kelsey has bent over backwards to accommodate their feelings, and how do they repay her? By blaming her for Corthie's death. It makes me angry.'

Cole eyed him.

Lucius took a breath. 'Apologies, Cole.'

They came over the crest of the hill, and saw the large buildings of Marchbrae spread out in front of them. The distillery was the tallest structure, but the brewery, warehouses, blacksmiths, copper works, cooperage and malting facilities were almost as large. Barrels were stacked up in their hundreds, and the tracks were full of wagons and carts. Smoke was issuing from three stone chimneys, and the complex was bigger than most villages in Southern Kell.

Lucius and Cole stopped to take in the view.

'Is it any wonder that Aila is the richest woman in Kellach Brigdomin?' said Lucius. 'She built this place from nothing. Have you been to Marchside recently? Aila has paid for every road to be paved, and she funds the library, a school, and a hospital. She's also the largest employer in Kell; the wages she pays look after hundreds of local families; and the raw materials Marchbrae buys in keeps the entire economy afloat. Think of that the next time you drink one of her whiskies.'

'Do you wish me to read Naxor's mind, sir?'

'Will he know if you try?'

'No, sir. I'm good at being quiet.'

'Then do so, but don't pry. All I want to know is if he is in any way involved in the murders of the two dragons; nothing else.'

Cole nodded.

They made their way down the gentle slope of the hill, and walked between long rows of warehouses, their walls blackened. They came to the office, knocked, and entered. Naxor was sitting at a desk next to two men and a woman, and he gave Lucius an exasperated expression.

'I'm a little busy right now, Constable,' Naxor said. 'Whatever it is, can it wait?'

'We won't take up much of your time, Naxor,' said Lucius.

The demigod gave an exaggerated sigh. He turned to the others. 'My humble apologies for this imperial intrusion. As you can see, the highest military authority in the Empire has deigned to grace us with his presence. Why don't you take a walk to the kitchens in the distillery? – the cooks there will provide you with some warm sustenance.'

The three Kellach got to their feet. Lucius and Cole stood aside to let them pass, and they left the office. Cole closed the door behind them, then he and Lucius sat down opposite Naxor.

Naxor smiled broadly. 'What can I do for you, gentlemen? Are you here for a tour of the facilities?'

'Have you been to Dragon Eyre recently?' said Lucius.

Naxor raised an eyebrow. 'Why? Has something happened?'

'I would be obliged if you answered the question.'

'No. I have not travelled to Dragon Eyre. I haven't been on that lizard-infested world for years, as it happens.'

'Have you instructed anyone to go there?'

Naxor smiled. 'These questions are starting to intrigue me, Constable,' he said. 'Might I try to guess what has occurred? Something awful has happened, yes, and someone has pointed the finger at me? Am I close? Let me make a full and frank statement – I have not commissioned any acts of sabotage, mayhem, bribery, robbery, skulduggery or anything remotely criminal upon Dragon Eyre. Does that cover everything?'

'Has anyone borrowed your Quadrant? Do you have it in your possession?'

'No and yes. I never allow anyone to touch my Quadrant, and it is currently in an inner pocket of my coat.'

Lucius smiled. 'Thank you for seeing us, Naxor; that will be all.'

'Is that it? Aren't you going to tell me what this is about? What happened on Dragon Eyre?'

Lucius got to his feet, and Cole stood up next to him.

Naxor glared at them.

'Is the whisky shop open?' said Cole.

'So you do speak?' said Naxor. 'I assumed you were being quiet so that you could surreptitiously read my mind. Yes, of course the shop is open. The locals round here would riot if we closed it. You'll have to pay full price, though, as a punishment for not telling me what's going on.'

'Thank you again, Naxor,' Lucius said, then he and Cole left the building.

'Is there anything I need to worry about?' Lucius said, as they took a path leading to the distillery shop.

'No, sir,' said Cole. 'He was telling the truth – he had no idea what we were talking about.'

'And his Quadrant?'

'He never lets anyone near it, sir.'

'Then we can rule him out. To be honest, I didn't regard him as a credible suspect, but at least we can tell Bailey that we have checked.'

They arrived at the shop – a squat, low building attached to the side of a massive warehouse. They went inside, and Lucius gazed at the shelves filled with the various produce from Marchbrae. There was a vast selection of whiskies on offer, but there was also gin, ale and cider, along with cheese, honey and oatcakes from the Clackenbaird farm.

An old Kellach woman glanced up from behind a counter. 'Do ye need any help, lads?' she said, not recognising either of them.

'We're fine, thanks,' said Lucius.

'Yer not local,' she went on. 'Did ye come by carriage?'

'By Quadrant,' said Lucius. 'We were visiting Lord Naxor.'

He plucked a bottle of Lachellan Fourteen Year Old from a shelf, then he selected a bottle of Strathlanach Twelve Year Old for himself. He placed them onto the counter, as Cole eyed the shelves of gin.

'Are you getting something?' said Lucius.

'Alva likes gin,' Cole said, 'but I don't know anything about it.'

'Is this Alva a Holdings lassie?' said the old woman. 'If so, try the new seaweed gin. It's destined for the Holdings, but none has left Marchbrae yet, so she'll be the first to have it.'

Cole saw the bottles she was referring to, then he eyed the price.

'Aye, it's expensive,' the old woman said, 'but the seaweed comes all the way from the bottom end of Lach. It's the only gin in the world made with it.'

'I'll get it,' said Lucius. 'I know how much you were paid in Rainsby.'

'I'll pay you back when I get my first wages as secretary,' said Cole.

'You will not,' said Lucius. 'Consider it a gift to celebrate your promotion.'

'Thank you, sir.'

Lucius handed over an exorbitant sum to the old woman, and she placed the three bottles into a straw-lined box. Lucius glanced out of the shop window, and saw that the rain had started again. He took out his Quadrant, as the old woman eyed him.

Lucius eyed her back, then he triggered the Quadrant, and he and Cole appeared in the Teal Garden. Three dragons were in the gardens next to the middle bridge, and one was much larger than the other two.

The huge old dragon gazed down at Lucius.

'Greetings, Lord Greysteel,' said Lucius. 'Maddie mentioned that I might be seeing you today.'

'Young Frostback and Halfclaw have been showing me the new palace,' said the old dragon, 'and the quarters where I shall be living.'

Lucius raised an eyebrow, then he saw Kelsey and Chancellor Fenu close by.

'Lord Greysteel is the first to be appointed to the Provincial Council,' said Kelsey.

'I was due to become ambassador,' said Greysteel, 'but I shall instead be a member of this new council. I am also here to issue a formal invitation to the Empress. Queen Blackrose has requested that Empress Thorn comes to the Eastern Rim. We have been a part of this Empire for seven years, and my queen believes it is time that the Empress and her court pay us a visit.'

'The Empress has accepted the offer,' said Kelsey. 'Fenu is going to arrange the details, as Brogan is away.' She eyed the box in Lucius's hands, then she smiled and took a purse from her pocket.

'You don't need to give me any money for the whisky,' Lucius said.

'No, I'll pay for it,' she said.

'It's fine. Call it a gift.'

'No. Let me pay for it.'

'No, I insist.'

'I don't care if you fucking insist, Lucius,' she shouted; 'I'm paying for the damn whisky.'

The others in the hall fell silent. Lucius placed the box onto a bench and opened it. He passed the gin to Cole, then he handed the Lachellan to Kelsey.

'I'm going to Rainsby for twenty minutes,' said Cole.

Neither Lucius nor Kelsey spoke, so Cole shrugged, then he activated his Quadrant and vanished.

Kelsey counted out some money and set it down onto the bench.

'Could you not accept his gift, my rider?' said Frostback. 'It seems rude to pay for something bought by another out of friendship.'

Kelsey simmered with anger, but ignored the silver dragon.

'Will fifty cover it?' she said to Lucius.

Lucius said nothing.

'Well,' she said, 'fifty is what you're getting. It's all there. You can count it if you want.'

She turned, the bottle of Lachellan clutched in her hands, then she walked away, leaving the hall by a rear door.

'I do not approve of my rider's behaviour, Lucius,' said Frostback. 'She should have accepted your gift.'

'She's proud,' he said. 'She doesn't want to owe me anything.'

'She is stubborn,' said Frostback. 'When you first began to argue with each other, I was firmly on Kelsey's side. Now, though, I feel that this has gone on for long enough. I have seen you try to make amends, but each attempt has been rebuffed. You have my sympathy, soldier.'

Lucius inclined his head. He picked up the bottle of Strathlanach and walked towards the stairs, leaving the fifty coins sitting on the bench.

CHAPTER 21
SECOND OUTING

Jezra, The Western Bank – 5th Balian 3441

Konna kept her head down as she walked along the fog-filled streets of Jezra. She had spent the morning picking off a few greenhides from the battlements of the Fortress of the Exiles, while Maxwell had been posted to one of the other large forts under construction, which lay several miles to iceward.

Her work had been brought to a halt when Seaspan had alighted on the fortress to inform her that the commander of the Brigades wanted to see her in his office. The dragon had carried her down to Lower Jezra, depositing her onto the roof of the Common Rooms, leaving her a five minute walk through the thick, grey fog.

She could guess why she had been summoned. Four days had passed since her brother had forced Esher to kill the two dragons, and the draughtsman's absence at his place of work would have been noticed. She had seen no sign of Cairney in that time, and part of her hoped that he had abandoned his stupid plan. The other part was worried about Esher. What they had done to him was wrong, and she knew it.

She found the building, and entered through the front door. Her hair was glistening wet from the fog, and the building had a damp feel about it. She made her way upstairs to the office of the commander, and knocked. A clerk told her to wait, so she took a chair in the passageway outside the office, and went over the story she was about to tell. She needed to stay calm when they berated her for her stupidity, as they surely would; then she needed to take any punishment with good grace. That would be the hard part.

The clerk reappeared. 'The commander is ready to see you, ma'am,' she said.

Konna got to her feet and walked into the small office. The clerk bowed her head, then she left the room, closing the door behind her.

The commander gazed up at Konna, his features a little tenser than usual.

'Please take a seat, Miss Holdfast,' he said.

Konna sat.

'Do you know why I have asked you to come here?' the commander went on.

She shook her head.

'You were seen speaking to one of the draughtsmen a few days ago,' he said. 'In fact, as far as we can gather, you were the last person to talk to him.'

'Which draughtsman, sir?'

He kept his gaze on her. 'Reece.'

'Oh.'

'His colleagues have stated that they saw him leave the office with you, Miss Holdfast, and no one has seen him since.'

She narrowed her eyes, and tried to look shocked. 'What?'

'What did you say to him?'

Konna forced her features into a frightened expression. For her story to work, she would need to look scared – scared of what she had done, and scared of the consequences.

'I... I'm so sorry,' she began. 'Please, I didn't mean it. I thought...'

'Slow down,' he said. 'Tell me what happened.'

'Maxwell told me Reece's real identity, sir. I tricked him when he was drunk – he didn't mean to tell me; it's not Maxwell's fault. And then... well, I didn't believe it. I had to find out for myself, so... I...'

'Yes?'

'I told Reece that I wanted to talk to him, and then...'

The commander's eyes darkened. 'And then what, Miss Holdfast? What did you say to him?'

'I told him who he really was, sir. I'm sorry. I'm really sorry. I couldn't believe that it was true, and I was treating it all as a big joke, but Reece... he grew angry; then he ran away.'

'Where did he go?'

'I don't know. He ran off, along a corridor in the building where he works. I... I thought it was funny. I mean, it isn't true, is it? It can't be true. Reece isn't a mighty all-powerful god. That would be ridiculous.'

The commander rested his head in his hands and exhaled. 'I will have to report this to the palace in Pella.'

'The palace?' cried Konna, in her best terrified-sounding voice. 'But... am I in trouble?'

'You might be. What in Malik's name possessed you to tell a stranger some rumour that you had heard about him? Reece has been absent from his place of work for four days, and he hasn't been in his quarters. He could be anywhere. He might have caught a ship to Ooste, and walked through the damn portal to the Star Continent for all we know.'

'But, Reece isn't actually... I mean he's not really...?'

He met her gaze. 'Tell me who you think he is. I want to hear you say the name.'

Konna lowered her voice. 'Esher.'

'And Maxwell told you this? He will be in as much trouble as you, miss, for he has broken an oath. Do you realise that, apart from you and Maxwell, I am the only person in Jezra who was aware of Reece's real identity? There are fewer than a dozen of us in the entire City. Now, try to remember – what exactly did he do or say after you told him?'

'He said... He said he didn't believe me, that the Ascendants were evil, and that he wasn't one of them. Then he got angry. He said he had to go, and he hurried away. That was it; that's all that happened between us. He hurried away, and I haven't seen him again. I have been back at the Fortress of the Exiles since then, killing greenhides.'

'You are extremely good at killing greenhides, and I wish you had stuck to that. Miss Holdfast, what you have done might well be irreparable. Reece is utterly harmless. He has no god powers, and he has no memories of his old life. Effectively, he is a mortal man, just like me.' He chewed his lip for a moment. 'Go back to your quarters,' he said, 'and stay there until further notice. I will be in touch after I inform the palace of what has occurred.'

'Is it all right if I go to Maxwell's apartment?' she said. 'I've been staying with my cousin when I'm not fighting along the Jezran Wall.'

'That's fine,' he said, 'but stay indoors. You may leave.'

Konna kept her bewildered and scared expression on her face until she had left the building. As soon as she was back in the midst of the thick fog, she relaxed. That hadn't been too bad. Pretending to be scared had been a little embarrassing, but it could have been far worse. She might have been immediately deported back to Kell, or even locked up in a prison cell while they conducted an investigation.

She walked to the building housing Maxwell's apartment, climbed the stairs, and unlocked the front door with the set of keys Maxwell had given her. She went through to the spare room, where she had been sleeping, and changed out of her army gear. If she had the rest of the day off, she was going to enjoy herself. She picked out a simple dress, pulled it over her shoulders, and went back into the main living area. She rummaged in a drawer, and found Maxwell's stash of dreamweed. She took it to the couch, then she brought over the bottle of Taran brandy that had been a gift from the Brigades following the destruction of the greenhide nest. She sat down, poured herself a drink, lit the weedstick, and put her feet up.

She was thoroughly drunk by the time Maxwell got home that evening. He walked into the living area, and raised an eyebrow.

'Hey, Maxie,' Konna cried. 'How was yer day?'

'It was much the same as yesterday,' he said. 'I killed about forty greenhides.' He sat. 'I walked back from the fort.'

'You walked?' she said, starting to laugh. 'All the way?'

'Yes, all the way. I couldn't face asking Seaspan to carry me here, not again. He would have grown suspicious. When Cairney gets back, I'm going to have to insist that he hands over the Quadrant.'

'You do that,' she said. 'How long did it take ye to walk here?'

'Well over an hour,' he said. 'Coming down the cliffs in the fog was the worst part; I nearly fell a hundred feet.'

'Ye would've survived, but,' she said.

'When did you get home?'

'Before lunchtime, not that I've eaten anything. Actually, now I think of it, I'm fucking ravenous. Could ye pop out and get me some food? I'm not allowed to leave the apartment.'

He narrowed his eyes, then he noticed the bottle of brandy. 'Are you drunk?'

'Aye. I've also smoked half yer stash.'

'I could smell the weed from the bottom of the stairs,' he said.

'How do ye even get weed in the City? Ye dinnae grow it here.'

He shrugged. 'It comes through the portal, I guess. Go back a bit – did you say that you weren't allowed to leave the apartment?'

'Aye, that I did, Maxie. We've been rumbled. I was hauled in front of the Brigade commander and asked about Esher.'

Maxwell's features paled.

'Dinnae worry, big man,' she said. 'I stuck to the story.'

'Did he believe you?'

'Aye, I think so. He'll be wanting to speak to you next, but. I told him that I got ye drunk, and then tricked ye into telling me Reece's real identity. I made out that it wasnae yer fault, but yer probably still likely to get yer arse kicked. I was told to stay indoors, while he tells the palace in Pella what's happened.'

'Shit.'

'It'll be fine,' she said. 'They're more worried about poor wee Reece, wandering about on his own, confused and angry.' She paused, as guilt at what they had really done to Reece surfaced in her mind. 'They'll be looking for him.'

'Of course they'll be looking for him,' Maxwell cried. 'He's the Ninth Ascendant!'

He got up and started to pace the floor.

'Ye look a wee bit vexed, Maxie,' she said.

'I should turn myself in,' he said. 'I should report to the commander, and confess everything, before he sends soldiers here to arrest me.'

She raised an eyebrow. 'Ye broke an oath,' she said; 'ye didnae burn down Jezra. Ye'll be fine if ye make a grovelling apology, just like I did.'

'And you told him that you forced it out of me? How exactly did you do that?'

'I got ye drunk,' she said, 'and tricked ye.'

'How? How does one do that?'

'Fuck knows. Tell them that ye were so pished that ye cannae remember how it happened.'

'But I have self-healing – why would I be that drunk?'

'Do I have to think of everything? Make something up. Tell them that it's a Kell tradition; actually, it is a Kell tradition. A drinking game, just like the one we played in Clackenbaird. It was against the rules to use our self-healing to sober up.'

Their front door was knocked, and Maxwell jumped.

'They're here for me,' he whispered.

'Quit whining and answer the door,' said Konna.

Maxwell walked over to the door. He hesitated for a moment, then swung it open. Standing outside was a massive greenhide, its claws dripping red blood onto the landing. Maxwell stepped back, his eyes wide. The greenhide vanished, replaced by Cairney, who laughed loudly and walked into the apartment.

'That was fucking hilarious,' he said, as he sat down next to Konna. 'Is that dreamweed?' He picked up a half-smoked weedstick and held up his right hand. Sparks flew across his fingertips, then he shot out a slender tendril of flame, lighting the stick of dreamweed.

He inhaled, as Maxwell closed the door, and walked over to the couch.

'That wasn't funny,' he said to Cairney.

'I happen to disagree,' said Cairney. 'What's the matter; did ye wet yer pants? Is that shite I can smell?' He laughed again.

'I want my Quadrant back,' said Maxwell.

Cairney ignored him.

'I said I want my Quadrant back.'

Cairney eyed his sister. 'What's wrong with Maxi-boy? Did ye rile him up?'

'He's worried,' said Konna. 'I was questioned about Esher.'

'So?' said Cairney. 'Did ye stick to the story?'

'Every word.'

'Then ye'll be fine.'

'I need my Quadrant in order to do my job,' said Maxwell.

Cairney's smile faded, and he stared at Maxwell, his head shaking. 'Ya selfish wee bastard,' he said. 'Oh, Maxi-boy, while you've been sitting here scratching yer arse and worrying about yer wee job, I've been trying to bring justice to the Empire. Have ye any idea how busy I've been? Have ye the slightest clue how many disguises I had to put on in order to discover the location of those two dragons, or how much work I've done to prepare today's outing?'

Maxwell narrowed his eyes.

'You will let me keep the Quadrant,' Cairney said; 'and ye'll stop complaining about it. That's an order.'

Maxwell blinked, then he glanced away.

Konna powered her self-healing, and she sobered up in an instant.

'Where's Esher?' she said.

Cairney turned back to face her. 'What's with all the questions? First Maxi-boy, and now you. Do ye not trust me?'

Konna snorted.

'Esher is ready and waiting,' Cairney went on. 'Ye'll see him soon.'

'How did ye discover the location of the dragons?' she said.

Cairney shrugged. 'I impersonated a palace guard in Ulna,' he said.

'I was standing in Blackrose's hall, a dozen yards from the nearest dragon, and not one of them suspected who I was – all those stupid lizards saw was my disguise. Dragons talk among themselves. Sometimes, I think they forget that their guards and servants are close by. That's where I first heard about the secret meetings. I then had to pretend to be a servant's boyfriend to get into her office, and the stupid bitch had written down the location in a ledger book.'

'Ye pretended to be someone's boyfriend?'

Cairney changed his appearance, into an older, shorter man with fair hair. 'Like this,' he said. He dropped his powers, and appeared as he was again. 'Anyway, I didnae come here to sit and chat. I want ye both to watch something.'

He got to his feet and took out the Quadrant. Maxwell eyed the device, but said nothing.

Konna stood. 'Do I need to put my boots on for this?'

'Ye'll be fine as ye are,' said Cairney. He swiped his fingers over the Quadrant, and they appeared within a small chamber. Dust coated every surface, and the few items of furniture were wreathed in sheets.

'Where are we?' said Konna.

'Go to the window and ye'll see,' said Cairney.

Konna and Maxwell walked up to the room's only window and gazed out. Ahead of them was a large, wide forecourt. On the left were two square keeps, while, on the right, the pink and peach tiers of the Summer Palace stretched up into the cloudy sky.

'What the fuck are we doing on Colsbury, brother?' Konna whispered. 'Are ye out of yer mind?'

'Calm yerself,' said Cairney. 'Karalyn isnae here. She hasnae been here in over a year; neither has the Empress, for that matter. The island is crawling with lawyers and clerks, all toiling away in their offices for Shella's convention.'

'Are we in the Spire?'

'Aye. It's locked up, and nobody ever comes here. We can watch the mayhem without being disturbed. I have decided that Colsbury is where the Dominion will take revenge for the murder of their dragon on Alef; and we shall witness it.'

Konna kept her eyes on the forecourt. She remembered being in the Summer Palace when she had learned of her father's death, and the place made her feel both angry and queasy. A few people were out walking by the two keeps, but the palace was locked up.

'Are ye ready to see Esher again?' said Cairney.

'Aye,' said Konna, turning.

Cairney laughed. 'Could ye have answered that any quicker, sis? Are ye developing a wee soft spot for the Ninth Ascendant, eh? Do ye like him now that he's young and handsome?'

'I preferred him when he looked older.'

'So ye say.'

He walked over to a set of stairs that ascended into an attic.

'Esher,' he called out. 'Come down.'

Konna gazed up as the thirty-thousand-year-old god walked down the stairs. He was wearing leather armour and a steel chestplate, but his eyes were glazed over. He came to a halt when he reached the bottom of the steps, and faced Cairney.

'Good lad,' said Cairney. 'I've got a wee job for ye. Yer gonnae go outside, and yer gonnae start killing everyone. No, not everyone – leave a few survivors. Use battle-vision, death powers, fire powers – whatever ye fancy, and kill, kill, kill. Then, when just a handful of survivors are left, I want you to give them a message. Tell them that you are a god from the Doomed Worlds, and tell them that ye were sent here by Edgar to get revenge for the murder of Lord Limnan. Then get yer arse back here.'

Esher did not respond.

'All right; go,' said Cairney.

Esher turned and walked past Konna and Maxwell on his way to the main staircase. He went down the steps, and disappeared out of sight. Konna hurried back to the narrow window, and Cairney and Maxwell crowded next to her. A crashing sound came from the ground floor of the Spire, then Esher appeared, walking across the forecourt.

'I don't understand,' said Konna. 'What have the poor bastards living on Colsbury done to deserve this?'

'Nothing,' said Cairney. 'The Dominion, in its cruelty, has chosen to massacre innocent civilians. In any case, that's what the Empire will think.'

Esher approached a group of clerks. They glanced over at him, then Esher raised his right hand, and the heads of the clerks exploded in a flash of red, their blood and brains spattering over the cobbles in a wide arc.

'Flow powers, eh?' said Cairney. 'Nasty.'

Soldiers from the gatehouse rushed over. Several of them aimed their crossbows at Esher, and some loosed. Esher stumbled back a step as two bolts hit his chest, then he ran at the soldiers. He pulled a crossbow from one's grasp and used it as a club, battering the soldiers until the wooden stock snapped. He ripped a spear from a soldier's hand, and slaughtered the others, his movements a blur.

'Esher's getting the hang of this,' laughed Cairney. 'Is anyone keeping count?'

Esher turned left towards the two keeps, and disappeared behind a wall.

'Bollocks,' muttered Cairney. 'Now we cannae see what's going on.'

'Where's Shella, brother?' said Konna.

'Why?'

'She's never done us any harm.'

'She's out on the lake with her pirate boyfriend.'

Konna gasped in relief. 'Thank Pyre for that.'

'I waited until she had gone out for her daily trip in their wee boat,' he said. 'Her flow powers might have stopped Esher in his tracks, and I couldnae have that.'

'You mean ye didn't do it to spare her?'

Cairney laughed. 'Yer getting soft in the head, sis. I couldnae give a shit if Shella lives or dies; I was protecting my asset.'

He took out the Quadrant, activated it, and they appeared on the roof of the Great Keep. The screams were the first thing Konna noticed, and she ran to the edge of the roof and looked down. Esher was killing everyone he saw, and bodies were covering the ground by the base of the Lesser Keep. Some of the convention's staff were trying to run towards the walled garden, but Esher lifted a hand, and they fell, blood pouring from their ears and eyes. Esher gazed up at the Lesser Keep. Dozens of faces were staring down at the carnage from the keep's many windows.

'You need to stop this, Cairney,' said Konna. 'This is too much.'

'Did ye think getting revenge would be bloodless, sis?' he said. 'How are we supposed to provoke the Empire into retaliating without a few deaths? And they're only mortals; they'd be dead soon, anyway.'

'No,' said Konna. 'You have to stop Esher. There are fifty bodies down there already; that's enough.'

'I'll judge when it's enough,' said Cairney.

Maxwell glanced at the two siblings, but said nothing, his features pale.

'Look – he's entering the Lesser Keep,' Cairney went on. 'This might take a while.' He sat down and stretched his legs out. 'Do ye remember the last time we were here?'

'Of course I remember,' she said.

'Do ye mind seeing Da's body?'

Konna said nothing, refusing to answer such a stupid question. More screams were reaching her ears, from the interior of the Lesser Keep. A window on the fourth floor was smashed open, and Esher appeared. He began throwing corpses out of the opening, and they piled up in a heap on the ground below.

'I knew that day what I was going to do,' Cairney went on. 'As soon as I saw Da's face, I knew that I would be the one to take vengeance for his death. Not you, Konna, and not any of our other brothers and sisters. I knew it would be me.'

'A boat is docking at the harbour,' said Maxwell.

Cairney jumped to his feet and ran to the far side of the roof.

'Shit,' he cried. 'It's Shella. She must have heard the screams.' He turned to Konna. 'Stay here.'

He clutched the Quadrant, swiped it, and vanished.

Konna walked across the roof to look at the island's little harbour. Olo'osso's yacht was alongside the pier, and the old man was securing the ropes, while Shella was hurrying towards the forecourt. Konna ducked low, in case the old Rakanese woman glanced up, then she rubbed her face, feeling sick.

'Why don't you stop your brother?' said Maxwell.

'Why the fuck don't you try to stop him?' cried Konna.

'He's too strong for me.'

'Well, there's yer fucking answer.'

'They'll think that we helped him.'

'We are helping him, ya dozy twat. This is a nightmare.'

Cairney arrived on the roof with Esher by his side; then he activated the Quadrant again, and they all appeared in a cave. The walls of the rough cavern were lined with supplies, and Konna could see palm trees and a blue sky through the entrance.

'We got away just in time,' said Cairney. 'I thought that Rakanese cow was gonnae see us.'

He turned to Esher, who still had two crossbow bolts protruding from his breastplate. Cairney reached up, and pulled them both from the Ascendant's chest.

'Ye did well,' said Cairney. 'Did ye pass on my message to the survivors?'

'Yes,' said Esher, his voice flat and emotionless.

'What did ye say to them?'

'I told them I was sent by Edgar to take revenge for Limnan.'

'Good lad. Now – forget everything that has happened today, then lie down and take a wee nap.'

Esher blinked, then he yawned, his eyes confused. He glanced down at the hard stone ground, then he lay down, and his eyes closed.

'Please tell me that was the last time we do anything like that,' said Konna. 'Killing two dragons was bad enough; but you slaughtered dozens of innocent people today.'

'I didnae slaughter them,' said Cairney. 'A wicked god from the

Doomed Worlds did it, on Edgar's orders. I didnae do fuck all. And it was probably hundreds of people, not dozens. The inside of the Lesser Keep was like a fucking abattoir. But who gives a shit? They were only mortals.'

'I don't want to be part of this any more,' said Maxwell.

'Oh, Maxi-boy,' said Cairney; 'it's a little late for second thoughts. Here are yer choices – ye stick with me and Konna, and do what we say, or ye try to grass us up. The second of those options will result in yer immediate death. I'll torture ye first, but, for being such a prick.'

Maxwell cowered back a few steps, his eyes wide.

'My plan is working,' Cairney went on. 'When the Empire finds out what happened on Colsbury, they will order a retaliatory attack on the Dominion. Edgar will have no choice but to strike back at the Empire, and then war will break out. Karalyn will not be happy.' He laughed. 'She'll be fucking raging.' He eyed his sister. 'In other words, that might have been our last outing with Esher,' he said. 'If the plan works, we won't need him to kill for us any more.'

'And if it doesn't work?' said Konna. 'The Dominion will deny everything. What if Cael reads Edgar's mind? They'll know it wasnae him.'

'Then Esher will be carrying out a few more atrocities,' said Cairney, 'but that won't be my fault. I'll be keeping a close eye on what the Empire does next. If they send someone to talk to Edgar, I'll be watching. I'll let nothing prevent the war we need to bring down Karalyn's almighty wrath.'

'But Cael might...'

'Cael Holdfast is overrated,' said Cairney. 'He has no death powers or battle-vision; and he cannae heal himself. I'll kick Cael's arse, if it comes to it. That goes for all of the Colsbury Holdfasts; apart from Sable, of course. I have no argument with Sable.'

Konna shook her head.

'Are you also getting second thoughts, sis?' said Cairney.

Konna gazed down at the unconscious form of Esher. He looked at peace, despite the spatters of blood staining his armour and face. Thanks to Cairney, he would remember nothing of what he had done.

Konna tried to work out what to do next. She was repelled by Cairney's actions, but she also wanted to see Thorn be humbled. If Cairney's plan worked, and the Empress fell, then did Konna care if a few mortals lost their lives? As her brother had said, they were all going to die anyway; did it matter when or how?

'I'm with ye, brother,' she said. 'Let's just hope the Empire takes the bait.'

Cairney grinned, then he activated the Quadrant, and they appeared back in Maxwell's apartment.

'Make sure you two scamps behave yerselves,' Cairney said, then he vanished.

Konna and Maxwell sat on the long couch. They said nothing for a while, then Maxwell reached for the brandy and the weedsticks.

'Have you got a light?' he said.

'I thought ye were going to hand yourself in to the Brigade commander.'

Maxwell snorted. 'And have Cairney hunt me down? No thanks. If they come for me, I'll play along with the plan. After all, Cairney will still be around a hundred years from now; the Brigade commander won't. If I have to please one of them, then I know which to choose.'

She passed him her matches. He struck one, and lit a fresh weedstick.

'Your brother's a maniac,' Maxwell went on; 'but he's immortal. There's nothing we can do.'

Konna said nothing. It was too late for words. She had seen Cairney at his worst, and she hadn't tried to stop him. She was complicit, and if Karalyn came for her, there would be nowhere to hide.

CHAPTER 22
DENIALS

Plateau City, The Plateau – 15th Day, First Third Autumn 552

'Thanks for breakfast,' said Cole. He leaned his elbows on the kitchen table, as Nestorian made more coffee by the stove.

'You're welcome,' said Rosie. 'Are you liking your new apartment?'

'I don't have any furniture,' he said. 'Am I supposed to buy it myself? Where did you get yours?'

'We brought ours from our old house,' said Nestorian.

'You must have a bed,' said Rosie.

'I have a mattress,' said Cole. 'I bought it in the Old Town yesterday, and then I had to drag it all the way up to my quarters.'

'But you've had months to plan your move to Plateau City,' said Rosie.

'My rooms in Rainsby came with furniture,' he said.

'And so you assumed that the palace would be the same?'

Cole nodded. 'That's exactly what I did.'

'The army has done this to him,' said Nestorian. 'He expects to be fed, housed and clothed wherever he goes. The lads who retire from the Banner of the Sapphire Throne are just as clueless about how to live as civilians.'

'Am I a civilian?' said Cole. 'I don't recall leaving the army. I'm still a captain, as far as I know.'

'Do you want me to take you shopping?' said Rosie. 'I'll help you pick out some things for your apartment, so you won't look completely hopeless if you bring Alva Longhold round to visit.'

Cole frowned. 'Who told you about Alva?'

She smiled. 'Cael. Don't be angry with him – he's happy for you.'

'He thinks I'm sad and lonely,' said Cole; 'he thinks I need to be fixed. I wasn't sitting in Rainsby feeling sorry for myself, and I wasn't looking for anyone. It just... happened.'

Nestorian poured fresh coffee into three cups, then he brought them over to the table.

'Are you working today?' he said.

'I'm not sure,' said Cole. 'There's no Chief of Staff, and Lucius Cardova is always busy. I don't have a set schedule, but I have to stay here in case I'm needed.'

'Would you rather be in Rainsby?' said Rosie.

'I'm sure you can guess the answer to that; I've barely seen Alva in three days. But, you know, duty comes first.'

'Get married, and your problems will be solved,' said Rosie. 'Nestorian and I live together, and so do Cael and Arrosa. If you were married, your wife would be able to move into the palace.'

Cole laughed. 'It might be a little early for a proposal. Let's see if we can get through a few thirds before I frighten Alva away.'

A bell pealed throughout the palace, and Rosie shared a glance with Nestorian.

'What does the bell mean?' said Cole.

'It's how the Empress summons the Imperial Court for an impromptu meeting,' said Rosie. 'You and I will have to go upstairs to join the others.' She got to her feet.

'I haven't had my coffee,' said Cole.

'Take it with you,' said Rosie. 'We'd best not keep the Empress waiting.'

She leaned over and kissed Nestorian, then she led Cole out of their apartment. They walked down a flight of stairs past a trellis of thick vines, and entered the Teal Garden. The sun was shining through the vast section of glass in the exterior wall of the tower, but rows of open windows were keeping the humidity caused by the fountains and waterfalls at bay. Cole and Rosie followed a path to the row of steam platforms by the eastern wall of the cavernous hall, where Lucius Cardova and Cael were already standing.

'Good morning,' said Cardova.

'Do we know what this is about, sir?' said Rosie.

'Perhaps Her Majesty is testing out the bell, to see how quickly we can all gather in the upper audience chamber.'

'Is this the first time the bell has rung?' said Cole.

'It is,' said Cardova.

Cole eyed Cael. 'I hear that you are incapable of keeping a secret, cousin.'

Cael smiled. 'I've also told Arrosa.'

'Have you seen her recently?'

'I went to Gunst yesterday,' he said. 'Brogan is pleased with how things are going, but the Gunstians have placed Gifted agents among them to see if our delegates are telling the truth. Arrosa isn't too happy about it. They asked her a lot of questions on their first day, but she's been left alone since.'

The door to one of the steam platforms slid open, and a porter gestured for them to enter.

'The Empress's private gardens, please,' said Cardova.

The porter bowed, then he closed the door and moved the lever. The platform juddered into life, lifting its five occupants up through the heart of the palace.

'Where are the hounds?' said Cole.

'I left them in the apartment,' said Cael. 'The Empress doesn't like them jumping up on people, especially her.'

The platform came to a halt, and the porter slid open the door. The small party walked out and came into a set of gardens at the very top of the tower. It was Cole's first time on the upper levels of the palace. The private gardens of the Empress were like a smaller version of the Teal Garden, and a few servants were tending the flowering shrubs and the neat lawns. To the south lay a large section of glass wall, and Cole caught a glimpse of the panoramic view. They were towering over Plateau City, and even the tall spires of the university seemed tiny. They entered a grand hall, where the other members of the Imperial Court were waiting, along with several dozen courtiers. Every member of the court was there, apart from those who had travelled to Gunst. Cole kept an eye on Kelsey, to see how she would react when she saw Cardova, but the Herald kept her expression neutral. He had witnessed them arguing over the bottle of whisky, and he suspected that there was more to it.

They were about to take their seats when the Empress entered the hall via a rear door. The members of the court bowed their heads as Thorn sat on her throne.

'Herald,' said the Empress, 'inform the others what has happened.'

Kelsey remained on her feet as the others sat. 'I have just returned from Colsbury,' she said. 'I was there to talk to Shella, to ask her some questions about the Provincial Council...' Her voice trailed away, and her eyes darkened. 'There is no easy way to say this – several hundred of those working on Colsbury for the constitutional convention have been massacred.'

The others gasped.

'A god carried out the slaughter,' Kelsey went on. 'We don't know which god, but witnesses saw death powers and battle-vision. Self-healing, too. The god was walking about with two crossbow bolts in his chest. He entered the Lesser Keep, and killed everyone he could find, and then, suddenly, he was gone, leaving those who had been on the upper floors alive and unharmed. Shella is fine. She was out with Olo'osso on their yacht, but over three hundred delegates were killed. I don't yet have an accurate figure, as they were still counting the bodies when I returned here with the news.'

Chief Jurist Nardini broke down and began to weep, and Fenu put her arm over his shoulder.

'Was anyone able to get a good look at the god?' said Cardova.

'We have a description from the survivors, but no name,' said Kelsey. 'The god also left a message. He told several groups of survivors that he had been sent to Colsbury by Lord Edgar, to avenge the death of Limnan.'

Cardova's eyes narrowed. 'Do we believe this message? Lord Edgar would not send an assassin to massacre innocents, not in my opinion.'

'I tend to agree,' said the Empress. 'This does not seem like something Edgar would do. However, we must be prepared. Whoever killed the delegates may strike again. If their aim is to provoke a conflict between the Empire and the Dominion, then their next target may be upon Athumia – a massacre that they will blame on us. We must go to the Dominion at once. Lord Marshal, I want you to travel to Zamata, and then, with Lord Bailey's permission, proceed onwards to Nom Karta. The Imperial Secretary shall accompany you. Discover the truth, and then report back.'

Cael and Cole got to their feet and bowed.

'Take care, lads,' said Kelsey.

Cole and Cael walked past the crowd of courtiers and left the audience chamber, then they made their way through the gardens of the Empress towards the steam platforms.

'Shouldn't we leave from here?' said Cole.

'I need to warn the nursemaid that I'll be gone for a while,' said Cael. 'She has Cowie and the dogs to look after, and I told her I wouldn't be longer then ten minutes.'

Cole narrowed his eyes. 'Should so many courtiers be present for meetings of the Imperial Court?'

'Kelsey's blocking abilities stop any god or mages from using their powers,' said Cael.

'She doesn't stop my powers, or yours.'

Cael eyed him as they approached the steam platforms. 'Kelsey doesn't block your powers? Since when?'

'Since always. I assumed it was because I have a small amount of dream powers. Me, you, Sable and your sister have never been affected by Kelsey's presence.'

'Why didn't I know that you were immune?'

'Probably because I barely used my powers for years,' he said. 'And then I was in Rainsby. Anyway, I'm not comfortable with so many courtiers hanging around during meetings of the Imperial Court. They should be conducted in private. What if one of them is a Dominion spy?'

'Every one of them has been vetted, Cole. I think we're safe.'

They took a platform back down to their own level, and Cole waited in the hallway while Cael spoke to his maid. He returned after a few moments with a Quadrant in his hand.

He nodded to Cole, and swiped his fingers over the device. The air shimmered, and they appeared in the forecourt of Colsbury Castle. Rows of bloody bodies had been laid out in front of the two keeps, and groups of delegates were clustered together, weeping, or staring around in shock. Shella was comforting some of the grieving delegates, and Cael made straight for her.

'Aunty Shella!' he cried.

Shella waited for Cael and Cole to approach. She had been crying, but was putting on a brave face for the others.

'I'm sorry, Aunty,' said Cael.

She nodded.

'I need to speak to someone who saw the assailant,' he went on. 'Cole and I are about to go to Athumia, and I want to have a clear image in my mind of who did this.'

'Why, in case he really does work for Edgar?'

'Aye,' said Cael. 'I need to know what he looks like.'

Shella gestured to one of the surviving delegates, who stepped forward.

'Did you see the god?' said Cael.

The man nodded.

'May I go into your mind?' said Cael. 'You won't feel a thing.'

'If it helps to catch him,' said the man, 'then do so.'

Cole stood back as Cael stared into the man's eyes. He glanced down at the bodies, and saw signs of different god powers. Cael nudged his arm.

'I have the image of who did this,' he said.

'Do you recognise him?' said Cole.

Cael frowned for a moment, then he shook his head. 'Are you ready for Zamata?' He triggered his Quadrant, and they appeared outside the monastery of Zamata Gataza. There was no sign of Bailey, so Cael activated his Quadrant again, moving him and Cole up into Bailey's private quarters. The god was stretched out on a couch with an open book over his face, dozing.

Cael kicked the side of the couch, and Bailey sat up, the book falling to the floor.

'We need to see Edgar,' said Cael. 'We need to see him now.'

Bailey rubbed his face, his gaze on the cousins. 'Is this a two-Holdfast emergency?' he said. 'What has occurred?'

'You'll find that out when you take us to Inopei; I don't want Edgar pre-warned.'

'Ah, then you suspect that Edgar may have done something?'

'Let's just say I'm keeping an open mind.'

Bailey eyed Cole. 'Why are you so damn quiet?' He got to his feet, and stretched his arms. 'Well, I suppose we had better be off.' He took out his Quadrant, then he examined his reflection in a mirror. He adjusted his cuffs, and straightened his necktie, then he began to brush his hair.

'Don't make me beat you,' said Cael.

Bailey snorted, then he straightened his back and triggered his Quadrant. The three of them appeared inside Queen Famula's palace in Nom Karta, in the same reception hall where Cole had met the dragon rulers of the Dominion. Famula and her close kin were there, along with Edgar and Kyra.

Bailey bowed low. 'Greetings, Your Majesty,' he said. 'Not one, but two Holdfasts have just bullied me into bringing them here.'

Cael stepped past the god. 'Your Majesty,' he said to Famula, then he turned to Edgar. 'An immortal being has carried out a massacre on the island of Colsbury,' he said. 'The same immortal being told the survivors that he had been sent by you, Lord Edgar. Would you care to comment?'

'A massacre?' said Edgar. 'How many?'

'Over three hundred civilians,' said Cael.

Edgar's eyes widened.

'Take out one of your eye guards,' said Cael.

'There is no need for that, brother,' said Kyra. 'I would know if Edgar was guilty of this crime. He is not.'

'You misunderstand, sister. I have an image of the murderer in my head that I took from one of the survivors. The Empire suspects that Athumia might be his next target, if he is indeed trying to provoke a new conflict.'

'Could he be the same god who slew Limnan and Honeytail, Holdfast?' said Famula.

'I believe so, Your Majesty,' said Cael. 'Someone seems determined to undermine the peace treaty.'

'Put the image into my head,' said Kyra.

'Come and get it,' said Cael.

Kyra looked into her brother's eyes, and nodded. 'I have it,' she said. 'The face does not match any god or demigod from the Doomed Worlds, brother, but...'

'But what?'

Kyra frowned. 'I think I may have seen his face before, but I can't remember where.'

Cael lowered his gaze. 'I thought the same. Could we have met this god a long time ago?'

'Might I see the image?' said Bailey. 'I have a good memory for faces. May I enter your mind to see if I recognise the suspect?'

'All right,' said Cael.

Bailey gazed into Cael's eyes for a moment.

'Speak, Bailey,' said Edgar. 'Do we know him?'

'Unfortunately not,' said Bailey. 'He is not a god I have ever seen before. And you say that he left a message, Cael?'

'Aye. Just what I said – he had been sent by Edgar in response to the death of Limnan.'

'Does the Empress believe this to be true?' said Edgar.

'She does not,' said Cael. 'Her Majesty sent me here primarily to warn you, as we think this god may strike again, this time against the Dominion. If he does so, then he might try to blame the Empire for the attack. Please know that we have no hostile intentions towards the Dominion. Could we work together to bring this murderer to justice?'

'Perhaps,' said Queen Famula. 'For now, I wish to express my condolences for this tragedy. The lives of three hundred innocents have been lost, and we would like the Empress to know that we are sympathetic. We also wish to thank you for the warning. I, too, deem it likely that some wicked party is trying to drive a wedge between us.'

'Might we discuss the deaths of Honeytail and Limnan for a moment?' said Edgar. 'Kyra has scanned the minds of all those in the Dominion who knew about the secret meetings that were taking place. None of them were aware of the exact location.'

'We now believe,' said Cael, 'that the location was leaked by someone in the Empire.'

'What a scandalous lapse in security,' said Lady Abda. 'We trusted the Empire to keep Lord Limnan safe, and you allowed this vile murderer to discover his whereabouts.'

'We formally apologise for this lapse, my lady,' said Cael, 'but we are yet to understand how it was done. I have interviewed everyone on our side who knew the location, and have found nothing remiss. I admit to being perplexed as to how the information was discovered.'

'That isn't good enough, Holdfast,' said Abda.

'I know, my lady,' said Cael; 'it isn't. Cole and I will find the answer, though – be assured of that. Might we depart in peace?'

'You may,' said Famula.

Cael and Cole bowed, then Cael activated his Quadrant. The air crackled, and they appeared on the Dragon Bridge of the Blue Palace.

'What I am about to say goes no further, cousin,' Cael said. 'I do have an idea of how the location was leaked. Some of the dragons in Blackrose's court are a little loose with their tongues. I questioned Maddie, and she told me that she had heard several dragons talk about the meetings while the hall was filled with others, not all of whom have been vetted. However, she also told me that the location was not mentioned. I was reluctant to say anything in front of Edgar and Famula, as I didn't want to sound as though I was blaming Blackrose.'

'Understood,' said Cole.

'What do you think?'

Cole gazed at the view of the southern half of the city. 'What Bailey said was significant. If he doesn't recognise the face of the murderer, then that should narrow our options. I would have thought Bailey would remember most gods from Implacatus, because we are dealing with a god – not a demigod or a mortal mage. I saw evidence of vision, flow and death on Colsbury. Only a powerful, full god could wield all of those powers. But from where would such a god originate, if he is unknown to Bailey?'

'He can't have known every Ancient. There were thousands of them.'

'Even so, Bailey's memory is considerable. Should we rule out the Doomed Worlds?'

'I think we need to. I believe Kyra – she would know if Edgar had anything to do with the murders.'

'Then where should we look?'

Cael lit a cigarette. 'Perhaps we should concentrate on the imperial Quadrants,' he said. 'If we assume that every Quadrant in existence is owned by someone from either the Dominion or the Empire, and that Edgar is correct when he says that none of theirs have been misused, then the killer has one of our Quadrants. Naxor was definitely telling the truth, aye?'

'Naxor is very possessive about his Quadrant. I was in his head when he told us that he never allowed anyone else to touch it. He wasn't lying.'

'Then we're going to have to check them all,' said Cael. 'And by check, I mean we are going to have to visit every Quadrant owner, and ask them to show us their device, to prove that they still have it. Then we'll need to read their minds to see if they have lent it to anyone. This cannot be done quickly. We'll start with the Star Continent. 'I'll take the Holdings if you want to take the Plateau.' He smiled at Cole. 'You can begin in Rainsby. I think a certain Lieutenant Alva Longhold is in possession of a Quadrant. Can you ensure that she is keeping it safe, Cole?'

'I think I could manage that,' he said.

'After Alva, check the Quadrant owned by the governor of Rainsby, then do the same for Westport and Stretton Sands. That will probably take the rest of the day, so I will see you back here for breakfast tomorrow and we can compare notes.'

'Breakfast will have to be in your apartment,' said Cole. 'I still haven't got any chairs. Or a table. Or any way to make breakfast.'

Cael stubbed out his cigarette. 'I'll report to Her Majesty before going to the Holdings. See you tomorrow.'

Cole took out his Quadrant as Cael walked towards the Western Tower of the palace. Cole swept his fingers over the device, and he appeared in a long hallway within Madden's Tower. He tucked his Quadrant away, and nodded to a group of passing marines. He knocked on the door to his old office and waited.

'Enter,' said Alva.

Cole opened the door and walked into the room.

Alva smiled. 'I was hoping you might drop by today,' she said, as she got up from her seat. 'Do you have another present for me?'

'Did you enjoy the gin?'

'I haven't finished it,' she said; 'but yes, I am enjoying it. Audrey wants a bottle the next time you're in Kell.'

He put a hand on her waist and they kissed.

'I missed you,' she said. 'How is life in the capital?'

'I have no furniture,' he said. 'Apparently, I should have known that I had to buy some. At the moment, I have a mattress and four large empty rooms. But, I have a great view of the Teal Garden. My apartment is on the twenty-second floor.'

'Can you stay for long, or is this another fleeting visit?'

'I have to go to Westport and Stretton Sands before the end of the day, but I'm not due back in Plateau City until tomorrow morning.'

'I see,' she said.

'Can I sleep on your couch?'

'I'm sure we can arrange something.'

'I also have to see the governor of Rainsby. Before I go, though, I need to ask about your Quadrant.'

She went over to her desk and opened the drawer. 'It's here.'

'Don't take any of this personally,' he said. 'We'll be asking the same questions to every Quadrant owner in the Empire. Here goes – have you ever allowed anyone to borrow your Quadrant?'

'Never.'

'Has it ever gone missing, even for a short time?'

'Not that I am aware of. I keep it locked in my desk when I'm in the office, and it stays in my bedroom when I go to sleep.'

'Have you ever used the Quadrant to travel to Colsbury?'

'No.'

'How about Dragon Eyre?'

'Yes, but I was with you at the time. To be honest, Cole, I've barely used it since you went to Plateau City.'

'Now I'll have to tell you the reason for the questions,' he said. 'Sit down for this.'

They took seats by the desk.

'A god slaughtered over three hundred delegates from the constitutional convention on Colsbury,' he said. 'He walked into the Lesser Keep and killed everyone he saw. He also wiped out a small detachment of soldiers who were on duty by the gates.'

'A god did this?' she said. 'Are you sure?'

'We're sure.'

'A Dominion god?'

'They are denying it. Cael and I were in Nom Karta twenty minutes ago. They say they had nothing to do with it; and I believe them. Edgar isn't so rash that he would send one of his gods to massacre innocent civilians. He knows that Karalyn would see it as a breach of the treaty. Besides, Kyra wouldn't have allowed it to happen. She isn't fond of the Empire, but she wouldn't sanction a massacre.'

Someone knocked on the door.

'Come in,' said Alva.

The door opened, and a tall Holdings marine entered the room.

'Ma'am,' he said; 'sir.'

'How can I help you?' said Alva.

The marine smiled. 'I'm here to tell ye both that it's time for a good long nap.'

Alva's eyes rolled up into her head, and she slipped off her chair and onto the floor. Cole remained awake, his hands by the sides of his head as he fought the compunction to sleep. The marine punched him in the face, and removed the Quadrant from his pocket. Cole gasped, as blood streamed from his nose, and he felt himself start to succumb. He dropped to his knees, then toppled sideways, his eyes still open.

'You're a tough wee fighter, Cole,' the marine said. 'I'm impressed.'

Cole gazed up at the figure, then he blinked as the marine changed into Cairney Holdfast.

Cairney kicked Cole in the ribs, 'Sleep, ya bastard!' he shouted.

Cole's eyes closed, and he fell into darkness.

Cole awoke when a bucket of seawater was thrown over his face. He spluttered and tried to move, but his wrists and ankles had been bound, and he had a gag over his mouth.

'Wakey-wakey, Cole,' said Cairney.

Cole glanced up. He was in a narrow cave, and sunlight was entering through a small entrance to his right.

'I've blocked yer vision powers,' said Cairney. 'Try them, if ye like; it'll do ye no good.' He grinned. 'Right now, ye'll be thinking – *but Cairney cannae read folks' thoughts* – and ye'd be right. I don't need to go into people's heads, Cole. I just tell folk what to do, and they do it. You're one of the few who can resist, but I'm stronger than you, in every respect. Now ye'll be thinking – *what has that handsome bastard done with wee Alva?* She's a pretty lassie, right enough. Do ye want her to stay pretty? I can re-arrange her face for her, if ye decide not to cooperate. Her safety is in your hands, Cole. Be a good wee boy, and she'll be fine. Right – I know ye went to Nom Karta with Cael. Tell me – did the Dominion deny killing those folk on Colsbury? Nod or shake yer head.'

Cole nodded.

'Does the Empire believe it was the Dominion who did it?'

Cole shook his head.

'Fucking bastards!' Cairney cried. 'Those stupid numpty arseholes!'

Cole remained calm as Cairney swore and raged in the cave. Was a sixteen-year-old behind the murders? But Aila had vouched for his presence in Kell. He was supposed to be camping.

'Here's another question,' said Cairney. 'Does the Empire have any idea who carried out the killings?'

Cole shook his head.

'Well, that's something, I suppose,' said Cairney. 'It's not much, but it's better than a kick in the teeth. What's the Empire's plan, then?'

Cole looked at him as if he was stupid.

'Oh aye, the gag,' said Cairney. 'I'm not taking it off, so I'll have to think up some more yes-or-no questions for ye. Here's a good one. Does the Empire know that Esher is missing?'

Cole's eyes widened, and he shook his head.

'Braw,' said Cairney. 'Next one – do they know I managed to get my hands on a Quadrant?'

Cole shook his head again.

'I have three Quadrants now,' he said; 'mine, yours and wee Alva's.'

Cole attempted to get into Cairney's mind, but the boy had been speaking the truth. His vision powers were unresponsive. He took a breath. He wasn't about to panic. His priority was to free himself and Alva, and to escape. Nothing else mattered.

Cairney held up a Quadrant. 'I'll be leaving ye now. Don't be crawling away. Alva's not on this island, and there's nowhere to go. It's basically a rock in the middle of the ocean; no one's gonnae find ye. When I come back, I'll bring food and water, and if ye behave, we can have a proper chat.'

He hovered a hand over the Quadrant, then he hesitated. 'Yer only still alive because yer not one of the Colsbury Holdfasts I blame for Da's death. I thought ye should know.'

His fingers moved over the device, and he vanished.

CHAPTER 23
UNFORGIVEABLE

Great Gunst, Gunstian Empire – 25th Luddinch 1605

Arrosa gazed out of her room's narrow window. The small panes were warped, and there were tiny air bubbles trapped within the glass, and it was difficult to see much of the city. She turned to her simple quarters and made her bed. She had only been in Great Gunst for three nights, but already she wanted to leave. Brogan and Claudian, each in their own way, were content with the progress that had been made in the talks they had been having with various departments of the Gunstian government; but Arrosa was still angry about how she had been questioned when they had first arrived. On the Star Continent, Arrosa was viewed as relatively pious; her Gunstian ways seeming overtly religious to many – but in Gunst, she was a faithless apostate, someone who had been shown the saving light of Chadura and had then rejected it. The Gunstians despised unbelievers, but they reserved their worst hatred for those who had abandoned the faith.

She glanced out of the window again. Where was he?

She smiled as the air shimmered in the corner of the room, then she realised immediately that something was wrong.

'Are you all right, Cael?' she said.

Her husband kissed her, then he glanced away, as though distracted.

'Cole didn't turn up for duty in Plateau City this morning,' he said. 'He was going to spend the night in Rainsby, so I assumed he had slept in, but he isn't in Madden's Tower. Alva Longhold isn't there, either. I found a few marines who had seen Cole go into her office, and then nothing. He was supposed to visit the governor, but I checked with him and he hasn't seen Cole.'

They sat on the bed.

'I don't suppose that they have run off together?' said Arrosa. 'Everyone knows that Cole was reluctant to move to the capital.'

'I can't believe he would have done something like that,' said Cael. 'I had a look around Alva's office, and her quarters. Her Quadrant has gone, but everything else is there – her clothes, all of the little things she brought from the Holdings – everything.'

'Have you been to Hold Long?'

'Not yet. I wanted to see you first, to make sure you were fine.'

'Everything seems to be going well here. Brogan met with a few industrial guilds yesterday evening, and they were very eager about forging closer trading ties to the Empire. We are far more advanced than Gunst in several areas, and they are keen to catch up. In fact, they were the most enthusiastic people we've met here. The government is wary, and many of the priests seem a little hostile.'

'Have they been asking you any more questions about your faith?'

'No, not since the first day. Perhaps the prayer I recited at the welcoming dinner satisfied them. I felt like such a hypocrite, but it might have allayed a few of their suspicions.'

'You can always leave if you feel uncomfortable.'

'And how would that look?' she said. 'Brogan and Claudian are happy with the negotiations so far, and I don't want to leave them here answering questions about why I have disappeared. The Chamberlain thinks we'll be here for another three days, so I just need to remain patient for a little while longer. How is Cowie?'

Cael nodded. 'He's fine. Rosie and Lucius have been helping out, and old Caelius has been taking care of the dogs.' He paused. 'I might have to go back to Nom Karta, and this time remain invisible. If one of Edgar's gods has taken Cole, then I... You know what I'll have to do.'

'Be careful,' she said. 'Kyra and I may have had our disagreements, but I cannot believe that she would allow Cole to be taken.'

Cael took her hand. 'I had better go.'

'Let me know about Cole when you have any news.'

They kissed, then Cael got to his feet. He triggered his Quadrant and vanished.

Arrosa stayed where she was. For all her own problems, she knew that Cael was trying to deal with the murder of the dragons, the slaughter on Colsbury, and the absence of Cole. Others might have cracked under the pressure, but she knew Cael would never give up. Neither would she. She would remain in the Gunstian capital until Claudian and Brogan were satisfied with the negotiations, and then she would leave Gunst, never to return.

She checked her reflection in the mirror, then she left the room. Two courtiers were waiting to escort her to breakfast, and they bowed.

'Did you sleep well, my lady?' said one.

Arrosa smiled. 'I did, yes; thank you.'

They led her through the dark, winding passageways towards the guests' dining room, and they entered the chamber where the imperial delegates and their staff ate their meals. The low, vaulted ceiling was being held up by dozens of broad stone pillars, and tables were laid out between them. Arrosa walked to where Claudian and Brogan were sitting, and took her seat. Claudian nodded his greetings, then he filled a bowl from the communal pot in the centre of the table and handed it to Arrosa.

'We have another busy day ahead of us,' Claudian said. 'I have been invited to tour some of the city's military facilities, and then I have a meeting with a few senior officials to discuss mutual cooperation against the Dominion.'

'Remember not to give away any of our secrets,' said Brogan.

Claudian smiled. 'Naturally, ma'am. The Gunstian army and navy are organised around their Gifted warriors, and they have their own secrets to keep. Besides, without a treaty, these tours and meetings are informal affairs, meant to lay down a foundation if any agreement is reached.'

'What are you doing today, ma'am?' said Arrosa.

'I am spending another day with various merchant guilds,' said Brogan. 'Most are optimistic that the Empire will be able to begin trading with Gunst even if no treaty is signed. The biggest problem is that they have very little to offer us. It is no exaggeration to state that the Empire is superior in almost every material respect. We have a far wider range of goods to sell than the Gunstians can provide.' She lowered her voice. 'In my opinion, the Gunstians are far too reliant upon their Gifted, and they have made very little progress in other areas. Their agriculture is backward, for instance, as are their construction methods, and their garment industries. I fear that any deal would consist of us allowing them to obtain our latest technology. They have no printing presses, and the quality of their steel is very poor. The size of their population is another problem – they have so many poor peasants for cheap labour that they see no need to make their industry more efficient. The question is – do we want the Gunstians to catch up with us?'

'They must have raw materials they could offer in exchange for technology,' said Claudian.

'None that we are lacking,' said Brogan. 'There are large deposits of coal and iron, but the reserves on the Star Continent are greater. They pride themselves on ship-building, but have so far been unable to construct any vessel that could cross the ocean to Aucteran. The Dominion has nothing to fear from Gunst.'

'Is the opposite true?' said Arrosa.

'If Edgar so wished it,' said Brogan, 'he could send gods, dragons and armies to these shores, but the Gifted would defend Gunst ferociously, as they have done in the past. But why would Edgar do such a thing? Even if an invasion was successful, the Dominion would have to govern millions of Chadura-worshippers who hate them. I cannot see any benefit for the Empire in getting too close to Gunst.'

'With one exception,' said Claudian. 'If the Empire had access to a few Gifted warriors, then we could easily repel any attack by the Dominion. Do you recall how effective Lahnos Laimos was when he was working for us? Imagine a dozen like him in the Imperial Army.'

'Should I suggest that as a trade?' said Brogan. 'We give them technology in return for them sending us a detachment of Gifted? How would we ensure their loyalty?' She leaned in closer. 'What if they refused to work for *unbelievers*?'

'Cael visited this morning,' said Arrosa.

'Did he?' said Brogan. 'How are things in the Empire?'

'Cole has gone missing,' she said.

Claudian and Brogan stared at her.

'He was supposed to be in Plateau City today. Cael went to Rainsby to look for him, but he wasn't there.'

'Does Cael suspect Dominion involvement?' said Claudian.

'He is going to explore that possibility.'

'He had better be careful,' said Brogan. 'He can be a little reckless at times; no offence, Arrosa.'

'Let's not jump to any conclusions,' said Claudian. 'I am sure that the Herald will sort it all out.'

'If something has happened to Cole,' said Arrosa, 'then I doubt even Kelsey would be able to restrain my husband.'

Claudian frowned. 'Should we cut short our stay here and go back to the Star Continent?'

'Let's wait to see if Cole is quickly found,' said Brogan. 'It might be nothing. Cael will let us know when he visits tomorrow.' She glanced at Arrosa. 'What do you have on for today?'

'Another cultural visit,' said Arrosa. 'I am to see the oldest temple in Gunst.'

Brogan smiled. 'Rather you than me.'

They finished their breakfast and got to their feet. Groups of Gunstian officials had entered the dining room and were waiting for the three delegates by the main door. Army officers were there for Claudian, and several merchants in rich robes greeted Brogan. Arrosa glanced around to find that day's escort, and a party of priests approached her.

The tallest among them gestured to an older man in dark brown robes. 'My lady,' he said; 'this is Archpriest Paltanai, who shall be your guide today.'

Arrosa inclined her head. 'It is a pleasure to meet you, Archpriest.'

'Lady Arrosa of Zamata,' said the old priest; 'today it is our great privilege to take you to the most sacred site on Athumia – the thousand-year-old Temple of the Martyrs.'

Arrosa smiled politely. 'I would be honoured to visit such a place.'

'Of course,' said the old priest; 'just like yesterday's visit to the crypt, only those belonging to the Gunstian faith are permitted to enter the Temple of the Martyrs; therefore, your courtiers will not be able to accompany you. I am sure you understand.'

Arrosa hid her feelings as the priests led her from the dining hall. The last thing she wanted to do was see another temple. On the previous day, she had been taken to a vast underground crypt, where the preserved body parts of dozens of ancient holy men were interred. Skulls, hands, thigh bones and all manner of other human remains had been encased in gold, and were arranged on deep shelves carved out of the bedrock beneath Great Gunst. Each reliquary had been fitted with a little hatch that opened, allowing the faithful to kiss the precious remains. Arrosa had been shown the skull of a man dead for eight hundred years, and she had pretended to kiss it, just as she had gone along with every other aspect of the Gunstian religion since she had arrived.

The priests escorted her along the wide hallways of the massive temple in which they had been staying, then they emerged out into a cloudy morning. The paving slabs of the plaza were wet from the morning rain, and a chill wind was blowing over the vast open space. They went down a street to their right, and came to a walled compound set amid houses and shops. Gunstian soldiers were on duty by the compound's only entrance, and they eyed Arrosa as she was led through.

The priests stopped in front of an ancient building, where two other priests were waiting for them.

'Do you know much of Gunstian history, my lady?' said Paltanai.

'Not as much as I would like,' said Arrosa.

'One thousand years ago,' he went on, 'Gunst was ruled by a monarchy, and it so happened that a new king was crowned – a king who had been deceiving his family and his people for many years. That king was Hardin the Apostate, cursed be his name. In his youth he pretended to be one of the faithful, but his wicked heart concealed a dreadful truth – that he had abandoned the true faith. He scorned the blessed Chadura, calling her nothing more than a false god, and he proclaimed himself to be the font of all wisdom. For six terrible years, he persecuted the devout followers of Chadura, martyring hundreds in his cruel desire to see our religion destroyed, until Chadura decided that our time of testing was at an end. Upon that day, the faithless king was ambushed here, in this very location. The righteous surrounded him, and they tore his godless body to pieces while his soldiers stood by and did nothing – praise be to Chadura!'

'I had not heard of this king,' said Arrosa.

'We teach his story as a lesson to all,' said the old priest, 'and as a warning to the faithful not to be corrupted by the evil ways of those who seek to tear down our religion. The blessed Chadura loves her people, but she hates those who abandon her teachings; she hates them with a violent and unremitting passion. One can always make excuses for the unbelievers – for they are ignorant, rather than evil; but there shall be no forgiveness for those who have seen the light and yet have turned from it. Their souls will burn forever in the fiery pits, and their suffering shall be eternal. Do you agree, my lady?'

'I bow to your superior knowledge of these matters,' said Arrosa.

The archpriest smiled, and gestured towards the low entrance to the temple. Arrosa went to the ancient doorway, and walked into the dark interior. As she passed the two priests by the door, her Gift of Kenning sensed that one had the Gift of Truth, and the other had the Gift of Pain. The two men bowed as she entered the temple, then followed her in with the other priests. Inside, candles were partly illuminating the sanctuary. Smoke-stained murals depicting the gruesome martyrdom of the faithful adorned most walls, while the largest picture was reserved for the horrible death of the apostate king. In it, pious Gunstians were holding him down as his skin was being scraped off by sharpened shards of pottery; while above, a representation of Chadura was smiling down benignly as she watched.

Behind Arrosa, the door was closed.

Archpriest Paltanai smiled at her. 'How long have you lived among the unbelievers, my lady?' he said.

'I left Zamata after the Gunstians there were massacred,' she said. 'That was seventeen years ago.'

'Why did you not flee to Gunst?' he said. 'You must have known that you would be forced to dwell among those who do not worship the blessed Chadura.'

'I fled Zamata on the only ship I could find,' she said. 'It happened to sail to Aucteran.'

The old priest kept a smile on his face as they explored the interior of the temple.

'I have been told,' he said, 'that a Gunstian priest conducted your marriage to the son of the Demon Witch; is that true?'

'It is, yes.'

'So I might assume that your husband has converted to the faith?'

'I would question your presumption, holy father,' she said; 'and I would prefer not to discuss my personal life.'

'Nothing is personal in the eyes of Chadura, my lady,' he said. 'Before her gaze, all secrets are revealed; all deceptions laid bare. Were you aware that many among the priesthood are opposed to any treaty with the Empire of the Sapphire Throne? Our military men thirst for your Empire's new weapons, while our merchants abase themselves in their greed for yet more wealth; but the priesthood remains influential. If we instruct the government to reject any such treaty, we shall be heard. For what use to us are weapons and wealth if our souls are lost in the process?'

'Weapons would allow Gunst to defend itself from the Dominion,' said Arrosa, 'while wealth would raise many here out of poverty.'

The priests next to her eyed her with contempt, and she wondered if she should be afraid. She glanced at the entrance, but it was sealed and barred, and she was alone with a dozen men, two of whom had Gifts, and all of whom were dressed in the robes of the priesthood.

'But the faith is what matters,' she went on.

'We have no need for the weapons of the Holdfasts, nor their money,' said Paltanai. 'The blessed Chadura sent us Gifts – Gifts we can use to defend ourselves; Gifts that we could use to destroy every nation of unbelievers upon this world and the others. You have three Gifts, my lady. Do you use them to honour Chadura?'

She glanced up, and noticed that the priest with the Gift of Truth was listening to her every word. She turned back to Paltanai, but kept her mouth shut.

'We require a demonstration of your faith,' the old priest went on, 'since you are refusing to answer our questions. Some among us have begun to suspect that your prayers and devotions are nought but a sham; that, within your heart, you have abandoned the true path. Is this so?'

Arrosa narrowed her eyes. 'Is this how you treat an emissary from a fellow nation? Have I not done what the Gunstian government requested? Did I not bring a delegation to Great Gunst? How dare you question my faith?'

'We dare, my lady, because we have to be sure that your motives are pure. If, as some suspect, you have committed the grievous crime of apostasy, then we shall cut all ties with your Empire, for we shall never entangle ourselves with a nest of demon-worshipping renegades.'

'I think I shall return to my quarters,' said Arrosa. 'Please escort me there.'

The old priest moved a little closer to her. 'We shall not, my lady; not until you answer a few simple questions. Do you not honour the truth? If your faith is sound, then you have nothing to fear. Tell me – do you believe in the one, true god?'

Arrosa moved away, until her back was against a wall. She calmed her thoughts.

'Yes,' she said.

The other priests glanced at the one with the Gift of Truth.

'She did not lie,' said the man.

'Praise Chadura!' cried the tall priest. 'Do you see? Arrosa is blameless. We have been suspicious for nothing. She has held on to her faith.'

'Wait,' said Paltanai. 'Arrosa – tell me more. Who is this god in which you believe?'

'There is only one god,' said Arrosa.

'Go on.'

Arrosa felt fear rise within her, along with a surge of defiance. There was no way she was going to be able to continue to trick the priests with half-evasions and platitudes; they would be content with nothing less than a full confession.

'There is but one true god,' she said, raising her chin, 'and her name is Karalyn Holdfast.'

The priests shrieked and wailed, some tearing their garments and beating their chests. Arrosa bolted for the door, slipping under the lunging arms of an old man. She reached the entrance, her hands pulling at the handle, but the door stood firm.

'Apostate!' the old priest shouted. 'Seize her.'

Arrosa turned, ready to defend herself, and a wave of Pain hit her. She saw the Gifted priest with his hand raised in her direction, and she clattered to the stone floor, convulsing in agony. She reached for her Quadrant, and another priest stamped on her hand.

'Be careful,' hissed another. 'She has the Gift of Vitrification.'

The Gift of Pain ceased, and the old archpriest leaned over and scooped up the Quadrant. He gazed down at the copper device, as Arrosa curled into a ball on the floor. Paltanai's fingers went out, and he touched several of the engraved images. The air crackled and shimmered, and the old archpriest disappeared.

The other priests cried out in terror, and one drew a knife. He held it close to Arrosa's throat.

'Where is he?' he shouted. 'What have you done with Archpriest Paltanai?'

Arrosa said nothing.

'Kill her!' cried another.

The tall priest pushed the others back. 'No,' he said. 'If she dies now, we may never see Paltanai again. She has used witchcraft to entrap him, and he will be lost forever. There is but one answer – we should take her in chains to the government, and confess what we have done this day.'

'We cannot,' shouted another. 'We have attacked an emissary. Our enemies among the army will use this against us – and what of the other delegates? We must conceal what has transpired here, but we must also press this woman to reveal what she has done with the archpriest.'

The tall priest nodded. 'If we follow this course,' he said, 'then not one word of this must leave the temple. Arrosa must disappear without a trace. We will say that she... that she ran away from us; or that she panicked and used her device to vanish.' He eyed the priest with the Gift of Pain. 'Subdue her until she loses consciousness.'

The priest nodded, and raised his hand again. Pain swept over Arrosa. Her mouth opened, but no sound came out, then she slipped into darkness.

When Arrosa awoke, she was still within the Temple of the Martyrs. Her wrists had been bound behind her back, and she was lying on the stone floor next to a sacrificial altar. The same dozen priests were gazing down at her, some with fear in their eyes, others with contempt.

'She is awake,' hissed one.

The tall priest stepped forward. 'Where is Paltanai?'

Arrosa gazed up from the cold floor, still dazed and groggy from the Gift of Pain.

'What have you done with the archpriest?' said the tall man.

'He could be anywhere,' said Arrosa. 'You saw what he did. He touched the Quadrant's surface. He could be a hundred yards away, or a hundred miles. He might be at the bottom of the ocean, or buried within a mountain; or he might be unharmed, if he's lucky.'

'Bring him back!' cried another priest.

Arrosa laughed, a bitter sound to her ears. 'And how would I do that? He has the Quadrant, not I.'

'Ask her how she left Athumia,' said another. 'Remember what we agreed. How did she leave this world and reach the Star Continent in the first place?'

The tall priest tilted his head. 'Answer my colleague's question, Arrosa.'

She kept her eyes on the priests. 'The Demon Witch took me,' she said.

The priests eyed each other.

'Were you on Zamata at the same time as the Demon Witch?' said one.

'I was.'

'Were you there when the great demon Lahnos Laimos destroyed the Gunstian fleet, slaughtering thousands of our kinsmen?'

'I was.'

The priests eyed each other again.

'Can it be true?' whispered one. 'Is Arrosa the Gunstian girl from the tales; the one seen in the presence of the great demon?'

'She spoke no lie,' said the priest with the Gift of Truth.

The tall priest crouched by Arrosa. 'Were you a friend of Lahnos Laimos?'

'I am still his friend,' she said.

The tall priest lowered his gaze, while the others whispered.

'She is a traitor, as well as an apostate,' said one of them. 'We should kill her now.'

'She deserves to die,' said another. 'She has betrayed our nation, and she has betrayed the blessed Chadura.'

'Maybe so,' said the tall priest, 'but she must not die here, and she must not die by our hands. This information will see us exonerated, my friends – don't you see? The government will not punish us for striking an emissary, not when they discover that she is a wanted traitor. They will applaud our actions, and Paltanai will be elevated to martyrdom.'

'Praise be to Chadura!' cried a priest.

'What of the other delegates from the Empire?' said another. 'They will return home to spread the news that we have arrested one of their number.'

'Their objections will be silenced when they discover that Arrosa is a traitor to Gunst,' said the tall priest.

'Perhaps they already know,' said another; 'perhaps they are here to spy on us, or to do us harm.'

'As representatives of a foreign land, we have no jurisdiction over them,' said the tall priest; 'but that does not apply to Arrosa. She is Gunstian; she is one of us, and we have every right to punish her for her crimes. Her execution shall serve as a lesson to the Empire of the Sapphire Throne; and it shall put an end to all foolish talk about a treaty with the unbelievers.' He glanced at his colleagues. 'This is a grim day, my friends. We have lost Archpriest Paltanai, may Chadura preserve his soul, but we shall have this one consolation – we shall see Arrosa burn.'

CHAPTER 24
THE PEACE OFFERING

Plateau City, The Plateau – 17th Day, First Third Autumn 552

'Get your shoes on, Caitlyn,' said Lucius. 'The tutor will be here in a couple of minutes to take you and Carden to school.'

'But I haven't finished my breakfast,' said the nine-year-old girl.

'And where is Carden?' Lucius went on, as he gazed around the apartment.

'He's gone to the toilet,' said Caitlyn.

'You and your brother are going to be late again,' said Lucius. 'How is it so difficult to get ready each morning? All you have to do is get dressed and eat some breakfast.'

'It was the same with my own children,' said Cowie's nursemaid, as she fed the young boy a spoon of yoghurt. 'It was always a mad rush in the mornings.'

Caitlyn slipped off her chair, and Lucius handed the girl her shoes.

'Put them on,' he said, 'then get your bag.'

'I don't know where my bag is,' she said.

'Where did you leave it yesterday?'

'I can't remember.'

Old Caelius chuckled from his armchair, which had been positioned next to the open entrance to their balcony.

'I think I saw it by the front door,' he said. 'Will you help me take Arrosa's dogs out after the children have gone to school?'

'If I have time,' said Lucius.

'My back's getting sore from controlling all three of them,' said Caelius. 'Rosie helped me yesterday, but she's busy today.' He reached down and scratched Maisie behind the ears. 'You're a good girl, but you're bloody strong.'

'Mind your language in front of the children,' said Lucius, as he watched Caitlyn tie her laces. Carden emerged from the bathroom, shoeless, and sat down at the table to resume his breakfast.

'You haven't got time for that,' said Lucius. 'The tutor will be here in...'

There was a knock at the door.

'Shoes, Carden; now,' said Lucius, as he walked to the entrance. He opened the door, and saw the children's tutor standing in the palace hallway. 'They will be just another minute.'

The tutor nodded, as though he had expected a delay.

Lucius picked up Caitlyn's bag from the floor by the door, and handed it to the girl.

'That's one ready,' said Lucius. 'Carden, get your shoes on.'

'I'm doing it,' cried the boy.

'Then do it faster.'

The boy finished lacing up his shoes and got to his feet. He picked up his school bag, and Lucius escorted both children to the door.

'Here they are,' he said to the tutor.

The man bowed. 'Thank you, sir. Come on, children; let's get to class.'

Lucius puffed out his cheeks as he watched the tutor leading the children towards the stairs.

'Work hard at school,' he called out, then he went back into the apartment and closed the door. He walked over to a side table in the sitting room, and poured himself another mug of coffee from the silver pot. He took the mug to a table on the apartment's long balcony, then he sat, lit a cigarette, and gazed at the view of the Teal Garden. He had five minutes to himself every morning – the small amount of time between the children leaving for school and the start of another working day.

The nursemaid frowned at the smoke rising from the cigarette, and carried Cowie into another room. Old Caelius gestured towards the three dogs.

'After this,' said Lucius, holding up his mug.

'That's your third this morning,' said Caelius.

'I'm glad to hear that you can still count,' said Lucius.

Caelius laughed. 'I haven't lost all of my faculties, you cheeky bastard; not yet, at any rate. Do you want to know another number that I've been counting? It's been fifty-five days since you last saw your wife.'

Lucius shrugged. 'She told me that she might be gone for a while.'

'Is that it? That's your response? You're bringing up those children on your own.'

'Hardly. They have tutors, and the nursemaid, and even you, Caelius.'

'You know what I mean. Caitlyn and Carden need their mother. For all Karalyn's regret about not being around for Cael and Kyra, she is repeating the same mistake.'

'Her earlier absences weren't *mistakes*, Caelius. She got stuck going to Lostwell, and then, for the second absence, Bastion murdered her.'

'That makes it worse,' said Caelius. 'She couldn't help being away from the twins. This time, it's her choice. You might have to accept that she doesn't want to be a wife or a mother any more.'

'And what would *acceptance* look like?'

Caelius gave him a sly smile. 'You find yourself another woman, lad. I happen to know one who lives a few flights of stairs up from here.'

'I was wrong,' said Lucius; 'you have gone senile. Are you seriously suggesting that I replace Karalyn with her sister? For a moment, let's leave aside the fact that Kelsey hates my guts, and try to imagine what Karalyn would do when she got home to discover me with her sister. She would kill us both.'

'Fear is not a reason to stay married to someone. And Kelsey doesn't hate you, Lucius. She's angry with you, and there's a big difference.'

'And what would your son say?'

'Van is a bloody imbecile,' said Caelius. 'I love him, of course; he's my son, but he was an idiot to throw away what he had with Kelsey. And now he's with someone young enough to be my granddaughter.'

Lucius finished his coffee and stubbed out the cigarette.

He stood. 'This has been enlightening, Caelius, but I'd better go to work. I have Her Majesty's visit to the Eastern Rim to organise.'

'Oh yes? And when will that be?'

'A few days from now.'

The air shimmered a few yards away, and Cael appeared on the balcony. The three dogs leapt to their feet and bounded towards him, whimpering, whining and barking. They jumped up at Cael, and he scratched the head of each in turn as they began to calm down.

'Have you had any luck?' said Lucius.

Cael shook his head, the anger and frustration evident in his eyes.

'Can I have some of your coffee?' he said.

'Help yourself,' said Lucius.

Cael walked into the sitting room and filled a mug, while the three dogs followed him, wagging their tails. He put in four sugars and a splash of milk, then he walked back out on to the balcony and lit a cigarette.

'Where have you been looking?' said Lucius.

'Rainsby, Hold Long and the Hold Fast estate,' said Cael, as the dogs sat by his feet. 'That was yesterday. Last night, I visited Nom Karta, quietly. There's no sign of him there.'

'Did Kyra detect your presence?'

'Maybe,' said Cael, 'if she happened to be looking in the right place at the right time. I kept my thoughts focussed on finding Cole, so if she read my mind, she would understand why I was there.' He eyed Lucius. 'Is Cowie here?'

'He's with his nursemaid in another room,' said Lucius. 'I would leave him there, if I were you, at least until you've finished that cigarette.

The maid doesn't like smoke around the children. Have you been to visit Arrosa this morning?'

'Not yet,' said Cael. 'I was in Clackenbaird at dawn.'

'Why?'

'I was ruling out any involvement by the Marchbrae Holdfasts,' said Cael. 'I saw no sign of Cole, but I did find something strange, within Aunty Aila's mind.'

Lucius narrowed his eyes. 'What did you find?'

'Someone has... altered her memories. I couldn't sense which ones, or when it had happened, but I could feel the lingering presence of the powers of persuasion. I know that I haven't touched Aunty Aila's mind, and I'm pretty certain Kyra wouldn't do it. Who does that leave? Sable? My mother?'

'Might we have another Daimon on our hands?' said Caelius. 'That little bastard could alter memories; might there be a new dream mage somewhere in Kell?'

'I would have sensed it; I'm sure,' said Cael.

'Did you read Naxor's mind?' said Lucius.

'Briefly,' said Cael. 'There was nothing in there to alarm us; just the usual nonsense. He still believes that Aila and Corthie's children should be patient; that they should wait until we all die off before they make any move.'

Lucius nodded. 'It might be time to make the search for Cole official,' he said. 'It's been two days since he was last seen. Perhaps we should notify every agent in the Empire.'

'But that would also alert whoever took him.'

'That's if he has been taken; and, if he has, then his abductor will already guess that we'll be looking for him. Let's assume that the same god who killed the dragons and the convention delegates took Cole and Alva. He's likely to be hiding somewhere, but what does he want? He has a Holdfast and a vision mage – what will he do with them?'

'He might demand a ransom,' said Caelius. 'Either that, or poor Cole might already be dead.'

'I'm not giving up,' said Cael. 'Give me one more day to find him before we make it public. One day, Lucius.'

'All right. Where are you going next?'

Cael eyed him. 'I was hoping you might have some suggestions.'

'From what distance would you be able to sense Cole's powers?'

'The same distance that I can vision to, but where do I look? It would take me a third to scan the Star Continent from end to end.'

Caelius leaned forward and peered over the edge of the balcony. 'Something's going on down on the Dragon Bridge,' he said. 'Greysteel seems quite agitated.'

Lucius and Cael turned. Greysteel was standing on the sturdy bridge, his wings extended, as though he had been surprised by something. Next to him was a woman.

'What in Pyre's name is my sister doing here?' said Cael.

Greysteel gestured towards the Teal Garden with a forelimb. Kyra turned, and saw the three men gazing down at her from the balcony. She raised a hand in greeting, then she appeared in the middle of the apartment's sitting room. The dogs jumped up and barked at her, and Cael ordered them to lie down.

Kyra walked out on to the balcony, and Lucius got to his feet.

'Greetings, Kyra,' he said. 'Is this an official visit?'

'Apologies for not going through Bailey, Lucius,' said Kyra, 'but I need to speak to my brother. Might I stay for a few moments?'

'Of course,' said Lucius. 'Does Edgar know that you are here?'

'He does,' she said. 'By the way, the layout of the palace is quite ingenious; I was unable to access the upper floors, hence my arrival on the bridge.'

Lucius smiled. 'It was designed to prevent strangers from arriving by Quadrant without an invitation. Coffee?'

'No, thank you.' She turned to Cael. 'Bailey lied to you, brother. Two days ago, when you and Cole were in Nom Karta, he deliberately withheld the truth from you. He recognised the image of the god in your mind.'

Cael's eyes tightened. 'Why would he lie about it?'

'He claims he was too bewildered to properly understand what he had seen. He confessed this to Edgar and myself earlier this morning. He is quite ashamed of himself, as he should be. He also said that he simply could not accept what he had seen.'

'Why couldn't he accept it?' said Cael.

'Because he firmly believed the Ninth Ascendant to be dead.'

Cael blinked. 'What? Esher? Esher killed the delegates on Colsbury? – but that's impossible. His powers were blocked and his memories wiped clean. We were there, sister; we saw what Mother did to him.'

'I understand this, brother,' she said, 'but that is what Bailey told us. Edgar went into his mind, and he confirmed that the god in question appears to be a young version of Esher. The Esher that Edgar remembers was an old man, long before the days of salve.'

Cael turned to Lucius.

'As far as I know,' Lucius said, 'Esher is still working in Jezra, under an assumed identity. He is known there as *Reece*. He is monitored, but with a light touch. He has a job with the Brigades, and an apartment of his own.'

'This doesn't make any sense,' said Cael. 'If it's really Esher, then someone must have unblocked his powers.'

Kyra raised an eyebrow. 'Don't look at me, brother. I haven't been to the City of Salve for years. You should know that Edgar is quite angry with Bailey over this.'

'Is he, aye?' said Cael. 'Did you know that Cole was abducted after we left Nom Karta? Perhaps if Bailey had been honest, then Cole wouldn't be missing.'

Kyra lowered her gaze. 'Cole is missing? Mother wouldn't have done anything to Esher, would she?'

Cael stubbed out his cigarette and began to pace up and down the balcony. 'Someone has also been changing Aunty Aila's memories.'

'You know me better than to think that I would go anywhere near Aila,' said Kyra. 'She still loathes me for what I did to escape Colsbury.'

'I didn't say it was you,' said Cael; 'but someone did it.' He stopped, and faced Lucius. 'I'm going to Pella, then Jezra. I need to see Esher with my own eyes. He should look around forty by now, aye?'

'I would imagine so,' said Lucius.

'The god who was witnessed on Colsbury looked around twenty,' Cael said. He took out his Quadrant, then he glanced at his sister. 'I will deal with Bailey later.'

Cael swept his fingers over the surface of the Quadrant and vanished.

'Thank you for coming here to let us know,' said Lucius.

Kyra nodded.

'How is Lord Edgar these days?'

'He is well,' said Kyra, 'and enjoying being a father again. So this is the famed Blue Palace? It's a little on the large side, don't you think? How many schools and hospitals could have been built if the Empress possessed less hubris?'

Lucius smiled. 'The imperial treasury can afford both.'

'Aye, since you sold half of the Plateau to the Rakanese.'

'I didn't realise that you still studied the politics of the Empire, Kyra,' he said. 'Is the Dominion interested in joining? I could arrange that.'

'Are three worlds not enough for you, Lucius? Is the Empress anxious to ensure that everyone on every world submits to her rule?'

'The Empress is gradually introducing democracy to the Empire,' said Lucius. 'The Plateau will be the next province to be enfranchised. Tell me – do the dragons of the Dominion allow the Aucterians to vote? It's a little ironic that you fled to an empire far more despotic than the one you left. And who is really in charge? Is it Queen Famula or is it Lord Edgar? That always confused me.'

'Well, you were always easily confused, Lucius.'

Caelius laughed. 'This is like the old days.'

Kyra eyed him. 'Where do Cael and Arrosa live? I would like to see my nephew.'

'Cowie is in this apartment,' said Lucius. 'Arrosa is away on imperial business.'

Kyra gazed into his eyes. 'Gunst.'

'That's right. We informed Edgar of this, if you recall.'

She nodded. 'I was on Zamata when your delegates told us. To be honest, I would rather see Cowie without Arrosa looking over my shoulder.'

Lucius walked into the neighbouring room and gestured for the nursemaid to bring Cowie. Kyra gazed at the two-year-old child. The nursemaid glanced at Lucius, who nodded. Kyra took the offered child, and held him for a few moments.

'He looks like his father,' she said. 'I can't see any Arrosa in him.'

'You can if you look hard enough,' said Lucius. 'Do you want to go upstairs to pay your respects to Her Majesty while you're here?'

Kyra handed Cowie back to the nursemaid. 'I do not,' she said. 'Tell my brother that I hope he finds Cole. Goodbye, Lucius; goodbye, Caelius.'

She vanished.

Lucius eyed Caelius. 'I had better go upstairs to let the Herald know that Kyra was here, and what she told us.'

'But the dogs, Lucius,' said Caelius. 'They need to go on their... you know.'

'Sorry, Caelius,' he said. 'You're on your own.'

He nodded to the nursemaid and left the apartment. He took a steam platform to the upper levels of the palace, and walked into Kelsey's quarters. He knocked on her office door, and it swung open.

Kelsey glanced up from the book she was reading.

'Hard at work, I see,' said Lucius.

'Shut it, smart arse,' she said. 'This book is research.'

Lucius glanced at the spine. '*A Guide to the Gunstian Religion*?' he said.

'It was written by an Aucterian,' she said, 'so it's biased. All the same, the Gunstians appear to be quite deranged, and I'm not sure we should sign any treaty with them.' She frowned. 'What do you want? I assume you want something?'

He sat. 'Kyra was here. Bailey thinks it was Esher who slaughtered the delegates on Colsbury. Cael has gone to the City to investigate.'

'Esher, eh? That seems unlikely. He would have needed someone to unblock his powers. We know the folk who can do that, but why would any of them have gone near Esher? And who knew he was alive and well in Jezra? I need a list of names.'

'Let's see what Cael finds. Bailey might have been mistaken. Perhaps we should be looking for one of Esher's sons or grandsons. Albany looked very similar to Arete, for instance.'

Kelsey raised an eyebrow. 'That was an interesting example to choose. Have there been any sightings of Albany... I mean Karalyn?'

'You're as hilarious as ever, Kelsey.'

'I didn't hear you laugh.'

'Caelius reminded me that it has been fifty-five days since Karalyn was last here.'

'I didn't think the old bastard could count past ten. Are you busy right now?'

'Why?'

She opened a drawer and took out two glasses and the bottle of Lachellan whisky that Lucius had bought for her in Kell.

'Let's have a drink,' she said. 'We need to talk.'

Lucius said nothing as she opened the bottle and poured out two small measures. She slid one of the glasses across the table to him.

'It's a little early to be drinking,' he said. 'Are we celebrating something?'

'No. Are you still angry with me?'

Lucius frowned. 'Am I still angry with you? I think you might have that the wrong way round.'

'You were pissed off when I tried to pay for the whisky.'

'That's because I meant it as a gift.'

'Aye, but I asked you to get me some Lachellan so that I could share it with you, as a peace offering. I could hardly ask you to pay for my own fucking peace offering, could I?'

'Maybe if you had explained that, then we wouldn't have argued.'

She nodded. 'Drink the damn whisky, Lucius.'

He picked up the glass. 'Thank you.'

'You're welcome. I've been thinking.'

'Is that wise?'

'Shut up for one moment,' she said. 'Those reforms you suggested to the Empress – you were right. If we are going to deliver democracy to the Empire, it will need to be done gradually. It might take years, maybe decades. So, that's what I wanted to say.'

'I want to say something, too,' he said. 'Despite what you think, I support the new constitution. I want the people of the Empire to have a say in how decisions are taken. I voted for a postponement to avoid civil strife, not because I'm opposed to the reforms. It has to be gradual, as you said.'

Kelsey glanced out of her window at the view of the private gardens of the Empress. 'It's taken me a while to get over what you did that day,' she said. 'I'm still angry about it. The Empress says that I'm angry because you're my best friend, and she's right. Don't ever hide your feelings from me again, Lucius, not about something that I worked on for years.'

'I won't,' he said. 'I regret that; it was a mistake. I didn't want to interfere, but I went about it in the wrong way.' He sipped his whisky. 'This stuff's pretty good.'

'No shit,' she said. 'I prefer the single malts to the blends. How much did it cost?'

'Ninety.'

'Ninety fucking sovereigns?' she cried. 'And I thought the fifty I offered you was generous. Aila will bleed us all dry at this rate, the cheeky bitch. I can get Severton for a third of the price.'

'Yes, but this is probably three times better than Severton.'

'Aye, but you drink it just as fast. Ninety? Pyre's tits.'

'Naxor refused us a discount.'

'Aye, I'm sure he did, the wee radge. Fifty-five days, eh?'

'I thought we had moved past that point in the conversation.'

'I was circling around it,' she said. 'You have to tell her how you're feeling, Lucius, you know, when she eventually turns up. You can't live like this.'

'It was different for you and Van,' he said.

Kelsey stared at him. 'Why would you bring up that prick?'

'Because you were married to him, and we were discussing marriage. You and Van always felt free to shout at each other. You were never cautious about holding back your feelings.'

'And? I assume there's some convoluted point you're trying to make?'

'Can you imagine Karalyn engaging in a stand up row? Karalyn and I have never once had a raging argument. She has been angry with me from time to time, usually over politics, but she never raises her voice. It is almost impossible to argue with her. She closes up. One time, when I was trying to tell her something she didn't want to hear, she vanished, while I was mid-sentence.'

'She doesn't like confrontation, but you still need to tell her what you think.'

'What was it like for you and Van?' he said. 'When did you know it was over?'

'That's easy,' she said. 'I can remember the exact moment – it was when he took Calpurnia and Caelius to the City without my permission, and then he wouldn't bring them back. That was it for me. I could forgive a lot, but I wasn't prepared to forgive that. Why are you still friends with that numpty?'

Lucius finished his whisky, and Kelsey refilled their glasses.

'Are you sure we should be drinking another one?' he said.

'After the Empress,' she said, 'we are the two most powerful people in the Empire. Who's going to stop us from having a drink? This is a peace offering, or had you forgotten? The Empress won't need me for the rest of the day. What have you got on?'

'I'm supposed to be organising the trip to Dragon Eyre.'

She laughed. 'It's all in hand, Lucius; relax. Let the Chamberlain's staff take care of it.'

'Fair enough,' he said, picking up the glass.

'So,' she went on, 'I noticed how you deftly tried to avoid my last question. I want an answer. Van stabbed me in the back, and you're still his friend. Why?'

'We go back a long way,' he said. 'I met him at roughly the same time I met you, back when the Banner of the Lostwell Exiles was founded. Think about everything we've been through since then; all the experiences we've shared. You can't cast that aside; well, I won't cast it aside, not even when Van does something stupid. Do you think Van and I agree on everything? We have had several major disagreements over the years but, fundamentally, we are there for each other if we need help.'

'But I'm your best friend, aye?'

He laughed. 'Yes, Kelsey – you are my best friend.'

'Why isn't Van your best friend?'

'Possibly because he was my superior officer for several years when we first met. That put some distance between us. Besides, I can't talk to him the way I can talk to you. You get me, while Van doesn't really understand how I think. He thinks I'm too nice to get anywhere in life.'

Kelsey laughed. 'The twat. You're the fucking commander of the entire imperial army, while he's an unemployed ambassador. When it comes to Karalyn, though, the prick might have a point. You are too nice. As a husband, I mean. What would Karalyn have to do to make you stand up to her?'

Lucius drank his whisky. 'I think she may have already done it. I can't pinpoint the exact moment in the way that you could with Van, but I've moved beyond hoping that my marriage will recover. It's hard to accept, but I know that Karalyn doesn't love me any more. And there's no point in staying together for Caitlyn and Carden, because we aren't together. I have no idea where my wife is; no idea where she has been for fifty-five days.' He drained the glass. 'It's over.'

Kelsey puffed out her cheeks. 'Shit, Lucius; I'm sorry.'

'It's fine. In my heart, I've known it for a long time.'

'I wonder what my mother would think,' she said. 'Of the famed Daphne Holdfast's four children, three had failed marriages, and poor Corthie, who was the only one of us whose marriage worked, is dead.'

'I think that Karalyn still loves Lennox,' he said. 'I don't think she has ever really got over that; I was the replacement and, in her eyes, I never quite measured up to him.'

'I don't know if that's true,' said Kelsey. 'I'm sure that Karalyn loved you when you got married, but if she thinks that, then she's an idiot. Do you remember Nurian?'

Lucius shook his head.

'He was a captain in the Banner while we were living in the City,' Kelsey went on. 'Van assigned him as my liaison officer, when I was sleeping in the quarries on the Iceward Range with Deathfang and the other dragons from Lostwell. Van chose him because he thought that we would get on, and he was right. It sounds terrible to say this, but I was more fond of him than I ever was of Van. Nurian had the same interests, the same sense of humour; he was the opposite of Van in many ways. It broke my heart when he was killed by a greenhide. If things had worked out differently, I might have married him instead of Van.'

Lucius nodded.

'All the same,' Kelsey said, 'I don't hold on to the past like my sister does. To me, Nurian is a fond memory, but Karalyn clings to an idealised version of Lennox – the perfect man. It was tragic what happened to him, but Karalyn has never been able to put it behind her.'

'All I have to do now is tell her that it's over between us,' he said. 'Do you think she'll care?'

'She'll care, but not as much as you would hope. I don't think she loves you any more; she might not have loved you for some time. And then what? Have you thought about what might come after Karalyn?'

Lucius took a breath. Perhaps it was the whisky, or perhaps it was

Kelsey's direct question about the future, but he knew the time for complete honesty had come.

'Earlier,' he said, 'you told me to never hide my feelings from you again.'

'Aye,' she said, 'that's right.'

'Kelsey,' he said, 'I love you.'

She spat her whisky out over the desk and began to choke. Her features flushed, and she tried to stand up. She gave up, coughing.

'What the fuck, Lucius?' she cried. 'This is a joke, aye?'

'It's not a joke,' he said. 'It's always been you, Kelsey. If you and Van hadn't got together, then I would have told you years ago.'

'But you married my fucking sister!'

'I loved her. I had given up on you by that point; I had moved on. My love for Karalyn wasn't a lie. But, now that I know my marriage is over, I've had time to think about what I really want. It's you; I want you.'

She stared at him. 'I can't do this,' she whispered. 'I think you should leave, Lucius. I could never... I could never betray my sister, even though...'

'Even though?'

'Please, Lucius; go. You need to go.'

He got to his feet. 'I'm glad I said it. I'm sick of pretending. Thanks for the whisky.'

He turned and left her office, then he took a steam platform back down to the floor upon which his apartment lay. He walked through the front door, and saw Caelius struggling with the leashes for the three dogs.

'Those damn hounds!' Caelius cried. 'One of them saw a dragon, and she damn near pulled me over the side of the bridge.'

Lucius went to a cupboard in the sitting room, as the dogs ran to their beds. He opened the cupboard, and withdrew the bottle of Strathlanach whisky.

Caelius eyed it. 'That looks interesting. Are you opening it?'

Lucius nodded. He set down two glasses, cracked open the seal on the bottle, and poured.

'What's the occasion?' said Caelius, as he eased himself into his armchair.

Lucius brought the glasses and the bottle over to where Van's father was sitting, and took a chair opposite him. He handed Caelius a glass.

'I've just told Kelsey that I love her,' he said.

'Oh,' said Caelius. 'How did she take it?'

'How do you think?' said Lucius. 'Drink up.'

CHAPTER 25
BLUDGEONED

Jezra, The Western Bank – 7th Balian 3441

'It's only been seven days,' said Konna, 'but I already hate this fog. What kind of shithole has fog for an entire month? I cannae take much more of it.'

'It's not the fog that's getting you down,' said Maxwell. 'Your brother has done this to your mood. You've been staring out of that window for two days, ever since we got back from Colsbury.'

'It's partly the fog,' she said. 'I don't like the way it hangs over the streets like a shroud. It makes Jezra seem dead. I cannae wait for winter to start.'

'Would you go back to Kell if I still had my Quadrant?' he said.

She shrugged.

'Maybe you should travel over to Ooste and walk through the portal,' Maxwell said. 'You can get a porter to take you to Kell, just like we did back at the beginning of Sweetmist. You aren't trapped here.'

'I'm not sure I'd be able to look Ma in the eye,' she said. 'And I cannae leave you here on yer own, not if Cairney might appear at any moment.'

'I don't think he likes me very much.'

'That's because ye let him walk all over ye. Stand up to him, and he might start to respect ye.'

'Or he'd kill me.'

Konna laughed. 'Aye, maybe. Shall we go to a tavern and get hammered?'

'I suppose so.'

'We could go out on the pull.'

Maxwell squinted at her. 'What does that mean?'

'It means we go out looking for somebody to get off with,' she said. 'I'd try to snag a good-looking lad, and you'd chase the girls. Or boys. Whatever ye fancy.'

'It would be girls,' said Maxwell. 'I just want to make that clear.'

'We've got thousands of years ahead of us,' she said; 'keep an open mind.'

Maxwell rolled his eyes, then he got to his feet and walked away from the window.

'Where are ye going?' she said.

'To get my boots on,' he said. 'I'm not walking to the taverns in my bare feet.'

'Fair point.'

Konna also stood, and she joined Maxwell by the front entrance to the apartment, and they both pulled their boots on and laced them up.

'Remember to tell everyone that we're cousins,' she said; 'I don't want anyone thinking we're a couple.'

'Everyone knows who we are,' he said. 'It's the immortality that will scare people off.'

'Is that what ye've found?'

'Sometimes. There are girls who like the idea of being with a god, while others don't see any future in it, so they stay away. What about you? Many boyfriends in Kell?'

'Nah, not really. For me, it's the family name that does it. People are intimidated by the word *Holdfast*. All the lads knew who my father was, and most gave up before they'd even tried.'

'My mother has much the same effect on people.'

'Do ye ever wonder about going to Athumia?' she said.

'Why would I want to go there?'

'Why do ye think? It's the only place left that still has lots of gods and demigods. If we're going to meet someone, it'd probably be there. Where else is there?'

'But don't they all hate the Empire?'

'My cousin Kyra is married to Lord Edgar, ya numpty. We'd be fine. The Sapphire Throne is a mortal empire; the Dominion is run by dragons and gods. Do ye not think we'd be better off there?'

Maxwell lowered his gaze. 'I don't know,' he said. 'When I was being brought up, I was always told that it was my duty to defend the City from the greenhides.'

'All right – what about after we destroy the last two nests on this side of the Straits? That would free the City from greenhide attack for decades. If ye stayed here, ye'd have fuck all to do.'

'Deserting to the enemy seems a bit radical, though. And remember your brother's crazy plan – if he gets his way, there will be another war between the Empire and the Dominion. And then Karalyn will descend from on high, and smite us all.'

Konna laughed.

They took their coats down from their pegs, then the air shimmered behind them. Konna sighed.

'How did you know I was coming?' said Cairney. 'Ye've got yer boots on, but ye won't need yer coats.'

Cairney triggered the Quadrant, the air shimmered again, and the three of them appeared on a beach somewhere on Dragon Eyre. Behind them was a fringe of palm trees, then the sheer sides of a cliff rose into the blue sky. At the base of the cliff was a cluster of dark cave entrances, almost hidden by the thick, green foliage.

Konna held up her coat. 'Ye didnae give us a chance to put them back on the pegs, ya bellend.'

Cairney raised his palms and gazed around at the view. 'Is this not better than fog, sis? I rescued ye from the shite weather in the City, and brought ye to the world of never-ending sunshine. I dinnae hear Maxi-boy complaining.'

'Why are we here?' said Maxwell. 'I don't want to watch another massacre.'

'Relax,' said Cairney, putting his huge arm round Maxwell's shoulder. 'I just thought ye both deserved a wee break from Jezra. I've gathered food and drink, and ye can swim in the sea, or lie on the beach.'

Konna narrowed her eyes. 'Is that it? No ulterior motive?'

'Ya cynical cow, Konna,' said Cairney. He pulled out a bundle of weedsticks from a pocket. 'Do ye want some dreamweed? And there's whisky in a crate under that palm tree over there; and it's not the shite stuff, either. I stole it from a warehouse last night.'

'Ye were back in Kell?'

'Obviously. Do ye think I'd bother to steal anything from Severton? Kell whisky is miles better.'

'Technically, it's Lach whisky,' said Konna. 'We only mature and blend it. Most of it is distilled in Lach.'

'Shut up, ya fucking killjoy. I try to do something nice for ye both, and all ye do is whine.'

'What ye mean is that ye were bored out here on yer own,' said Konna; 'still, I appreciate the gesture, brother. It does feel good to have the sun on my skin again. And I'll take one of those weedsticks.'

Cairney grinned, and handed her one. She placed it to her lips, and Cairney shot out a tiny spark of fire, which lit it. They walked over to where Cairney had laid down a few blankets on the sand under the shade of a palm tree.

Konna smoked the weedstick for a minute, then she passed it to Maxwell.

'What have ye been doing for the last couple of days, brother?' she said.

'This and that,' said Cairney. 'I was in Plateau City for a while, pretending to be a courtier. I got as far as the fucking audience chamber – can ye believe that? I heard them talking about Colsbury. The Empress sent Cael and Cole scurrying off to Nom Karta, to tell Edgar that the Empire doesnae blame him or the Dominion for the deaths of the delegates.'

'Shit,' said Konna. 'Then the plan didnae work?'

'They think somebody is trying to stir up trouble between the two sides.'

'That is exactly what you've been doing,' said Maxwell, 'but the leaders of the Empire aren't stupid.'

'I've thought of something else we can do,' said Cairney; 'something that will kick off a proper war. Check this out.'

Cairney appeared to change his form in front of them, morphing until he looked like Cael Holdfast.

'Pretty convincing, eh?' he said, changing back to his own likeness.

Maxwell got to his feet, then he staggered and nearly fell over. Cairney cackled.

'That weed is strong,' said Maxwell, 'but I need to pee.'

'Use yer powers to sober up,' said Konna.

Maxwell frowned. 'I thought that was against the rules.'

'Leave him be, sis,' said Cairney. 'It's funny to watch him stumble about. Go behind a tree, Maxi-boy; and don't get lost.'

Maxwell nodded, then he swayed and started to walk towards the line of palm trees.

Konna turned back to Cairney as soon as Maxwell was out of sight.

'I'm gonnae regret asking this,' she said, 'but why would ye want to look like Cael Holdfast?'

'I was about to tell ye, sis, now that Maxi-boy's away for a piss; but first,' he said, 'I have a wee confession. After Cael and Cole were sent to Nom Karta, I went to Rainsby, and waited for Cole to visit. I knew he wouldnae be able to resist seeing his wee lassie there. It turns out that I can control Cole – it's easy for me. I can order him about. So, now that ye know that, have a guess what I might do while appearing as Cael. Imagine the faces of the Dominion dragons, when me and Cole kill a few dozen of them. We'll leave some alive, of course, so they can tell Edgar and Kyra what happened. Genius, eh? The Dominion will have to retaliate.'

Konna narrowed her eyes. 'Can ye just answer this one question for me?' she said. 'Where is Cole right now?'

Cairney laughed. 'That would be telling. He's in a secure location. I took his lassie, too. It always helps to have a hostage – it weakens Cole's will to resist. But here's the best part – while Cole and I attack the Dominion, Esher will be attacking the Empress and her court on Dragon Eyre. That's right – the fucking Empress herself is going to Ulna tomorrow.'

'If the Empress is going to Dragon Eyre,' said Konna, 'then why don't ye order Esher to kill her? Why go to the bother of starting a war?'

'Simple, sis. Esher is highly unlikely to be able to get close enough to the Empress to do her any real harm. Kelsey will be there, so most of his powers won't work; and the real Cael will be around, naturally, along with a shitload of soldiers and dragons. Esher will be commanded to throw himself at them until he's dead, and his death will destroy any link he had to us. It's a clean way to get rid of the evidence.'

'Wait,' said Konna. 'Yer gonnae order Esher to kill himself? I thought you said he was one of us – a god?'

Cairney smiled. 'Did I say that? Oh well. I guess that's tough shit for Esher, eh? Just think, though – most folk thought that he was already dead, so what difference will it make?'

'I think it might make a lot of difference to Esher,' said Konna. 'We would have been better off leaving him as Reece.'

'But if we keep using him to kill folk,' said Cairney, 'then somebody, eventually, is going to recognise him, especially when the City of Salve admits that they've lost him.'

'The Aurelians might have already told the Empire,' she said.

'They'll be embarrassed about having misplaced an Ascendant,' said Cairney, 'and they'll want to conduct their own search first. But aye – it's only a matter of time before they have to tell folk. That's why Esher has to go. It's a shame, so it is; but what can we do? At least the bastard will go down fighting, eh?' He paused. 'What about the wee laddie; can we trust him, sis?'

'Maxwell? Aye. He's sound.'

'I'm not certain ye understood me,' Cairney went on. 'There was a reason I waited until he was away before telling ye the plan. Are we sure that Maxi-boy will keep his mouth shut if he gets questioned by a Colsbury Holdfast?'

'Could ye not use yer weird voice powers to block his mind from being read?'

'Maybe, but how long would it last? We might have to face another sad truth – Maxi-boy's a fucking liability. Me and you can keep the Colsbury Holdfasts out of our heads, but Maxwell is weak. He doesnae have any dream powers, and his mind would buckle, even if he was determined to say nothing.'

Konna rolled her eyes. 'The answer is no, Cairney. We're not killing Maxwell.'

Cairney withdrew a bottle of whisky from a crate, opened it, and took a long swig.

'Pyre's arse, brother,' said Konna. 'That's eighteen-year-old. Uncle Naxor is going to miss a crate of fucking eighteen-year-old.'

'He'll assume that one of the Marchbrae workers has stolen it.'

'Until he reads their minds and discovers their innocence. Ye dinnae think things through sometimes, brother.'

Cairney shrugged. Maxwell returned from the trees, his eyes wild.

Konna frowned as the young god approached. 'What's up?'

Maxwell gazed at Cairney. From his expression, it was clear that he had used his powers to sober himself.

'Why is there an unconscious woman tied up in the caves?' said Maxwell.

Cairney's eyes darkened. 'I fucking told ye not to get lost, ya halfwit. What were ye doing in the caves?'

'I thought a dark cave would be more private,' he said.

Konna got to her feet and peered towards the cave entrances. 'There's a woman tied up in there? Cairney, what the fuck?'

'It's Alva Longhold, ya twat,' said Cairney. 'I've already told ye about her. I'm keeping her as a hostage.'

'A hostage?' said Maxwell. 'What do we need a hostage for?'

'Never you mind, Maxi-boy,' said Cairney.

Konna began walking towards the caves. Cairney muttered something under his breath, got up, and followed her. Konna passed through the lines of palm trees, and approached the closest cave.

'Try the one on the right,' said Maxwell.

Konna veered to her right, and gazed into the dark entrance. Lying a few yards within the cave, a dark-skinned woman had been bound. Her arms were tied behind her back, and more rope had been used to secure her legs. Her eyes were closed, but Konna could see her chest rise and fall.

'She's fine,' said Cairney.

'How long has she been here?' said Konna.

'Two days. I've been waking her up now and again so she can drink some water; I'm not a fucking savage.'

'She reeks, Cairney,' said Konna. 'Ye cannae leaving her lying on the ground like that. She's only Holdings; a mortal – she'll get sick.'

'So what if she gets sick? We only need to keep her alive until Cole has helped me with the next attack. After that, I'll snap her neck. It'll be quick; I promise.'

'No,' said Konna.

Cairney laughed.

'I'm serious, brother,' she said. 'Ye cannae kill her. What has she ever done to us?'

'It was her bad luck to be going with a Colsbury Holdfast.'

'Aye, but that Colsbury Holdfast is Cole – someone who has never hurt us. We've talked about this. I thought we'd agreed that Cole was one of the good ones?'

'Aye – and that's why the bastard is still alive,' Cairney cried. 'I would have ripped his head off if he was one of the bad ones.'

'Are ye planning to kill him after the attack?'

'Of course not! I'll command him to die in the assault on the dragons. I won't kill him myself.'

Konna put a hand on her hip and stared at her brother. 'You have lost yer way.'

'Shut the fuck up.'

'Yer acting like a maniac, and yer making mistakes – mistakes that will get us caught. The other Holdfasts will be searching for Cole and Alva – ye've made it personal.'

'It is personal. I thought this was what ye wanted, sis? To get revenge? And now yer getting squeamish on me? Well, it's too late for you and Maxi-boy. If I go down, we all go down.'

'What have we done?' Maxwell wailed.

'Shut it, ya fud,' said Cairney. 'I've had it with you two. All ye do is whine and complain, when I'm the only bastard with the balls to see this through to the end. Ya ungrateful wankers.' He pulled out his Quadrant. 'I'm taking ye back to the fog, so ye can moan and complain without me having to hear it.'

The air shimmered, and they appeared in the sitting room of Maxwell's apartment.

'Ye can both fuck off,' said Cairney, then he vanished.

'Oh shit,' cried Maxwell. 'How did we let this happen? We're screwed, Konna, completely screwed. If the Holdfasts don't get us, then your brother will.'

Konna gazed out of the window at the thick fog.

'What are we going to do?' Maxwell went on.

'First of all,' she said, 'you need to calm yerself. Panicking isnae gonnae help. Then we pack, and get a boat to Ooste. We could still make the evening portal if we hurry. Once we're in Plateau City, we can lie low for a while, or...'

'Or what? Should we hand ourselves in and confess everything?'

'Absolutely not,' said Konna. 'Cairney's an arsehole, but he's my brother, and ye don't betray yer own family. We'll hide until things settle down. We're immortal – we can wait a few decades. Time means nothing to folk like us.'

Maxwell gazed down at the floor. 'All right. I'll start packing.'

He walked into his bedroom, closing the door behind him. Konna's shoulders sagged. She had been bold in front of Maxwell, but her nerves were frayed, and anxiety was making her chest ache. The sight of the Holdings woman in the cave had been bad enough, but Cairney's assertion that he would snap her neck had almost broken Konna. Was her brother really so callous? Konna knew that Alva was only a mortal, and that mortals died every day, but it was still wrong.

The air shimmered behind her, and Konna prepared herself. She would tell Cairney that she would not allow him to murder Alva – it was a step too far, and she would stand her ground.

'Good evening, cousin,' came a low voice.

Konna's blood froze. She turned away from the window. Cael Holdfast was standing a few yards in front of her. He wasn't as tall or as broad as Cairney, but there wasn't much in it; and his eyes held a deep darkness. For a brief moment, she wondered if Cairney was playing a trick on her, but she could always faintly sense his powers being used when he changed his appearance.

It was Cael – there was no doubt, and Konna felt fear for the first time in years.

'I think you know why I am here,' said Cael. 'Cooperate, and I'll spare you.'

'I don't know what you're talking about,' she said.

Cael nodded. 'Are you going to make me enter your mind, Konna? You don't want that – believe me. I will stamp upon your thoughts; I will rip your consciousness to pieces and bludgeon the remains. Where are they? Speak.'

Konna's hands trembled. 'Where are who?'

'Esher, Cole, Alva and Cairney,' he said. 'This is your last chance. I know you're involved. If you willingly help me, I will see that you are reprieved the fate I have in store for your brother.'

'Leave my brother alone.'

A wry smile flitted over Cael's features. 'Cairney's psychotic, but he's also an amateur. I know what he did to your mother's mind; changing her memories so that she would think he was camping in Kell. I know that he's been here – that he was with you when you talked to Draughtsman Reece; and I know it was Esher who massacred the delegates on Colsbury.' He took a step closer to Konna. 'Your brother can change his appearance, can't he? How long has he been hiding that? What else can he do? How does he persuade people to do things? What are his plans for Cole? Where is he, cousin?'

The bedroom door opened and Maxwell walked out, a packed bag slung over his shoulder. He gazed at Konna and Cael, then he shook his head.

'Stop fooling around, Cairney,' he said. 'We know it's really you.'

Cael clicked his fingers. Maxwell screamed, his eyes rolling up into his head. He fell to his knees, howling in agony, then he collapsed to the floorboards, his body convulsing.

'Dragon Eyre,' said Cael. 'Cairney is on Dragon Eyre, and you saw the body of Alva. She's alive. That is good, Konna. If she was dead, then you would also be screaming in pain. Upon which island group is Cairney hiding?'

'I don't know!' Konna cried. 'Honestly – Cairney didn't tell us.'

She backed away, feeling for her battle-vision. If she pretended to be terrified, she might be able to catch Cael unawares. She gasped. Her battle-vision was gone. Was her cousin already in her mind? She felt for her other powers – but they were all blocked.

'Do you want revenge?' said Cael. 'Here I am. Your father died in my arms, Konna; do you think a day goes by when I don't mourn him? And yet you and the others blame me. You blame all of us, don't you? – the Colsbury Holdfasts. Take your revenge, cousin. Come on.'

'You arrogant bastard,' cried Konna. 'You and the others sent my father to Na Sun Ka, and then you abandoned him. That bitch Kelsey, and the fucking Empress – they deserve to die for what they did to my Da.'

'Naxor has warped your mind, cousin,' he said. 'He has driven a wedge into our family, splitting it in two. He has poisoned your thoughts against your own kin.' He shook his head. 'You are wasting my time. Prepare yourself; this is going to hurt.'

Konna flinched back, raising her palms uselessly as she tried to ready her mind to face an imminent assault. The air shimmered in the corner of the room, and Cairney appeared.

Cael turned, as Cairney's mouth opened. The two cousins stared at each other, then Cael smiled.

'Get away from my sister,' Cairney growled.

'I have no need to invade her memories,' said Cael; 'not now that you are here in person, Cairney.'

'I command you to sleep!' Cairney shouted.

Cael blinked and took a step back, then he frowned.

'Sleep!' Cairney cried. 'Sleep!'

Cael staggered, but remained on his feet. He raised his right hand, and Cairney's face twisted in pain. Konna stared at the two men, their faces straining with effort as they stood three yards apart. Cairney changed his form into that of a greenhide, but Cael brushed the vision away. Cairney tried to charge at Cael, his muscular arms stretching out towards his cousin's neck. Cael grunted, and Cairney was forced down to his knees, his eyes bulging.

'I will kill you!' cried Cairney.

'I am stronger than you, Cairney,' said Cael, 'and you know it. You are shielding your thoughts well, but I will tear down your defences, piece by piece, and then I will scour you clean. You will be like a bairn again, helpless and innocent.'

'No!' cried Konna. 'Please, Cael; don't do it.'

'Stay out of this, cousin,' said Cael. 'It's not too late for you, but Cairney's reign of mayhem is over.'

Konna picked up a heavy glass ashtray, and swung it at Cael's head. He ducked, and the blow battered off his shoulder and neck. Cael flinched, his concentration broken for a moment. It was enough. Cairney reached into his pocket, took out the Quadrant, and the air shimmered.

Konna found herself back on the beach, close to the caves where Alva Longhold was being kept. Next to her, Maxwell was lying unconscious on the sand, while Cairney was on his knees, gasping in pain. Konna staggered over to him, then Cairney raised his head and laughed, long and hard. He fell backwards onto the golden sand, his laughter echoing up through the palm trees.

'Do you think this is funny?' said Konna.

'It's fucking hilarious,' Cairney wheezed. 'That was amazing. Did ye see us? Me and Cael – a proper fucking dream mage, and he couldnae break me.'

'Are you out of yer mind, brother?' Konna cried. 'He was about to scour you.'

'Was he fuck,' said Cairney. 'I was just letting him believe that. I only brought us back here because I was worried he might do something to you. I was protecting ye, sis. I could have taken him.'

Konna shook her head. Did Cairney believe that?

'My powers have gone,' she said. 'He even took away my self-healing.'

Cairney raised a hand from the sand. 'Yer powers are back. Feel them – and tell me I'm right.'

Konna felt a wave of her brother's powers pass through her body as soon as he had spoken the words. Her self-healing returned, along with battle-vision and death. She gazed at her hands.

'Well?' said Cairney.

She nodded.

'Cael won't want to mess with me again,' he went on. 'I fucking showed that wee prick.'

Konna sat on the sand next to her delusional brother.

'What now?' she said.

'That depends.'

'On what?'

'Did Cael manage to read our plans from yer mind?'

'If he could block my powers, then he must have been inside my head,' she said.

'Aye, but yer memories are shielded, too. It would have taken him some effort to get past all of the layers of protection that Karalyn put in there when we were babies.'

'Then,' she said, 'if I had to guess, he doesnae know the plan. He was just about to rampage through my thoughts when ye arrived.'

'Thank fuck for that,' said Cairney. 'The answer to yer question is obvious – we carry on with the plan. Cael doesnae know where we are, because I didnae tell you or Maxwell the exact location.' He gazed around. 'This island is called Serpens, and it's just a wee bit south of Ulna. In other words, we're hiding right under Blackrose's nose. It's the last place they'll look.'

'Cael knows we're on Dragon Eyre,' said Konna. 'He read Maxwell's mind.'

'Did he? Then it's just as well I didnae tell him the plan, eh?'

Cairney got to his feet, and brushed the loose sand from his clothes. Konna joined him, and they glanced down at Maxwell's unconscious body.

'We'll let him sleep it off,' said Cairney. 'We can tell him the plan when he wakes up.'

'Is that wise?' said Konna.

'It'll make no difference,' said Cairney. 'He won't be leaving Serpens again until it's time to put the plan into action. Come on.'

Cairney led Konna to the cluster of caves, raised his arm, and pointed to the entrance on the left.

'Cole's in that one,' he said. He pointed to the next one along. 'And Esher's in there. Alva, as we know, is in the cave on the right – that leaves one, where we can stay until we're ready to attack Nom Karta and Ulna.' He fixed Konna with a stare. 'Are ye with me, sister?'

She eyed the caves, then lowered her head. 'Aye, Cairney. I'm with you.'

Cairney grinned. 'Then we should relax for the rest of the evening – tomorrow's gonnae be a big day.'

CHAPTER 26
UNDER THE STARS

Serpens, Ulnan Archipelago, Eastern Rim – 6th Luddinch 5273 (18th Gylean Year 24)

Cole awoke with stars shining down upon him. He tried to move, but his wrists and legs had been tightly bound. He was in a cave, but there was a large aperture a few feet above him that was letting in the cool night air. He turned his head, and saw the cave entrance. Through it, palm trees were swaying in the sea breeze, and the foaming waves were glistening in the starlight.

Dragon Eyre – it had to be. The sound of voices drifted through to him, and he lay in silence, trying to pick out any words. The accents were unmistakable – Kellach – one man, and one woman. Cairney must be there, along with someone else. Another voice spoke, one with a softer accent. Cole couldn't make out the words, but the man sounded as though he came from the City of Salve. A Pellan, maybe. A hint of smoke reached Cole's nose. Dreamweed mixed with keenweed.

Cole felt the ground beneath him, but the floor of the cave was too smooth to be of any use in cutting his bonds. He went over his priorities, listing them. Escape. Alva. Violence. He felt for his powers. Somehow, when he had been captured, Cairney had been able to block his vision, and Cole examined his own mind. He could see the blocks that had been put in place. They were powerful, but they were also clumsy. If he focussed hard enough, he might be able to unpick them. He got to work, and a bead of sweat trickled down his face from the effort. It occurred to him that he had never thoroughly investigated his own powers. He knew what Karalyn had said; that he had latent dream abilities, but he had never asked her, Cael or Kyra to unlock them. He wondered how they would feel, and what extra powers they would give him. He never felt tired or in pain after using his vision, and he had always guessed that this might be related to his latent powers. Was that the sum total of his dream abilities?

He unpicked a strand of Cairney's blocks, and pain flooded his head. Cole grimaced, and carried on. His vision powers were connected to his eyes, which made sense. When hooded, or with his eyes closed, he couldn't vision. Cael could use his powers even while blindfolded – that was a trait of being a dream mage, so Cole closed his eyes as he worked.

Time passed, and Cole's headache grew.

A voice spoke from above him.

'What's he doing?' said the man from the City.

Cairney laughed. 'It looks like he's trying to have a shite.'

Cole opened his eyes and relaxed.

'Have ye shit yerself, Cole?' said Cairney.

Cole looked at the three faces peering down at him. Konna was standing next to her brother, while the other man was Maxwell, Amalia's son. Konna crouched down with a cup of water, and held it to Cole's lips. He ignored her.

'Drink,' she said.

Cole's immediate response was defiance, then he started to run through what might happen if he pretended to go along with what they said. What if he put on an act of abject terror? What if he wept and begged? They might get complacent, and he only needed a single opportunity.

'Thank you, Konna,' he gasped, then he allowed her to pour some of the cool water into his parched mouth. He started to cry. 'Where am I? What is happening to me?'

Cairney laughed. 'Look at him – greetin' like a wee bairn. I thought ye were tough, Cole.'

Konna eyed Cole, as though she wasn't quite convinced by his act.

'Please,' he said. 'Is Alva all right? Don't hurt her; please. Konna – is she all right?'

'Aye,' said Konna. 'She's tied up like you, but she's alive.'

'Thank you. Maxwell, is that you? Where are we?'

Maxwell glanced away, as though he would rather be elsewhere.

'Talk to me, Cairney,' Cole said. 'What do you want with me?'

'You'll see, laddo,' said Cairney. 'I'm gonnae turn ye into a fucking legend. By the time I've finished with ye, every bastard in the Empire and the Dominion will know yer name.'

'Will you let Alva go if I help you?'

Cairney frowned, and Cole wondered if he was taking the act too far.

'Will you let me see her?' he said. 'Let me see that she's all right, and then we can talk.'

'I kicked Cael's arse earlier today,' said Cairney. 'What do ye think about that?'

Cole suppressed an urge to laugh. Instead, he tried to appear amazed by Cairney's words. Was Cairney's giant ego his weak point?

'How?' Cole gasped. 'Cael is powerful; how did you beat him?'

Cairney grinned. 'He tried to scour my mind, but I fought him off. He gave it his best shot, but I was too strong for him.'

Cole noticed Konna look away, and he knew from the expression on her face that Cairney was lying.

'And then I managed to rescue Konna and Maxi-boy right from under Cael's nose,' Cairney went on. 'Ye should have seen the look on Cael's face – he couldnae believe it!' He paused. 'Aye; all right – ye can see Alva, but just for a moment.'

'Thank you.'

'Grab his legs, Maxi-boy,' said Cairney.

Konna stood to the side as Cairney and Maxwell lifted Cole's body. They carried him through the cave entrance and out into the open air, then they set him down by the base of a palm tree. Cairney pulled him up by the shoulders until he was in a sitting position, with his back to the tree trunk. Konna pointed towards another cave.

'Alva is in there,' she said. 'Can ye see her?'

Cole stared into the gloom of the cave. Lying on the ground, still and quiet, was the shadowy form of a woman. Anger that was far from fake swept over him, and it was difficult to keep his expression fearful. He lowered his gaze. They had already made a mistake. Cairney had told him that Alva was on a different island, and yet there she was, just ten yards in front of him. His fingers touched the rough bark of the palm tree, and he began to gently rub the cords binding his wrists against the ragged surface.

Cairney, Konna and Maxwell sat down on a blanket that had been laid out to Cole's left. Cairney lit a weedstick, and swigged from a bottle of whisky.

'Why did you wake me?' said Cole.

'Water,' said Konna. 'It was time for you to take a drink.'

'What do you need me to do?'

'Right now,' said Cairney, 'I'd rather ye just sat there and kept yer mouth shut.'

Cole nodded, not too displeased with Cairney's words. If they allowed him to sit in silence, while they talked, then he could continue unpicking the blocks in his mind, as well as attempting to wear down the ropes binding his wrists. He concentrated on his vision powers, while keeping his face still. He had seen much of Alva's powers while he had been training her, so he focussed on any differences between his mind and hers. Alva was a genuine Holdings vision mage, with no trace of any dream abilities; therefore, he reasoned that any differences might be related to his latent powers. He could sense a slender strand of powers beneath his vision, a strand absent from Alva's mind. What was it doing there? What could it do? He unpicked another part of Cairney's blocks, and cried out in pain, unable to stop himself. He quickly turned his cry into a sob of misery and fear, as the others glanced over at him.

'Stop that fucking racket,' said Cairney.

'Could I have some of that weed, please?' Cole said.

'Aye, if it'll make ye shut up,' said Cairney. 'Maxi-boy, pass Cole yer weedstick.'

Maxwell got up, and walked over to Cole. He held out the weedstick and Cole inhaled.

'I know this isn't your fault,' he whispered to Maxwell. 'I know he is making you do this.'

Maxwell stared at him, but said nothing. Cole took another draw, then Maxwell returned to the blanket.

'What a braw night,' said Cairney, stretching out on the blanket. He glugged from the whisky bottle. 'This is better than fog, eh, sis?'

'Aye,' Konna muttered.

'It's a pity that I'll have to leave ye for a wee bit,' Cairney went on. 'I have things to do to prepare for tomorrow – it cannae be helped.'

'How long will ye be?' said Konna.

'Just a couple of minutes,' he said. 'I'll be back before ye know it.' He handed the whisky to Konna and got to his feet, then he stared down at Maxwell. 'Stay here,' he said in a commanding voice, 'and make sure Cole doesnae try to escape.' Cairney frowned as he looked down at Cole. 'My blocks are strong,' he said, 'but maybe we should be taking a few wee precautions if I'm not gonnae be here.'

He walked over to the palm tree, reached down, and ripped the sleeve from Cole's left arm. He looped it round Cole's face, covering his eyes, then he tied it at the back of his head.

'That'll stop him getting up to any tricks,' he said. 'All the same, Maxi-boy, make sure ye watch him.'

Cole listened, but heard no more of Cairney. Had he gone? He recalled the way he had spoken to Maxwell – there had been a tone of authority in his words. Was that how Cairney did it – through the power of his voice alone? As far as he knew, only Karalyn possessed that particular ability. She could order people to do things without being in their minds, and she was always obeyed. Cole remembered back to Rainsby. Cairney could also change his appearance, just as his mother could do. Only, with Aila, Cole wasn't fooled by her powers; yet Cairney had managed to deceive him. The combination of Cairney's various skills made him a formidable opponent, but he was also rash and clumsy, as well as over-confidant. Cole was ten years older than him, and the age difference showed. Cole concentrated. He unpicked the last of Cairney's blocks, and managed to stop himself from crying out. He rode out the pain, feeling it torment his mind until it passed.

He listened for Konna and Maxwell, but they were sitting in silence. Cole had removed Cairney's blocks, but with his eyes covered, he would be unable to use his vision. He went back to examining his own mind. He perceived his freed powers, and noticed something else – the strand that was missing from Alva's mind. It was moving – spreading through his mind, making new connections and embedding itself across his consciousness. Had the removal of Cairney's blocks unwittingly unlocked his latent abilities?

He closed his eyes, and tried to see.

His vision arose from his body, and he had a view of the beach, the caves, and the fringe of palm trees from above. It was no ordinary vision he was using, he realised; it was something more – dream vision. He revelled for a moment in his new abilities, then he focussed on what he needed to do next.

Cole turned to face the cave entrance where Alva lay, then he slowly and carefully pushed out his new vision powers. They shot over to the cave, and Cole looked down on Alva's unconscious body. Anger surged through him again, and he fought to control his emotions. He would get nowhere if he lost his self-control. One of Alva's eyes was open a crack, and Cole entered her mind.

Alva was dreaming. In her dream, she was being pursued by unknown assailants through the dark and narrow streets of an unfamiliar city. She looked over her shoulder, but her pursuers were out of sight.

Cole made an image of himself appear in front of her, and she ran into him.

She stared up. 'Cole?'

'I'm here,' he said, gazing down at her. 'I am inside your mind, Alva.'

'Are we in Rainsby?'

'We are on Dragon Eyre. Do you remember what happened?'

Alva looked confused. 'A woman gave me water,' she said.

'Konna Holdfast,' said Cole. 'She and her brother have brought us here. I am also a prisoner, but I have managed to free my vision powers, and now I am going to do the same to you. It might hurt. I'm sorry.'

She took his hand. 'Am I dreaming? Is this only a dream? You have been in my mind many times, but this feels... different.'

He nodded. 'Your body is lying in a cave, but I can see you, even though I have been blindfolded.'

'What?' she said. 'But... that should be impossible.'

'I think I might have unlocked something within me,' he said. 'I have spent hours removing Cairney's blocks from my head, and I think I disturbed something else. Listen – I am sitting by a tree just a few yards from you. I will distract them, and you will lie still, and send out your powers. Try to find someone, anyone. Tell them to look for us; show them where we are. Will you do this?'

'Yes, Cole.'

'Try not to cry out when I remove the blocks,' he said.

She smiled at him. 'Once again, Cole, I am slightly disturbed by how calm you are. Does nothing frighten you?'

'I am frightened,' he said, 'but I will not let fear stop me.'

'Don't lie to me,' she said. 'I can sense your thoughts – you are angry, very angry, but you aren't scared.'

'Maybe there's something wrong with me,' he said.

'There is nothing wrong with you, Cole. Remove my blocks. I will do what is required.'

They kissed, then Cole turned to the blocks overlaying her powers. They were similar to the ones that he had removed from his own mind, but Alva was lacking the extra strand. He steeled himself, then he tore through the blocks, ripping them from Alva's mind. She gritted her teeth as pain flashed through her, but she didn't cry out.

'It's all right, Cole,' she said. 'I know you didn't want to hurt me. Let me work. I will find someone.'

Cole withdrew from her head. He watched her as she opened her eyes in the darkness, then he sensed her vision powers fly out over the ocean. Cole turned to glance at Maxwell and Konna, but neither had noticed anything. He went into Maxwell's mind, and quietly blocked up the god's death powers, then he fashioned another block, one that would prevent Maxwell from hurting Alva in any way. He plunged into Maxwell's memories, piecing together what had happened, and gleaning Cairney's plans for the following day. He saw that they were on the island of Serpens, then he dug deeper, and paused.

Esher?

Cole hesitated, then he pulled out of Maxwell's head and entered a different cave. Lying on the ground was another body – a man, a well-built man in leather armour. An Ascendant. Esher looked as though he was also dreaming, and his face was twitching. Both of his eyes were fully closed, and Cole had no way in, so he returned to Maxwell's head.

Cole wondered if he also possessed any powers of persuasion. He would start small, with a mere suggestion, to see if that would suffice.

Maybe Esher is thirsty, Cole insinuated into the young god's mind.

Maxwell frowned. He glanced over his shoulder at the cave where Esher lay, then he looked at Konna.

'Does Esher need some water?' he said.

'What?' said Konna.

'Do you think Esher is thirsty?' said Maxwell. 'We gave water to Alva and Cole, but not to him.'

Konna sighed. 'Give him some water if you want to, but don't be long.'

Maxwell got to his feet. He picked up a water skin and poured some into a cup, then he walked over to the cave, as Cole remained in his mind.

Maxwell knelt by Esher. A few drops of water dripped from the cup, splashing on the Ascendant's face. His eyes opened, and Cole drove his powers into Esher's mind. He filled it with rage and panic, and tore away the blocks sealing up the Ascendant's self-healing and battle-vision.

Esher roared out in terror, then he pulled his arms apart, breaking the cords that bound him. His right hand went to Maxwell's throat. He squeezed, breaking Maxwell's neck, then he tossed the body aside and ripped the ropes from his legs. Konna stared at the cave entrance as Esher walked out. He stared back at her.

'Where is the one who brought me here?' Esher cried. 'Where is he?'

Konna said nothing, her mouth falling open.

Esher gazed up at the stars, his eyes wide with confusion, then he saw Cole. 'Why is he tied up?' Esher said. 'Is he also a prisoner?'

Konna got to her feet, her right hand raised. 'Come no closer.'

Esher stared at her. 'I remember you. It was you who told me to follow you, that day in Jezra. You told me to come with you, and then the other one took me away. Why? What did I ever do to you?'

Cole returned to his own mind, but kept his new dream powers working, so that he could see what was happening in front of him.

'Konna is not to blame,' he called out. 'Her brother is forcing her to do these things. We are all his prisoners.'

Esher gazed down at his hands. 'I think I killed someone in the cave. I didn't mean to. I saw a man leaning over me in the darkness, and I panicked. I throttled him.'

'Maxwell has self-healing,' said Cole. 'He'll be all right.'

'That was Maxwell?' said Esher. 'The son of the God-Queen?'

'He is not our enemy,' said Cole. 'The one responsible has gone for now, but he will be back soon.'

'Shut up!' Konna shouted. 'Shut yer fucking mouth, Cole. I knew yer terrified weeping was an act.'

'It fooled your brother,' said Cole. 'What are you going to do now, Konna? Cairney could be back at any moment. Free my wrists and legs, and I'll make sure you are treated fairly by the Empire.'

'That's exactly what Cael said to me before Cairney turned up in Jezra,' cried Konna. 'You and Cael are just the same; full of threats and promises.'

Cole laughed. 'Was I supposed to believe that Cairney defeated Cael? What really happened, Konna?'

'Cael nearly scoured him; what do ye think happened? We had to flee here.'

Esher slumped down to the sand. 'Who am I?'

Konna turned to him.

'Do either of you know?' Esher said. 'Tell me.'

'You are the Ninth Ascendant,' said Konna. 'Yer real name is Esher, not Reece.'

'So it's true?' said Esher.

'Karalyn Holdfast wiped yer mind,' Konna went on. 'We told you this, after we took ye from Jezra.'

'My mind has been filled with pain and confusion ever since. I thought I had dreamed that part.'

'Well, ye didnae. Yer a fucking Ascendant – the last Ascendant.'

'No.'

'I thought we were doing it to rescue ye,' said Konna. 'I didn't know what my brother had planned.'

'Rescue me from what?'

'Yer miserable, mortal life,' she said. 'Ye deserve better than sitting in some damp office in Jezra.'

'Is this better?' he said. 'I have slaughtered hundreds of people. My memories are mixed up, but I can recall some of it. I tore innocent people to pieces with my bare hands. In what way is this better?'

'Cairney has been using you,' said Cole. 'You have been a weapon in his hands, but the Empire is closing in. Tomorrow, Cairney intends to send you to your death. He will order you to attack the Empress's party on Ulna, and he will command you to fight until you have been cut down.'

Konna stared at him. 'How did ye know that?'

'What bothers me, cousin,' Cole said, 'is that you went along with it.

Do you hate the Colsbury Holdfasts that much? Would you happily watch the Dominion and the Empire go to war to get revenge on Kelsey and the Empress? Do you think you'll be able to deceive Karalyn? Cairney is insane, but you are almost as bad. I actually thought you were my friend, Konna. I guess that makes me the stupid one.' He turned to Esher. 'I would be grateful if you would remove the blindfold, and the cords binding me.'

Esher stared at him, then at Konna. Just then, Maxwell staggered out from the cave, a hand rubbing his neck.

'That hurt,' he hissed.

'I am sorry,' said Esher.

Maxwell eyed Konna. 'He has battle-vision, he must have. I saw the way he ripped the cords from his wrists.'

'But how?' said Konna. 'All of his powers should be blocked.'

Esher got to his feet, and began to walk towards the tree where Cole was sitting.

'Stop him!' cried Maxwell.

Konna remained where she was, her eyes unsure.

Esher crouched by Cole. He reached out, and removed the sleeve that was covering his face.

'What is your name?' said the god.

'Cole Holdfast.'

Esher nodded. 'Will I be executed by the Empire?'

'None of this was your fault,' said Cole. 'You will not be harmed; I give you my word as a Holdfast.'

'Are we not enemies? The Ascendants and the Holdfasts fought many battles, until you destroyed them. I said *them*, when I should have said *us*.'

'You are not the same as you were,' said Cole. 'When Karalyn scoured your mind, she created a new man. Nothing remains of the old Esher; nothing but your powers, which Cairney has blocked. I can unblock them. Do you want the ability to kill people from a distance? The ability to see things from hundreds of miles away?'

Esher bowed his head. 'I don't want any of that. I want to be Reece.'

He leaned forward to untie the cords binding Cole's wrists, when a fist connected with the side of Esher's head. Cairney lunged forward, his features enraged, and he punched Esher again, then he kicked the god in the face.

'Stay down!' Cairney commanded, and Esher fell limp to the sand. 'All of your powers are blocked. Sleep.' He turned to Maxwell and Konna. 'What the fuck has been going on here? I leave for ten minutes, and the whole thing comes crashing down. How did Esher get out of his cave, eh? Will somebody fucking answer me?'

Konna's eyes shone with fear.

'Are you fucking with me, sister?' shouted Cairney.

'It was Cole,' said Maxwell. 'It must have been. Cole's powers must be back.'

'Impossible,' said Cairney. 'Cole was wearing a fucking blindfold. Was it you, ya wee prick? Was it you, Maxi-boy? Did ye think ye could stab me in the back and get away with it? Konna – speak, before I kill this little bastard.'

Konna lowered her gaze. 'It wasn't Maxwell,' she whispered. 'It... it might have been Cole. He knows about the plan for tomorrow; how could he know that? We haven't talked about it since he woke up. Maybe the blindfold slipped from his eyes. He must have read Maxwell's mind.'

Cairney turned from Maxwell, and faced Cole. 'Is this true?'

'Is what true?'

'Don't test me,' Cairney cried. 'Is yer vision working again?'

'Your only hope is to flee, Cairney,' said Cole. 'Find yourself a new home on one of the Doomed Worlds, and wait for everyone else to die. If you don't, there will be no escape from what's coming for you. They'll put a restrainer mask on your face, and throw you into a deep pit, if you're lucky.'

Cairney pointed at him. 'Yer powers are blocked.'

Cole grimaced as he felt new blocks appear in his mind. They clamped down onto his vision powers, smothering them and the strands of dream skills, undoing all of his earlier work.

Cairney clenched his fist and punched Cole in the face. Cole's chin took the brunt of the impact, and his head cracked back against the trunk of the palm tree. Pain shot through his face, and he spat out blood.

'I should fucking kill you right now,' Cairney screamed at him, 'but yer death will have to wait for tomorrow. I will laugh when I see you getting ripped to shreds by dragon claws. I will order you to attack, and ye won't be able to resist me.'

Cairney kicked him in the stomach, and Cole fell to the side, away from the tree. Cairney drove his boot down, stamping on Cole's chest, then he glanced over to the nearest cave entrance.

'Maybe we should make Cole watch as we hurt his wee lassie,' he said.

'There's no need, brother,' said Konna. 'Everything is back to normal. Sit down and have some whisky. The drama's over.'

Cairney frowned, then he walked over to the blanket and sat. Konna handed him the whisky and a fresh weedstick. Maxwell came over. He sat down at the opposite end of the blanket from Cairney, his eyes fearful.

'I wasnae really gonnae kill ye, Maxi-boy,' said Cairney.

Maxwell said nothing.

'Come on,' Cairney said; 'let's get fucking hammered.'

Cole closed his eyes, and got back to work.

Cole judged that it was well past midnight by the time Cairney had fallen asleep on the blanket under the stars. Maxwell had retired to a cave by that point, after Cairney had forced him to bind Esher's wrists and ankles again. Esher's body had been left out in the open, just a couple of yards from where Cole lay. Cole had spent the hours trying to remove the blocks again, but the pain in his head and stomach had been too distracting, and his efforts had failed.

Cole gazed up at the night sky. When dawn came, he would fight Cairney's ability to command, but he would probably lose. He had no alternative – if he wanted to survive, and if he wanted Alva to be safe, he would have to stay awake, and fight the blocks in his head all night.

He heard movement next to him, and saw Konna close by. She was peering down at him, her face veiled in shadow.

'Sorry,' she whispered.

'For what?' he said.

'For telling Cairney about yer powers. I thought he was gonnae kill Maxwell, but I knew that he needed you alive for tomorrow.'

'Untie my hands.'

'I can't. Cairney would know it was me.'

'Where is his Quadrant?'

'I'm not sure. He hid it before he fell asleep. He doesn't trust me or Maxwell any more. He watched me do nothing when Esher was going to free you.'

'Listen to me, Konna – untie my hands and legs, and I will take Alva and run to the other end of the island. There will be boats somewhere; I think there's a fishing village on Serpens. Alva and I will sail to Ulna and warn Blackrose. I will tell the Empress that you and Maxwell helped us escape. We're family, Konna; you and I.'

'Cairney is also family.'

Cole said nothing.

Konna gazed into the distance. 'No. I'm sorry, Cole, but he's my brother. I'll not betray him.'

A huge dragon soared down from the dark sky, his great wings outspread. With one forelimb, he batted Konna away, sending her tumbling through the air towards the ocean; then with the other, he picked up Cole.

'Where is the Longhold girl, Holdfast?' said the dragon. 'She called for aid.'

'In the cave, down there,' Cole cried.

Cairney's eyes opened, and he stared up at the dark form hovering over the palm trees.

'What the fuck?' he shouted, jumping to his feet. He raised his right hand. 'Die, you lizard bastard!'

The dragon opened his jaws and sprayed Cairney with flames.

The palm trees exploded in an inferno that lit up the night sky. Cairney fell screaming, his clothes and hair ablaze. The dragon reached into the nearest cave with his free forelimb, and plucked Alva from within. With his wings still extended, he rose into the air, and Cole gazed over at Alva, who was clutched within the dragon's claws. Their eyes met as the dragon ascended.

'To where, Holdfast?' the dragon said.

'To Ulna,' Cole cried, 'and thank you, dragon; thank you.'

'It was nothing,' said the dragon, as he turned for the north. He shot off across the sky in a surge of speed, leaving the flames of Serpens behind.

CHAPTER 27
A SLIGHT INCONVENIENCE

Great Gunst, Gunstian Empire – 27th Luddinch 1605

'Bring in the accused,' said the clerk of the court.

Arrosa was led into the dark, windowless chamber, her wrists shackled. Her hair had been cut short, and she was wearing a drab grey prison gown, with thin sandals on her feet. She eyed the five judges sitting behind a long desk at the far end of the room, as she was escorted by Gunstian soldiers to a small platform. She stepped up onto it, a soldier positioned by each shoulder, as priests, officials and clerks crowded the chamber.

'Who has the list of charges?' said a judge.

'I have, Your Honour,' said a clerk. He leaned over and passed each of the judges a handwritten copy of the crimes Arrosa had committed. There was silence for a moment as the judges read the list.

'We may begin,' said a judge.

A lawyer stood. 'I wish to petition the court that this case be immediately thrown out, Your Honours,' he said. 'The accused is a member of a diplomatic mission to the Gunstian Empire and, as such, she does not fall under our jurisdiction. Furthermore, Gunst risks its reputation in this affair. If the other nations learn that we have arrested and charged an emissary, then none will treat with us. I have this very morning received delegations from several merchants' guilds, all requesting that the case be dismissed on these grounds.'

The lawyer sat, and a priest rose to his feet.

'If I may, esteemed judges?' said the priest. 'The crimes committed by Arrosa of Zamata were carried out before she fled Athumia; and they are of such magnitude that it would be irresponsible not to have this case heard. We have already agreed that this hearing be held in private, as a concession to those overly worried about our reputation. Treason. Apostasy. The worst crimes imaginable – and both committed while Arrosa was a citizen of Zamata. As per the imperial statutes formulated centuries ago, all Gunstians resident upon Zamata are subject to the law of Gunst, and Arrosa of Kaugatz is no exception.'

The priest sat, and the judges conferred in hushed tones for a few moments.

'This case shall be heard,' said the one in the middle. 'It is a hearing, not a trial, and thus we can disregard any notions of diplomatic immunity. Arrosa of Kaugatz and Zamata, how do you plead to the charge of treason?'

'Not guilty, Your Honour,' she said.

'And how do you plead to the charge of apostasy?'

'Guilty.'

Several voices clamoured around the chamber at her words.

'Do we need to hear any more, esteemed judges?' said the priest, as he rose to his feet again. 'The penalty for apostasy is death. Does it matter if we hold a trial for treason? The holy church would be content to drop the charge of treason if we can move swiftly to sentencing.'

'I want to hear the accused explain herself,' said the judge on the right; 'and I have a few questions of my own.'

'Of course, Your Honour,' said the priest.

'I wish to ask about Archpriest Paltanai,' said the judge. 'If you return him to us unharmed, Arrosa, we may be prepared to show you some clemency.'

'I cannot bring Paltanai back, Your Honour,' she said, 'because I have no knowledge of his location. He accidentally triggered my Quadrant and vanished.'

'That is unfortunate.'

'Indeed, Your Honour.'

'Arrosa,' said another judge, 'it states here that you were married to an unbeliever, but that the service was conducted by a Gunstian priest. Is that true?'

'It is, Your Honour. I did not become an apostate while living upon Zamata, despite what the priest asserted. I carried my faith all the way to the Star Continent. I wanted to be married in the Gunstian tradition, though my husband was and is an unbeliever.'

'Were you aware that you were committing the crime of blasphemy?'

'I was, Your Honour.'

'Tell me – when did you lose your faith?'

'It was a gradual process, Your Honour. It culminated when I saw the body of Theodora, the First Ascendant. Lord Bailey, her younger brother, has had the body interred upon Zamata. It was then that I reconciled myself to the fact that Chadura was dead.'

The five judges frowned and shook their heads in dismay.

'Need we hear any more, esteemed judges?' said the priest. 'My heart is breaking at this evil woman's words.'

'Her testimony is relevant,' said the judge on the right, 'no matter how painful it might be to hear. If, as she states, she became an apostate while living on the Star Continent, then she cannot be tried by this court. Shall we move on to the charge of treason? Arrosa, it is alleged that you helped Lahnos Laimos before and after he destroyed the Gunstian fleet in the Cyasarta of Zamata. Is this true?'

'It is, Your Honour. I was eight years old at the time. I'm not sure how much use I was to Lahnos. I also do not accept that the defence of Zamata from any invader can be considered as treason.'

'I want to return to the subject of her husband,' said the judge in the middle. 'Arrosa, it is alleged that you are wed to a son of the Demon Witch, one Cael Holdfast. Is that correct?'

'It is, Your Honour. If you doubt it, then you can ask him yourself when he comes to collect me. He may even bring a few other Holdfasts with him.'

'Is that a threat?' said the judge.

'It certainly is, Your Honour. Do you think the Holdfasts' reputation is ill-founded? What do you think they will do when they discover that I have been treated so shabbily? My husband is the Empress's choice as heir to succeed her, which means that, one day, I may be Empress. If that does come to pass, you can be sure that I will remember what has happened here. If, on the other hand, you execute me, then I fear for all of Gunst. The wrath of the Holdfasts shall descend upon this land as night blots out the sun.' She turned to a priest in the crowd; one that she knew possessed the Gift of Truth. 'Was that a lie? Tell the court.'

'It was not,' said the priest, his eyes wide.

Arrosa raised a hand, her index finger extended. 'Release me now, and I will forgive you. I will persuade my husband that this was all a terrible misunderstanding, and I will plead with him to show you mercy.'

The crowd sat in a stunned silence.

'And I haven't even mentioned the Demon Witch,' Arrosa went on. 'You know what she did to Gahad; did you also know that she treated me as a mother treats a daughter; that she brought me up? Anger her at your peril. Fear her, as the only god that matters – as the only god that exists. Karalyn Holdfast is slow to anger, but her rage is implacable when someone hurts her family. Kill me, and you will soon discover this immutable fact. Are there any more questions?'

The judges conferred again, whispering to each other behind the long desk. Arrosa scanned the others in the chamber. She could see raw fear on the faces of a few, and that pleased her. The rest were staring at her with pure loathing, as though they wanted to kill her with their bare hands.

The central judge cleared his throat. 'I am recusing myself from this hearing,' he said. 'It is clear to me that Arrosa is guilty of apostasy, but the implications of her conviction and execution are a political and religious matter. This hearing is therefore suspended, pending a decision by the high council of the Gunstian Empire.'

Arrosa smiled as the five judges filed out of the chamber.

The two soldiers led her down from the platform, and through the crowd of hostile priests and officials. Some spat on her as she passed them, but Arrosa did not flinch, nor did she pay any attention to the vile insults being thrown her way. She was a Holdfast, and such things were beneath her.

The soldiers escorted her down a long dark passageway, and she was placed back into her cell. The barred door was closed and locked, and the soldiers eyed her.

'You should burn for what you said in there, girl,' muttered one.

'Do your worst,' she said. 'I do not fear you. I pity you. Desert your posts and go home, and you might survive this day.'

The soldiers snorted and walked away. Arrosa sat down on the low wooden bench. She was unsure of the exact time, having caught no glimpse of the sun since she had been led into the Temple of the Martyrs two days previously. She was a little annoyed that Cael had not turned up on the day before, while she had been languishing in the cell. Something must have happened to steal his attention, and she wondered if it was connected to Cole's disappearance. She also had no idea where Brogan and Claudian were. Did they know that she had been arrested? If so, why had they not come to visit her? Perhaps they had been forbidden, in which case, she imagined that they would have returned to Plateau City with all speed, to report what had happened to the Empress. There were too many unanswered questions, but she remained serene. Cael would come; it was only a matter of time.

The hours passed. The cell was in almost complete darkness, and no one had been to see her in that time. She knew what was happening – the high and mighty of Gunst would be debating what to do with her. She was guilty, that was clear, but what would they do? If they were going to release and deport her, she hoped it would be soon, before Cael arrived.

She heard a noise, and looked up to see an old priest approach her cell.

'Good morning, Arrosa of Kaugatz,' he said.

'Good morning,' she said. 'Has the sun long risen?'

'It has just cleared the horizon.'

'Are you here to tell me what the judges and priests have decided?'

'No, my girl. That argument is far above my station. A hundred high priests and officials have gathered in the Temple of the Martyrs to discuss your case. I am here for another reason, a more spiritual reason. Will you listen to what I have to say?'

'I will if you bring me a cup of water.'

The old priest smiled. 'I shall return in a moment,' he said.

He walked out of sight, and Arrosa got to her feet. She walked up to the bars of the door as he came back into view. He passed a metal cup between the bars, and she drank.

'Thank you,' she said.

'You are welcome, Arrosa,' he said. 'I want to ask if you are willing to give your heart back to the blessed Chadura, child. You do not need to die. If you repent your apostasy, and return to the holy faith, then the judges will not condemn you to death. The treason charges are ludicrous, for how can you be held responsible for acts you carried out when you were eight years old? Repent, Arrosa, and your life will be saved.'

'Would the blessed Chadura be convinced by an insincere repentance?'

The priest looked pained.

'I cannot change what I believe, holy father,' she said. 'I cannot force myself to believe in something I know to be untrue. Were I to repent, it would be a sham. I would be lying, and any priest with the Gift of Truth would know that I was being false. I was crushed when I learned the true identity of Chadura. I was heartbroken to realise that my religion was built on an unstable foundation. Chadura did create this world –

that is true, but she was never an almighty god. She was one among twelve Ascendants, of whom all but one are now dead. The Holdfasts killed most of them, but Chadura was betrayed and murdered by her faithless husband – Edmond.'

'My poor, deluded girl,' the priest said. 'I fear for your soul in the afterlife, for the blasphemies that have just left your lips would shame the most pious among us. Chadura cannot die; she is eternal, ever-living.'

'Her body is buried under a Zamatan monastery,' said Arrosa. 'There is only one person who can claim to be ever-living; only one who lives on after death; who can take a new body to inhabit when the old one has been destroyed. The Demon Witch. Karalyn Holdfast can do this. She will never die.'

'When the Demon Witch came to Great Gunst, Arrosa,' he said, 'she was not endowed with any godlike powers. She was easily captured, and taken away by a woman by the name of Albany. How could such a weak woman ever be divine?'

'The body she dwelt in at that time lacked any Gifts or godlike powers,' she said. 'Do you know whose body she now inhabits? Albany's. Albany killed the Demon Witch's mortal form, freeing her soul to rise again, and her soul extinguished Albany's life, and took her body as her own. This is Karalyn's third body. If it is destroyed, she will find another.'

'That cannot be,' said the priest.

'Perhaps it should not be,' said Arrosa, 'but it is. I have seen her with my own eyes. It is I who should be trying to convert you to the truth, holy father.'

'Do you pray to the Demon Witch, Arrosa?'

She smiled. 'No. Karalyn wouldn't like that. She wants to be treated as an ordinary person, but her immortality is taking a toll on her humanity. At the moment, she is busy creating new worlds, and I hope she remembers how much her family loves her.'

'Real gods do not have human bodies or human families,' the priest said. 'Can Karalyn see everything at once; does she know the heart of everyone alive or dead; can she hear the prayers of the faithful whispered at night? Is she listening to us right now?'

Arrosa smiled. 'Probably not. She is not the same as how the Gunstians imagine Chadura to be. I pity her, in some ways. I love her, but it must be hard being Karalyn.'

The old priest nodded. 'Thank you for talking to me, Arrosa of Kaugatz.'

'Thank you for listening without haranguing me,' she said. 'Also, I am not known by that name, not any more. I am Arrosa Holdfast.'

He bowed his head. 'Then farewell, Arrosa Holdfast.'

He walked away into the darkness, and Arrosa returned to the wooden bench.

Another hour had passed before the air shimmered in the hallway outside the cell. Arrosa got to her feet as Cael appeared, a guilty look on his face.

'I'm sorry,' he said, as he took a set of bloody keys from a pocket. 'I should have been here yesterday.'

'You left me waiting for an entire day,' she said. 'Is Cole all right?'

'I haven't found him. I almost subdued Cairney yesterday evening, but Konna hit me with a damn ashtray, and they escaped.'

He pulled the door open, and entered the cell. She gazed up at him. He was taller than anyone in Gunst, his Kellach build towering over her. He put his arms round her, and they kissed.

'Thank you for coming for me,' she said, 'but you should be looking for Cole. His life may be in danger.'

'Cole is my best friend,' he said, 'but you are my wife.'

'How many Gunstians did you kill to get here?

'Seven,' he said. 'It's not enough. Gunst needs to be punished for what they have done to you, starting with whoever did that to your hair.'

'Don't you like it?'

'No.'

'Me, neither, but at least hair grows back. Do you know if Brogan and Claudian are all right? I haven't seen them since my arrest.'

'They are back in Plateau City,' he said. 'They returned as soon as they heard what had happened to you, to request assistance. I came as quickly as I could. Cowie is also fine. I have been managing to see him for a few hours each day.'

'Were you serious about punishing the Gunstians?'

'Aye. Do you have any objections?'

'None,' she said. 'I tried to warn them, but they wouldn't listen.'

'Any ideas about who we should target, or should we rampage our way through the Temple of the Great Mother?'

'There are a hundred priests and government officials discussing my case inside the Temple of the Martyrs. That seems like a nice round number.'

'The Temple of the Martyrs?'

'It's a walled compound, with an ancient temple – the oldest in Gunst, apparently. Destroying the building will hurt them more than the deaths of those inside. It's close by. Look into my mind and you will see it.'

She concentrated on the temple building as Cael gazed into her eyes.

'Got it,' he said. 'We will need to stop off somewhere first. Are you ready?'

'I am.'

Cael activated his Quadrant, and the air crackled. They appeared within the shadows of a large stone warehouse, and Arrosa heard the cries of gulls coming from outside.

'We're inside a marine base on Yearning,' Cael said, as he glanced at the stacked shelves and crates. 'What happened to your Quadrant?'

'I was attacked by the Gift of Pain, and an archpriest took it from me.'

'We will have to make sure we collect it when we go back to Great Gunst.'

'That might be difficult,' she said. 'The archpriest accidentally triggered it and vanished.'

Cael laughed.

'Here we are,' he said, stopping by a row of shelves. He took down a large weapon, and slung the leather strap over his shoulder.

'What is it?' said Arrosa.

'A Mark Seven Battanara,' said Cael. 'Who needs battle-vision when you can have one of these?' He picked up a leather satchel, and filled it with long projectiles. 'The marines call these *Skinnies*,' he said, 'presumably because they're slimmer than the earlier ones. Can you carry the bag?'

She nodded, and he passed her the satchel. He took out his Quadrant.

'I have made us both invisible,' he said. 'We are going to appear by the edge of the plaza close to the Temple of the Martyrs, but no one will be able to see us.'

Cael touched the Quadrant, and Arrosa found herself standing under the wide eaves of a housing block on the northern flank of the plaza, fifty yards from the walled Temple of the Martyrs. Crowds of civilians were out in the plaza, and many were walking along the street that ran next to the walled compound.

'Let's check who's inside the temple first,' he said.

Arrosa felt Cael's presence in her mind, then he pulled her consciousness out of her body, and they rose up, their thoughts intertwined. Cael shot his vision towards the temple, and Arrosa was brought along with him. They went over the outer wall, and entered the building through a narrow slat in a set of window shutters. They passed the painted chapel where Arrosa had been ambushed, and came to a crowded hall, where dozens were engaged in a fierce argument.

'There are more than a hundred people in here,' said Cael. 'More like three hundred.'

'The priest who told me about the meeting was probably only counting the important ones – the rest will be soldiers, servants and clerks, I imagine.'

Cael cut the vision connection, and Arrosa found herself back in her body. Cael took a missile from the satchel, and loaded the Battanara.

He smiled at her as he placed the weapon onto his right shoulder. 'Get ready to witness a mass panic.'

He aimed along the sights, and pulled the trigger. There was a loud thump from the Battanara, and the missile streaked out from the weapon. It struck the outside wall of the temple compound, obliterating a large section of it. A roar of noise erupted as debris and smoke filled the air. Screams rang out all over the plaza, and on the street that ran by the temple. Civilians started to flee, as Cael reloaded the weapon. He fired again, and the missile passed through the gap in the outer wall and impacted against the side of the temple. Arrosa watched the flames and smoke rise, as Cael fired another three missiles into the ancient structure. When the fifth had exploded, he swiped the Quadrant, and they appeared on a high balcony overlooking the undamaged half of the temple. Cael loaded, aimed down, and fired. The missile hit a central dome, directly above the hall where the meeting had been taking place, and the temple roof collapsed. Cael reloaded and fired, again and again, until the satchel was empty.

Arrosa stared down at the destruction wrought by her husband. In ten minutes, he had turned the oldest temple in Gunst into a smoking crater of blackened rubble. Bodies littered the ground in every direction, and wounded men and woman were staggering through the smoke. Arrosa felt her stomach turn. Despite having suggested the Temple of the Martyrs as a suitable target, she had not appreciated how terrible the slaughter would be. She glanced at her husband, but he seemed unperturbed by the violence he had unleashed.

Cael gazed at the destruction, and slung the Battanara back over his shoulder.

'That should do it,' he said. 'Now we need to let everyone know who did this, and why.'

He swiped the Quadrant, and Arrosa appeared next to Cael on the wide steps leading up to the massive Temple of the Great Mother. A great crowd of Gunstians were streaming past them, running away from the burning ruins of the smaller temple.

'We are visible to them,' Cael said. He raised his arms. 'People of Gunst,' he cried, his persuasion powers surging outwards in a great arc to cover most of the plaza; 'you will listen to me.'

Arrosa swayed on her knees as she felt the power of Cael's words flow over her. The crowd halted, and turned to stare, their attention captivated by the sight of Cael and Arrosa on the steps.

Cael pointed at what remained of the Temple of the Martyrs.

'Today,' he said, 'Gunst has been justly punished. For laying hands upon my wife, I, Cael Holdfast, son of the Demon Witch, have punished the church and government of Gunst. For subjecting a Holdfast to wrongful arrest, the Empire of the Sapphire Throne has responded in kind. Touch one of us, and you all suffer. Be glad that Arrosa Holdfast was not tortured or executed, for then my wrath would have razed this entire city to the ground, grinding it into dust. The lesson is this – the Holdfasts protect their own. You would be wise to remember that.'

The crowd stared at him in silence, as plumes of smoke rose up into the grey sky. Cael took Arrosa's hand, and raised it into the air, and they stood together for a moment, as the great mass of Gunstians watched them with a mixture of terror and awe.

Cael triggered the Quadrant, and they appeared inside the comfortable rooms of the Holdfast townhouse in Plateau City.

Arrosa gazed out of the tall windows leading to the balcony in the sea walls. 'Why have you brought us here?'

'It's quiet,' he said, 'and our old rooms still have many of our clothes. I guessed that you might want to change out of that prison gown before we go to Nom Karta. We need to inform the Dominion leadership of what we have done.'

'Why do we need to tell them anything?'

'Two reasons,' he said. 'They share the same world as the Gunstian Empire, and it's only polite to inform them that we have eliminated a good portion of the Gunstian priesthood and government.'

'And the second reason?'

He eyed her. 'To let the Dominion know what happens if anyone fucks with the Holdfasts. I'll make some coffee and breakfast if you want to take a shower. There's plenty of hot water.'

She nodded, and opened a wardrobe. Racks of her clothes were still hanging inside, and a pile of towels sat at its base. She picked up two towels, and selected a dress and some clean underwear. She walked to the bathroom door, and entered the tiled room. She showered under the warm water, washing away the two days of grime and sweat, then she dressed in the fresh clothes. She stared at her reflection in the steamed-up mirror. Her hair had been badly cropped by a prison guard, and she hated how it made her look. She would need to visit a professional stylist when she got back to the Blue Palace, to see if they could do anything to fix it. She wondered what Kyra would make of the way she looked, then she realised that she didn't care. She stepped out of the bathroom, and looked around for Cael. He was standing on the balcony, smoking a cigarette as he gazed over the Inner Sea. On the table next to him, food was sitting on plates, along with a silver coffee pot.

Arrosa gazed at him. She had done her best to warn the Gunstians, but they had refused to listen, and she doubted that the horror of what she had seen her husband do would ever leave her. At the same time, she was also glad that the Gunstians hadn't taken her advice; she was glad that Cael had taught them a lesson they would never forget. They needed to know what kind of man he was; and they needed to understand the true nature of the Holdfasts.

She walked to the balcony door, and Cael tossed the cigarette butt into the sea.

'Are you hungry?' he said.

She took his hand, and glanced towards the large bed at the far end of their old room. He looked into her eyes, and followed her back inside.

CHAPTER 28
FOREWARNED

Udall, Ulna, Eastern Rim – 7th Luddinch 5273 (18th Gylean Year 24)

The air crackled and spat over the town of Udall, and three dragons appeared in the cloudless blue sky. Three humans were harnessed to the shoulders of each, and Lucius gazed down from Halfclaw, as more dragons rose up from the bridge palace to greet them. To his left sat the Empress, and Claudian was seated on the far side of the leather harness. Frostback was circling close to their right, bearing Herald Kelsey, Chamberlain Brogan and Chancellor Fenu; while Greysteel was carrying Rosie Jackdaw the Imperial Quartermaster, Treasurer Slaeon and Chief Jurist Nardini.

'If this doesn't impress Queen Blackrose, nothing will,' said Claudian. 'Nine members of the Imperial Court, all gathered on Ulna.'

'There would have been more,' said Lucius, 'if Cael, Cole and Arrosa were with us. It worries me a little that we left Plateau City without knowing if Cael's mission to Gunst was a success.'

'Have a little faith in the Lord Marshal,' said the Empress.

'I have great faith in him, Your Majesty,' said Lucius, 'but Cael has a tendency to take matters into his own hands from time to time.'

'Shall we discuss what to do if Arrosa has been wounded, Your

Majesty,' said Claudian, 'or even executed? Apostasy carries the death penalty in Gunst.'

'If those savages have harmed her,' said the Empress, 'then we shall allow Cael to deliver vengeance on our behalf.'

Claudian puffed out his cheeks. 'Then we can say goodbye to the prospects of any treaty, Your Majesty.'

'A treaty was always unlikely,' said Thorn. 'It became impossible as soon as Arrosa was arrested. How dare they? Is their faith so fragile that they would try to punish someone who turns from it?'

'In what condition is their military?' said Lucius.

'They have a truly massive army, sir,' said Claudian; 'three or four times greater in size than the armed forces of the Empire. They have several elite regiments of infantry, but most are conscripted peasants, and they are badly-equipped, badly-trained and barely literate. Their cadres of Gifted, on the other hand, are potent indeed. Imagine hundreds of men and women with the abilities of Lahnos Laimos. They are powerful shock troops, and even better at defending territory. They pulverised the Dominion forces when they last invaded, some seventeen years ago.'

Blackrose ascended to their altitude, flanked by two other large dragons.

'Greetings, Empress,' said the black dragon. 'Welcome to the capital of my realm. And greetings to you, Halfclaw; you have grown since last we met.'

Halfclaw tilted his head. 'My queen.'

'We are delighted to be here, Queen of the Eastern Rim,' said Thorn.

'With the arrival of nine members of the Imperial Court,' Lucius said, 'Udall shall temporarily become the capital of the entire Empire.'

'There are ten members of the court here,' said Blackrose, 'as one has arrived before you.'

The Empress narrowed her eyes. 'Who?'

'Cole Keir-son,' said the black dragon. 'A dragon living on a small island between Ulna and Throscala bore him and Alva Longhold here this morning. Come; let us land. Cole is waiting in the palace.'

The six dragons soared down from the sky. They banked over the wide, brown river, and alighted onto the large platforms that sat on the roof of the bridge palace. Crowds of courtiers were standing by the edges of the platforms, bearing trays with food and drink, and the imperial party climbed down from the shoulders of the dragons.

Lucius glanced over at Kelsey as she descended from Frostback's flank. They hadn't spoken since he had told her how he felt on the previous day, and he was still feeling the effects of too much whisky. Kelsey caught him looking at her, and their eyes met, before both glanced away.

Thorn frowned at him. 'I saw that look, Lucius,' she said. 'I don't know what it meant, but it meant something. Are you still fighting with my Herald? I thought you were friends again.'

'We didn't fight, Your Majesty,' he said. 'It was far worse than that.'

'I intend to ask her what happened,' she said. 'This is your chance to give me your side of the story.'

'I told her what I truly thought of her, Your Majesty.'

Thorn's eyes tightened. 'And what was that?'

'I told her I loved her.'

Cole appeared on the platform, and Lucius walked forward to meet him, leaving the Empress staring at his back. Kelsey had clearly had the same idea, and she approached Cole from the other side.

'Let's hear it,' said Kelsey, avoiding Lucius's gaze. 'Where's Alva?'

'She's sleeping, ma'am,' said Cole. 'She's had a rough few days.'

'But she's all right?' Kelsey said. 'You're both all right?'

'A little bruised, but we're fine, ma'am. We were being held on Serpens by Cairney Holdfast.'

Lucius frowned. 'I thought he was camping in Kell.'

'It was Cairney who organised the attacks on Alef and Colsbury,' said Cole; 'and now he intends to use Esher to attack the imperial party in Udall.'

'Esher?' said Lucius. 'The Ninth Ascendant?'

'Yes, sir. Cairney can persuade, even without vision powers. He can also block and unblock powers. It's his voice that does it. He is far more powerful than we had been led to believe. Konna is also there, as is Maxwell from the City of Salve; though neither are enthusiastic supporters of Cairney. They fear him.'

'I find it hard to believe that a sixteen-year-old has been orchestrating events,' said Kelsey. 'Is Cairney still on Serpens?'

Blackrose lowered her giant head. 'Serpens has already been scouted by my kin this morning,' she said. 'They found a camp on the beach, but there was no sign of the three errant godlings.'

'It was Alva who saved us,' Cole went on. 'She was able to contact a small community of dragons on an island halfway to Throscala, and one of them came to help us.'

'Why didn't you use your own vision?' said Kelsey.

'My powers were blocked by Cairney's voice, ma'am.'

'And Alva's weren't?' she said. 'There's something you're not telling me.'

Cole glanced away. 'I was able to unpick the blocks in my head, and I reached out and did the same to Alva. Then, I distracted them for a while so that she could look for help.'

'I knew it,' said Kelsey. 'Don't underplay your contributions, Cole. You're far too modest.'

'Well done, Cole,' said Lucius. 'Cael has been searching for you for days.'

'I was expecting to see him here, sir.'

'He rushed to Gunst,' Lucius went on. 'Arrosa has been arrested by the priests there.'

'Should I go?' said Cole. His hand went to a pocket, then he frowned. 'Alva and I lost our Quadrants, sir. Sorry. Cairney has them.'

'These things happen,' said Lucius. 'The fact that you are both safe and well outweighs the loss of a couple of Quadrants. Can we go back to Esher? I assume that Cairney worked out who he was, and was able to unblock his powers?'

'Yes, sir. Esher is... confused and frightened. He knows nothing of his past life as an Ascendant, and he just wants to go home to Jezra. Cairney is forcing him to kill. Cairney's powers are too much for him – they were too much for me. But, he's stupid. He's young, and he makes mistakes.'

'I have alerted the town militia, and dragons are patrolling,' said Blackrose. 'If we are attacked by an Ascendant, then your presence will be essential, Kelsey.'

'Has Sable been summoned?' said Lucius. 'She has the most experience of dealing with Ascendants.'

'Sable is somewhere out on the ocean at present,' said the black dragon. 'She and Lara are taking their new vessel for sea trials.'

'I have tried to look for her,' said Cole, 'but the ocean is a big place.'

'You look tired,' said Kelsey.

'I have been up all night, ma'am, removing Cairney's blocks for a second time.'

'You should get some rest,' said Lucius.

'With all due respect, sir,' he said, 'I will remain on duty for the rest of the day. I am the only one among us who has faced Cairney.'

'I'll let the Empress know the situation,' said Kelsey. 'It might be wise to withdraw Her Majesty from Ulna for a few hours. Perhaps Claudian could give her a tour of the new base on Yearning.'

'Would that be acceptable to you, Queen Blackrose?' said Lucius. 'If Udall is facing imminent attack by an Ascendant, then we should remove the Empress from danger.'

The black dragon eyed them. 'Let us wait to see what the Empress thinks of Kelsey's suggestion.'

Kelsey nodded, then she disappeared through the crowd of people on the platform.

Blackrose turned to Lucius. 'I can sense that all is not well between you and the Herald, soldier,' she said. 'What is at issue?'

'How did you sense anything?' said Lucius. 'We were acting normally. Weren't we acting normally?'

Cole looked away.

'Even Keir-son can detect the tension between you,' said Blackrose.

'Be careful that my rider does not learn of this, as she would no doubt be very eager to get to the truth. Maddie can be extremely persistent.'

Lucius gestured to Claudian. 'Arrange a portal to bring a regiment of imperial marines through to Udall, Adjutant,' he said. 'Have them arrayed by the river.'

'An entire regiment, sir?' said Claudian.

'I will explain the reasons when I brief the regiment's officers. Do it quickly, but quietly. Try not to cause any alarm. Have them bring a few Battanaras.'

Claudian saluted. 'Yes, sir.'

He turned and entered the crowd.

'I am still waiting, Lucius,' said Blackrose. 'What lies between you and the Herald? A fracture at the very top of the Empire's leadership bodes ill. Can it be repaired?'

Lucius lowered his gaze. 'I said something that I should have kept to myself.'

'It must have been something terrible,' said Blackrose, 'for Kelsey is known to brush off most insults. She is as proficient in receiving them as she is at giving them.'

They fell silent as Kelsey returned through the crowd. She eyed Lucius, a slight frown on her features.

'The Empress is refusing to leave Udall,' she said. 'She says she will not run away and hide on Yearning; if Esher comes, she trusts that the defences of Udall will suffice to defeat him. Her Majesty also reminded me that she has powers of her own, though none she can use in my presence.'

'I suspected her reaction would be thus,' said Blackrose. 'The Empress has courage.'

'I have ordered Claudian to bring a regiment of marines through by portal,' said Lucius.

Kelsey nodded, not meeting his gaze. 'Good.'

'I insist that you inform me of the nature of your dispute at once,' said the black dragon, her red eyes burning like coals. 'If my realm is facing an assault by an Ascendant, I need to know if the Empire's Herald and its Constable are able to work together.'

'There is no dispute,' said Kelsey, her voice low.

'Lies!' cried the dragon.

'Don't blame Kelsey for this,' said Lucius. 'The fault is mine. I made an inappropriate advance towards her; one that she rejected.'

The dragon's head lifted a foot, her eyes wide.

'Did I hear that right?' said Maddie, as she and Rosie approached from the left.

'It wasn't exactly an advance,' said Kelsey, her arms out. 'He told me something; he wasn't trying to seduce me or anything.'

'What is this?' cried Frostback, barging her way forward.

'But he is wed to Karalyn,' said Blackrose. 'Lucius Cardova, explain yourself.'

Lucius gazed around. Several dragons and a few dozen humans had turned to see what was causing the noise, and every eye was upon him. The crowd on the roof platform parted for the Empress, who walked up to where Lucius, Kelsey and Cole were standing.

Thorn came to a halt in front of Blackrose. 'I would rather we discussed how Udall shall be defended from the Ninth Ascendant. What goes on between Lucius and Karalyn, and between Lucius and Kelsey, is no one else's concern. I have every faith that my Herald and my Constable are fully able to carry out their duties.'

'I have but one question, Empress,' said Blackrose. 'Is Karalyn Holdfast liable to become enraged when she discovers what, if anything, has been going on between your two highest-ranked ministers of state?'

'Nothing has been going on,' said Thorn. 'Nothing has occurred that will cause Karalyn to act recklessly. I would be grateful if we all allowed them some privacy. Let us go down into the interior of the palace, if we may, Queen of the Eastern Rim, to plan our defence of Udall.'

Blackrose tilted her head. 'To the great audience hall,' she said, and those on the platform began walking down the wide ramp into the palace.

'Thank you, Your Majesty,' Kelsey whispered, as the dragons descended the ramp.

'You two remain here for a moment,' Thorn said. 'Thank you for your service, Cole; please go downstairs with everyone else.'

Cole bowed, and joined Maddie and the others on their way down the ramp. The Empress waited until the platform was empty, then she turned to Lucius and Kelsey.

She shook her head at them. 'Well? Did I speak the truth just now, or did I lie to Blackrose? Is anything going on?'

'No,' said Kelsey.

'I told her how I felt, Your Majesty,' said Lucius; 'that was all. Nothing happened.'

'Oh Lucius,' said Thorn, 'you are married to her sister. How could you say such a thing to Kelsey?'

'I believe that my marriage to Karalyn is over in all but name, Your Majesty.'

'Stop calling me that while we three are alone,' snapped Thorn. 'We are talking as friends. I care about both of you deeply. Talk to me as you would talk to any other friend, Lucius.'

'All right. I told Kelsey my marriage was over, and she asked me about the future. I told her that I wanted to be with her; that I loved her, and then she kicked me out of her office.'

Thorn glanced at Kelsey, who nodded.

'But you two have been best friends for years,' Thorn said. 'How long have you had these feelings, Lucius?'

'That's hard to answer. I loved her back in the City of Salve, but she was with Van, so I said nothing, and did nothing. I moved on. I met Karalyn and we fell in love. For a while, I barely saw Kelsey but, over time, we started to work closely together again. She divorced Van, and I began to see less and less of Karalyn. When I realised that I no longer loved my wife, I also realised that it was Kelsey I wanted to be with; it was Kelsey I loved.'

Thorn eyed Kelsey. 'Will you please say something?'

'I can't,' said Kelsey. 'If I talked about how I felt, I would be betraying my sister. I can't do this; I can't do anything about this. I'm sorry, Lucius, but there's nothing I can do.'

'I know,' he said, 'which is why I shouldn't have said it. When Karalyn next returns, I will tell her that I want to end our marriage. I think she might even be relieved to hear me say it – it will free her to live as she pleases.'

'And the children?' said Thorn. 'What will become of Caitlyn and Carden?'

'I will continue to bring them up, if Karalyn agrees,' he said. 'If she doesn't, then we'll have to work something out.'

'When did they last see their mother?'

'Fifty-six days ago.'

Thorn shook her head. 'It seems perverse of me, but I am greatly angered by that. Twice, I was the guardian of Cael and Kyra, and twice Karalyn appeared and took them from me. I submitted willingly, of course – they were her children, not mine. And now, to think that she has walked away from Caitlyn and Carden fills me with rage. Why is she behaving in this manner? How could she be so desperate to hold on to Cael and Kyra, and yet so negligent when it comes to Caitlyn and Carden?'

'Immortality,' said Kelsey. 'Karalyn is struggling with what her life now means. Can you imagine living as she does? Knowing that if she dies, she will be able to take another body? She's already on her third – what has that done to her sense of who she is? Who does she see when she looks in a mirror?'

'I am sure you are right, Kelsey,' said Thorn. 'It can't be easy. I am going to leave you both alone for a moment. Sort out how you are going to work together, then join us in the audience hall.'

The Empress turned, and walked down the ramp. Lucius lit a cigarette, then he and Kelsey leaned on the platform railings and gazed out over Udall.

'Can we pretend it never happened?' he said.

'I don't know if I'll be able to look at you in the same way,' she said.

'I'm much too tall for you, anyway.'

She laughed. 'Aye. I'd sprain my neck looking up at you. And you smoke. It's a disgusting habit.'

'It's never too late for you to restart smoking, Kelsey. I know you secretly want to.'

She eyed him. 'Say I did secretly want to, but I knew it would be bad for me. Would you still advise me to do it?'

'It's your life.'

'Aye, but others might be hurt if I started... smoking. What would Calpurnia and Caelius think?'

'I think they would be happy to see you happy.'

'I wish it were that easy. I will not hurt my sister. My brothers are dead; my parents are dead. Karalyn is all I have left of the family I knew as a child. If the price for not hurting her is a life of being alone, then I will have to accept it. Can you accept it, Lucius?'

'I will do what I must.'

She frowned. 'Let's go downstairs.'

Lucius stubbed out the cigarette, and they walked down the ramp and into the palace. They entered a long, wide passageway, and came to the large, domed audience chamber. Over a dozen dragons and several hundred people had crowded in, and most were arranged around Blackrose and the Empress, who were both standing on a raised platform. Blackrose saw Lucius and Kelsey enter the hall, and the crowds parted to allow them to reach the platform.

'We have reached a few decisions,' said Blackrose. 'As we do not know where and when the Ascendant will appear, we have decided that the bridge palace shall be evacuated. All civilians shall depart, along with most dragons. The regiment Adjutant Claudian is bringing shall remain outside; those remaining inside shall cluster around Kelsey, here, in the heart of the palace.' She turned to the Empress.

'My Herald and I shall act as bait,' Thorn said. 'We are both loathed by Cairney Holdfast, and I believe that Esher will be sent against us, to kill us if possible. Cole has informed us that Cairney will command Esher to throw his own life away in the assault, so do not expect to see him retreat. Esher will not be fleeing; he will be trying his best to slaughter everyone he sees in the palace. And yet, I pity the Ninth Ascendant. For nearly two decades, Esher has lived a quiet, peaceful life in the City of Salve, his memories obliterated and his powers blocked. He is blameless, his mind corrupted by Cairney Holdfast's powers to command him. If it is possible, I want Esher subdued and captured, not killed. Let us remove Cairney's weapon from his hands.'

'And what of Cairney himself?' said a red dragon. 'How do we intend to eliminate the threat he represents?'

The Empress gestured to Cole, who stepped up onto the platform. He looked exhausted, but his eyes still shone.

'I believe that Cairney's plans are in tatters,' Cole said. 'He chose Esher to disguise his own designs against the Empress and her Herald, and he wanted the Empire and the Dominion to blame each other for the murders that he commanded Esher to carry out. He had no desire to be revealed as the instigator of our troubles. He must know by now that he has failed. He watched as Alva Longhold and I were borne away to safety, rescued by a dragon from the Eastern Rim. He knows that I was aware of his plans, and he may change them. Esher might not be coming here this day. Cairney may decide to find another use for him. Cairney is powerful; he is one of the most powerful Holdfasts alive, and he is a demigod. He is also young, and unpredictable. He can alter his appearance, as his mother Lady Aila is able to do; and he has the ability to force people to act against their will. He also has death powers and battle-vision; and he has self-healing. We are fortunate that he has decided to turn on us at the age of sixteen. Had he waited ten years, he might have become too powerful for anyone but Karalyn; but now, right now, Cael remains stronger than him, and I am able to resist him, to a certain extent. I will also be able to remove Cairney's control over Esher, if I can get close enough to him.'

'Thank you, Cole Keir-son,' said Blackrose. 'Should we not make every effort to ensure that Cael is here? If he is able to overpower Cairney, then the same would be true regarding Esher.'

'We have looked for him, Your Majesty,' said Claudian. 'He is not on

Zamata, nor is he in the Blue Palace. I fear we must do this without him.'

Blackrose tilted her head. 'Then I will now order the evacuation. All must leave the palace, excepting those the Empress and I have asked to stay. Kelsey and Lucius – you were not here when we listed those to remain, but you were both included. Stay here, while the others depart.'

Several dragons began to make their way out of the hall, followed by the palace courtiers and guards. Most of the Imperial Court was escorted out by Halfclaw and Greysteel, leaving only Lucius, the Empress, Kelsey and Cole behind. The Jackdaw sisters said their farewells to each other, as Rosie left, while Maddie remained by Blackrose's side. The hall quietened as it emptied, then it fell into silence as the last of the evacuees departed.

'We must all remain within one hundred yards of Kelsey,' said Blackrose. 'Frostback, you shall defend your rider; while I defend the Empress. Lucius will stand watch over the entrance to the hall, and you, Cole Keir-son, you will hide in the shadows, ready to invade Esher's mind as soon as he gets here.'

'What should I do?' said Maddie.

'It would probably be best if you stayed back a little,' said Blackrose, 'and remained out of danger.'

Lucius tilted his head towards Blackrose, and walked across the hall to the large, arched entrance. He glanced over his shoulder. He was about fifty yards from Kelsey, which was well within her range, but Esher would have battle-vision, and he would need to react quickly. He leaned against the wall, and waited.

Two hours passed. The silence within the palace was almost complete, as the two dragons strained their hearing, listening for any sign that Esher had arrived. To pass the time, Lucius tried to forget about Esher; instead, he concentrated on what he would say to Karalyn. How, exactly, did one go about divorcing the most powerful being in existence? Tactfully, he imagined. He would be straightforward and honest with her, as she hated it when people danced around a subject. He would tell her the truth, but not all of the truth. He would admit that he no longer loved her, but he would neglect to mention Kelsey.

'He is here,' said Cole. 'He has arrived by Quadrant on the same platform that we were standing on before.'

'I do not hear anything,' said Blackrose.

'He is creeping down the ramp, Your Majesty. Lucius, sir, keep a watch out to your left. Esher is armed.'

Lucius edged out through the archway, keeping close to the wall. He gazed to his left, where the bottom of the ramp appeared at the far end of the dragon-sized passageway. A man came into view. He looked like one of the Ancients with battle-vision that they had fought during the war against the Ascendants, but his breastplate was of steel, rather than compressed stone. An imperial longsword was in his right hand, and he was padding softly along the passageway. He caught sight of Lucius, and raised his left arm.

Nothing happened. Esher came to a halt, and then he gazed at his hand as though he sensed that something was wrong.

'I am in his mind,' whispered Cole, 'but I will need a few minutes.'

Lucius nodded, then he stepped out into the passageway.

'It's over, Lord Esher,' he called out. 'Lay down the sword and surrender.'

'My name is Reece,' said the man, 'and I am here for the Empress and her Herald. Do not stand in my way.'

'You are being manipulated, Reece,' said Lucius. 'Cairney Holdfast has corrupted your mind.'

'I know,' said the man. 'I cannot resist.' He gripped the sword in both hands, and his eyes darkened.

Lucius remained where he was, then Esher began to move, charging towards him at a speed Lucius could barely comprehend. Lucius stepped back, but Esher was on him before he could retreat into the hall. Esher swung his sword at Lucius's head, and a great dragon forelimb shot out, shoving Lucius to the side as the sword bit deep into the black scales. Blackrose grunted in pain, then she swiped at Esher.

The Ascendant rolled under the swinging forelimb and sprinted into the hall. Frostback opened her jaws, sending flames down onto him, but Esher kept moving. His clothes were aflame, and yet on he came, racing towards the Empress. Maddie screamed. Blackrose tried to move back to protect Thorn, but Esher was faster than anyone else in the hall. Frostback lunged forward to shield Kelsey, and Esher dealt the silver dragon a savage blow, his sword slicing through her left flank. Esher raised his sword at Thorn, who remained calm, her eyes unyielding.

'For Corthie,' cried Esher, as he prepared to swing.

Lucius stared in horror as he watched from the floor by the hall's entrance, then Esher staggered. The sword fell from his grip, and he collapsed, falling two feet in front of Thorn.

Maddie puffed out her cheeks. 'Malik's ass, Cole, could you have cut it any finer?'

Thorn smiled at Cole, who was standing on the low platform, his eyes half-closed from the effort.

'I had every faith in my Imperial Secretary,' she said.

Cole looked up, then he toppled off the platform and fell onto the floor. Lucius got to his feet and ran towards Cole. He knelt by him, and checked his breathing.

'Is he all right, Constable?' said the Empress. 'Does he require a healing?'

'He's unconscious, Your Majesty,' Lucius said, 'but he's suffering from exhaustion, not from an injury that can be healed.' He turned to gaze at Blackrose. 'Thank you, Dragon Queen. You saved my life by the entrance. And thank you, Frostback. You both took wounds meant for us.'

'I will heal you both,' said Thorn. She touched Frostback's flank, and the injury closed up, then she walked across the hall and placed her hand onto Blackrose's forelimb.

'You are most welcome, Empress,' Blackrose said, as her injury was healed. 'We have subdued Esher, as you commanded – what now shall we do with him?'

Lucius stood, then he picked up the fallen longsword, and placed the tip against Esher's throat.

'Should we wake him?' said Kelsey.

Frostback nudged the Ascendant with an extended claw, then Kelsey slapped him across the face.

Esher opened his eyes.

'Do not move,' said Lucius, 'if you wish to keep your head.'

Esher stared around, his eyes wide.

'Can you still feel Cairney's orders in your mind?' said Lucius.

'Yes,' said Esher, 'but they are more like a faint memory. Did I kill anyone?'

'You did not,' said the Empress, 'though not through want of trying.'

'Are you the Empress? Is it really you?'

'It is I,' she said.

Esher started to weep. 'I'm sorry. Take my head, for I have slaughtered innocents and I deserve to die. I don't want to live like this; I don't want to be a god. Cairney has destroyed me.'

Thorn glanced at Lucius, and he pulled the blade away from Esher's throat.

'Why would you spare me?' said Esher.

'Because you are innocent,' said the Empress. 'You are absolved of your crimes, for you were not in control of your actions. Stand, Esher; you are free.'

Lucius extended a hand. Esher took it, and got to his feet.

'What will Cairney do now?' said Lucius.

'I don't know,' said Esher. 'He expected me to die in this attack.'

'Do you know where he is?' said Kelsey.

'He moved us to a different island,' he said. 'I don't know why, and I don't know which island.'

Cole groaned and opened his eyes. Lucius went to his side and helped him stand. Esher gazed over.

'Was it you who stopped me?' Esher said.

Cole nodded.

'Thank you,' said Esher. 'Have you blocked my powers?'

'All but self-healing,' said Cole.

Cole staggered, and Lucius put an arm round his shoulder to support him.

'Will you take me to see Alva?' Cole said.

Lucius nodded. 'I think Cole might need to sleep for a while.'

'Alva Longhold was moved to a small cottage in Udall,' said Blackrose. 'Take him there, and let him rest.'

'And the evacuees, Your Majesty?'

'They will remain out of the palace for the moment,' said the black dragon. 'Cairney will not be pleased by what we have done this day. I sense he may wish to make an appearance of his own.'

'If Cole is no longer able to help us,' said Thorn, 'then perhaps we should order the marines into the palace, in case Queen Blackrose's suspicions prove correct.'

'I will see to it, Your Majesty,' said Lucius. He tilted his head, then he helped Cole walk towards the entrance. He gazed over at Kelsey, and their eyes met. She gave Lucius a crooked smile, then he and Cole left the hall.

'Aunty Kelsey can't tell you what she wants, not out loud, Lucius,' Cole said, as they made their way to the stairs, 'but the truth is staring you in the face.'

'What truth?' said Lucius.

Cole turned his exhausted features to him. 'You belong together.'

CHAPTER 29
SEEING IT THROUGH

Nom Karta, Inopei – 27th Luddinch 1605

The air crackled, and Konna found herself within a dark chamber. She was underground; she could sense it, but where? Bright sparks arose from Cairney's left hand, then he shot a thin strand of fire up into a wall lamp. The wick burst into flames, illuminating the large, empty cellar.

Maxwell gazed around at the bare walls. 'Where are we?'

'Nom Karta,' said Cairney. 'Where else? I told ye that I was planning to come here, Maxi-boy.'

'Aye,' said Konna, 'but we weren't expecting to come along.'

Cairney shrugged. He was wearing steel armour that he had stolen from somewhere, and the breastplate was shining in the reflected light of the lamp.

'I thought it might be better to keep ye where I can see ye,' he said.

'Ye don't trust us, in other words,' said Konna.

'Have ye given me any reason to trust ye, sis?' he said. 'Tell me – why didn't ye try to stop Esher untying Cole's bonds? Why were ye just standing there, doing nothing? I knew Maxi-boy was a coward, but ye've gravely disappointed me, sister.'

'But yer plans have gone to shit, Cairney,' she said. 'Where do ye think Cole will be right now? He and Alva will be telling everyone what we've done.'

'Relax,' he said. 'Esher will be in Ulna by now, and I ordered him to make sure he kills everyone he sees. Cole's probably dead.'

'Are you out of yer mind?' she shouted. 'If the Empress is there, then Kelsey will be there!'

'Good. I hope Esher rips them both to pieces.'

'But...'

'Esher will still be able to use battle-vision,' Cairney went on, 'even if Kelsey is standing right next to him. Cael isnae there, and Sable isnae there – Esher will tear through the rest of them nae bother.'

'A dragon has most likely incinerated Esher,' said Maxwell. 'Face it, Cairney, the Empire will not be going to war with the Dominion, not if they know that you were behind the deaths.'

'Then we'll have to make sure that the Dominion attacks the Empire,' cried Cairney. 'That's why we're here. The plan took a blow when Cole escaped, but it'll still work if the Dominion thinks Cael Holdfast has gone berserk. You two just need to stay calm. I'll put on a show disguised as Cael, and the Dominion will be forced to retaliate.'

'And then what?' said Konna. 'If Karalyn comes down to sort out any trouble, how long do ye think it will take her to realise what's been going on? Do ye think she's stupid? All she'll have to do is read Cael's mind, and she'll know it wasn't him.'

Cairney glared at his sister, his eyes dark. 'But what else is left? What else can we do? We have to keep going. Once we're finished here, I can look for Cael, and kill him before Karalyn can read his mind. What about that? That would work.'

Konna lowered her gaze. She cursed her indecision during the previous night. Cole had asked her for help, and she had refused, only for a dragon to soar down and carry both him and Alva Longhold away. Konna had been struck by the dragon's forelimb, and had crashed into the waves of the ocean. That had saved her from the flames that had enveloped Cairney on the beach. Maxwell had also been spared a roasting, as he had been sleeping in a cave at the time. Konna had waded back onto the beach as soon as the dragon had flown away, and she had seen the smouldering remains of her brother, his scorched and burnt flesh, and his bald scalp, where the hair had been burned away. It had taken Cairney almost an hour to fully recover from the burning, and his temper had not cooled since.

Cairney drew a black-bladed sword, then he tossed the empty scabbard to the floor.

Maxwell stared at the weapon. 'That's a Fated Blade,' he said. 'Where did you get it?'

'Is it not obvious, Maxi-boy?' said Cairney. 'Sable has one of them, and I was hardly likely to steal it from her, was I? I took this from yer quarters in Jezra. Right – listen. I want ye both to stay behind me when we go upstairs. Don't draw any attention to yerselves; I want all eyes to be on me.'

'Maybe we should stay down here,' said Maxwell.

Cairney laughed. 'No chance. I know ye'd betray me the first opportunity ye got, Maxi-boy. In fact, let me do something about that.' He stared into Maxwell's face. 'You will be loyal to me this day,' he said. 'You will be my loyal lieutenant, and you will obey every order that comes from my mouth.'

Maxwell blinked and staggered back a step.

Cairney turned to Konna.

'Yer tricks won't work on me, brother,' she said.

'Are ye sure?' he said. 'My powers have grown over the last wee while with all the practice. I'm stronger now than ever.' He took a step towards her, and she edged back. He laughed. 'Are ye frightened of me, sister?' he said.

'Stay away from me.'

He stared into her eyes. 'You will be loyal to me.'

Konna felt a wave of power strike her, and she stumbled backwards, falling over and hitting the cold, stone floor. The sensation in her head wasn't painful, but it felt as though there was another presence in her mind, one that was trampling all over her free will. She looked up at Cairney. She would be loyal; she had no choice. She closed her eyes, fighting to resist the controlling force invading her thoughts.

'How does it feel, sis?' said Cairney. 'Are ye gonnae behave?'

Konna writhed on the floor of the cellar.

'It'll be easier if ye stop fighting it,' Cairney said. 'Just accept it, sis. It'll wear off on its own, though fuck knows when. Stand up.'

Konna's body started to obey her brother's words and, before she could control herself, she was back on her feet. She glanced at Maxwell, but his eyes had almost glazed over.

'It's time,' said Cairney. He smiled, then his appearance altered to that of Cael Holdfast. Only his head had transformed – the rest of him remained the same, the steel armour unchanged.

'Follow me,' he said, then he turned and made for the cellar's only doorway.

Maxwell and Konna kept pace a couple of yards behind Cairney as they hurried through the sprawling basement.

'A dozen dragons live in this palace,' Cairney said. 'Most of them are out of favour with Queen Famula for one reason or another, and they keep to themselves. We'll slaughter a few, but we'll make sure the survivors see who did it.'

He paused at the foot of a set of stairs leading up. He eyed Maxwell, then he withdrew a Quadrant from behind his armour.

'This belonged to the Longhold lassie,' Cairney said, 'or it might have been Cole's; I cannae remember. Take it. If anything happens to me, I'm depending on you to get us the fuck out of here.'

Maxwell took the Quadrant. 'Where will I take us if that happens?'

Cairney smiled. 'Call me *boss* when ye speak to me.'

'Sorry,' said Maxwell. 'Where will I take us if that happens, boss?'

Cairney stretched out his left hand and mimicked the actions above the surface of the Quadrant.

'Have ye got that?' he said. 'Move yer fingers like this.'

Maxwell nodded. 'Understood, boss.'

He dropped the Quadrant into a pocket, and Cairney turned back to the stairs. He hesitated, and Konna tried again to free her mind of his influence. She could see what he had done to her sense of will, but remained unable to resist. All the same, she told herself, there was a reason her brother hadn't trusted her with a Quadrant. He knew that her mind was stronger than Maxwell's; and perhaps he was unsure how long his influence over her would last. She had to keep fighting.

Cairney raised the Fated Blade, and ran up the stairs.

Maxwell and Konna raced up after him. They came to another wide passageway, and headed towards the entrance of a large hall, from where light and voices were emanating. They reached the tall, arched entrance, and Konna caught a glimpse of several dragons. Most were adults, but there were infant dragons mixed among them.

'I am Cael Holdfast,' Cairney cried, 'and I am here to take revenge for the crimes of the Dominion.'

The dragons stared at him.

Cairney raised his left arm, and Konna sensed his death powers being unleashed. Three dragons screamed, their eyes bleeding, and their scales withering as they collapsed to the floor of the hall. One of the three dragons was a mere child, and Konna stared as she watched him die. A blast of fire burst out from the jaws of a large purple dragon, and Cairney raced forward, leaving Konna and Maxwell to be bathed in flames. Konna dived to the floor, her clothes on fire, as her self-healing got to work. She glanced up, her scalded body in agony, and saw Cairney's Tempest-bladed sword slice clean through the long neck of a green dragon. The head crashed to the floor, then Cairney rolled to avoid a lunging swing of claws aimed at his head. He pointed at a young orange dragon, and her head exploded, showering the others in the hall with blood. Cairney laughed, his eyes wide, then Konna blinked. It was Cairney she was seeing, not Cairney disguised as Cael. His appearance had reverted to his own, but he hadn't seemed to realise.

'I am Cael Holdfast!' he shouted again, as he raised the Fated Blade.

'You are not,' said a voice from the entrance to the hall. 'Your illusions don't work on me, Cairney. Get on your knees; it's over.'

Konna turned her head. Kyra Holdfast was standing by the arched entranceway, Edgar by her side. Cairney fell to his knees, as though compelled. He dropped the sword, and it clattered over the stone floor. The purple dragon raised her left forelimb, ready to tear Cairney to pieces.

'No, Lady Sigra,' said Edgar. 'We will be taking this vile criminal into custody.'

'But he murdered five dragons, my lord,' said the purple dragon; 'including two little ones. He deserves to die.'

'He does,' said Edgar, 'but not before Karalyn sees the truth of what has happened.'

Kyra stared at Cairney. 'Did you think you could use your powers here without me noticing?' she said. 'You are a fool.'

'Fuck you!' Cairney cried. 'Maxi-boy – now!'

Konna glanced over at the burnt form of Maxwell on the floor a few yards from her. The flesh on his hands was bloody and smouldering as they gripped the Quadrant Cairney had lent him. Maxwell's fingers moved, as Kyra and Edgar turned to him.

The air crackled. Konna fell a few feet and crashed into cold water. Her head went under the surface, the water soothing her burnt skin. She kicked out, and rose back up for air. She was thirty yards from a beach. Maxwell was on her left, while Cairney was over to her right, the heavy armour weighing him down as he began to swim towards the shoreline. The three young gods struggled and swam until they were able to wade out from the ocean. They staggered up onto the beach, then each one collapsed onto the warm sand.

'Pyre's cock,' Cairney muttered. 'Nice one, Maxi-boy; ye fucking saved us back there.'

Konna stared up at the cloudless sky. Her self-healing had almost repaired the damage caused by the flames of the purple dragon, and the pain was starting to recede.

'I hate Kyra Holdfast,' said Cairney. 'I fucking hate that bitch.'

Konna sat up. Her clothes were in tatters, and she could smell the burnt hair that was still being re-grown. Maxwell was also healing, and his skin was starting to re-form. He was gazing down at the Quadrant in his hands, as though he was desperate to flee, but was being forced to do whatever Cairney told him.

'Do you now accept that it's over, brother?' Konna said. 'Kyra and Cael both know what we've been doing; and Cole will have told everyone else.'

'The plan has gone to shit, right enough,' said Cairney, who was still lying on his back on the sand.

'We should hand ourselves in,' she said.

Cairney eyed her. 'Aye? You'd be all right, but, eh? Ye'd tell them that I forced ye to help me, and they might let ye off. Same with Maxi-boy – you two cowardly wee fuds won't be punished; but did ye not hear Edgar? The bastards are gonnae kill me if they catch me. I killed five dragons, including two bairns. They'll not forgive that.'

'Then why the fuck did ye do it?' cried Konna.

'I was being Cael Holdfast; it was Cael who killed them, not me.'

'Yer a fucking nutter, Cairney.'

'Aye, maybe,' he said. 'There's only one thing left to do. We're going to Ulna. If we're lucky, then Esher will have already slaughtered the Imperial Court; if not, we'll have to do the job ourselves.'

Konna stared at him.

'Yer right,' Cairney went on. 'There's no hiding behind Esher any more – they all know it was us. We've been rumbled good and proper. We cannae hide, because they'll find us. If we surrender, I'll be strung up, or they'll put me in a restrainer mask for a few centuries – either way, I'm fucked. If we go to Clackenbaird, the Colsbury Holdfasts will follow us there, and I cannae risk putting Ma and our brothers and sisters in danger. Carter would probably try to help us, the stupid wee radge. There's no going back, Konna. We have to see it through to the end.' He eyed her. 'This is what we've wanted, but – a chance for revenge. Let's strike the Empress down ourselves, and her Herald, and the whole bloody lot of them. Let's spit on the corpses of the bastards who sent our father to die.'

'Karalyn will kill us if we do that,' she said.

'Karalyn is probably gonnae kill me anyway. What have I got to lose?'

'What about me and Maxwell?' she said.

'Leave us here when you go to Ulna, Cairney, please,' said Maxwell. 'You don't need us to go with you.'

'Yer a wee shitebag, Maxi-boy,' said Cairney, as he got to his feet. 'Is that how ye want to live? If I leave ye here, the Empire will probably spare yer life, but they'll never trust ye again. It was you who told us about Esher – it was you who started this whole thing. If ye'd kept yer big mouth shut, then none of this would've happened. But just think – what if we go to Ulna and win? What if we wipe out the entire Imperial Court, assuming Esher hasnae already done it? We will have avenged Corthie Holdfast; we will have taken revenge for what those bastards did to my Da. Is that not worth it? Konna – is that not what ye've always wanted?'

Konna said nothing.

'I asked you a question, sister,' Cairney went on. 'Have ye given up? Does Da's death mean nothing to ye? Remember how ye felt when ye saw his body laid out before us in Colsbury Castle – his wounds, his face. I know ye remember it; could ye not feel the same way for one more day? Ye can give up tomorrow, when we've finished what we started. Ye can go back to Kell after we've killed the Empress, and ye can tell Ma what we've done. She'll be so proud of us, Konna. Come on; stand up. Ye can alter yer appearance, and ye've got battle-vision and death powers – it's fucking time to use them. Hey – I've got an idea. If you pretend to be Arrosa, I'll pretend to be Cael, and we'll be able to slip into Blackrose's palace. The Empress won't know what's hit her until we bury our fists in her face. Remember – she's a soulwitch, so she'll take some killing. We'll have to behead her to make sure. Kelsey will be easy – we'll snap her fucking neck like a twig. Aye – let's make Kelsey our first target. If we can get her, then we'll be able to use our other powers. Aye. Let's go. Maxwell – on yer feet.'

Maxwell stood at once, but Konna remained sitting on the sand, her brother's hold over her starting to weaken. She gazed up at Cairney, and shook her head.

'I'm done,' she said. 'I hate the Empress, and I hate the Empire, but what's the point? Why are we wasting our time worrying about mortals? Thorn and Kelsey will be dead soon, no matter what we do. Uncle Naxor was right – we should have been more patient. The Empire would have fallen into our hands if we had held our nerve for a few decades; we could have ruled it together as soon as the mortal Holdfasts had died out. And now we've fucked it all up.'

'Then we should go out in a blaze of glory, sister,' Cairney said. He eyed her, but she didn't move. 'I cannae believe yer forcing me to do this to ye twice in one day,' he said. 'Ye've left me no choice – Konna, you will obey me. Stand.'

Konna got to her feet, her body moving before she could do anything about it.

'Konna,' Cairney went on, 'today, you are going to fight by my side. You will attack everyone you see in Blackrose's palace, and you will use all of yer powers to strike down our enemies. You will not surrender, and you will show no mercy. Kelsey first, then we'll slaughter everyone else. Maxwell, you will also fight. Stay back until Kelsey is dead, then use yer death powers on the dragons; defend me and Konna while we kill the Colsbury Holdfasts.'

Konna closed her eyes, feeling Cairney's powers batter her free will. Her conscious mind remained untrammelled, but she had lost control over her actions.

'Take on Arrosa's appearance,' said Cairney.

Konna did so, her powers convincing all who saw her that she looked like Cael's Gunstian wife.

Cairney transformed back into Cael.

'I dropped the Fated Blade in Nom Karta,' said Cairney, 'so we'll have to get ourselves some new weapons. That's our first priority. Weapons, then Kelsey.' He took out the Quadrant from behind his breastplate.

'Do ye know how to get to Blackrose's palace?' said Konna.

'Of course I do,' said Cairney. 'I've been there a few times, disguised as a courtier, but the dragons are clever; they usually sense that something's not quite right, so we'll need to be quick. I'll take us to a wee apartment in the human part of the palace. We're gonnae be sneaky, and fast.'

He swept his fingers over the Quadrant, and the air shimmered. They appeared in a small, empty bedroom, and Konna peered out of the window. They were in the bridge palace in Udall, and she could see the brown river, and the harbour. Hundreds of imperial marines were down by the road leading from the palace to the quayside, and dozens of dragons were circling overhead. There was also a large crowd of civilians, but the marines were blocking the road, keeping them from entering the palace. Cairney joined her by the window.

'It looks like they've evacuated the building,' said Cairney. 'I wonder if that's good or bad. I don't hear any screaming.'

He walked over to a wardrobe, and opened it. Leaning against the back wall was a sheathed militia sword, and Cairney picked it up. He threw the sheath away, and brandished the sword in his right hand.

'It's a shite blade,' he said, 'but it'll do until we can get something better.'

'The marines are on the move, boss,' said Maxwell. 'They're marching towards the palace.'

Cairney went back to the window, and his eyes tightened. 'Let's pay the marines a quick visit,' he said. 'Stay here, Maxwell. Stay here, and remain quiet.'

Cairney activated the Quadrant, then he and Konna appeared by the base of the bridge palace, on the banks of the brown river. Several marines turned in surprise, then an officer bowed his head.

'Lord Cael, Lady Arrosa,' he said, 'are you aware of what has been happening in Udall today?'

'I am aware,' said Cairney. 'I am here to ensure that none of you enter the palace, not until I give the word that it's safe to do so.'

'But, sir,' said the officer, 'we have received orders to enter the palace to protect the Empress.'

'And I'm countermanding those orders,' said Cairney. 'Stay the fuck outside.'

'Understood, sir,' said the officer.

'Arrosa and I are now going into the palace,' said Cairney. 'If Cairney comes, we'll be ready for him.'

He triggered the Quadrant again, and he and Konna appeared in the same small bedroom from before. Maxwell was standing by the window, his eyes still glazed over.

'Now we won't be interrupted,' said Cairney. 'Ye did well there, Miss Arrosa.'

He walked to the room's only door, opened it, and peered out.

'It's clear,' he said.

Konna and Maxwell followed him out into a corridor. Cairney headed to the right, and Konna's legs kept moving, keeping pace with her brother. Inside, her mind was submerged by Cairney's powers. Part of her felt as though she was screaming, though no sound was coming from her mouth. She wanted to flee, flee and hide, but her body was no longer hers to control.

Cairney led them up a flight of stairs, then they paused by the top, where the passageway opened out into a dragon-sized hall.

'We're entering the dragon part of the palace,' Cairney whispered. He lifted his left hand, and sparks shot between his fingers. 'We're still out of Kelsey's range, if she's alive.'

They carried on, keeping to the thick shadows of the hallway, and moving as quietly as they were able. Cairney paused at another junction, and tried to spark. Nothing happened. He glanced at Konna, and nodded.

They crept along another hallway, then the sound of dragons talking came out from a large chamber to their right. Cairney led the others to the corner of the arched entrance, and they peered inside. Four dragons were present within the cavernous hall. Konna recognised Blackrose and Frostback, but not the other two.

'And when will it be safe to bring the civilians back into the palace, Your Majesty?' said one of the unfamiliar dragons.

'We shall wait to see if Cairney makes an appearance,' said Blackrose; 'until then, it remains unsafe for everyone else. I will not risk my people's lives while that vile god is on the loose.'

'But you are risking your own life, Your Majesty.'

'I am the Queen; it is my duty to protect my people. We have already taken care of the Ninth Ascendant this day, and the Empire's marines will soon be here; I do not fear Cairney.'

Cairney pulled back from the entrance, his eyes downcast. 'They got Esher,' he whispered. 'The bastards got him.'

He crept away from the entrance and raced towards a smaller, human-sized doorway that lay next to the great hall. Konna and Maxwell reached his side just as Cairney was opening the door. They came into a long room, where two women were sitting by the far wall. Both glanced up. It was Maddie Jackdaw and Kelsey Holdfast.

'Cael!' Maddie cried, as she got to her feet. 'You're back. Hello, Arrosa. You missed all the excitement.'

Cairney shoved Maxwell forward, pushing him so hard that he fell to the floor.

'We caught Maxwell,' Cairney said. 'The wee bastard was shitting his pants when we found him. Where is the Empress?'

Kelsey got to her feet.

'I almost nabbed Cairney,' Cairney went on, 'but he was too quick for me. Is the Empress here?'

Kelsey nodded, her features steady. She knows, Konna thought; Kelsey knows that something is wrong. It hit her – Cairney's illusion would not work on the Herald; she would see through it in an instant. She tried to warn Cairney, but his grip over her movements was keeping her mouth closed.

'I'll let the Empress know that you're both here,' Kelsey said, as she walked towards a side door. 'Maddie, you should tell Blackrose.'

'Eh?' said Maddie. 'You can tell her. I want to speak to Arrosa.' She peered at Maxwell. 'So this is Amalia's son, yeah? Wow.'

Kelsey took another step towards the side door, but it opened before she could reach it, and Lucius Cardova walked in.

His eyes widened. 'You found her, Cael? Good job. You have arrived just in time; how was Gunst?'

'Gunst?' said Cairney. 'It was... fine, I guess.'

Lucius frowned.

'They caught Maxwell,' said Maddie. 'He looks like his mother, a little bit. Is he dangerous?'

Lucius glanced down. Maxwell was whimpering on the floor of the room, his hands over his head.

'So, Cael,' said Kelsey, 'is the Gunstian government happy with the terms of the treaty we agreed with them?'

'Eh, aye, Aunty,' Cairney said. 'They were happy enough.'

Lucius moved a little further into the room, as though he wanted to check on Maxwell, but Konna could see that he was putting himself between Kelsey and Cairney.

Cairney powered his battle-vision, just as Maddie decided to walk over. The Jackdaw woman seemed oblivious to the tension in the room, and she moved in front of Cairney, so that she could get a better look at Maxwell.

Cardova bundled Kelsey out through the side door, half-dragging her as they ran. Cairney cried out in rage. He shoved Maddie out of the way, sending her flying, then he raced after Kelsey, his sword raised. Konna went after him, and they rushed through the side door, and into a long, dark corridor. Lucius was backing away, his arms out-stretched, keeping Kelsey behind him.

'Help!' Kelsey shouted.

'No one is coming to help you,' cried Cairney, shedding his disguise. 'No dragon can get into this corridor. This is where it ends, Kelsey. You destroyed my family; you killed my Da. I've been waiting for this moment for years.'

'Run!' Cardova cried. 'Run to Blackrose. Protect the Empress.'

Kelsey stared at him, then she bolted down the hallway and through another door. Cairney charged forward, then he drove his sword into Cardova's stomach, pushing the blade in deep. Blood spilled down the front of Cardova's clothes. He gasped, then Cairney ripped the sword free. Cardova staggered back, then he collapsed to the floor, his hands on the wound by his waist.

'I hope that fucking hurts,' Cairney screamed in his face.

He glanced at Konna. 'With me.'

They raced past Cardova, leaving him bleeding on the floor, and went through the other door. They came into another human-sized room, where food and drinks were laid out on a table. The meals looked half-eaten, and steam was rising from an untouched cup of black coffee.

'Where the fuck is she?' said Cairney.

He went to the only other door in the room, and opened it. A black dragon forelimb burst through the entrance, smashing the doorframe. It gripped Cairney and pulled him out of the room. Konna ran to the broken entrance. Blackrose had Cairney held tightly in her grasp. Next to her, Frostback opened her jaws. Konna dived to the left, as a blast of flames tore through the room, incinerating the table and its contents. Konna cowered in the corner, waiting for the flames to stop, then she crawled back to the entrance. Cairney was still being held in Blackrose's grip, but the face of the black dragon was twisting in pain.

'You are filled with agony!' Cairney cried. 'Sleep!'

Blackrose's eyes dimmed, then she crashed to the floor of the cavernous hall. Cairney rolled from her grasp and pointed at Frostback.

'I order you to kill your rider,' Cairney shouted.

Frostback looked stricken, and she raised her claws towards Kelsey and the Empress, who were sheltering behind the fallen body of Blackrose. The silver dragon gazed down at her rider, her red eyes filled with torment.

'Do it!' Cairney screamed. 'Kill Kelsey.'

'I will not,' cried Frostback. 'You will not defeat me, foul wretch. My will is my own.'

'Then it's naptime for you, ya useless lizard,' said Cairney.

Frostback toppled over, her body slumping down next to Blackrose.

'Fucking dragons, eh?' said Cairney, as he eyed Kelsey and the Empress. 'Well, as I always say, if ye need something done...' He picked up the militia sword. 'I'm gonnae kill you first, Kelsey,' he said; 'so I can use my powers to tear the Empress to shreds.'

'I am not afraid,' said Thorn.

Konna got back to her feet, her burns healed for the second time that day. She stayed by the smashed doorway, as Cairney walked toward Kelsey and the Empress.

Cairney laughed. 'I'm gonnae enjoy this.'

CHAPTER 30
THE ARBITER

Udall, Ulna, Eastern Rim – 7th Luddinch 5273 (18th Gylean Year 24)

Cole lay on the bed fully-clothed, unable to sleep. It was warm in the small cottage, even with the windows open, and his mind was too busy to allow him to rest. He sat up, and glanced over at the other bed in the room. Alva was sleeping under the blankets, her face peaceful. Cole got up and sat down on the bed next to her.

Her eyes opened.

'Sorry,' he said; 'I didn't mean to wake you.'

'It's fine,' she said. 'What's happening?'

'You missed Esher. He attacked the palace, but everyone is all right. We caught him.'

'Where is he? Actually, where are we? This isn't the room where I fell asleep.'

'Claudian has Esher under guard somewhere in the town,' he said. 'Blackrose wanted the palace evacuated, so they moved you by Quadrant, while you were sleeping.'

She gazed at him. 'You look tired, Cole.'

'So I keep getting told,' he said. 'I'll be fine. I tried to get some sleep, but my head is wide awake.'

'Has there been any news of Cairney?'

'None. He must have realised by now that we know he was behind everything. I reckon he'll run away, and try to hide.'

She looked down at her clothes. 'I'm a mess,' she said. 'I would do anything for a bath and a warm meal; and a coffee. Have you got any keenweed?'

'None. We'd better stay here, though; we might be needed.'

'I thought you said that Cairney would run away.'

'Yes, but I could be wrong.'

He lay down next to her and put an arm over her shoulder. She moved closer, and they embraced. Cole closed his eyes. He had never been so exhausted. The effort of bringing Esher under control, so soon after he had spent hours removing Cairney's blocks had drained him. He had also managed to free his other powers at the same time. They had helped him sense Esher's approach when he had first appeared in the bridge palace; but the act of removing Cairney's control over the Ascendant had been a struggle; one he had barely overcome. He was just starting to drift off when there was a loud knock at the door.

Cole got to his feet. He walked through the small cottage to the front door, and opened it. A marine officer was standing outside in the street, a Quadrant in his left hand.

'Sorry to bother you, sir,' he said, 'but Adjutant Claudian heard that you had lost your Quadrant; and he sent me here to give you this.'

He held out his hand, and Cole took the device.

'Thank you,' said Cole.

'The Adjutant also thought you should know that Cael and Arrosa Holdfast have just arrived in Udall.'

'They're here?' said Cole.

'Aye, sir. They have ordered the marines to remain outside the palace for now.'

'Thanks for letting me know.'

'No problem, sir.'

Cole closed the door, then an idea formed in his mind as he returned to the bedroom.

'What was that you were saying about a bath?' he said. 'Cael and Arrosa are in the palace; which means that they can guard the Empress for the next ten minutes. How about I take you to Plateau City? You can have a bath, food, coffee, maybe even some keenweed.'

Alva sat up. 'Will you take me to your new rooms in the Blue Palace?'

'Maybe not,' he said. 'I still haven't got any furniture. Wait – I know somewhere in the city that will be perfect. It'll be quiet, and there's food and clothes, and a great big bath. I'll drop you off, and then come back here.'

Alva got out of bed and stretched her arms. 'That sounds wonderful, but won't we need a Quadrant?'

Cole smiled, and held up the device the marine officer had given him. He swiped his fingers over the copper surface, and the air crackled. They appeared in the main drawing room within the Holdfast townhouse in Plateau City.

'This is nice,' said Alva.

'The Holdfasts have had this place for nearly fifty years,' said Cole. 'It's narrow, but tall; let me show you the best thing about it before I head back to Ulna. Come on.'

He led her out of the drawing room, and they turned for the staircase. They ascended one flight, and Cole pushed open the door that led to the master bedroom.

Cael glanced up from where he was pulling on his boots. 'Don't you ever knock?' he said.

Arrosa was standing a yard from Cael, fastening the catches on her dress.

'I'm glad you didn't barge through that door a few minutes ago,' she said.

Cole stared at them, his mouth falling open. His gaze went over Arrosa. 'What happened to your hair?'

'I went to the worst hairdresser in Gunst,' said Arrosa. She smiled at the woman standing next to Cole. 'You must be Alva,' she said. 'It's nice to meet you at last.'

'Never mind that,' Cole cried; 'you're supposed to be in Udall. Shit. We have to go. The marines told me that you had both just arrived; we have to go. Now.'

'What?' said Cael, standing.

'It must be Cairney,' Cole cried. 'Cairney must be impersonating you, and Konna must be appearing as Arrosa. They're in the damn bridge palace.'

Cael and Cole reached for their Quadrants at the same time.

'Use yours,' said Cael, as he slipped his own away. 'I'll go straight for Cairney.'

'Wait,' said Alva. 'What if he uses his voice on us? That's how he controls people.'

Arrosa walked over to a desk, and picked up a lump of red sealing wax. She massaged it between her fingers, and ripped it into small pieces.

'Take two pieces each,' she said, 'and plug up your ears.'

'But how will we communicate?' said Alva.

'Cole and I will use our vision,' said Cael.

'I might have accidentally unlocked the latent dream powers I possess,' said Cole.

'After twenty-seven years, you managed to switch them on by yourself?' said Cael. 'Are you sure?'

'I'm sure, cousin. I'll need them if we're going to bring Cairney down. He's strong; too strong for ordinary vision powers.'

'Can I look into your mind later to see what's changed?' Cael said, as he plugged up one ear with wax. 'Can you vision with your eyes closed?'

Cole nodded, then he took two pieces of wax from Arrosa, and pushed them into his ears. His hearing became muffled, and he gazed down at his Quadrant.

Are you ready? said Cael in his mind. *Give us a countdown on your fingers.*

We will be going straight to the audience hall, said Cole.

Cael nodded.

Cole counted down from three, then activated the Quadrant. The air crackled, and they appeared next to the unconscious bodies of two dragons – one black, one silver. By the back wall, the Empress was standing next to Kelsey, as Cairney approached, a sword in his right hand.

Cael raised a hand, and Cairney came to a halt. He turned, and his face flickered with fear, before he hardened his features.

Cairney said something, but the words were too faint to hear. Even so, Cole felt the power of the young god battering against his mind. He staggered back a step, along with Arrosa and Alva, but Cael stood his ground. Cairney's face contorted with pain; but he also stood his ground, as the two Holdfasts – one mortal, the other immortal, each used their powers to try to batter the other into submission.

Cole turned, and saw Konna standing by a smashed doorway, her eyes wide. Cole forced his way into her mind. She cried out, her hands going to the sides of her head, as Cole examined what Cairney had done to his sister's mind. The orders he had imprinted were similar to those he had put into Esher's mind, but Konna was stronger, and had faint dream powers of her own. Without hesitating, Cole tore through Cairney's handiwork, freeing Konna from his spell. She fell to her knees, gasping for breath; then she leapt to her feet and charged at Cairney, her battle-vision thrumming. Cairney and Cael were staring at each other, neither flinching, as Konna barrelled into Cairney from the side, knocking him off his feet, his sword falling from his hand.

Cael ran over as Cairney tried to push his sister off. He punched Cairney in the face, then he gazed into the young god's eyes. Cairney thrashed around. He reached up to grab Cael's throat, and Konna drove his arm back down. Cairney struck his sister with his other hand, but she remained where she was, as Cole rushed forwards. He gripped Cairney's free arm, helping to hold him down. Cole entered Cairney's mind, and found Cael already there. The layers of protection in Cairney's mind were stronger than anything Cole had experienced, and he knew that, on his own, he would have been unable to defeat his younger cousin. Cole added his powers to those of Cael and, together, they stripped away Cairney's savage resistance to their powers until, at last, his body went limp, and Cairney slipped into unconsciousness.

Cael sat on the floor, and plucked the wax from his ears. Cole did the same, then he gazed down at Cairney, hardly able to believe how powerful he had become.

Kelsey and the Empress hurried over.

'Thank you,' said the Empress.

'You're welcome, Your Majesty,' said Cael.

'Is Cairney sleeping?' said Kelsey, as she looked down at him. 'How long will that last?'

'We rendered him unconscious,' said Cael. 'He won't be waking up for a while.'

'Gunst?' said Kelsey.

'All taken care of, ma'am. I taught them a few hard truths.'

The Empress eyed Arrosa. 'Did they hurt you?'

'Anything they did to me, Your Majesty,' said Arrosa, 'has been repaid a hundredfold.'

Konna staggered to her feet.

'Thank you for your help, cousin,' said Cael. 'Are the dragons all right? Did anyone get hurt?'

'Lucius Cardova,' whispered Konna.

'What did you say?' said Kelsey.

'Cairney stabbed him,' said Konna. 'I couldn't do anything to stop him.'

'Show me,' said Kelsey.

'I will come with you,' said the Empress.

Konna led Kelsey and the Empress away, and Cael got to his feet.

'Go with them,' he said to Cole. 'I'll watch Cairney.'

Cole glanced at Alva.

'Go,' she said. 'I'll awaken the dragons and see if they need any help.'

Cole hurried after the Empress. He was sure that Konna's intentions were benign, but there was little point in taking any risks when it came to the safety of the Herald and the Empress. He caught up with them in a long corridor. Lucius Cardova was lying on the floor in a pool of his own blood, while Kelsey knelt by him, his hand in hers. Lucius's eyes were closed, and silent tears were falling down Kelsey's face.

'Move aside, Herald,' said the Empress. 'I shall need to touch him in order to heal him.'

Thorn crouched down, and placed a hand onto Lucius's forehead. She closed her eyes, and Cole sensed a great burst of her powers entering Cardova's body. Lucius convulsed, then he vomited up a stream of blood as he opened his eyes. The Empress got back to her feet, her right hand dripping blood onto the floor. Kelsey continued to weep as she and Lucius gazed at each other.

'Let us give them a moment together,' said Thorn. 'Is Maxwell also here, Konna?'

'Aye,' she said. 'We left him in the next room.'

'Thank you for your cooperation,' said the Empress.

Konna snorted. 'I may have stopped my brother from killing you, Empress,' she said, 'but that doesn't mean I like you. Your warmongering and greed led to my father's death; and that is not something I will ever forgive.'

'I appreciate your honesty,' said Thorn. 'Now, Maxwell?'

Konna gestured towards a door, then she and the Empress walked towards it. Cole kept his gaze on Lucius Cardova and Kelsey for a moment. To his mind, it was obvious that they were in love with each other, and he guessed that the Empress also knew the truth. He heard Maxwell groan aloud, and followed the Empress and Konna into the other room. The Empress was tending to Maddie, who was holding a sore arm, while Maxwell was on the ground, shivering with fear and confusion.

'Cairney's commands are still gripping him,' said Konna. She eyed Cole. 'It was you who freed me, aye? Can ye do the same to Maxwell?'

Cole gazed down at Maxwell's face. His eyes were wide, and Cole drove his powers in. Maxwell's mind was weaker than Konna's; weaker even than Esher's had been in his reduced state.

Cole sat down on the floor. 'This will take a moment,' he said.

Cole closed his eyes and focussed on Maxwell's battered mind. Cairney had given him repeated commands that had spanned several days, and each layer needed to be removed. Cole unpicked one of Cairney's blocks, and Maxwell whimpered. It occurred to Cole at that point that he would be able to scour Maxwell's mind clean – his unlocked dream powers would make it easy, far easier than removing Cairney's blocks.

Cole blinked when he finished clearing Maxwell's mind of Cairney's influence. Maddie and the Empress had left the room, and Konna and Maxwell were gazing at him.

'Thank you,' said Maxwell. 'Am I under arrest?'

'That will be up to the Empress,' Cole said, 'but I will tell her that your mind was being manipulated; I will say the same about you, Konna.'

Konna shook her head. 'I betrayed my own brother,' she said. 'I helped you subdue him.'

'He was insane,' said Maxwell.

'He might have killed the Empress and the Herald if you hadn't intervened,' said Cole.

'So?' said Konna. 'Do ye think I would have mourned them? I stopped him to prevent Karalyn from killing us all. And now my own mother will hate me, for helping the Colsbury Holdfasts take Cairney into custody. What am I supposed to do?'

They got to their feet.

'You could live in the City with me, cousin,' said Maxwell. 'We could kill greenhides together.'

Konna said nothing as they walked into the long corridor. Lucius Cardova was on his feet, talking to Kelsey, Maddie and the Empress. They saw Cole and the others approach.

'Feeling better, sir?' Cole said.

'Much, thank you,' said Cardova.

'Let us ensure that Cairney has been safely secured,' said the Empress.

They entered the large audience hall. Frostback and Blackrose were on their feet, and both were staring down at Cael, who was leaning over Cairney. Arrosa was crouching next to him, while Alva stood a little further away, her eyes troubled.

Cael had a long nail clutched in one hand, which he was holding over Cairney's face, while another nail lay ready by his side.

'What the fuck are ye doing?' cried Konna.

'I'm making my own restrainer mask,' said Cael. 'If I don't, then Cairney will be able to break free of my blocks when he regains consciousness. Would you rather I scoured his mind clean?'

'Could we not blindfold and shackle him?' said the Empress.

'His battle-vision is almost as strong as his father's was,' said Cael. 'He might be able to escape from any shackles. I've blocked his powers but, as I said, there's no guarantee that he won't be able to recover his use of them. Cairney is stronger than he has any right to be. If I scoured him, then I could rebuild him in a way that would keep him weaker, but...'

'Get yer fucking hands off him,' Konna shouted.

'Your brother must be punished,' said Blackrose. 'His crimes require a response. Tell us, daughter of Corthie – what should be done with him?'

Konna clenched her fists. 'I don't know, but he doesn't deserve to have his mind scoured – he's only sixteen; he's a boy.'

'Then it's the nails,' said Cael.

He raised his hand, ready to drive the first nail into Cairney's face.

'Stop,' came a voice.

Everyone in the hall froze as Karalyn appeared, Kyra by her side.

'Put the nail down, son,' Karalyn said. 'You have done well today; do not blemish your actions with an act of cruelty.'

'What are you doing here, sister?' said Kelsey.

'Kyra summoned me,' said Karalyn. 'She told me what Cairney had been doing; she also told me about Esher. Where is he?'

'He's resting in a house down in the town,' said Kelsey.

Karalyn nodded. 'I can sense him.'

She gestured to a clear space next to her, and Esher appeared. His eyes widened.

'Do not be afraid, Reece,' said Karalyn. 'None of this was your fault. I am Karalyn Holdfast, and I want to help you.'

'Will you take me home?' said Esher.

'I will not be taking you back to the City of Salve,' she said. 'Too many people now know who you really are; you will not be able to live a peaceful life there. My daughter has a suggestion. Kyra?'

'I live with Edgar, the brother of an Ascendant,' said Kyra. 'We dwell among the last gods and demigods from the Doomed Worlds, and we could help you. You could live with us, in peace. Edgar would guide you; instruct you in the ways of immortality.'

'Woah,' said Kelsey. 'Hold on a moment. Are you seriously suggesting that the Dominion shelters an Ascendant? An actual Ascendant, with all of his powers?'

'How is this different from Belinda, sister?' said Karalyn. 'Esher is not the same as he once was – he was reborn that day in Tara when I wiped his mind clean. He is innocent. Why should he not be permitted to live among those who also have immortality?'

'But with Belinda,' said the Empress, 'you sealed up her powers and released them gradually. Who will do the same for Esher?'

'I will take care of that,' said Kyra. She glanced at the Ascendant. 'The choice is yours, Esher. I can take you back with me to Nom Karta. Edgar and Bailey are there. They remember you from the olden times, and they both hope that you will come and stay with us, even if it is only for a short time. Will you try it?'

'Doesn't this break the treaty?' said Kelsey. 'If the Dominion suddenly gets itself an Ascendant, that puts us at a disadvantage.'

Karalyn smiled. 'I decide the terms of the treaty, sister; I alone. And doesn't the Empire now have a range of dangerous new weapons – ones capable of killing gods? Isn't that the case? This would balance things a little. This is my will – if Esher agrees, then he can go to Athumia.'

'I will try it,' said Esher. 'I will go to Inopei, and try to learn who I am.'

'What about me?' said Konna. 'Can I go, too? I want to live among gods.'

'I was going to send you back to Kell, Konna,' said Karalyn. 'You are not to be punished for your role in Cairney's crimes. The same goes for you, Maxwell; you are absolved.'

Cole noticed Kelsey, Cardova and the Empress exchange glances. They looked unhappy that Karalyn was dictating her terms, but remained silent.

Cael got to his feet. 'What are you going to do about Cairney, Mother?'

'Wait,' said Karalyn. 'I hadn't finished speaking. Aila will have missed you, Konna.'

'She will hate me when she finds out that I helped the others defeat Cairney,' Konna said. 'Please, Karalyn, let me go to Inopei, if Kyra will allow it.'

'I thought you hated me,' said Kyra.

Konna gave her a wry smile. 'No offence, Kyra, but you'll be dead in a few decades, and I can put up with you until then. It's the gods I want to live among.'

'Then you are welcome to come back with me,' said Kyra.

'All right,' said Karalyn. 'Daughter, you may take both Konna and Esher to Nom Karta. Thank you for summoning me.'

'Wait,' said Konna. 'What will happen to my brother?'

'Kyra will give you the details,' said Karalyn. 'He will not be executed, nor will he be placed into a restrainer mask.'

Kyra tilted her head, then she vanished, along with Konna and Esher.

'I assume you wish to go home, Maxwell?' Karalyn said.

'Yes,' he said. He glanced at the Empress. 'I'm sorry about everything. This was my fault. I told Konna about Esher, and then Cairney found out. I... I didn't mean for any of this to happen.'

'Give him his Quadrant, son,' said Karalyn.

Cael frowned, but he reached into a pocket and handed Maxwell a Quadrant.

'You may go,' said Karalyn.

Maxwell bowed his head, then he activated the device and disappeared.

'Are you going to forgive Cairney as well, Mother?' said Cael, as he removed the Quadrant from behind Cairney's armour.

Karalyn eyed her son. 'Are you angry with me? Of course I am not going to forgive Cairney. Not yet, at any rate; perhaps in a century or so. But neither shall I torture him with a mask.'

'Then what?' said Kelsey.

'I have been making worlds,' she said, a light in her eyes appearing; 'beautiful worlds. I have one in mind for Cairney. It is filled with plant and animal life, but there are no humans, nor any sentient species. I shall place Cairney there, and leave him. He will have all the time he needs to reflect upon his actions. I will inform Konna of this, and perhaps I will allow her to visit her brother from time to time, but Cairney shall not be permitted to leave this world, not until I command it.' She glanced at Blackrose. 'Does that satisfy you?'

The black dragon tilted her head. 'It does.'

'And you, Empress?' said Karalyn. 'Do you object to my decision?'

'If the Empire is safe, then I am content,' said Thorn.

'The Empire will be safe from Cairney,' said Karalyn, 'but I am not altogether sure that it is safe from you. I will go now, and take Cairney with me.'

'Wait a moment,' said Cole, stepping forward. 'Do we mean nothing to you any more, Karalyn?'

Karalyn looked confused.

'I am your brother's son,' Cole went on, 'and yet you have said nothing to me. You cared for Arrosa for years, and you haven't even glanced in her direction. Have you seen what the Gunstians did to her hair? And this is Alva Longhold, in case you were wondering. And that's Maddie – remember her? And... and isn't that your husband standing next to Aunty Kelsey and the Empress? Have you nothing to say to him?'

Karalyn glanced at the faces watching her.

'Might we talk for a moment?' said Cardova.

Karalyn's eyes pierced him. She began to frown, her eyes darkening, then she turned to Kelsey.

'I see,' said Karalyn. 'Do you want my husband, sister?'

'Kelsey has rejected me,' said Cardova; 'she has behaved with honour, and out of love for you.'

Karalyn ignored him. 'Kelsey, do you love him? Answer me, and speak the truth.'

Kelsey lowered her gaze and nodded. 'Aye,' she said. 'I love him, but I know that nothing can ever happen.'

'Why not?' said Karalyn. 'Lucius's suspicions are correct – I no longer love him, and I can see that he no longer loves me. This is hard to take, but I accept your offer of a divorce, Lucius. We had many good years, and I will always remember you with fondness, but our lives have gone in different directions. I accept much of the blame for this; I am no longer the woman you married.'

Lucius bowed his head. 'And the children?'

'Are you happy to keep caring for them?'

'I am.'

'Then do so. I will see them both when they are older, and we can spend millennia together. Your time with them is short – enjoy it. As for you, Kelsey, I want you to be happy. Lucius loves you; I saw it clearly in his mind. Be together, without any guilt. I wish you both well. Arrosa, you will always be dear to my heart, but I get so distracted with things. I was in the middle of building a new world when Kyra interrupted me, and I long to return to my work.' She glanced at Cole. 'Thank you for reminding me of my obligations.'

She gestured towards Cairney, then both of them vanished.

The Empress exhaled. 'These meetings with Karalyn get ever more fraught,' she said.

'She's bloody terrifying, you mean,' said Maddie; 'and she doesn't even know it.' She turned to Kelsey and Cardova. 'You two, eh? I should have seen that coming. So, how did Kyra summon her mother? How did that happen? Do we know how to summon her? Not that I want to, but, you know, if we have to?'

'Let us hope we never need to,' said the Empress.

'Shall I instruct the evacuees to re-enter the palace?' said Blackrose. 'I had planned for a day of feasting.'

'Please do so,' said Thorn. She eyed Kelsey and Cardova. 'Do you need some time before the others get here?'

Kelsey smiled. 'Aye. I think so. Lucius, we need to talk. Maybe we should include the children, too.'

'We could go back to the Blue Palace,' said Lucius, his gaze on her.

She took his hand. 'All right. We'll be back soon.'

'Take your time,' said the Empress.

Cardova took out a Quadrant, activated it, and they vanished.

Cael laughed. 'Lucius and Kelsey – my adopted father and my aunt. That was your doing, Cole – don't think I didn't notice where your little speech ended. If you hadn't spoken up, then my mother would have been none the wiser.'

Cole shrugged. 'I do what I can. Your Majesty, I promised Alva a bath and some clean clothes. May we also be excused for a short time?'

'You may,' said the Empress; 'but I have another task for you when you return.'

'Are you going to the Blue Palace?' said Cael.

'I don't think that's a good idea,' said Cole.

'You need to get some furniture for your quarters,' said Arrosa.

Cole smiled. 'I know,' he said, then he triggered his Quadrant.

He and Alva appeared on the roof of Madden's Tower in Rainsby. The sun was high in the sky, and a cold wind was blowing over the town. He put his arms round Alva.

'I could sleep for days,' he said.

'Don't let the Empress work you too hard,' she said.

'Do you regret getting involved with a Holdfast?' he said. 'Cairney would never have taken you if you weren't connected to me; and I can't promise you a peaceful life. The next time there's an emergency, Cael and I will be back on duty.'

'I know,' said Alva. She shivered. 'Could we go somewhere warmer? Hold Long, perhaps?'

'Do you want to see your parents?'

'I want them to see you, Cole. I want to tell them that we're together. Are you ready to be a part of the world?'

He smiled. 'With you, Alva, I'm ready for anything.'

EPILOGUE

Marchside, Kell – 19nd Day, First Third Autumn 552

Aila opened the front door of the farmhouse and walked inside, leaving the blustery rain behind. She took off her overcoat and her boots, and arranged them neatly by the door. The house was quiet. With her three eldest children absent, and the others at school, only Naxor and the cook would be indoors.

She walked into the sitting room, but it was empty, so she turned and went to the kitchen. Also empty. She saw a note on the table from the cook, explaining that she had gone down to Marchside to buy some extra provisions. Aila frowned. Part of the reason for having so many children was that she liked a noisy, busy house; and being alone made her think of Corthie, which was never wise. She went to the counter, filled a kettle with fresh water, and placed it on to the hot stove. She would make some coffee, and try to enjoy the solitude.

She gazed out of the kitchen window as the water began to warm. The weather had been awful that day, and spring was a long time away. She wondered why she had persisted with living in Kell. Long before, she had promised herself that she would return to the City when Corthie passed away, but she had decided instead that she wanted her children brought up in the vast rolling countryside of Southern Kell.

The City was so small in comparison, while Kell had space in abundance. Perhaps, when they had all grown up, she might reconsider.

The air shimmered behind her, and Naxor appeared, with Killop next to him.

Aila smiled. 'Killop,' she said, reaching out for her son.

'Ma,' he said, embracing her. He kissed her on the cheek. 'Are we alone in the house?'

'We are,' she said. She glanced at Naxor. 'Thank you for bringing him here but, next time, warn me in advance.'

Naxor laughed. 'I do it to see the expression on your face, cousin. Killop has some things he wants to tell us.'

Someone thumped on the front door.

'Sit down,' Naxor said to Aila and Killop. 'I'll answer the door.'

'You sit,' said Aila to her son, as Naxor left the kitchen. 'I was making coffee. It is very nice to see you.'

'I'll take a coffee, thanks, Ma,' he said, taking a chair by the kitchen table.

Aila went back to the stove and prepared a coffee pot.

'We have a visitor,' said Naxor.

'So I had assumed,' said Aila.

'A visitor from the Empress.'

Aila frowned, then she turned to see who it was.

'Ma'am,' said Cole, tilting his head. He eyed Killop. 'Cousin.'

'What can we do for you, Cole?' said Aila.

'I have bad news for you,' he said. 'Cairney has been arrested for several counts of murder.'

Aila snorted. 'Don't be ridiculous,' she snapped. 'The boy has been camping in the nearby hills. Who has he murdered – some sheep?'

Aila felt Cole's powers pass through her mind, and she blinked, her false memories removed. She narrowed her eyes. Cairney wasn't in the hills; she had no idea where he was.

'Cairney was using his abilities to make you think that,' said Cole. 'In reality, he was with Konna and Maxwell, Amalia's son. They told Esher his true identity, and then they manipulated him into killing many dragons and people. We caught them yesterday, when they tried to kill the Empress.'

Aila said nothing.

'Konna and Maxwell have been exonerated,' Cole went on. 'Cairney was manipulating them, too.'

'Where is my daughter?' said Aila.

'She has decided to go to Athumia with Kyra. Esher has also gone there.'

'She went with Kyra?' said Killop.

'She did, cousin. She wants to live with other gods – that's what she said. She helped us subdue Cairney, and she was worried that you would think she had betrayed your family.'

'And Cairney?' said Aila. 'What has the Empress decided?'

'The Empress had no say in it, ma'am. Karalyn has taken Cairney into exile. He will be unharmed, but he will not be allowed to leave the world upon which Karalyn has placed him – not until she decides to release him.'

The kettle on the stove boiled, its whistle sharp. Aila remained where she was, so Naxor walked over to the stove. He picked up the kettle, and filled the coffee pot with hot water.

'I have lost two of my children,' said Aila.

'Both are alive and well, ma'am,' said Cole.

'Am I allowed to see either?'

'You may be able to arrange a meeting with Konna, perhaps on Zamata, if you ask Lord Bailey. As for Cairney, he is out of our reach. Only Karalyn knows where he has been exiled; only she can bring him back.'

'Was he close?' she said.

Cole frowned. 'Ma'am?'

'Did he get close to killing the Empress?'

'Yes. He got very close. Another few seconds, and he would have murdered Her Majesty and Aunty Kelsey. We got to him just in time.'

Aila nodded. Her poor boy.

'I assume that you are not staying for coffee?' said Naxor.

Cole smiled at the demigod. 'I will take my leave,' he said. 'If you have any questions, I will be in the Blue Palace.'

Cole swiped his Quadrant and vanished.

Killop put his head in his hands.

'Did you have any idea of what your brother was doing?' said Aila.

'None,' said Killop. 'Cairney and Konna don't trust me with their secrets, not since I've been pretending to like the Colsbury Holdfasts.'

'You have paid a price for what you have been doing,' said Naxor, as he poured coffee into three cups, 'but it will all be worth it in the end. And before you ask, cousin – no, I didn't know what Cairney was doing, either. He manipulated an Ascendant, eh? That lad is powerful now; just wait a decade or so – he will be unstoppable.'

Aila stirred sugar into her cup. 'Another few seconds, that's what Cole said. Cairney was so close to bringing us revenge, despite all of your advice to my children, telling them to be patient.'

'Yes,' said Naxor, 'but had he succeeded, then I fear Karalyn's justice would have been far harsher. Cairney has been exiled, not executed, and for that we must be thankful.'

'But how do we get him back?' said Killop.

'That, my boy, will require patience. Why don't you tell us how things have been going on the Hold Fast estate?'

'It has been going well, Uncle,' said Killop. 'Celine is desperate to retire; she'll be seventy years old soon, and she's tired of managing the estate. I have been learning everything as quickly as possible, and I think I've been doing a good job. Kelsey is adamant that only a Holdfast should run the estate, and I'm in a good position to be selected as the next manager.'

'Does Celine trust you?' said Aila.

'Aye, she does. I'm already making her life easier, by taking some of the more arduous jobs off her hands, and she seems happy that I'm there.'

'Good work,' said Naxor. 'Once Celine has retired, and you have taken over, we shall control the two largest sources of income for the Holdfasts. One or two of your younger siblings could go up to the Holdings to assist you, and to entrench our hold on the estate. Carter, perhaps, or Clova.'

'Not Clova,' said Killop. 'I was pretending to be sympathetic towards the Colsbury Holdfasts; Clova really does like them. We should keep her here, where she can't cause us any problems.'

'She is only twelve,' said Naxor. 'I am confident that we shall win her over to our way of thinking. We don't just want to destroy the Colsbury Holdfasts, we also want to inherit their great wealth and influence. Controlling the Hold Fast estate is a vital part of that.'

'One day, Killop,' said Aila, 'you will be Holder Fast. You must keep up the pretence until then. Give Kelsey no reason to doubt you. We shall outlive the mortal Holdfasts, and take over their name.'

'And then,' said Naxor, 'the Empire shall be ours.'

AUTHOR'S NOTES

JULY 2025

Thank you for reading ***The Lost Ascendant***; I hope you enjoyed it.

In some ways, this was an unplanned book, as the original conception of the end of Magelands Empire was to jump fifteen years between the end of ***Sapphire Throne*** (Book Nine of Empire) and ***Yearning for Evermore*** (the first book of the final trilogy). However, the more I looked at the story, the more I realised that this gap was crying out for a book to fill it. There were important events that would have been missed had I moved straight to ***Yearning for Evermore***, and so ***The Lost Ascendant*** was born. As such, it now occupies a unique place with the Magelands arc – as the only book (with the possible exceptions of the two Origins novels) that does not stand within a trilogy or four-book sequence. It is the only *standalone* book in the main arc and, to emphasis this quality, I decided to focus on characters who would be familiar, but who had never had their own point-of-view story told before.

RECEIVE A FREE MAGELANDS DOMINION SHORT STORY

Building a relationship with my readers is very important to me.

Join my newsletter for information on new books and deals and you will also receive a Magelands Dominion short story that is currently EXCLUSIVE to my Readers' Group for FREE.

www.ChristopherMitchellBooks.com/dominion

ABOUT THE AUTHOR

Christopher Mitchell is the author of the Magelands epic fantasy series.

For more information:

www.christophermitchellbooks.com
info@christophermitchellbooks.com

Printed in Dunstable, United Kingdom

65586017R00272